TO CONQUER— OR DESTROY!

"We can strangle the Directorate and at the same time destroy these barbarian Romanans they bring with them." The First Citizen of Sirius laughed at the thought. "Imagine, Stone Age warriors . . . against *our* Home Legions? The Patrol marines I would worry about. But these cow herders? Fodder for our men. Stupid targets to be—"

"They need not even be allowed to land, First Citizen."

"No! I think it wise to let some through. We need to destroy them on the planet—"

"They will cause substantial damage. It means lives, First Citizen."

"And lives, my friend, will make martyrs for Sirius. Martyrs drive the people harder than any threat by government. Keep in mind that those who have nothing to lose, those who think themselves already dead, they make the *finest* soldiers. . . ."

THE
WAY
OF
SPIDER

W. MICHAEL GEAR

DAW BOOKS, INC.

DONALD A. WOLLHEIM, PUBLISHER

1633 Broadway, New York, NY 10019

DAW Book Collectors No. 767.

First Printing, January 1989

1 2 3 4 5 6 7 8 9

PRINTED IN THE U.S.A.

TO WILLY "J" JENKINS AND
THE HONORABLE H. GENE DRIGGERS
THIS YARN IS DEDICATED

WITH THANKS FOR YOUR ENDLESS
SUPPORT DURING THE PURPOSELESS HELL THAT
WAS GRADUATE SCHOOL.
I HAVEN'T FORGOTTEN.

ACKNOWLEDGMENTS

The production of this manuscript in its present form would have been impossible without the vital input of a handful of key people. I owe a great deal to my cherished wife, Kathy, who spent countless hours reading, commenting and correcting. You wouldn't be reading this were it not for her. Sharon Jarvis, my agent at the time, did a wonderful job working with DAW. My ex-editor mother, Katherine P. Cook, provided her years of journalistic insight and keen judgment. And finally, editors remain the overworked, unsung heroes of the publishing business. With pleasure, therefore, I would like to acknowledge Sheila Gilbert, of DAW Books, for the incredibly perceptive comments and salient suggestions she provided. The book is stronger as a result.

Thank you all.

CHAPTER I

Spider would decide the fate of a planet.

Men and women peered upward into the flickering darkness, anxious, mouths working silently as jagged fingers of actinic death ripped the soundless heavens above. Evil strobes of violet boiled from one part of the heavens, searing the cloud cover, rolling across the arch of the night to pulse in weird lavender.

Star lightning—frightening in its unworldly silence—wove back and forth over the village as starships flashed death beyond any Romanan's comprehension.

Hushed voices, abstracted and unreal, whispered in awe to either side of Susan Smith Andojar. She looked around her as another streak of violet illuminated angular, weather-hardened faces; their strength, spirit, and character betrayed by the squint of an eye, the set of a hard mouth. Tension—so common to her violent people—crackled in the air.

Wrinkled, age-battered old men, dark eyes gleaming, peered upward, fighting their failing vision. Twisted mahogany lips pulled over toothless gums in a rictus of dread and hope.

Silent, terror-locked women—some young, some old—stood, helpless. Others sat on gay-colored wool blankets spread over hard-packed dirt, or perched in the beds of wagons and leaned against pillows made of coats, packs and hides. Here and there arms cradled an infant who slept soundly, heedless of the searing arcs of death overhead.

The few warriors glared helplessly upward. Impotent agony glazed their eyes. At each flash of the star weapons they shifted, shaking rifles futilely at the cloud-masked sky, fingering the human-hair coups dangling from their vests and belts—knowing they missed the greatest opportunity for status and honor to befall the People since the revolt against the Sobyets so long ago.

Man, woman, and child, they prayed to Spider—prayed the star death would end, leaving their world alive.

7

Susan snugged her worn blanket tightly around her shoulders and walked slowly from the crowd. Even while death glittered in the skies, she existed separately, alone, mocked by Spider. As so often before, she sought sanctuary within, away from her dead parents' people. In the deadly dancing lights, she followed the way she knew by heart. Climbing up on the corral poles, she leaned against one of the big posts, watching the eerie skies, waiting, wondering.

The clouds had drifted, scudding rapidly to the east. A painful actinic brilliance burst across the tortured sky. She pulled the coarse wool blanket over her head. Terror breathed close. Would her soul go to Spider in that last hellish instant?

The chill of the spring night crept into her. Scents of woodsmoke and dung-fed fires intermixed with horse, manure, rot and spices drifted on the wind. Not even the blanket could hide the macabre presence of the star weapons.

The renegade ship *Bullet* still fought. Worse, the Prophets said nothing! Two had gone with the star men in their AT and risen into the heavens. The other two sat in their room in the ancient wreck of the *Nicholai Romanan* and waited, nodding, smiling, driving the People mad with their refusal to talk of the future.

Susan chewed her lip, wondering what the stars looked like from so high in the death-laced sky. Even if the Spider warriors and their star friends won, she would never know. Her heart skipped a beat. Only what if. . . . Quickly, she clamped down on the idea, driving it from her mind. Such things were not for a woman of the People.

Her uncle, Ramon Luis Andojar—disgusted by her odd ways and dreams—already pushed her to marry Willy Red Hawk Horsecapture. Through bride price, he hoped to get some return on the burden of her existence. Susan grimaced under the security of her blanket. She hated Horsecapture. He might be a noted warrior. Many eyes followed him through the camp. People spoke well of him. Only he never hid his arrogance. Something sinister lay behind his hot black eyes: a menace of evil and dishonor.

Marry him? *Never!*

No one understood! Susan could hear and feel her molars grinding in frustration. Another light flashed, brighter than the last. Peeking out from under her blanket, she looked up at the heavens, seeing a small rain of meteors. The death of one of the star ships? The breeze rustled with the soft nervous cries of the People.

A bleak future stretched before her. Death from star weapons—or marriage to Horsecapture. She had no escape. Better a quick burning finality as star weapons blasted World rather than a slow death of drudgery. The thought of Horsecapture pawing her body, his child growing within her. . . .

Physically sick, Susan Smith Andojar clutched herself, trapped. She couldn't put Horsecapture off forever. Not with her half-crazy uncle—his eyes on Horsecapture's prize horses—demanding she marry and cease being a burden to him, his family, and her clan.

She clenched long brown fingers into a fist and sought to quiet the feelings of frustration and anxiety. Spider had given the People law. Spider had decreed that men should behave one way and women another. Spider had freed them all from the Sobyets and brought the People here to World to live unfettered those many centuries ago.

She could not fight Spider. She could not outsmart him, trick him, or out-argue him like she did her kinsfolk. She had to obey. Spider was God.

Even in her depression she realized the lights of death had gone black. Looking up, she saw nothing but stars and the first moon rising beyond the clouded Bear Mountains to the east. Faint yellow flickers streaked like meteors, the ATs, the Attack Transports of the star men.

Who had won? Would she live? Perhaps the star men in the village would know! She jumped lithely to the dung-soft dirt, calmed the horses, and darted off between the dark houses.

The star men had assembled in one of the meeting halls. Susan stopped in the doorway, suddenly frightened by her temerity. They knotted around a machine that showed pictures. One of the men saw her from the corner of his eye. A white uniform covered him from throat to foot, while his hands were bare. The wide belt at his hip carried curious metal boxes and hoops of wire. Wide-set blue eyes studied her from a face oddly pale as if it had never been in the sun. His mousy hair, close cropped, wouldn't be worth a coup.

He straightened and turned, fatigue and concern lined into his face. Though his voice was pleasant, he addressed her in incomprehensible star speech.

"I want to know who won," Susan told him, keeping her eyes lowered appropriately for an unmarried woman speaking to a man.

The glance had been enough. Never would she cease to wonder at the incredible clothing they wore—dazzling whites of soft, body-conforming light material. Never did they wear heavy hides or scratchy wool. Odd metal things hung at their belts, mysterious with magical qualities, allowing them to see or talk across immense distances. The star men themselves displayed a wealth of variations in their skin tones and hair colors. Even their eyes came in all shades of green, blue, gray, and brown.

The man picked up a small box from the table. Attention centered on her now and she wished she could sink into the rough pole wood planks of the floor. It had been a mistake to come here. She turned to go, cursing herself for a fool.

"Wait!" The voice came in the tongue of the People. She turned, startled by the mechanical sound.

While the others watched for her reaction, the man talked into the little box he held between his hands. The words sounded tinny, oddly inflected. "Your people are fine. The starships have ceased fighting. There is a truce."

"They will not destroy the Settlements?" Susan's heart beat rapidly.

"No one else will die," the box intoned after the man had spoken.

She heard with dull acceptance. Uncle Ramon would be more adamant. Horsecapture had been involved with the star men since the beginning. Ramon would tell her to accept Horsecapture. If she didn't, the clan council would intercede and just give her to him—possibly without bride price: humiliation on top of everything else.

She looked at the star people, wondering again at the women among them, now tight-faced, staring at her with curiosity in their eyes. She'd seen the female marines and marveled, wondering if they were for the men's pleasure at first. Then she'd seen them with their blasters, walking as tall and proud as the men. In fear, she'd hesitated to speak to them.

The big ship they called *Bullet* had come from the stars half a year earlier, kicking off immediate warfare between the Spider and Santos tribes. At the same time the star men had tried to conquer the People. With rifles and raw courage they fought back against the ATs and blasters, screaming their devotion to Spider, dying with honor as violet bolts charred and exploded their flesh. Spider had been honored—their souls had returned to God.

John Smith Iron Eyes, the greatest Spider warrior, had saved them, by forging an alliance between the tribes and the star men. An uneasy peace existed while Spider and Santos warriors trained in the remote mountain camp called the Navel. They had gone to the starship and the star Colonel, Damen Ree, had decided to fight for the People. Rumors spread that Spider had spoken to him through the Prophet, Chester Armijo Garcia, and made him one with Spider.

When other star men came from the blackness, *Bullet* had fought for the People. Because of *Bullet,* the People would live. So said this star man with his talking box. Spider had saved his People again. There would be no Sobyets to come and make them prisoners.

She knew what these star men saw as she stood, cowering in the doorway. A tall, thin girl with long black stringy hair, her dirt-shiny blanket—a castoff she'd found—hiding her body. But they could see her haunted eyes, the bruises from Ramon's frequent beatings.

"I give you thanks," Susan murmured under her breath turning to leave again.

"Wait!" Again the box called to her. She kept her eyes lowered. "You have been out among the people. Are they mad at us?"

Susan looked up. "I don't understand." She frowned. "Why would they be mad at you? The star men with John Smith Iron Eyes fought for us. You are our friends. You have done the People honor! We salute you."

The man paled, shifting uneasily. Susan looked around the table, seeing men and women avoid her glance, afraid to meet her suddenly curious stare.

"You do not know?" a woman asked.

"Know what?" Susan shook her head.

"We refused to fight," another man said through the translator. "We couldn't go against our oaths. Bear arms against the Patrol. We are called traitors."

She could see shame on their faces. "Then why are you here?" Susan demanded, feeling her blood rise. Were these cowards? The thought chilled her. Could star men . . .

The first man had a wry smile on his lips. "We were placed here as hostages to keep your village safe. Colonel Ree hoped the Directorate wouldn't destroy you if we were in the way." His face reddened; but ironic amusement danced in his eyes. "I think we're just as glad it worked out this way."

"Are you cowards?" she asked, scorn edging her voice.

The man listened to the machine translate and calmly shook his head. "No, we just had a different loyalty. We did what we believed right. Is that cowardice?"

The sudden thought of her own outcast status crossed her mind. She didn't bow to the will of the People and accept her place as a woman. Perhaps these star men were the same?

"No," she whispered.

A question nagged at her. Screwing up her nerve she asked, "Why do you have women with you?" Susan looked at the females where they stood, heads cocked at her question.

The sudden chatter of voices confused the translator. Finally one of the women asked, "Why wouldn't we be here?"

Susan caught the note of uncertainty in her voice before the translator uttered it.

"Because a woman's place is different." She sounded sullen and knew it.

One of the women, older, with steel-gray eyes walked forward. "A woman can do anything a man can . . . if she's willing to work to be as capable."

Tightness caught at her heart, a sudden leap of hope. "You . . . are a warrior?"

The woman grinned. "I am. I'm a corporal—an officer. Uh, I suppose like your war chiefs."

"Like a war chief?" Susan gasped, fingers to her lips in awe. "How? How did they let you?"

"Let me?" the corporal mused, face lined. A hardness glittered in those gray eyes. "I just . . . well, they accepted my application to join the Patrol. I studied hard, passed the exams, and proved—"

"But, the men, didn't they try and . . ." Her voice froze as she looked in fear at the star men, all of whose eyes were focused on her.

The corporal nodded, clasping her hands together. "Ah, I see. Your Romanan ways are different from ours. Our technology . . . uh, the machines we use to alter our environment . . . have freed us from sexual role differentiation. We don't—"

For a brief moment, the room seemed brighter. "Could

I . . . Could I come with you? Be a warrior? Go among the stars with—"

"*Susan!*" Her uncle's voice cut like a lash. "*Get away from there!*"

She turned as her uncle closed—ducked the backhanded blow he aimed at her head—and scuttled into the darkness.

"You will *never* learn to be a woman! *You are shameless!*" he shouted after her. "How could my beloved sister bear such a one as you?"

Behind her, she heard his whining tones as he apologized to the star men. Then she rounded the corner of the building, bare feet pounding the dirt as she ran into the safe arms of the night.

A room of swirling blue, seemingly endless, without depth or dimension, faded into forever. Director Skor Robinson stared absently at the cerulean haze, frightened by the thumping heartbeat in his chest. He twisted slightly in the zero g environment, the catheters which kept him alive bending like snakes behind him.

Fear: It filled him, pulsing along his veins, shivering up and down his atrophied spine.

War! Death! Violence in Directorate space! A battle stopped at his discretion. On his responsibilility, he'd concluded a pact with barbarians and traitors.

What have I wrought, Prophet? he'd asked the Romanan shaman, Chester Armijo Garcia.

Freedom . . . freedom . . . freedom . . . The words echoed hollowly through Skor Robinson's huge brain. In one fleeting moment, with one decision to spare the Rebel ship, *Bullet,* and the Romanans it sheltered, his universe changed, transmuted to a different reality. *Freedom . . . freedom to fear!*

I have learned, Prophet . . . Skor echoed to himself, each of his many segments of mind reacting, evaluating, afraid, *. . . that freedom is the ultimate condemnation. Yes, I shall learn from the universe. What will it teach me? What horror is loose with your Romanans?*

Skor winced, grunting, as he forced himself to raise his reed-thin arm to touch the gray metal headset encapsulating his huge bulbous cranium. Pain lanced up his arm—the legacy of muscles unused since birth. The sensation of touch awed him, the cool feel of the headset strange under his bone-thin fingers.

A caricature of a man, Skor floated, weightless. The most powerful man in human space, he shuddered under the impact of his thoughts. *Alone! I am a mutant! Grown in a culture vat, tailored to interface with the Gi-net computers, I can never be fully human!*

Skor blinked, trying to flex atrophied limbs, feeling the sting as residual strands of muscle strained.

Director? Assistant Director Semri Navtov's call sought again to interrupt. Strands of inquiry began wheedling into Skor's mind as other urgent requests for information prickled at the edges of his consciousness.

I am free. Condemned.

Skor firmly denied the frantic calls jamming the QED switches of his Gi-net interface. A vast feeling of emptiness filled his mighty mind as he studied the effects of the message still filtering through space.

Leeta Dobra had wreaked havoc before her death in the fight over World. She had broadcast the entire story of the Romanan expedition out into human space, bypassing the Gi-net—just as her suicidal lover, Jeffray, had once threatened to do. Now, all humanity questioned the actions of the Directorate, upset, curious. *How do I defend genocide? Thank God the Romanans lived.*

But what other choice did I have? he wondered. *Sirius is in revolt. I have made a pact with barbarians and traitors to subdue a Directorate world. Social unrest stirs through human space. Subspace transduction jams the iota-regga dimensions, humming beyond gravity and mass. How can I save civilization?*

Even the incredible systems of the Gi-net were strained by the number of requests for information: Had the Directorate really ordered the genocide of an entire people? Ordered the destruction of an entire planet? Confusion reigned. At the core of the Arcturian Gi-net, Skor felt the tremors of the frightened billions.

And Sirius burned—a chancre of revolt.

Order has fled. Skor continued to feel the headset with his delicate fingers. *They call us pumpkin-heads. They call us freaks. Did we do so badly by humanity and its needs?*

He sent a mental query through the system, replaying the battle between *Bullet, Victory,* and *Brotherhood* above the gemlike planet of World. Again, he watched as Damen Ree and his renegade ship hurled itself, wounded and out-gunned, at his Patrol brethren. Blaster bolts laced the ships, hulls breaching, atmosphere, machinery and men boiling out into fiery death. Shields glared across the entire spectrum, wavering under the incredible energies.

Insanity! Nevertheless, Skor's heart pounded, pumping strange adrenaline into his bloodstream. Registering the change in blood composition, the Gi-net controlled monitors struggled to compensate, lowering his body's metabolism in response, keeping the balance.

"I wish they could see our eyes," Damen Ree was mumbling to himself under his breath. "They would see that they killed us, but—by Spider—they never defeated us!"

"Ree! What the hell are you doing?" Sheila Rostostiev, *Brotherhood's* commander, demanded, her face forming on *Bullet's* bridge monitors.

"We are all going to die," Ree told her, a curious serenity in his expression. "Unless, of course, you yield."

Odd, that serenity. So much like the inevitable knowing look in Chester Garcia's eyes. What is it about this Spider religion that possesses the Romanans? How can it be so infectious?

Maya ben Ahmad, Colonel in command of the Patrol ship *Victory*, cried, "You mean you would destroy your ship to kill us?" Her dark, ancient face screwed up in disbelief.

"I will keep you from destroying the Romanans," Ree insisted stubbornly. "I will win this battle and all your lives will be for naught." Ree laughed in a manner totally unbefitting the dire nature of the situation. "You can't get away before I set off the reaction. You're too close together."

"Oh, God, no!" Sheila shrieked, screaming rabidly at the screens, howling like some tortured animal.

Skor winced, swallowing hard, seeing the tension in tough Maya ben Ahmad's face as Sheila was pulled, kicking and slavering, from the bridge of *Brotherhood*.

Skor watched, fascinated as Ree continued his conversation with Maya. "Won't surrender? It's a chance, Maya." Ree bent his head curiously.

"Can't, Damen. On the odd chance you're bluffing, I'd feel like a fool. Just as you've chosen what you feel is right, I have to follow my orders. Just a quirk, you understand." Maya smiled at Ree, an odd warmth in her eyes, a fondness reflected there.

Respect! She can't help but admire Damen Ree even while he destroys her! Why? What does this mean? Skor stared, baffled, his magnificent mind stunned at the illogic of it all.

"We're too glorious for that damn Robinson, you know that?" And Ree saluted and opened the dead-man's box, his fingers gripping the big red toggle lever that would drop the stasis fields around the antimatter, releasing it to react with the matter of the ship.

Skor froze the scene in his mind, studying the expression on Ree's face. Almost rapturous, the Colonel's blocky features betrayed a certain internal glow—a man victorious. Maya, on the other hand, her ship having seriously wounded *Bullet*, looked drained. A curious interplay of grudging respect and admiration mixed with the impending horror of her own death along with that of her ship and crew. Skor studied the images, curiosity budding, reading Maya's dread of defeat.

"And I interrupted," Skor said aloud, strained vocal chords turning the utterance into a rasp. "I passed the cusp. Made the decisions to let them all live."

He blinked, a foreign twist of emotion in his chest. Skor waited until the computer regained control of his metabolism, feeling his heart slow, the strangeness of emotion draining from his exhausted body.

For yet another minute he studied their faces, trying to read their thoughts through expressions and postures—to peer into their very brains.

"Chester Armijo Garcia says I have lost my humanity." Skor swallowed dryly. "Is that what it means to be human?"

Director! Semri Navtov overrode his mental block. *You have ignored our requests for information! Are you well? We notice significant abnormalities in your physical chemical composition. Your body is unstable. If you do not respond within statistically acceptable parameters of logical ability, your control of the Gi-net will be terminated and I shall take over primary control.*

Skor returned to the present, allowing the image of Damen Ree and Maya ben Ahmad to slip into his subconscious. Rapidly, he accessed the system, pulling data from the biological monitors despite Navtov's sudden move to block him. He found what he expected.

I suggest you look at your own biological charts, Assistant Director, Skor replied scathingly as he accessed the readouts himself. *You and An Roque are both exhibiting abnormalities. Do not censure me when your own physical deviance is evident.*

We face a disaster! Navtov replied through the system—

ignoring the subject now that he'd lost. *Subspace is clogged! The pirate, Ree, has raised pandemonium! We can deny it happened, deny that we ordered the Romanans destroyed, but Ree continues to broadcast. Everything is public! Order is compromised! Social turbulence is rising to an unprecedented degree—jumping as much as ten statistical points among borderline populations. We see an increase of sudden deviance factors among the Arpeggians and Zionists. The worst rising index shows the Sirian position is strengthened. Ngen Van Chow is playing the Bullet broadcast to the Sirian rebels . . . making a mockery of the Directorate. Support among the conservatives has faltered. Less than eleven percent of the population continue to support us . . . and you pick this moment to ignore our calls?*

Skor Robinson studied the statistics Navtov forwarded. *Assistant Director, the time has come for us to deal with this on a rational basis. The Romanans are our only hope to quell the rebellion on Sirius. This Ngen Van Chow—this smuggler and felon—has been allowed loose too long. We—*

How did we miss his ability? Why did no alarm go off? Navtov hesitated. *Could it be that the Director allowed his preoccupation with the Romanans to blind him to the Sirian instability?*

Skor countered, *Could it be that the Assistant Director of Social Affairs failed to administer his area of responsibility?*

An Roque's intrusion into the thought channels came abruptly. *I hear discord! How can we maintain control when we ourselves are in confusion? I am considerably disturbed. I need to have predictability from both of you. From what source does this disharmony arise? I do not find rational decision making in your thoughts. If either of you persist in maintaining illogical mannerisms, you both must be removed.*

Skor ran his tongue over the roof of his mouth, curious at the sensation. *Director An Roque is correct. Assistant Director Navtov will resume his duties. In the meantime, let us regain control. I am instituting a program of plausible deniability. In the meantime, let us watch how these Romanans function. In the end, the threat of Damen Ree and the barbarians must be first softened, then blunted, and finally destroyed. I suggest you all bend your minds to that problem.*

Ngen Van Chow, First Citizen of the Independence Party chuckled lightly to himself as he watched the rolling crowds in the streets below. For the moment, the bustle of the city was stilled, the giant open-air holo projectors holding every citizen's rapt attention as they watched the illegal broadcast of the battle over the Romanans.

"Oh, this is good," he muttered aloud.

"I must say," Leona Magill agreed, her patrician features pensive, "the timing is perfect. How could the Romanan problem manage to fall into our hands so neatly?" She lifted a long, manicured thumb to her full lips, chewing it thoughtfully.

Lost in your reprehensible idealism again, Leona? Ngen wondered, letting his eyes trace the perfect line of her jaw. Such a beautiful woman. Too bad she didn't share his ends and means. But then, when everything came due, what was one beautiful woman more or less? And the future could never be counted on.

"Do not turn your back on luck," Pika Vitr added.

Dressed in black, he stood tall, thin. Elderly, his mop of white hair gave him a commanding look—one Ngen always chafed at, comparing it to his own medium build, swarthy skin, and flat features. Despite his limited imagination and talents, Pika looked the part of a dignified head of state. Ngen, no matter how he affected multicolored expensive clothes, never truly felt he'd shed the clinging reality of his orphaned childhood when he'd hustled on the docks.

He looked up at Vitr's aquiline features and lifted a shoulder. "Random chance may be rare, but look how it has worked for us. The conservative remainder is eroding. Like sand on a beach, Directorate support is washing away in the Romanan scandal."

The huge holo depicted courageous Damen Ree as he looked at Maya ben Ahmad. "We're too glorious for that damn Robinson, you know that?" Ree's voice filled the thronged streets. A cheer rose like ground swell.

"Cut," Ngen ordered.

The holo flickered and died, Ngen's own image appearing in its place. "There you see it, fellow citizens." Ngen's holographic eyes swept the crowd. Excellent how the recorder caught that sympathetic look. It melted the crowds every time. "We are not alone! True, the Directorate brought us three centuries of peace. Now, it chains us in a stagnant prison. Together we have united Sirius to become a new beacon for all humanity!" Ngen's voice boomed over the crowd, everyone's attention on his image as it began preaching revolution.

A soft swell of sound, repeating, "Ngen! Ngen! Ngen!" grew and filled every throat in the street below.

"I don't know how you do it," Pika said softly, shaking his head, pensively studying the crowd.

As his voice boomed out from the speakers, Ngen lifted a shoulder and sighed. "I spent a lot of time before the recorders, Citizen. That, and the docks, I learned to appeal to a man's heart, to make him want to believe."

"You were a con man," Leona told him tartly.

Ngen bit off a quick rejoinder. Forcing himself to remain calm, he met the reserved look in her green eyes. "That's all any politician is, Leona. A con man. A soother and persuader. A subtle and glib liar." *And one of these days, my idealistic alabaster darling, I am going to possess you . . . break you . . . feel you whimper in my arms.*

"First Citizen?" Giorj Hambrei called uncertainly from behind.

"Excuse me," Ngen bowed slightly, seeing the challenge in Leona's thoughtful gaze. He stepped back, allowing gray-complected Giorj to draw him to one side. "Yes?"

The sallow engineer raised his pale gaze. "I have news. The Directorate has just announced they have allied with the Romanans. Together, the Patrol and the barbarians are coming here . . . coming to destroy the revolt."

Ngen squinted his disbelief. "Allied? No, it's . . . impossible!"

The truth lay in Giorj's eyes.

"Very well," Ngen added quietly. "I trust we can handle the situation?" There would be new groundwork to be laid. The hero, Damen Ree, would have to be sullied. All in its time. A little manipulation here, some misinformation there— and presto! the Romanans have betrayed Sirius and the revolution!

Giorj nodded. "They will need time to get here. I estimate we have between six and nine months. Modifications to the captured ships will be complete by then."

"Don't let me down, Giorj." Ngen fingered his chin and chewed his lip. Romanans and Patrol? Allied? What did it mean? The other unsettling claim revolved around Romanan shamans seeing the future? What about this nonsense of prescience?

"I have heard from my mother, First Citizen. Her treatments are most satisfactory." Giorj inclined his head. "I have my things packed. Your private launch is ready and I am leaving immediately for Frontier on the matter we discussed earlier." At that, he turned and walked away.

"Yes," Ngen whispered to himself. "You know where your loyalty lies, don't you, Giorj. Do your job well, my man." He filled his lungs, turning to study his companions' backs. *Then I shall have to move quickly. By the time the Patrol arrives, Sirius must be mine—heart, body and soul! And as for the Patrol? Well, we have a little surprise for them, don't we?*

CHAPTER II

Susan sprinted through the dark village, seeing men and women working their way down the streets, finding their dwellings and seeking their beds. The battle ended, the question had been answered: the People would live.

In her misery, she didn't notice the air of relief in their happy voices.

Susan ducked through a corral, speaking soothingly to the horses, calming them. She worked her way to the manger and pulled herself on top of the straw. She sat for a moment, numb, biting at the knuckle of her thumb. Irritated, Susan shoved the hand far down into her blanket.

The star men had women who commanded—like war chiefs! She knew they had women marines. But women who commanded?

She knew she ought to go home. Uncle Ramon would be there . . . and yes, he'd beat her. Then Aunt Maria and the rest would ridicule her for her odd ways. Susan closed her eyes and leaned back on the hay, careful of any bayonet grass that might be in it.

The beatings weren't bad. Only rarely did Ramon Luis Andojar get carried away and really hurt her. Physical pain passed. Ridicule seemed to last forever. Her aunt's words would cut into her soul. And when Maria finished, the rest would deride Susan for days. Then—in the way of the Settlements—it would spread. People on the street would look at her with amusement, knowing her own family scorned her. The thought almost made Susan wish the Santos would steal her. She'd only have to endure rape and slavery—a future no different from her present one.

The star men have women war chiefs! The thought lulled her exhausted mind and body to sleep.

The morning sun didn't wake her where she curled under her blanket, but the sound of a piercing whistle brought her bolt upright, to smash her head on a low beam. Cursing, she pulled the blanket from over her rumpled black hair.

She blinked her way beyond the stable and tried to brush the hay from her blanket and calf-hide dress. A lean white AT hovered, settling slowly to the ground next to the wreck of the *Nicholai Romanan*—the Sobyet transport her ancestors had stolen and brought to this world centuries ago. From the ship, the star men had named her people: Romanans.

Men and women hurried toward the square, chattering excitedly. ATs remained a novelty—and these had just returned from war. Susan hurried along, sticking to the outskirts of the crowd, hoping to avoid notice, dreading to see her uncle or any of the rest of her family.

The familiar sight of the ramps dropping to the ground left Susan with a strange longing. The star men had women who went among them as equals. She had heard the tales of Red Many Coups, the star woman warrior who wore coups on her belt. From the stories, she had taken five in one battle—a feat only John Smith Iron Eyes might have equaled.

First the marines trotted down the ramp in shining white battle armor, blasters cradled in their arms. Susan heard a gasp from the crowd and strained to follow pointing fingers. She saw, clapping a hand over her mouth. The marines had spider effigies and crosses drawn on their reflective battle armor. And yes, there were women among them!

She crawled up on a cart to see better. Behind her, the Settlement stretched out in a hodge-podge—a cluster of rounded hide roofs, smoke spiraling from the smoke holes. Brown humps, they radiated out from the gray bulk of the *Nicholai Romanan*, warm in the sunlight of a new day. Horses were tied at entrances while irregular lines of pole tree corrals zigzagged out toward the herds of cattle grazing in lush grasses.

A shout distracted her and she twisted her head to see warriors bounding down the ramp. Their Romanan hide clothing contrasted with the reflective white of the marines, but the Romanan warriors were more colorful.

The crowd recoiled, a wave of muttering growing loud as they realized Santos warriors mingled with their own. Here—for the first time—Spider and Santos walked as brothers, arms about each other as they shouted and whooped at the blue sky. They sang medicine songs and pointed heavy rifles into the air—some shooting in the age-old signal of victory.

A carnival atmosphere swept the mass of spectators while overhead a second AT dropped from the sky, settling near Susan, blasting dust, hot air, and a curious odor over the packed people. Others circled out of the sky, whistling as they sought a place to land.

The stark white of the ATs glared against the dingy rusted hulk of the *Nicholai Romanan*—a comparison, Susan thought, of her life with that of the star men. They left her breathless —so shiny, brilliant, exciting and new. She wondered how star men married as she saw her uncle's lopsided head in the crowd, wrapped in soft hides. He'd had coup taken from him as a youth. Nevertheless, he'd finally killed the Santos who shamed him and regained his honor.

The ramp shot out from the second AT and more marines and warriors paraded off. Last came a big Santos prodded ahead by guards in battle armor with blasters at the ready. Possibly the biggest man Susan had ever seen, he sneered, spitting into the dirt. Hard dark eyes looked out contemptuously at the crowd, now so oddly quiet. Ripples of low conversation ran from person to person.

"It is Big Man." Susan overheard an awed voice. "He betrayed the People—his as well as ours, and the *Bullet* men."

She looked again at Big Man as he grinned wickedly at the crowd. Even over the distance, something about him sent a shiver down her back.

"John Smith Iron Eyes has sworn a knife feud!" a hushed voice added.

Another figure emerged from the AT. Sunlight glinted from red hair hanging down over her shoulders. "Red Many Coups!" the cry rose from the crowd.

Red Many Coups stood, hands on hips, at the foot of the ramp, meeting stares. Romanan hide clothing did little to hide the full curves of an athletic woman. She took in the crowd, a somber aura riding her shoulders like a mantle. Her green eyes held them, powered by some inner determination. The belt of human hair at her waist shimmered black in the sunlight—the status of a true warrior.

Susan strained to see. *She was real! It was true!* She forced her tight throat to swallow. She lost herself for the moment, imagining riding freely over the plains, rifle in hand, alert for Santos warriors and their rich horse herds.

A rough hand grabbed her ankle. Starting, she looked down into the wrath-lined face of her uncle. "There you are, bastard child of my sister," he growled. "*Get home!* Your aunt needs you. We are feasting Red Hawk Horsecapture this afternoon." His critical eye went over her. "Sleeping in the hay, eh? By Spider, you better have been alone! You embarrass us enough without another bastard child in my family!"

She felt herself toppled off the wagon and onto her butt in the mud. Someone laughed as she scrambled to her feet and glared wickedly at her uncle.

"Now, *go!*" Ramon Luis Andojar ordered, scornfully. "Worthless child." He raised his hands to the prying eyes of onlookers, perplexed. "It is only that I so loved my sister. What can an old warrior do, eh?"

More laughter grated on Susan's shamed ears.

"The star people treat women differently!" Too late. She clapped a hand over her mouth, terrified. A young girl *never* challenged her elders.

Ramon's face twisted, eyes queerly glazed. Brown lips pulled back to expose broken yellow teeth.

The blow came quickly, but she ducked it. He kicked at her and she barely twisted out of the way. Her agility caught the old man off balance and he stumbled into the side of the wagon, banging his elbow and cursing.

More people laughed.

Susan tried to jump away, but Andojar's grasping fingers caught the edge of her dress and sent her sprawling. Rolling, she came up on her feet, hemmed in by the crowd.

Ramon Luis Andojar had her trapped. "*DAMN you, girl!*" he hissed. "I'll break every bone in your body! What did you say about star men? You want to be like them, eh? Your mother's clan isn't good enough for you?"

"They don't beat their women!" Susan growled back, knowing it would hurt this time, but beyond caring. The crowd jeered, feeding Ramon's insane rage.

"If you strike me, I'll . . . I'll . . ." Susan heard herself cry.

"This is how you pay back your clan?" Ramon demanded.

She didn't duck quickly enough. The fist caught the edge of her cheekbone and sent her spinning. She tried to fight back, kicking, scratching, pummeling his heavy body with futile fists. A stunning blow clipped her under the jaw. There was a sudden flash of lights back of her eyes. She fell, senses reeling. Dirt clutched in her fingers as she tried to get up.

"You *filth!*" She barely heard her uncle howling. A kick landed in her side, stitching her with pain. "You are cursed, Susan Smith Andojar! No clan will have you! No man will have you! You said you will not live in my house? Well and good! By these witnesses, I throw you out! Out! You hear? My clan knows not your name!"

His spittle caught her full in the face.

She felt cruel hands on the back of her dress as he jerked her upright, and slapped her—the sting bringing back a fuller consciousness. Susan squinted into his red-rimmed eyes. Ramon's balled fist blasted lights through her brain, snapping her head back. Her skull clunked hollowly against the cart wheel. She whimpered, trying to see straight, panting in pain.

"Enough!" The voice carried authority.

Susan blinked desperately, trying to focus on her uncle. His eyes had gone wide. The fist dropped away. Susan slumped limply to the ground. With determination, she pushed herself up and dabbed at the blood that dripped from her nose, refusing to quit. He slapped her down as she dove at him.

"Enough, I said! Take her home," the voice ordered. "What is your name, old man?" Venom dripped from the tones.

"R-Ramon Luis Andojar."

"See that she's cared for. If you lay another finger on her, you'll deal with me." A woman's voice. The speech had a slight accent.

Susan looked up, wincing in the bright sunlight. She couldn't make out the face—haloed in red by the sun. She dropped her eyes and saw the string of coups hanging from the belt. Again she sought to concentrate on the face.

"You know who I am?" the woman asked, voice firm.

Ramon nodded slowly.

Vision clearing, Susan glared defiance at her uncle before looking to her savior. She met green eyes, grim now, commanding. And . . . pained? Tinged with sorrow and hurt?

"Good." Red Many Coups straightened. "See that you heed me." The star warrior turned on her heel and walked off, people hastening to shuffle out of her way. Whispers stole through the crowd as Susan pulled herself unsteadily to her feet, feeling the warm drip from her stinging nose.

Ramon Luis Andojar pushed himself against the wagon and puffed as he uneasily wiped his face. "They have no right to interfere with our ways," he threatened softly. The crowd evaporated.

He looked at her, hatred modeling his craggy features. "Go on, we have to feast Horsecapture this afternoon. Be of some use for once. I doubt he'll marry you after this—not and give me any horses!"

Susan stumbled as Ramon pushed her roughly away. She continued to dab at her nose as she staggered along, heedless of the drying blood. The curious stares hardly bothered her.

The house brought a feeling of strangulation to the base of her throat. Sturdy pole wood legs, hauled from the mountains, supported a roof of earth and stretched hides. Partly dug into the ground, perhaps ten meters long, it provided shelter from the cold winter winds—a miserable prison at best.

She ducked through the doorway and blinked in the darkness of the interior. The hushed chatter stopped. Only the smokehole and doorway provided light. Susan quietly went to the dirty pile of hides that made her bed. She knew the whole family watched her. Already word must have reached here. Angry condemnation burned in her aunt's hard face and the other children's—all younger than her but Raven. A warrior now, he would come later—black mood baited, eyes flashing when he heard what had happened to his father.

She dropped her head and bent to wash the blood from her face. No one said anything as she looked into the small, angular fragment of looking glass. The product of another world and a distant past, the reflective material had flaked off the back, leaving the mirror spotty. Like a reflection of her life.

A haunted, lean image peered back at her in the shabby glass. Her straight nose had swollen. A swelling knot formed on the firm lines of her jaw. The boys had called her pretty. They admired her body, whispering behind their hands about her firm breasts, the curve of her hips and the way her long legs moved. Any would have been more than willing to take her for a night—that was the way of men—but none would want her for a wife. They said, "Too wild. Too odd. No warrior's wife!"

Clean, she stepped outside with the dented metal pan, flinging bloody water to spatter in the street. Taking a knife, she cut steaks from the haunch that hung in the shaded part of the house and saw to their preparation, aware of the eyes that followed her every move.

She overheard them mumbling about Ramon disowning her—and how Red Many Coups sent her back. She steeled herself. Better had the star woman left her to beg in the streets rather than sending her back here, shaming Ramon all the more. Hatred hung heavy in the air.

Susan watched the flames licking at the meat as she cut the greens she'd gathered beyond the Settlements the day before while watching the cattle and sheep. Knowing the stew boiled right, she unrolled a hide, bending her back to the effort of scraping the unforgiving tissues free while the meat cooked.

I cannot stay. Ramon will kill me one day—him or Raven. There is no life here. I am a slave. She heard more whispering behind her.

But where? Where could she find a haven? What was left? No one would take her. Too many people liked Ramon Luis Andojar. He had been a fine warrior in his younger days. In the ways of the People, she was at fault. She had been taken in, fed, clothed, kept warm and sheltered. Now she shamed clan and household.

Placing the cuts of meat by the fire where they would stay warm, she bent her thoughts to the problem. The mountains were always there. Spring had come. Melon bushes would provide enough to keep her alive . . . if no bear found her. She shuddered at the thought. The huge native predators were two-tailed dragonlike beasts with suction disks to grab their prey.

Could she find one of the small groups that had split off from the Spiders and Santos? Maybe they would take her in and grant her some sort of shelter? What else was there?

Red Many Coups? Would the star woman want her? Without coup? A woman without family or clan? No, no great warrior would take her in. She had shamed her clan.

Ramon cried a greeting from outside, "Make ready! Willy Red Hawk Horsecapture is here!"

Susan swallowed, retreating to her bed at the back, trying to make herself small and unnoticed.

"Secure from damage control quarters," Damen Ree ordered, rubbing his face as the last of the ATs dropped toward the planet, taking so many of the Romanans with them. Shorthanded as they were and suffering casualities, rebuilding *Bullet* would take every waking hour.

Ree glared harshly at the screen showing *Victory* and her crippled sister ship *Brotherhood* several hundred kilometers away. History had been made. Patrol ships had shot at each other: the death of a civilization. How many qualified men and women were dead because of the pumpkin-heads? How many more would die?

"Where do we go from here?" Ree wondered, baffled by the turn of events.

He tried to massage life into his cheeks, looking up at the reflective surface of a black monitor. A haunted look in his eyes made him appear haggard, wary, and . . . old.

"Yes, that's really me," he whispered, feeling the exhaustion of too many hours in the command chair. How long since he'd slept? How many days? He blinked at his reflection, seeing a stout man, firm of body with craggy features, the planes of his face heavy around a stubby nose. His hair had been cropped close to his skull, leaving his bullet head a bony lump on beefy shoulders. Silver shot through his black hair now, the years of command graven deeply into his face.

"Me, I'm the first Patrol Colonel to have ever turned against his superiors." The nagging strains of an eternal headache clanged behind his eyes. *I need sleep.*

The comm personnel muttered softly to the system, continuing their endless duty. Endless? He'd seen two shifts change since the last shot had been fired. And they'd worked double stretches prior to the battle.

He sniffed irritably. "I guess there's no easy way along the road to treason." Treason? Yes, they'd crossed that line. An era had ended. Patrol had fired on Patrol.

"Five hundred years of honor . . . all shot to hell." He looked absently at the monitor, watching the dots of movement as tugs worked around the other ships, knowing *Bullet* looked the same.

"It would have happened eventually," he mumbled absently. "If not me, then Maya, or Toby, or someone else would have received an order they couldn't carry out. *Skor,*

you overloaded your grav plates when you ordered me to
burn the Romanans. That's all. Could have been anyone.

"Dry rot in human civilization . . . and now Sirius is
revolting, too." He grunted bitter amusement. "The beginning of the end, Skor. Like the old Terran empires. The
barbarians are loose. You're collapsing from the inside."

"Colonel?" Neal Iverson's voice came through comm.

"Here," he responded, mentally triggering the headset
that rested like a golden circlet about his skull.

"I can't seem to reach Lieutenant Sarsa, sir. I had a
couple of questions about the—"

"She's on the planet, Neal." Ree stifled a yawn, eyes
feeling gravel-filled. Treason had proved hard work.

"Uh, well, I'll try and get her down there, then. Maybe
the AT comm will—"

"Forget it, Neal." Ree pulled himself to his feet, looking
around the bridge, noting smoke-stained panels he'd never
seen in any condition less than spotlessly white. "Iron Eyes
has to finish Knife Feud with Big Man. Rita is our represen-
tative for that."

"Any ideas when she'll be back, sir?" Neal sounded perplexed. Hell! This Spider business perplexed them all.

"No." Ree rubbed the stubble of three days of beard.
"And I don't expect her back in a big hurry. Philip died
when the upper port gun deck decompressed." Ree rubbed
the back of his neck, attention caught by the spider effigy
Leeta Dobra had drawn overhead.

He added quietly, "A lot of people died, Neal. Give her
time to mourn." *We all need time to mourn.*

"Yes, sir. Uh, I guess I'll . . . I'll make it up as I go, sir."

"You're a good man, Neal. I have every trust that you'll
do fine coordinating the repair work. If you need me, give a
holler."

Surprise and appreciation filled the voice on comm. "Why
. . . thank you, sir!" The comm went dead, leaving him in
peace.

Ree chuckled absently, eyes refusing to leave the spider
drawn on the overhead panel. The melancholy returned.
"Ah, Leeta," he whispered, voice strained. "You were too
good for them all."

He studied the effigy. Despite the tension, she'd drawn a
perfectly proportioned spider, as if some artist had possessed her hand in those frenzied moments. *Bullet* became a
Spider ship under her hand.

"Time to mourn?" He shook his head sadly.

He'd watched from the monitor as her body, wrapped in white, was blown out the evacuation hatch. They'd shot her out separately from the others out of respect.

Hollowness gaped under his heart and he shook his head. A man shouldn't think of dead friends when fatigue rode his mind so heavily. It made the hurt worse; grief almost became palpable.

A private pushed a cleaning machine through the main hatch, saluting absently as he unlimbered the ionizing brushes and nozzles. Haggard like so many, he practically stumbled from fatigue. "Won't be but a minute and the bridge will be sparkling again, Colonel."

Ree nodded, seeing little left to do. The comm personnel—bleary-eyed like the rest—seemed to be in control of the ship, coordinating repairs, handling communications.

"I'm going to catch a couple of hours of shut eye," he called across to the comm station. "I'll be available for emergencies."

"Yes, sir," Tony called back. "Have a good rest, sir."

The private punched a button, starting his machine to whirring as he ran the nozzles over the smoke-stained cabinets and monitors.

"When I come back," Ree added, passing the youth, "that spider on the overhead panels better be there. If it's not, you're gonna . . . well, you'll regret it! I promise."

The private gulped, looked up at the spider, and nodded so hard he shook.

The corridors seemed strange, not at all like the old *Bullet*, but then, she'd been bloodied. For the first time in her three hundred and fifty years of service, *Bullet* had been hurt. So had they all. The Directorate, the Patrol, no one would ever be the same . . . least of all, Damen Ree.

He stopped at a burned section of corridor, a twisting pain in his soul as he looked at blackened paneling, melted steel, and gashed bulkhead. He'd underestimated the effect the damage would have on him.

"Oh, *Bullet*," he sighed.

You know, we'd make horrible lovers, Leeta's voice crept out of his memory. Damen stopped, clamping his eyes shut, leaning his forehead against the damaged plating of his ship.

"And I asked why," he told the cold graphitic metal, running callused fingers lightly over the heat-blistered plating, sharing pain with his ship.

He could picture her, staring at him over the rim of her glass as she coolly sipped at the Arcturian wine. Her blue eyes had been thoughtful, measuring, seeing him for exactly who and what he was. *I couldn't share you with your ship for one thing.*

Damen pulled air into his suddenly fevered lungs, slapping the buckled metal, looking around him. "And she was in love with Iron Eyes all along." The empty feeling in his gut widened. "But she was right. You always came first. Made that choice years ago.

"Yeah, well, old girl. We still showed 'em, didn't we? Out-gunned. Two to one, and we couldn't maneuver." He caressed the metal lovingly. "We still saved the planet, best ship."

And Leeta's charred body tumbled in vacuum, lifeless, the keen mind baked in that lovely skull. She'd fall into atmosphere within days. Ree had computed that, knowing her ashes would blow over the planet she'd connived and plotted to save. A fitting end.

Damen Ree smiled weakly feeling the ship shudder under his feet. "Well, *Bullet*, I promised Leeta Dobra once that I'd never let anyone have you. That Skor Robinson would never take you away from me." He paused, frown lines etching his brow as he pursed his lips. "I'll keep that promise."

Looking up and down the empty corridor, he quickly forced his palm against a steel sliver, puncturing the skin of his hand. Surreptitiously, he rubbed the blood into the metal.

"There, old girl. I've staked everything on us. That seals it. I promise here and now, I'll never let anyone take you away from me."

He winked at the corridor around him, a weight lifting suddenly from his tired soul. "Out-gunned and out-numbered," he repeated, walking down the corridor in his rolling spacer's walk. "And we still beat 'em!"

In his quarters, he got only a couple of hours' sleep before the dream of Leeta's charred body brought him awake, swinging out of his bunk. Cold sweat chilled him as he dropped his head in his hands, blinking in the silence of his quarters.

He swallowed hard. "Damn!"

Like a man condemned, he pulled his battle-stained uniform over his aching body and palmed the hatch, knowing duty would keep his mind off her.

CHAPTER III

The heavy steel plate might be thick, but it groaned as atmospheric pressure built. Corporal Hans Yeager winced, using his suit lights to double-check his safety line. They'd lost this section of deck once before when a bad sonic weld snapped. The decompression had blown Keech out into vacuum until somebody had taken EVA time to snag him back in.

Hans checked the sensor leads going into the holo box. All tight. The image on the small screen shifted, colors reflecting increased strain on the metal. Hans played his lights down the new section of hull. Looked fine.

How many hours without sleep?

First he'd survived the grating tension of the battle, the horror of the blasted decks where *Victory's* fire had holed them. Damn, he'd come so close to dying when a direct hit decompressed his section. Luck, and only luck, had saved his life while others were sucked out to violet death. Then more damage control orders came through. It had been hustle ever since.

Hans checked the monitor, read micro-changes in the steel, and leaned against a makeshift hull brace and let himself float. They had to restore the lights, temperature and artificial gravity before the powerlead crews could begin piecing the rest together. And after that came another three sections of deck. He closed his eyes while they waited, suit crackling around him as the pressure increased. He took a deep breath, sighing, floating . . .

"Wake up," Breeze grumbled sourly.

Hans jerked his eyes open and blinked dumbly down at his instrument. "It'll hold," he decided, studying the tension lines running through the repaired section of hull. "It's not good, but it'll hold."

"Yeah, well, once we've got atmosphere in here, it's easier to patch up." Breeze moved to undog his helmet and throw it back over his sweaty hair. A puff of fog rose in the

lights around his head. Breath condensed before his mouth
and nose. "Damn, it got cold in here!"

Hans slipped his own helmet back, reveling in the biting
chill. He checked his suit monitor before climbing over a
twisted piece of machinery and plugging a comm trace into
the system. Frost from the renewed atmosphere glittered on
every surface as the warmer air met super-cold plating and
instruments.

"Shouldn't bother you that much," he called. "It's only
sixty below." His own sweat-wet hair had frozen. His nose
began to smart. "That's long enough, better suit up."

"How long till we have heat?" Breeze grumped, suit
lights flickering in the blackness as he refastened his helmet.

Hans studied his gauges. "Uh, here it is." From his tool
kit, he pulled his lead tracers and cut a section from the
melted bulkhead. Plasma from blaster fire had torched the
metal and severed the thick cable beneath. "Maybe ten
minutes."

His skilled hands began the intricate task of joining the
severed leads. A cheer echoed in his helmet when he re-
joined the lead that powered the lights. Flooding the deck
with light didn't help—just exposed more damage. He stood
and leaned down to touch a sensor to the deck. The digital
readout clicked, slowly climbing up the Celsius scale. At the
next lead, he settled slowly, weight returning as the grav
plates energized.

"Take a break," Breeze ordered.

Hans sagged on a capacitor cover as Breeze and some of
the others walked over. "It'll all fall apart as the metal
warms and expands," he added glumly.

Breeze nodded wearily. "Yeah."

Two Romanans, awkward in suits, threaded an antigrav
laden with sections of pirated plating past melted equipment. Evidently, they'd waited until the lights were repaired—
not that Hans could blame them. Stumbling around in the
dark trying to navigate that much inertia on an antigrav
would have been murder.

"Romanans! Wouldn't have believed it." Hans shook his
head. "We were shooting at them a couple of months ago."
He yawned, fighting to keep his head from nodding forward.

"Huh!" Breeze grunted. "Figured you'd be down there
dickering for one of their women. You know, the stupid
ones who're used to cows and stuff and wouldn't know
you're—"

"Aw, cut it out!"

Breeze grinned. "Yeah, well, maybe they wouldn't know you were a blushing virgin! Might think—"

"Damn it, Breeze!" Hans waved. "I do okay!"

"Yeah, that why you turned so damn beet red when we set you up with Marla? Thought you'd—"

"Shut up! I . . . I just got . . . You know. It was a surprise is all. Just a . . . surprise." Hans swallowed, the gurgle in his throat loud enough to cause Breeze to roar hilariously. "Can it! I'm going back to work."

Despite his weariness, he began tracing comm leads, restoring the ship's ability to communicate through the blaster torn sections of bulkhead.

Damn 'em! Damn 'em all! God, I'm never gonna live that down. Every guy on the gun deck can get a date but me. Well, that's okay. I guess not everybody is made for women. Oughta be some gal who can't handle men either. As scared of me as I am of her!

Adrenaline pushed him, stirred by the memory of how they'd all been watching when the voluptuous marine, Marla Sash, had crawled into his bunk that night. Hans colored at the memory of his frantic fumbling retreat. Damn it! How could a guy get along after something like that? He'd become the laughing stock of the whole ship!

One thing was sure, he decided—rapidly splicing new comm line into a freshly welded section—those horny bastards might be greased protons in bed, but none of them held a candle to Hans Yeager when it came to comm repair!

Willy Red Hawk Horsecapture arrived with greetings, bear hugs, and reckless laughter. He pounded Ramon on the back heartily and playfully teased Aunt Maria. Horsecapture's thin hatchet face took in everything, eyes glittering when he located Susan in the back.

Tall and muscular, the four coups he'd taken from the Santos and other Raiders dangled on his vest. He looked every inch a warrior, from his broad shoulders down to his thin waist and bowed rider's legs. He moved with a certain catlike fluidity. The fighting knife at his belt gleamed in the firelight. His eyes still held that knowing cruelty. As he talked to Ramon, a mocking tilt touched the corner of his lips. The thin shape of his face suggested a constant smirk.

I don't trust him. He'd turn on Ramon as quickly as not. He is not one with Spider—he's different, grasping, a man who follows honor only so long as it suits him. His only loyalty is to greed and power. I will die before he has me!

Ramon took his pipe bag from where it hung on the wall. With careful fingers he pulled the long carved piece from the soft leather, gently tamping tobacco into the bowl. Face serious, Ramon began the ceremony of a victory feast. He sang softly as he lit it and smoked, and passed it to Horsecapture, both blowing smoke up to Spider.

After the prayers and songs, Horsecapture gratefully helped himself to the meat and greens Maria laid before him. Susan watched from the shadows as the food disappeared. Finally, Horsecapture looked up and burped politely, smiling at Maria who—of course—took all the credit.

"So you had a run-in with Red Many Coups?" Horsecapture looked speculatively at Ramon before glancing to where Susan crouched in the shadows, wishing she could crawl under the dirt and bury herself. "She has shamed you, Ramon. Thrown your own words—"

"Damn her!" Ramon spat, indicating his displeasure. "It is not right to see coups on the belt of a woman. All she needs is . . . is a good hard screwing to set her right. Some man like you will come along and thrash her bottom." Irritated, he added, "But instead, tell us about the fight in space!"

Horsecapture laughed. "I tried to paddle her bottom at the Navel. She beat me fairly and squarely, old friend. Do not count on finding their women so civilized as ours. It's like . . . Well, they're like the men on that ship. Some are war leaders like Red Many Coups. They can kill you just as dead . . . and just as quick," Horsecapture murmured, eyes narrowed to a squint.

"Just like the men?" Ramon scowled, shifting his eyes to where Susan sat. Then he laughed raucously. "They take their turns on top? They ask a man to marry? I don't see how . . . Who does the cooking? Who gets pregnant, eh? That is wrong, warrior. Spider did not mean for women to be as men. They are to serve us! Warm our beds at—"

"Perhaps, Ramon. Let me tell you this, old friend." He paused, lost in thought. "There are new times coming. We have been offered the stars if we will go with the *Bullet* men and fight some Raiders they call Sirians. That is why the battle stopped last night."

"A raid? Far off . . . among the stars?" A fearful longing

crept into Ramon's voice. "There will be many coups in this? If only I . . ."

"Many coups." Horsecapture smiled wickedly. "Not only coups, my friend, but we have been promised riches to bring home. We, too, will have things like the star men. Who knows where this will end? This Directorate of theirs has grown weak. They do not have many marines or many ships. They need us now where once they would have only been too glad to destroy us and the Prophets. There is much at stake that a brave man could . . ."

"Would that I were younger." Ramon's eyes closed, fire-light playing oddly on his wrapped head. "I would take honor to the stars."

"That is why there will be change, Ramon. It is the way of things. Our people will—"

"Spider will not change things." Ramon shook his head. "What would he do? Take that miserable excuse for a girl . . ." he indicated Susan, ". . . and make her a warrior? . . . like this Red Many Coups? Eh? Santos, take us!" He made a noise of disgust, gesturing as if he flung water from his fingers.

Susan jerked upright. She fought to lower her head . . . to keep from the old man's notice.

"Perhaps. I will find power out among . . ." Horsecapture stopped, frowning. "New ways are coming. What we have always had, always believed, will—"

"Bah!" Ramon spit into the fire and grinned as it sizzled. "It wouldn't be right. Spider won't let us fall from the path of strength and freedom. We have . . . have truth!" He pounded his bony knee with a gnarled fist.

"There are those who now call themselves brothers with the Santos. Who would have believed that?" Horsecapture demanded. "I tell you—"

"We have the stars." Ramon shrugged. "Perhaps we can get these star weapons for our own, eh? We would be . . . I mean we will no longer need these Santos. It is not right that the Spiders should make friends with them."

"Spider has taken one ship, Ramon." Horsecapture sat back, ignoring the old man's glare, and picked up a cup of tea. "The *Bullet* is no longer all a Patrol ship. There are men there who now pray to Spider and Haysoos. It is a mixture. Our world will become like that, too. Change—"

"The old ways are good enough!" Ramon protested. "By them, we are strong—"

"Are they?" Horsecapture interrupted mildly, raising an eyebrow. "There are wonderful things among the stars. I have ridden above the land like the wind. I have seen the stars from up close . . . seen this world from space. Things you cannot . . . Let's just say there is power there, old friend. And where there is power, there comes a man to take it!" Horsecapture's fingers closed into a tight fist.

Silence stretched.

The old man had listened carefully, face twisting with a scowl. "Have you spoken to the Prophets? Do they know of this great ambition of yours?"

Horsecapture waved it away. "The Prophets know of all great things to come. They see the future. Why do you think the star men wanted to destroy us?"

"You will go with the Santos?" Ramon shook his head. "There is no good in that. They do not have God. I have heard of Spiders and Santos praying together. That's a bad—"

"The Santos are not so strong in their beliefs." Horsecapture laughed wickedly. "Big Man tried to sell us out to the Patrol ships. Santos see betrayal in Haysoos. Power is with Spider. Big Man had a Santos Prophet with him. Haysoos is dying in the minds of men. There are Santos warriors who now pray only to Spider. Things change."

Ramon fingered his wrinkled chin. "And what of Big Man? He's a powerful . . . What will they do to him?"

Horsecapture grinned. "John Smith Iron Eyes has sworn knife feud—blood oath. He hates Big Man. They will fight at the Navel the day after tomorrow. And if Iron Eyes dies . . ." Horsecapture smiled at some hidden thought.

"That I would see." Ramon sipped his tea. "The greatest warrior of the Spiders and the greatest warrior of the Santos in knife feud. There will be honor in that. Yes, honor . . ."

Horsecapture's eyes glistened. "I'll not miss it. You and I should ride out there and watch."

The men sat silently for several minutes. Horsecapture finally sighed. "What of this girl who brings you so many troubles? What do you plan to do with her?"

Susan stiffened. Ramon spit into the fire again. "I would have thrown her from my house this morning. I curse this Red Many Coups for sending her back! Take her. No bride price. For our friendship, I do this—"

"I'm sorry, Ramon." Horsecapture raised a hand plaintively. "She has spurned me too many times for honor. I myself can no longer take her from your hands. I will bring back women from the stars to keep my house." He shot Susan a crafty look, smiling secretly. "She is the most beautiful woman in the Settlements. I had hoped to break that spirit out of her—tame her to a man's hand. I think she would bear strong sons—but after this morning?" He shook his head before adding, "Perhaps you could give her to Old Man Wattie?"

Susan couldn't stop the sharp intake of breath.

Ramon heard it and looked up, confusion blending into understanding. "Old Man Wattie? No one would give a woman to . . . to . . ."

"She shamed you in public today," Willy Red Hawk Horsecapture said absently. "You will get no horses for her. You might have to *give* horses to get rid of her." He steepled his callused fingers, studying Ramon through slitted eyes. "Why not pay her back? Why not let Old Man Wattie take her to his bed? She could live for a long time knowing your . . . um, generosity."

Ramon licked his lips, face lighting, "I will. *I will give her to Old Man Wattie. I will ask only the price of one horsetail quirt for her.*"

Susan tried to stifle the tears—to keep from shaming herself. Old Man Wattie had but one leg—the other lost in his youth when a jealous husband shot it off. A woman he'd tried to rape had blinded one of his eyes and beaten him within a fraction of his life. Shamed as a coward, Wattie lived at the edge of the settlements. He begged for scraps of garbage to eat and complained to any who would listen that he had never had a wife. Jokes claimed that a woman would be better off giving herself to the Santos.

Susan shot a frightened glance at Ramon. She met his narrowed eyes, horrified at the glitter of triumph and hatred. She would be another man's wife and no longer the problem or responsibility of the clan—no matter what Red Many Coups said.

Lungs heaving, she tried to stifle sobs. The ghastly sight of Old Man Wattie clutched her mind, the leering grin as he watched women pass, his dirty stump of a leg wrapped in rags, spittle slipping down his hairy chin as he winked with his one good eye.

She couldn't keep the image of his filthy, cracked hands from her mind. She imagined his excitement as he pulled himself toward her—could feel his hands lifting her dress, reaching for her soft skin.

Frantic, she broke and bolted, cursing as she ducked from her uncle's house and into the dying light of the setting sun. Behind her, Ramon's whoop of triumph shrilled loudly.

Half-insane, she ran, bare feet pounding, arms pumping as her long hair streamed out behind her. As night fell, she still ran, trotting periodically, pushing her long legs despite her gasping lungs, heading ever to the east and the mountains that lay there.

"Spider," she moaned. "Get me away! Take me from here and I will be yours for all my life!"

Flames jumped high from the big bonfire while whole calves turned on spits over red coal beds to either side, watchful women basting the animals in sizzling grease. People milled in the darkness, some singing, others laughing over the babble of voices. Here and there a jug of locally distilled sour mash floated from lip to lip.

Szchinzki Montaldo, late of the Directorate Planetology and Survey Service, grinned heartily as he shared his limited vocabulary with an old Yellow Legs woman who patted his stomach with bony fingers.

"Says she's glad you came," José Grita White Eagle translated. "Says you star men need Romanan food to fill you out."

"Uh, right," Montaldo nodded, a plastic professional smile on his face. He lost the old woman's babble as she waddled off into the crowd on thick arthritic ankles.

"Quite a spread," Montaldo added to White Eagle.

The Santos gave him a wry smile. "It isn't every day a world is saved by a space battle. No, the Yellow Legs had a couple of young men in the fighting. Friday Garcia Yellow Legs was one of those who took the reactor with Rita. Not only that, but he saved a bunch of lives when the gun deck took a hit. That sawed-off little runt crawled out on the end of a breached section with a horsehair rope—of all things— and lassoed a bunch of marines who'd been blown out in the decompression."

Montaldo nodded, remembering his own fear as he'd stayed at the anthropological field camp the night before, knowing that if *Bullet* lost they'd be next. The Directorate wouldn't want witnesses to genocide.

"Not only that," José waved around. "A party is the only social life they really have except for the Spider rituals once a year. Oh, maybe someone gets married so they can have a wedding feast, or killed in a fight and they can throw a funeral. Life for us Romanans is tough."

José shook his head. "I mean, the first tapes Red Many Coups showed us . . . Couldn't believe it. People *lived* like that? When you've never seen electricity before, when you've never seen anything fly, or a motor move a vehicle, the Directorate comes across as . . . as magic."

S. Montaldo smiled and nodded.

Grita waved. "Old Mama Yellow Legs, there, has worked ten hours a day, seven days a week, all her life. Not a tooth is left in her head. Never had a pain pill in her life. See how bent she is? That's from tanning hides, butchering cattle, bearing children, packing wood, cooking food, fighting horses and watching three out of every five children die in infancy. She thinks there are strings that hang from *Bullet* to each of the ATs. To her notion, that's how they fly."

"You sure seem to have learned a lot about ships and space war," Montaldo changed the subject.

White Eagle shrugged. "A lot of it comes from sleep stim and language training. I had a head start. Red Many Coups, uh, Rita Sarsa, started me on the first sleep stim they set up in Navel Shelter. As official Santos liaison, I have to pretend I know more than the rest."

The little old lady came waddling back, rocking from side to side on her stubby legs. Grinning toothlessly, she nodded to Montaldo and handed him a dripping leg of lamb, chattering all the while like an Arcturian mendicant.

S. Montaldo nodded politely, fighting to keep his smile, feeling warm juices running down his arms. José Grita White Eagle chattered Romanan back as the little lady thumped Montaldo on the back—heedless of her greasy hands—and puttered off, chuckling to herself.

"This is an ANIMAL leg!" Montaldo cried.

"Of course, eat it." White Eagle greeted a passing Spider warrior with quick phrases. The Spider leaned his head back and belched loudly.

Montaldo winced.

"The sign of good manners here," José explained. "Means the food is good—and speaking of which, if you don't start chewing on that, Mama Yellow Legs is going to be back looking hurt. She honored you with that meat."

"What about . . . *I mean haven't they heard of plates?"* Montaldo wondered. "Uh, forks, and something to keep this grease under control. By Haysoos! I don't even have a flippin' knife!"

"That's why God gave you teeth," White Eagle chuckled. "Look, I know you've never . . . Here." José took the meat and ripped a large chunk loose with his teeth, chewing heartily. He handed the heavy piece of meat back and ran a sleeve across his mouth. "There. Like that."

"Go barbarian, Doctor," Bella Vola, another of the anthropologists, appeared at his shoulder. "It's fun. Throw your manners to the wilds and have a good time. Hell, after last night we didn't think any of us would see this day." She flipped black hair over her shoulder, grinning. "Besides, if you're going to deal for the toron on this planet, then you'd better get used to the folks who own it."

S. Montaldo sighed, leaning his head forward and taking a bite. He chewed thoughtfully, horrified at the juices running down his chin. He swallowed and looked at the meat. "Hey, that's real different tasting. Uh, richer, you know. Got a fuller flavor."

"Yeah," Bella agreed. "Wasn't raised in a zero g stall, or grown from cloning. That's the real thing right off a crittur."

Montaldo swallowed. "Right off the . . . I'm going to be sick." Of course I do have to live here, he reminded himself. Got to learn about the natives sometime. Won't be many Directorate supplies coming in. And it really isn't bad.

He took another bite.

"Where's Marty Bruk?" José asked.

Bella lifted a shoulder. "Disappeared with Friday."

"Yeah," Montaldo added. "Isn't he supposed to be here? I thought he was the big hero at this fandango."

White Eagle began swaying from foot to foot as someone started banging a drum. "In this crowd, you could miss him. Friday's the smallest man I've ever seen who wasn't a boy. But then if he was here, people would be laughing at his jokes. That or someone would be screaming because he'd wrapped a dead rock leech in their blankets when they weren't looking."

"José?" Bella wondered, "How are you feeling about leaving for Sirius?"

The Santos shrugged, grinning. "Colonel Ree says there will be many coups. He says there will be riches beyond anyone's conception. I am ready to be a rich man. How do you feel about staying? Heard Chem was shipping out on a Fast Transport to Arcturus. You're in charge now, huh?"

"Mixed feelings, José. Losing Doc, well, that hurts." Bella took her turn to shrug. "I've got Marty, a whole planet of you quaint Romanan types to study and write about, and a transductor to send my reports back. I love the hell out of it. If only Doc hadn't been . . ." She closed her eyes. "Aw, hell!"

"There's Marty now," Montaldo added, hastening to change the subject, jerking his head Bruk's way since his hands were full of hot lamb quarter. Damn! They'd all loved Leeta. She'd been a tough customer, but a hole had emptied in S. Montaldo's soul when he learned of her death.

Marty Bruk—the physical anthropologist from Doctor Dobra's team—climbed to the top of an aircar, hollering, waving his hands around. People stilled, looking up. The only sound came from the crackle of the pole tree segments in the bonfire. Sparks swirled orange in the night air. Montaldo chewed his lamb leg, realizing he really did enjoy the meat.

In flawless Romanan, Marty sang out, "Warriors! Spiders and Santos! Last night the star ship *Bullet* bravely gave us a victory—saved our lives! Tonight we celebrate what that victory brought us." He waved down the ululations.

"As you all know, tomorrow, John Smith Iron Eyes will face the traitor Big Man in knife feud."

Montaldo noted the Santos warriors here and there began shifting nervously. Even José Grita White Eagle tensed. Not a good subject, Bruk.

Marty had his hands raised, face serious. "Now, we all know John Smith Iron Eyes will win. But I have just come from another hero of the People. A man you all know. In fact, he says he's the *bravest* man of all the People! No one is braver than him!"

Warriors whispered back and forth, beginning to frown.

Marty waved them down again. "Oh, I know. You mock him now! At the same time, the bravest Romanan warrior has been in high places, making medicine, gaining his power! As a result he has made himself powerful beyond his stature! He has sworn to chase down Big Man if John doesn't get him tomorrow!"

A ripple of voices went through the crowd. Someone cheered from one side.

"Not only that, but the *bravest* Romanan warrior has

become so powerful, he is now the biggest man on World—bigger than even Big Man!"

The murmur of the crowd grew restless. Montaldo's limited vocabulary made out a burly warrior sneering, "No man is that big! Who is this brave warrior?"

Marty turned, pointing in the darkness. "Old ones and young, I give you *FRIDAY GARCIA YELLOW LEGS!*"

Grita chuckled, "Friday? Big? The top of his head barely reaches my chest!"

Montaldo strained his eyes as something towering moved behind one of the Romanan huts, bobbing, swaying with each huge step.

"The *biggest* Romanan!" Friday's voice called as he came striding into the circle of firelight high above the heads of laughing people.

The burly warrior in front of Montaldo snickered and shook his head. "I should have known!"

"Where's that Big Man?" Friday roared from his high perch on pole wood stilts. "I'll rip him limb from limb!"

He plodded around the happy crowd, stilt legs shrouded in some light cloth to look like pants. "Let's see if he can whittle *me* down to size!" Friday thumped his hard muscular chest with a balled fist.

"Hey, Friday?" Bull Wing Reesh called, raising a jug of whiskey over his head. "What are you doing up there?"

"Tired of being hit in the eye by your kneecaps!" Friday howled while the crowd broke into guffaws. "Nope! Now, when I was up there in *Bullet* I looked out one of them view holes, you know? Saw what World looked like. Why, that was the first time I'd ever seen over a pile of horse dung—and by Spider, I liked it!" He clasped his hands over his head, shaking them in an age-old sign of victory.

"How you going to get down?" Marty Bruk called, evidently on cue.

"Like this!" Friday hollered. He reached down and did something. The tops of the poles exploded in a flash of light and smoke. Friday dropped like a rock, neatly somersaulting and ending up on his feet while the crowd roared and applauded.

"He always like that?" Montaldo wondered.

"Naw," José managed. "Lots of times he's worse."

"I think you'll have an interesting trip to Sirius," S. grunted. He took another big bite out of the meat, wiping his sleeve across his chin and grinning.

CHAPTER IV

Knife feud. Romanan justice. The body of the dead Santos warrior, Big Man, sprawled limp in the loose dust—a pool of red spreading under the corpse. Big Man's blood-streaked skull gleamed where Iron Eyes had deftly skinned hair and hide: treachery repaid.

Warriors rehashed the fight, voices low. Spider and Santos colors flashed gaily in the bright sunlight. Here and there, Patrol personnel stood talking, gesturing. They nodded respectfully to the victor as by ones and twos they drifted off. Romanans stepped into the saddle, reining horses, or joined the Patrol leaving in aircars. Others jogged out to waiting ATs.

John Smith Iron Eyes gasped and stiffened as Rita Sarsa sterilized and pinned the long gash in his shoulder. He looked up at her from hard black eyes. Wide cheekbones gave his face an angular look. His brow rose high while the broad nose betrayed his Arapaho Indian ancestry. Long black braids hung over muscular slabs of shoulders. Darkened by years in the fierce Romanan sun, his skin contrasted with Rita's. Thin-lipped, his mobile mouth was set tightly in a face lined by tragedy. Muscles rippled up and down his body as he turned.

An AT whistled shrilly as it rose. Final spatters of rain left a last reminder of the storm that had just passed—purifying the clear air of the world the Directorate knew as Atlantis.

Iron Eyes wiped Big Man's blood from where it had spattered on his face and cleaned the spider drawn on the front of his war shirt.

"I've never seen Sirius," Rita said slowly, throwing red curls over her shoulder.

"Me either," Iron eyes joked, wincing as he moved his shoulder. He got up and walked over to his black mare before catching up the red gelding. In spite of his wound, he lifted Rita into the saddle.

43

"I was afraid you'd lose," she reminded, gesturing toward Big Man's corpse—left shamefully unclaimed by his relatives.

Expression going taut, Iron Eyes muttered, "I don't like to lose."

She spurred the horse out—away from the big rock overhang that marked the ancient Romanan campsite called the Navel. Haunting fingers of grief tugged at her mind. Philip's face filled those dark shadows behind her. Together, they had dreamed of a new world, of honor, of wild chances— and for it, Philip tumbled in space: dead.

She blinked back the burning sensation behind her eyes. Until the day she died, the image of his limp body would live in her memory, a coldness. She would never forget his blood crystallizing and freezing in the foamy way of fluids in vacuum. Bugged-out eyes started from their sockets. Philip's pain and agony jerked in her helpless arms. Again she heard atmosphere whooshing from the breached hull of the starship *Bullet*—sucking the greatest love of her life forever away into the void.

He had been a safe harbor in her turbulent life.

Remember the way his eyes twinkled and how his tanned skin crinkled into laugh lines? See the depth of his soul betrayed by those soft brown eyes? You were a compassionate man, Philip. A gentle man. Warm pain settled behind her eyes. *Where will I find your like again?*

Philip Smith Iron Eyes had wanted the stars. As she hung there in the vacuum of a blasted gun deck, she'd let his corpse slip from her fingers, out . . . out into the dark of space.

Her first husband had destroyed himself in his search for a different dream. Would she always lose men to dreams? Afterward, she had navigated a course through a variety of males who did nothing to satisfy her cravings for a companion. Now she had lost another love. *Damn the dream!*

The boom of an AT breaking the sound barrier brought her back. One dream come true. A people lived because of her, and Philip, and John, and Doc.

Doc! Another anguish. Sarsa's eyes strayed to John, noting the deep hurt he bore with such dignity. John Smith Iron Eyes had loved the anthropologist. Unlike her and Philip, he and Doc hadn't had time. Who suffered the greater loss?

She snorted to herself, seeing Iron Eyes throw her a dead look—miserable and exhausted. "We're a hell of a pair, aren't we?" she asked bitterly.

"Spider must have his purpose. Perhaps the Prophets have the answer, Red Many Coups."

She shook her head. "As if *they'd* ever tell."

"They're men of God." Iron Eyes shrugged.

She ignored his casual acceptance. Instead, she glared up at the gray sky. "Well, no matter. I guess we just do the best we can."

"That is the way of Spider."

They rode in silence for a while longer. Then he looked up. "Is peace too much to ask? First I loved Jenny—my clan sister. She was forbidden . . . taboo. Incest to my People. Big Man killed her. Leeta came and turned my anger into love. She gave me a reason to live, to serve the People. Yet Spider takes her from me! It's not fair."

"The Prophets say we are placed on earth to learn . . . for God," Rita reminded.

Iron Eyes' flat eyes displayed a twisted humor. "I have learned pain rather well."

"But if . . . if we're tools of God, perhaps we are forged stronger by having been given victory at such a price? Huh? You think?" She squinted into the distance.

"Like the forging of a good rifle barrel." Iron Eyes jerked a quick nod. "Not done all at once." He paused. "That Spider forges so well, so tough, makes a man nervous about what lies ahead. Let us hope the steel doesn't turn brittle."

"Great thought. I can hardly wait," Rita grunted. For a woman who had once prided herself on acceptance of agnosticism, she had come to believe in this Romanan concept of Deity. She shivered. "Sure makes a person . . . wonder."

"I once asked a Prophet if he had followed me into the mountains." Iron Eyes adjusted the heavy rifle resting over the bow of his saddle. "He asked if he had followed me . . . or if I was in reality following him. The same problem applies when you try and anticipate God."

"You know, once I wanted to be a wife. Bear my husband's children, maybe pursue a part-time career." She hunched in the saddle, swaying with the gelding. "Maybe that wasn't such a bad idea."

"You would say no to Spider?" Iron Eyes raised an eyebrow. "You would avoid the destiny he has in store?"

Rita nodded slowly, eyes blank.

John Smith Iron Eyes couldn't hide his amusement. He said bluntly, "You lie, Red Many Coups."

Rita stiffened, whip-tense. "You know, not many people would have the guts to call me a liar."

Iron Eyes let his gaze roam over the rolling grasslands. "You wouldn't be here if you didn't seek your destiny. You and I, we are too much alike. Tools of God—we would not be lightly discarded. Pride drives us, Rita. That . . . and we wish to challenge God. Spider may do his worst to us and in the end we think we can overcome—"

"You seem pretty sure of yourself," Rita snorted—partly to cover the fluster his words brought. She shifted in the saddle, suddenly uneasy. *A form of hubris? Will it destroy me?*

"You once told me that—given the chance—you'd kick God's ass." He laughed. "Tell me *that* isn't a challenge!"

"And you said the attempt would do God honor." She lifted a red eyebrow.

He prodded his black mare ahead. "Like it or not, we're warriors, Red Many Coups. No matter what your words, you can't turn down the challenge of destiny. It is part of your free will. No matter what the hurt, you must see how far you can push . . . and what you can get away with."

"And you're the very same!" she shouted after him, pushing the gelding ahead, so she stayed by his side.

"I am that," he agreed, moving easily with the horse. "I'm no more than . . . *Careful!*" Iron Eyes pulled up on his mare, bringing her to a walk. "Someone is there." He pointed with his rifle.

Rita shucked her blaster from its holster and checked the IR sight. "One person." The grass wavered as a body slithered through it.

"Get up!" Iron Eyes called out, riding forward, rifle ready.

A head lifted from the green carpet to be followed by the rest of a blanketed girl rising magically from the grass. She stood slowly, staring sullenly and defiantly at John Smith Iron Eyes as he rode closer.

Rita came up from the other side, blaster easy. The girl's eyes darted to her and stopped, surprised.

"Who are you?" Iron Eyes asked, eyes hinting at kindness.

"S-Susan Smith Andojar." Cowed, she kept her eyes to the ground.

Rita studied the bruises on the side of the girl's face. "You're a long way from the Settlements." *Why did she look so damn familiar?*

"I'm sorry."

"Damn it, look at me when you talk!" Rita ordered. "Who ever taught you to stare at the ground that way?"

"She is unmarried," John Smith told her. "Such behavior is considered seemly."

"You ever known me to be seemly?" Then in a softer voice, "Look at me, child. Do I know you?"

The girl looked up through a tangle of dirty black hair. With a bath, a combing, and some decent clothes, she'd be quite attractive—beautiful in fact.

"I saw you in the Settlements just after the space battle. You saved me from a beating." The words came with difficulty.

"Who beat you?" Iron Eyes asked, leaning over the horn of his saddle.

The girl stood silently, lips pursed, eyes down. "He beat you again?" Rita asked, remembering the scene. A big man, gray-haired with a lopsided skull wrapped in rags, had been slapping the girl. Scarred by the grief of Philip's death, she'd stopped it.

The girl just looked down at the grass.

"Where were you going?" Iron Eyes asked. "There is nothing out here but the mountains. You would be eaten by a bear. Have you no people to take care of you?"

"Why was that old man beating her?" Rita asked, dismounting and walking up to the girl—surprised to find her half a head taller.

"Probably her father punishing her for dallying with one of her friends," Iron Eyes guessed casually.

"He wasn't my father," the girl whispered. "My father and mother are dead."

Rita put a finger under the girl's chin and lifted, staring into frightened eyes. "So where were you going?" Rita asked softly. "There's nothing out here but death. You were running away? Speak, I'll protect you."

Susan nodded, trying to lower her eyes again. Iron Eyes had stepped down next to her. "Why do you leave your clan?" he asked, concern in his voice. "They would take care of you."

"My uncle is Ramon Luis Andojar." She kept her eyes carefully lowered from John's. "He swore he'd marry me to Old Man Wattie." She shivered at the words.

Iron Eyes laughed softly. "No man would wish that for his kinswoman."

"Who's Wattie?" Rita demanded, fists on hips.

"A wretch who lives outside the Settlements." Iron Eyes' expression showed his distaste. "He has only one leg. Had a woman scratch out one of his eyes. Begs for scraps to live. His only service to the community is horse tail quirts he weaves and trades. No one would grant him a wife—no matter what."

"Ramon promised me in front of Willy Red Hawk Horsecapture," Susan said with conviction. "It is a matter of honor now."

"Horsecapture?" Rita wondered. "Why? Damn it, I don't . . ."

Susan Smith Andojar gave Rita a frightened glance. "To punish me."

"It would be a pretty serious punishment." Iron Eyes shook his head in disbelief.

"I want more than a husband. I want to be a warrior." Susan looked up at Iron Eyes for the first time, desperation in her eyes.

"It's unheard of," Iron Eyes said softly. "A woman has no place—"

"Why?" Rita asked suddenly, spinning on her heel, glaring hotly at him. "The kid wants the chance? So let's—"

"It's not the way of women." John Smith Iron Eyes shrugged. "Spider made men one way . . . women another."

Rita's lips twisted. "Susan, do you really want to be a warrior?"

The girl nodded quickly, face flushing with sudden hope and longing as she looked quickly at Rita's coups.

Rita got a subtle pleasure out of the ghastly look on Iron Eyes' face. "So Spider says, huh?" She laughed out loud. "Maybe I can't kick his ass—but if this girl wants a chance to learn to be a warrior, she damn well can."

Iron Eyes looked his misgivings. "It'll cause a stir among the clans."

"What can they do? Knife feud? You really think any of those boys could take me?" Her voice echoed disbelief.

"No one would care," Susan whispered. "My uncle is only concerned for my bride price. He says I'm ungrateful."

"What's bride price?" Rita asked, shooting a scornful look at Iron Eyes.

"Usually two or three horses." Iron Eyes cocked his head.

"Ramon said he'd give me to Old Man Wattie for a horsetail quirt." Susan's voice hushed with shame.

"I suppose I could swing that." Rita grinned. "Come on, kid." Rita swung up on the gelding and reached a hand down. Susan took it eagerly, face suddenly glowing.

"This will cause problems," Iron Eyes said dubiously as he swung his horse and followed the two women.

Colonel Damen Ree ducked under a huge section of steel he recognized as having once been part of a lock reinforcement. Welded to the gun deck frame, it now kept bent, creaking hull plates from blowing out into space. Even so, the damage control crew worked completely suited, helmets ready in anticipation of a breach. *Bullet* still reeled, badly hurt.

A lieutenant continued explaining something about welding to an eager Romanan. Quite a number of the young men had stuck with the ship to see it put back together. Ignorant, they clamored to know, and better still—to Ree's view—they molded themselves into crew. Ree spotted yet another spider effigy painted on the wall.

Two Romanans chatted easily, vibra-cutters removing sections of a melted blaster from where it canted sideways on the slaglike deck.

So much? My beloved Bullet, *will we ever make you right again?*

His headset alerted him to the call. "Colonel Maya ben Ahmad and Brevet Colonel Arish Amahanandras are arriving by shuttle in fifteen minutes."

Ree let his eyes play over what he could see of the reconstruction of the gun deck. They had taken so much damage. So many lives had been lost. *Victory* had scored one of those lucky hits that played random chance with the best of tactics.

As he turned and climbed over a twisted mass of metal, he saw a foot sticking out of the mess. The splintered ends of the tibia and fibula protruded through flesh now dried black and dessicating.

"Here!" Ree shouted at an engineer while he pointed at the grisly remains. "Get this out and have medical run an ID. They can see to a funeral."

The man trotted over, bent to see, and saluted before accessing his comm. Ree climbed over the rest of the wreckage and made his way to the hatch.

The battle had almost been over when the call came in from the Director. *Bullet,* badly damaged, guns out, shields failing, had turned to run between the two Patrol ships the Directorate had sent to kill the renegades. Ree had decided to take his foes with him by exploding his antimatter in a last desperate gamble.

In the lift he accessed his conference room, alerted the kitchen staff, and thought about the upcoming meeting. His old nemesis, Colonel Sheila Rostostiev, of the Patrol ship of the line *Brotherhood*, had broken under the stress of combat. Arish Amahanandras had replaced her—a new element to consider. Maya ben Ahmad, on the other hand remained a known quantity and Ree had more than a little respect for the old war axe.

Finding a seat at the head of his table, Ree positioned his chair so the other commanders would have to look up at him—tactical advantage. He checked his recorders and ordered a cup of coffee. Sitting for once, he realized just how exhausted he felt. The supervision of repairs had occupied every waking moment since the battle.

Brotherhood had suffered the most. By a fraction, her engineer had averted a failure of her matter/antimatter reactor. Of course, Ree had meant to kill the ship since it was Sheila's—an old grudge. In one stroke he had disabled the vessel and broken his old rival. *Victory* had disabled his own guns—turning the tide.

Ree watched the shuttle dock and followed the two commanders by monitor as they were escorted by a combined guard of marines and Romanan warriors. The interest his counterparts showed in the Romanans brought a wry smile to his lips.

The hatch opened and Ree stood as Maya and Arish entered, uniforms immaculate. Ree looked down at his own, wrinkled, spotted with oil, torn here and there, smudged with soot. The odor of his wrecked gun deck clung to the fabric.

Maya smiled wickedly at him. A small woman, her skin had the dark look of oiled walnut. Her face had been lined by years of command. A hard wryness added a tilt to her lips, but her blue eyes sparked electrically as she studied him, her graying hair pulled back severely.

He bowed to the women, the movement short, stiff—that of a commander among equals. His fierce blue eyes drilled Maya.

"Damen," Maya ben Ahmad saluted.

"Maya," he smiled back. "I am pleased to see you looking so fit. Excuse my appearance. I've been busy."

"You repairing this damn wreck by yourself?" Colonel ben Ahmad asked dryly. She dropped easily into a chair.

Ree ignored her and turned to Brevet Colonel Arish Amahanandras. "Welcome to the *Bullet*, Colonel." Ree bowed deeply, taking stock of the new commander of *Brotherhood*. Tall, perhaps fifty, she moved gracefully, black hair streaked by white strands, her large nose emphasizing black piercing eyes. From his study of anthropology, Ree guessed her Terran ancestry as South Asian.

"My pleasure, Colonel," Arish said in a deep throaty voice. She bowed in response.

"Please be seated." Ree indicated a chair and settled down himself. Not so long ago the room had been the center of heated arguments among scientists and anthropologists over the nature of Romanan culture. Here, Ree liked to remember Leeta Dobra, sharp-eyed, eager to be at her study.

"Let's get to the point and cut out the crap," Maya began. "Damen, we've got a problem." She turned to Arish.

"Colonel Ree, *Brotherhood* was badly damaged during our recent difficulties. My people are working around the clock. Nevertheless, it will be some time before we can complete repairs that would meet even minimum requirements for the jump. Given the schedule Director Skor Robinson mandated, we have to arrive at Sirius within six months standard time. Given the damage sustained and the number of casualties, I can't meet that deadline."

Ree smiled pleasantly as refreshments were handed to the officers. "I have personnel I would be more than happy to transfer to your command."

Maya cackled, "That bunch you put on the planet and sent out to whirligig their way over to us in the middle of the fight?"

"Exactly." Ree steepled his fingers. "Those who were planet born are still with the Romanans on World. I would be more than happy to send them up to *Brotherhood*."

Arish looked pleased as Ree ordered a personnel list with qualifications. "Most excellent! Indeed, most . . ." she mused to herself.

Maya leaned on her elbow, watching speculatively. "That way you've gotten rid of your traitors, correct?" She squinted slightly.

Damn her! Ree fought to control himself. "Let's just say I

don't think they could . . . work in harmony with my crew."
He pasted a bland smile on his lips.

Maya laughed a dusty laugh. "My, how the Patrol has
changed. In the wild days of my youth, no commander
cared so much for personal loyalty. Things were . . ."

"Different?" Ree gave her an irritated look. "In the days
of your youth you wouldn't have fired on *Bullet* either.
Nothing's the same, Maya. The Directorate is collapsing
around our ears. We ourselves have just made history."

Maya nodded. "Tell me, Damen, what do you . . . Why
these barbarian Romanans, for God's sake? Why did you . . .
go rogue? Our orders were to come, burn every living soul
on that planet and silence the scientists. When *Brotherhood*
jumped in, Skor Robinson ordered us to destroy you. That's
completely . . .

"Damn it, Damen! What the hell is going on?"

Ree reached for one of his Terran cigars and sniffed along
the edge. He lit it, puffed with satisfaction, and leaned
back, feeling the weariness pulling at his limbs.

"It all started," he began, "with a radio signal an un-
manned GCI cargo ship picked up. The information relayed
automatically to the Directorate Gi-net and *Bullet* was assigned to make a reconnaissance of this sector. We sent a
drone in the general direction from which the signals were
thought to come and found this planet.

"University sent along a team of anthropologists since it
appeared that this was a lost colony. As more data came in,
the anthropologists got to calling this place Atlantis. Sure
enough, when we arrived, a positive ID was made on that
ship sunk into the ground down there. It is the *Nicholai
Romanan*, a Soviet transport from the days of exile six
hundred years ago.

"The team of anthropologists sent down to the planet was
under the supervision of Doctor Leeta Dobra. The first
surprise we got came from one of the men they call Prophets. We traced him through the ship's sensors, of course.
The odd thing is, he traveled for a solid week to meet our
landing party." Ree paused. "For a week before we even
knew where we would land."

"I don't understand." Colonel Amahanandras frowned.

"Neither did we—but we found out soon enough." Now
for the blaster bolt. "You see, the Prophets know the future." Ree smiled into disbelieving eyes. "That's right, they
are prescient."

Maya squinted sourly. "Oh, come on, Damen! No one sees the future! Causality proves . . . You couldn't have convinced Skor Robinson of that!"

Ree nodded easily. "Exactly. That's why we sent Chester —uh, that's the Romanan Prophet—to Skor Robinson. After Robinson himself determined that these men actually do see the future, he ordered the destruction of this world and any witnesses who might compromise the situation. At the same time he used the Sirian trouble as a cover, diverting the attention of the other Directors away from us and the Romanans. Effective as an ion cloud, don't you think? Who'd ever know he'd committed genocide here? Only Sirius blew up in his face."

Arish sat silently, but Maya leaned forward and pointed a taloned finger. "Let's say I believe all this. Why destroy them? Why not just interdict the planet?"

"I did exactly that." Ree grinned, remembering. "Consider, Maya, the Directorate claims to exist to foresee economic shortages and keep governments from conflict, correct? How have they done that?"

Arish answered. "They use the computers to predict economic trends. That's all. The Directorate doesn't have any real power. Space is an open resource base. All they do is coordinate."

"Do they?" Ree asked, pointedly. "How did you get ordered here? How can an organization without power order you to destroy my ship?" He saw he'd scored.

Turning back to Maya he continued, "Imagine the effect on civilization when it becomes known that we have found men who see the future. If there was ever an unsettling influence in the galaxy, it's prescience. Consider, too, that the people who produce these Prophets are warriors who raid and kill each other for fun. Given those parameters, how many options do you think Skor had?"

"Genocide is against every law we've had clear back to the Confederacy and the fall of the Soviets!" Arish shook her head. "It's just . . . just impossible!"

Maya fingered her chin. "The release of the Romanans would have brought *total* social disruption. Of course Robinson ordered them destroyed. Think of the ramifications! Insurance would be obsolete. Why go into business? Why risk anything? It would be total chaos." For the first time, Damen Ree thought he heard a note of awe in her voice. "It would make crime impossible. You'd know who to marry." She grinned wolfishly.

Arish frowned. "There's a flaw. Why did you even fight?" She stared at Ree. "You would have known we were going to be called off."

He shook his head. "Doesn't work that way." Ree puffed on his cigar. "Our first thoughts were along the same lines. Why even bother living if someone can tell you exactly what's going to happen to you? Now keep in mind, not every Romanan can see the future—only a select few with an odd brain structure.

"The Prophets don't ever attempt to change the future themselves. If you ask one of those sly old men, they just nod and smile.

"But let me back up for a bit. There has always been a philosophical problem about the nature of God. That is, if God is truly omniscient, he knows the future." Ree saw them both nod. "Now, that means that there is no purpose to the universe since God would already know the beginning, middle and end. Everything would be predetermined. As a result of this argument, the nature of God has always been uncertain.

"These Prophets do see the future. At the same time— and I quote Chester Armijo Garcia—God takes great pains to protect free will. You see, there is not one, but many different futures which may exist. These Prophets never make changes for their own future benefit. If they did, they would fall into a trap whereby each choice they make affects an exponential number of future results—each of which can lead to a greater exponential number of alternatives. In short, they become lost in possibilities—sucked into the future. It's a mind-blowing eternity of choices they can make. The result is, they go mad with total self-absorption."

"So what's the point?" Maya demanded.

"The point is that they consider themselves teachers." Ree stabbed at her with his cigar. "They try and get us to learn as we make our decisions. We are what they call cusps and they don't want anything to do with influencing us. If they did, they would fall into that trap I just told you about. According to them, the purpose of life is what we learn. By making decisions of our own free will, our experience becomes God's. They call him Spider, by the way."

"Then God is not all powerful or all knowing in their cosmology?" Arish asked.

"All powerful, yes," Ree agreed. "All knowing, no."

"So where did they come from?" Maya leaned back, still skeptical. "Is this just a unique mutation?"

"The Prophets are descended from the Arapaho—a Native American aboriginal group. In the earliest ethnographies —documents that date back almost eight hundred years— anthropologists talk of the Prophets. During the acculturation and reservation periods, they claimed that the Prophets died out. Later, the ancestral Romanans fought a very successful guerrilla campaign against the Soviets who occupied North America. As a result, they were deported on the same ship with Mexican freedom fighters, occasional ranchers, and some other native peoples. Keep in mind they were fighting men from the start. They took over the ship . . . then they couldn't navigate it."

"Perhaps their Prophets got them here?" Arish asked, eyes veiled.

"It doesn't matter. The fact is they're here and Skor Robinson perceived they were a threat. He ordered them destroyed before they upset the Directorate applecart. In the meantime, I tried enforcing martial law. It didn't work. They wouldn't give up. They would rather die fighting with their rifles against our blasters and ATs.

"Doctor Dobra suggested that perhaps there might be a way for us to acculturate them while Chester was off talking to Robinson. We tried and it seemed to work. At the same time, I was unaware of a conspiracy between the anthropologists and the Romanans. In the end, one of my lieutenants, along with the Romanans, got aboard the ship. Lieutenant Sarsa captured the reactor room and threatened to blow us all up." Ree smiled. "It seemed that she had absorbed too much from the Romanans and—as the anthropologists say— went native."

"What about security?" Maya looked shocked.

"Security?" Ree thundered, pounding a fist on the table. "Security, hell! There were a bunch of primitive men down there riding horses! Not even our precious Sheila would have thought them a threat. They don't even fly kites down there! How could they threaten the ship?" He felt himself bristle and forced his body to relax.

"My second in command, Major Antonia Reary, tried to take over my ship and ordered an attack on the Romanans. That forced my hand. At the same time, the order came through to destroy them. Why should I do that? It was . . . against the policy I was pledged to protect. There were

men, women, and children down there. History can record
someone else as a playmate for Hitler and Genghis Khan
. . . not Damen Ree!"

"You still could have surrendered and left it in other
hands," Arish pointed out.

"No," Ree sighed. "You see, I learned from them, too. I
learned that humanity has lost something during the age of
the Directorate; we've lost initiative and daring. The Directorate suppresses personal achievement. Sure the stories go
around about a citizen saving a drowning kid, or flinging his
body into a pressure breach, but you never hear their names.
Who are they?

"At the same time, do you remember any major exploration during our lifetimes? No? Humans no longer travel
between the stars. Why? Most of the cargo ships are GCIs.
Only the Patrol travels the stars. Only the Patrol sees anything beyond a station or planet and every year there are fewer
and fewer of us!" He banged his fist against the table again.

Arish shook her head. "But we have order. Humanity no
longer has problems with piracy, warfare, or religion. We
have peace and security! There have been no—"

"At a price," Ree agreed. "I don't think the price is
worth it. There never seems to be a balance. I don't want to
go back to the chaos of the Confederacy, but at the same
time I would like to know that men are making progress. I
would like to recognize a composer who wrote a great piece
of music. I would like to know who the engineer was who
built a safer reactor."

"Ambition is a sin," Maya said wryly, repeating Directorate dogma.

"Uh-huh," Ree grunted. "And ambition got you to the
command of *Victory*." He looked at her curiously. "You
know, the rest of humanity thinks we're dinosaurs."

"Whatever we are, we have certain problems to solve."
Arish inclined her head and sipped her tea. "What is the
status of the Romanan mercenaries?"

"They're learning. In fact, most of them have spent their
lives making limited war. The sleep synch teaches them
modern combat techniques, and they are better marksmen
with a blaster than most of my marines—once you teach
them to hold on line of sight."

"You know that nonregulation personnel are a terrible
breach of Patrol regulations." Arish studied Ree through
slitted eyes.

"So was refusing Sheila's order to turn over my command." Ree kept his voice even. "The fact of the matter is that a new age has dawned for the Patrol." Ree watched her eyes widen in shock. Maya had a sour smile on her thin, bloodless lips.

"What are you talking about?" Arish asked uncertainly. "Do you now consider yourself above the law?"

Ree laughed. "Law? What law, Colonel? I received orders to destroy an entire planet of horse and cattle herders because their wise men saw things. And where is Patrol honor? Where is duty, Colonel? For the first time in the entire history of the Patrol we have *fired* on each other! We have killed our bunk mates. Blown holes in each other's ships over an order from *a big-headed freak!*" Ree glared angrily.

"Do *not* call the Director a freak!" Arish spat back.

"What the hell do *you* call him?" Ree demanded.

"*Enough!*" Maya slapped the table. She turned to Arish Amahanandras. "You're bucking to keep your command, Major. That Brevet Colonel business is just for appearances until it comes through from Arcturus. Keep that in mind!"

"Must be hard." Ree squinted at Arish. "You see, I'm sure that after we handle the problem of Sirius, Skor'll want to relieve me of my command. I'm sure you've been wondering about being tainted by my presence." Direct hit! He could see it on Arish's face.

"Very well," Maya sighed. "We'll send your discontents to *Brotherhood*. That should get repairs back on schedule and make up for her casualties. When can we ship Romanan mercenaries?"

"When do you want them?"

"How soon will their training be complete?" Maya spread her hands. She looked at the warriors at the door. "They look . . ."

"Complete?" Ree laughed. "Know what it takes to be a warrior in Romanan society?" He saw them shake their heads. "A man must either steal horses from another tribe or take coup."

"What is . . . coup?" Arish asked sullenly.

Ree lifted a finger and a Romanan trotted over. Damen pointed to the hair on the man's vest. "That is coup."

"Where did he get it?" Maya asked, looking unimpressed.

"He cut it from the head of the man he killed in combat." Ree let satisfaction flow through his body as his counterparts started and stared. "You see," Ree continued. "All they need to learn is zero g and our weapons systems. When it comes to fighting—they've seen more of it than all your marines put together."

After the shuttle had ferried the commander back to their ships Damen returned to his quarters to get some rest. As he lay on his bunk he stared up at the Romanan rifles he'd had hung on his wall. It was true—they would take his command away after Sirius—and that day deserved a little thought.

CHAPTER V

From the roof of his tower, Ngen Van Chow could see the whole of the Sirian capital, Ekrania, spread before him. He leaned back in the recliner and darkened his visor until the glare from the Sirian sun and its companion white dwarf no longer irritated his eyes.

The situation on Sirius seemed to be in hand. Nevertheless, what if it did go wrong? He pulled at a shock of shoulder-length black hair. No matter how good things looked, a dock rat kept an escape hole near at hand. And he did have that fast yacht of his. Nothing in the sector could catch him if he could get clear of the planet.

He stretched his long arms and sucked at a too-alcoholic lime drink. His information had been correct. The revolt had taken the Patrol completely off guard. No ships of the line could reach Sirius for at least six months. In the meantime, he had to keep pressure on the workers—an effort requiring more ingenuity every day.

They don't worry anymore. They haven't seen Patrol marines dropping out of the sky. Too many have begun to believe the danger is passed—that the Directorate is afraid of them. So how do I make them fear? How do I bend their minds to me?

Ngen frowned. Three events had forced his Independence Party into early revolt. First, the grain supplies had run out and no relief had been sent by the Directorate. Second, an anonymous donor had dropped a half-billion credits into their account. Last, but not least, the Directorate had been absorbed with Romanans.

What a stroke of luck that the Romanan thing had blown up in Skor Robinson's face! His frown deepened. Luck? He ran long tanned fingers down the wet sides of his drink, thinking of things in retrospect. An anonymous donation of a half-billion credits? Who?

Accessing his comm, Ngen reran the illegal broadcast that the woman anthropologist, Leeta Dobra, had sent from Atlantis. How had the Directorate allowed it all to get out of control? How had they failed to anticipate a reaction from the Sirians? Worse, his agents reported unrest sending tendrils through all the Directorate worlds and stations. People were clamoring for information on the Romanans.

"Pika?" he accessed through comm.

"Here, First Citizen." Pika's harried face formed on his visor screen.

"Like Damen Ree, we must broadcast our own revolution on an open frequency. We have the Directorate communications in our control. Send everything we have. All the speeches, the scenes of cheering people casting off the yoke of Directorate repression."

Pika smiled thinly, eyes narrowing in his long face. "Yes, of course. That will pitch the pumpkin-heads on their faces." He paused. "Why didn't we think of it before?"

"Training, Pika," Ngen mused. "How many other avenues available to us have been ignored because we thought they were beyond our control?"

Pika wet his lips. "I have no idea . . . but I'll have a team working on it immediately."

"Excellent." Ngen cut access.

He caught himself chewing on his lip—an annoying nervous affliction. He'd fought the habit ever since he'd been a dock urchin living in filth, walking that thin red line between starvation, the pimps, the psych, and the gangs.

Again he assessed comm. The image of First Citizen Leona Magill formed under his visor. "Greetings," he said softly. "I've been thinking."

Magill tossed black hair over her shoulder as her lips twisted. "Indeed?" her sensuous, contralto voice mocked. Green eyes studied his black ones pensively.

"It has been a month since we destroyed the offices of the Directorate. In that time, we have had no word from our rich friend. Doesn't that strike you as odd? I would have

thought he'd make a demand or two by now. That much
money does not come without strings—unless it's a trap."

"We considered that when the deposit was made," Magill
reminded coolly. "We knew the risks . . ."

"And we decided to take the money anyway." Ngen
narrowed his eyes. *You always seem to be made of ice. Did
you know, dear one, with my knowledge of anatomy I could
melt you? Whether you wanted it or not.*

"And tell me, Ngen, where would the revolution be today
without it? Wherever the money came from, it's too late to
be wondering now. We won. The results speak for—"

"I know. To have done anything different . . . Well, it
was the boost we needed. At the same time, we should be
very careful. The longer we wait without word from our
donor, the more worried I will become."

She shrugged, pert head cocked as her eyes gleamed. "No
matter. I was just about to call you. A curious development.
One of our sources in Arcturus has sent the most interesting
news. It would appear that the Directorate is training these
barbarian Romanans as Patrol marines." She laughed at
that, displaying white teeth. "What do you make of that,
Ngen? How do Romanans . . . Well, you pride yourself on
your ability to plot. So, what does this mean?

Ah! And I knew a week ago! "Most elementary, Leona.
You see, the Directorate no longer has the means to deal
with unrest. They have rotted from the inside out. They
must import barbarians—mercenaries. They can't even put
down a single planet's revolt without outside help."

Leona evidently hadn't gotten the response she'd anticipated. He could see disappointment on her face. "Should
we worry?"

"They ride horses, Leona my love. How could illiterate—"

"I am not *your love!*" Her perfect features frosted.

He smiled ironically and inclined his head. "Forgive my
forwardness."

"Let me know if you find anything." Green eyes regarded
him with thinly veiled disgust. A graceful hand brushed her
rich black hair over a white shoulder.

"I trust there are no problems with the *Hiram Lazar*?"
Ngen changed the subject.

"Your Giorj did a superb job with the plans. We have the
shields in place. The power source for the main blasters
depends on obtaining a couple of toron crystals. We can't

modify any we cannibalized from the GCIs, the specs are wrong. If only—"

"The toron will be here within a month. I've sent Giorj to bring it from *Gulag* as soon as he finishes at Frontier."

"Your private yacht? And you paid yourself well, I suppose." She snorted in derision. "With the crystals in hand . . . maybe two weeks to operational capacity. *Dastar* and *Helk* are similarly behind schedule. If we had more hyperconductor, we—"

"Strip it from the domestic systems. Sacrifice for the cause, you know. Anything else on your mind?"

"No. You've heard everything. Think about the Romanans," she told him, barely civil.

"And you think about that half-billion credits." he answered. Her image faded from comm.

A remarkably attractive woman—her adroit use of power excited him. Wouldn't it be a pleasure to break her? Turn that competence into whimpering submission? Indeed, any human body could be turned against itself. Surely he could find a way.

Ngen changed the angle of his recliner, bringing it upright, and accessed the information on the Romanans, scanning Leeta Dobra's report.

Their old men could see the future? Bah! Impossible! Someone's imagination had stretched. He studied the holos again. They were dark-skinned, but not as dark as many races of humans. They wore hide clothing—not particularly well tailored. Their weapons consisted of primitive single shot rifles with bores averaging between eight and ten millimeters. And finally, each man carried a long fighting knife of about forty centimeters in length.

They hand-forged their rifles from metals pirated from the wreck of the *Nicholai Romanan* and made a reasonable nitro-based powder. And that topped their technological capacity? According to the report, they had no flight capabilities at all—let alone space travel.

Yet the Directorate trained them as marines? Ngen frowned and sipped at his drink—forgotten since the call to Leona.

Parallels between Rome in the fifth century, the Soviets in the twenty-first, and Arpeggio in the decline of 2460 flashed through his mind.

He laughed hollowly. So, Directorate policies had finally borne fruit, and the harvest found only rot on the branches. The Directorate faced chaos for the first time in . . .

Of course! Skor Robinson had sent his Independence Party the half-billion credits. He'd been frightened by the Romanans. If he allowed the Sirians to get a little out of hand, attention would be diverted from Atlantis. Only the Romanans and the Sirians had both proved better than expected.

Thoughts—like a cool breeze—drifted through Ngen's mind. If the Romanans had surprised Skor Robinson—that big-headed freak—how much more easily could they surprise Ngen Van Chow—who didn't have a direct mind-link into the Gi-net computer system?

He sipped at his drink again and cleared his mind, trying to visualize the Directorate in its entirety. He imagined the immense interstellar society as it was, full of faceless, nameless beings. Pampered, fed, clothed, and choreographed day in and day out—their every need met.

And those were the innovative ones. The other half of the population floated about in their stations, oblivious to the rest of humanity. They produced just enough for their needs—tied to the rest of the species only by subspace transduction. They worshiped primitive fusion reactors as gods, studied kinship systems—and, for the most part, ignored the planet dwellers.

Only the accidents showed any initiative. Aberrations like Ngen Van Chow—who managed to escape the law and the psychs that would have made him into a happy, productive citizen. Ngen had learned ambition, pain, challenge, and hunger on the docks. He'd had to survive by his wits. The Directorate hadn't given him a thing he hadn't earned on his own.

And now I will take it all!

His one great fear had been that the Sirians wouldn't make soldiers. He sighed, "Now—a month into the revolution—my fears are almost confirmed. My rebellion is drying up around me. If the Directorate has to go to the Romanans to find soldiers, I have no one but my own milquetoast population to draw from. How does one make a soldier out of a spoiled lamb?"

He stared at the picture of the Romanan warrior displayed on his comm screen. Lean, trim, his dark eyes glittered deadly. No civilized world had bred such a specimen.

His mind clung to that thought. Yes! He chuckled to himself as he thought it all out. There lies the answer. A man who has everything need not strive. The Romanans had nothing . . . and somehow they had forced the Directorate to back down. If my Sirians have nothing to lose, will they, too, not become a force to be reckoned with?

"Indeed," Ngen whispered, eyes tracing the familiar lines of Ekrania. "My people, the time has come to learn the value of life. Yes, you will learn what it means to fear. I will give you a choice. Live through me—*or die!*

Chester Armijo Garcia had learned to deal with time. A man did not stand before it. Instead, he let it pass, allowed it to wash around, over, and through him.

He read the accounts of nameless physicists, learning that they perceived time to be motion and space, although their mathematical proofs were beyond him. Time—bent space or not—filled Chester's universe—became his element. Learning to cope with time had almost destroyed him at first, driving him to the brink of madness. A confusion of sights, sounds and sensations from the future had whirled him through a fearful maelstrom.

His ambition had originally been to breed cattle, make a reasonable reputation as a horse thief, and have many children to bounce on his knee in his dotage. That had changed the day the Prophet came and ordered Chester to follow along in his wake with his cousin Philip Smith Iron Eyes.

In the beginning, Philip appeared to be the one the Prophet sought. In the end—frozen with fear—he hadn't been strong enough to accept the visions. The temptation to change his future—to avoid pain and suffering—had been too great.

At the same time, Chester began to see with greater clarity; as if Spider had changed His mind and His selection. Under the tutelage of the Old Ones, Chester learned. Visions unfolded out of gray mists of the unknown in his mind. They came as stills to begin with, but as his senses developed and he learned to accept them, the visions began to move. Finally he began to see vivid action with sound and sensation to match.

The Prophets had always been enigmatic to the People. Now Chester understood why. To retain sanity, a Prophet had to submit, to passively let time come to him, accepting what would be without emotion or involvement. He had to let himself go completely, unresisting of time and destiny. He must forget his identity as Chester Armijo Garcia. He had to forget his humanity, become one with Spider and the universe.

Now, he smiled benignly at the three monstrous visages which formed in holographic relief before him. The beatific smile on his bland flat face became an expression of sympathy—an understanding of what it means to be human and strive valiantly against crisis not knowing the effort is futile. The smile hovered, bittersweet as that of a parent watching a child's struggle against the inevitability of growth.

The faces before him hung in the air, grotesque, out of proportion. He saw human caricatures on bloated skulls partially hidden by gleaming skin-tight helmets covering the balloonlike craniums. The Directors: they ruled. Genetically altered humans capable of interfacing directly with the Ginet computer system via their helmets, their decisions affected the whole of human space, controlled population growth, industry, exploration, and communications.

"Chester Armijo Garcia," the one with blue eyes greeted.

"Director Skor Robinson," Chester smiled, bowing his head slightly.

"These are my colleagues," Skor introduced. "Semri Navtov, Assistant Director." One of the huge heads bowed, dark eyes impassive. "Assistant Director An Roque." The third head nodded.

Chester smiled, feeling the tapestry of events as an inevitable force. "You are worried about the explosions on Sirius," Chester began. "There was little you could do about it. To have predicted the—"

"That information has not been released." An Roque's voice intoned flatly, as if he hadn't used his vocal chords for decades.

"You have read the reports concerning me." Chester continued pleasantly. "This is our first meeting, Director Roque; you must prove to yourself that what Director Robinson has told you is indeed true.

"At the same time," Chester assured them, "you are lost because you don't understand the purpose of the explosion. There is a lesson here for you. Do you wish to learn it?" He inclined his head, lacing fingers together in his lap.

"Teach us, Prophet." Robinson's voice cracked brittlely. Chester ignored the dislike in his eyes.

"While Director Robinson knows, the others of your kind do not," Chester added, voice warm, feeling the harmony of time. "As a Prophet, my mission is to teach. I will not advise you. Know therefore, that Ngen Van Chow is disciplining his people. The lesson is well known on my planet—

inhaled with the first breath, taught by our very existence. The reason you find the action irrational is due to your alienation from the rest of the species."

Director Navtov's face contorted painfully. It had been years since he had used his facial muscles. "I still do not understand. We did not kill his people as he has accused us of doing! Why does he broadcast such lies through all of space? What good does he do by causing unrest among others?"

Chester concentrated on the Director's face. "What he has done is very simple. Humans need motivation. They can be motivated by anticipation of either reward or punishment. Ngen has simply provided them with this motivation. It serves to teach them that the Directorate will punish the Sirians if it wins. At the same time they are taught that should Sirius win, they will be safe. As a result, their emotions are stirred and once again they become dedicated to their cause. The dead are that many fewer mouths for the Independence Party to feed while the desire for revenge reinforces the anticipation of reward. All in all, a very well executed social stimulus.

"The purpose of the broadcasts is to demoralize the rest of the Directorate, to weaken your forces, divide your people, and erode the support of your political base."

"If this is so, he is an abomination," Navtov snapped.

"Would you do any differently to survive?" Chester asked and smiled easily.

Navtov's eyes glittered. "He has killed his fellows. He blames *us* for the destruction of women and children. He destroyed a residential area. He claims we have threatened the Sirians with annihilation. *These are lies!*"

"But they are useful lies. His factories are producing again. The heart for revolution is back in the people."

Robinson had been silent through most of the dialogue. Now he asked, "Will we win in the end, Prophet?"

Chester shrugged. "Perhaps."

"What do you mean, perhaps?" Roque exploded, straining his atrophied vocal chords. "If you truly see the future—tell us. We order you!"

Chester spread his hands. "There is no way to tell. The Directorate is changing. Things have moved beyond your control. There are a multitude of cusps—decisions of free will—which will change the various futures. I cannot predict them, you know that, you've studied the reports. God guards free will jealously. You yourselves are cusps. That is why I find your analysis of Ngen Van Chow interesting.

"Let me warn you." Chester paused, allowing his words to sink in. "Beware your emotions, Directors. You have been long away from human beings. You live with your giant computers and you have forgotten your roots. Depending on the cusps, the Directorate may have as much as sixty years left. If you allow your egos to dictate your responses to men like Ngen Van Chow, you may lose every aspect of your civilization within a year. You have been warned. That is all I have to say."

Roque and Navtov's images faded. It was no surprise that Skor's remained. "I have taken a great risk, Romanan. I only brought you here to see what sort of thing you were before I had you and your people destroyed."

"Yet you face a situation of your own devising," Chester countered amiably. "You allowed the Sirian situation to become what it is. You made the decision of your own free will." Chester smiled again. "Have you learned anything, Director?"

"I have learned that you and your kind are a poison." Skor's face showed no emotion. "Perhaps I should order you destroyed after all?"

"The choice is yours, Director." Chester nodded.

"You should fear me." Robinson's blue eyes seemed tiny against the swollen mass of his skull. He waited for a reaction.

"Why?" Chester finally asked. "Can you change reality? Have you the power to harm my soul? Do you threaten God?"

"I could cause you much pain before you die." Robinson added, "Suffering is never pleasant."

"If you wish," Chester said calmly. "You realize if you did so it would be an admission of your own inability to deal with reality."

Robinson watched him with cold, fish eyes. Finally the Director nodded. "You are correct. Be warned that pursuant to your own elucidation of the Sirian problem, I have indeed learned. Ngen Van Chow has taught me well. Good day, Prophet." Robinson faded away, his words echoing hollowly. Chester relaxed, feeling the changes of a decision made, a cusp brought to fruition. He experienced a change in the matrix of the future and waited while it flowed toward him.

"Call me Rita, kid," Red Many Coups told her as she slid off over the rear of the red gelding. Before them, a huge gleaming-white AT rested on skids. Susan sucked in her breath as she followed Rita up the ramp, amazed by the size of the craft—over a hundred meters long, deadly, sleek; it swallowed her.

A Patrolwoman snapped a salute as they stepped inside and Susan's heart stopped. Could there be a greater wonder than this in all the world?

White, spotless, gleaming, the interior dazzled her.

"What is it, kid?" Rita asked, turning, green eyes cool and thoughtful. "Your mouth is hanging open like a fly trap."

"I . . . I . . ." She raised helpless hands. "People *made* this . . . thing?"

Rita chuckled in wry amusement. "Yeah. And this is just a crummy AT. You oughta see the stations. Huge . . . Well, never mind. Come on, let's get you some decent clothes."

Susan followed, awed, frightened by the monitors and the strangeness. Truly, an AT *must* be magical. How did the People ever find courage to fight this . . . this miracle?

Rita placed her hand on a white wall. Susan jumped when the doorway appeared—seemingly from solid wall. Nervous, cringing, she followed Rita in. Uttering a little cry as the wall slid shut again, she stared fearfully back at the vanished doorway, aware of a difference in color and texture where the portal had slid.

"Easy, Susan," Rita frowned. "You look like a scared cat."

"M . . . Magic?" she wondered, pointing at the door.

Rita Sarsa's teeth sank into her lower lip for a moment. "No. Not magic. Science. There is a device, uh, a machine, that senses my hand when I put it against the wall. It traces the patterns of my hand and triggers a motor to pull the hatch open."

Susan nodded, trying to comprehend, looking rapturously about the little compartment. Rita stabbed a finger to another section of wall and a clear round thing popped up. This she placed into a slight recess. Susan gasped as it filled with liquid.

"Water runs from the walls?" She blinked, shaking her head. "You are powerful people, you star men."

Rita drank from the bulb, sinking down on a small shelf Susan identified as a bed.

"Susan," Rita's voice dropped, those green eyes still cool. "Do you realize just how great your handicap is? I mean, you've lived all your life squatting cross-legged on dirt floors. You don't know a word of Standard. You've never seen an electrical circuit in your life. You look around and see comm and dispensers as magic."

Susan swallowed. "I would be a warrior," she whispered, awe seeping away, worry building at the tone in Sarsa's voice.

Rita nodded, grunting. "Maybe Iron Eyes is right. I could be biting off more than I can chew." Hard eyes focused on Susan. "You want to be a warrior? How much? What would you give?"

Susan dropped her eyes, shoulders slumping. "Everything," she answered hollowly. "I would die. If I don't become a warrior . . . go with the star people, I will die anyway—one way or another."

Sarsa growled, "Look at me when you talk."

Susan looked up reluctantly, feeling awkward, trapped.

Sarsa exhaled explosively, slapped her thighs, and got to her feet. Harrier eyes pinned Susan, frightening her more. *"All right, damn it!"* Sarsa rasped. "You've got your chance . . . but on one condition."

Susan nodded, gut queasy from nerves and fear.

"You promise me," Sarsa began. "You promise, on your very life before Spider, that you'll do what I say. Hear? You promise that my word is your law!" A freckled finger pointed within inches of Susan's nose.

"I . . ." she struggled to swallow the knot in her throat. "I promise, Rita." Blood pulsed in Susan's ears. She looked for relief in those horrible green eyes. Not a flicker could she find. Could Red Many Coups be that hard?

"Good," Sarsa hissed, "because you'll have to be perfect, Susan." The voice turned deadly. "You won't be allowed a single mistake, hear? You represent the chances for every woman on this ball of rock. You let me down, and by Spider, I'll kill you!"

Susan trembled. The clicking sound came from her teeth. Horrified, she clenched her jaw. Every ounce of her courage spent itself keeping her eyes locked with Rita Sarsa's—but she managed, barely.

"You look scared," Rita mumbled, dropping her gaze, pulling a section of wall open and rummaging through piles of multicolored star fabrics.

"I am," Susan responded, regretting it immediately, hand over her mouth.

Sarsa laughed at her wide eyes. "Relax, Susan," her voice felt friendly this time. "You should be scared. Fear is the first thing a warrior learns—despite all the bragging to the contrary." She threw something blue and shimmery to Susan. "Here, keep it. Strip and step in there. It's called a shower. You eaten?"

Susan shook her head, catching the soft material, gasping at its beauty. She caressed it, hesitating, blushing.

"Go on," Rita rumbled, irritated by her reluctance. "I'm another woman, for god's sake. We're all built alike." She grinned. "Besides, modesty isn't a Romanan virtue."

No way to argue with that! Susan shucked her calf-hide dress and stepped into the narrow crevice Sarsa had indicated. Rita's fingers danced over colored spots on the wall.

Water shot over Susan's skin, warm and caressing. She yipped as invisible fingers ran down her body, pushing water ahead and into a hole in the white stuff of the floor.

Trembling, she stepped out, aware of the tingle in her skin. Clean! Totally! Her hair gleamed. From Sarsa's fingers, she took the star fabric and pulled the blue material over her head—amazed at its lightness.

"Damn it!" Rita grumbled, annoyed once again as she caught Susan's round-eyed stare at the shower. "It's just a damn shower! Nothing to it."

Susan nodded and swallowed. *Am I unchanged? Did it take my soul with it? What wonders these star people control! They must be perfect to have so many God-powers at their fingers!*

"Come here." Rita pointed at a row of colored beads on the wall. "This is a dispenser. Not magic, hear? Each of the buttons are color-coded. You'll learn to read the menu later. Push the red button. Don't be afraid."

The thing Sarsa called a button gave under Susan's finger. Involuntarily she jumped back as a dish, filled with stew, slid out of the wall.

"I told you," Sarsa grinned. "It's a machine. *You* control it."

The aroma brought a growl from Susan's stomach. How long since she'd eaten? Three days now? Fingers trembling, she took the bowl, hesitant, afraid, and sipped. Hot, it burned her lips. Mouth watering, hunger overcame pain.

"Sit." Rita pointed at the chair. Susan sat, maneuvering herself into it, feeling awkward. She ought to be on the floor on a blanket.

"Civilized people don't sip out of bowls. Like this," Rita continued. She sat down opposite the Romanan, using a strange implement to eat with, handing Susan one just like it.

Susan mimicked, bending awkward fingers around the little cup on a stick. Strength and warmth filled her, seeping into her limbs and bringing relief from the fear and pangs inspired by hunger.

"Looks like you've been without a meal for a couple of days," Rita noted. Susan nodded, returning for another bowl, eating slowly to keep it down. Minutes later she smiled, looking closely at the eating implement.

"Now, come here." Rita unfolded something from the wall that turned into a chair. A dull black glass stared at her as she slid into the seat, still awkward with the position.

"This is a headset," Rita told her, dropping a golden circlet over her head. The black glass flickered to life making her gasp and stiffen.

"Relax!" Rita cocked her head. "Say the following words." She carefully enunciated two words in a language Susan didn't understand. It took her three tries to get the pronunciation right, when, to her surprise, the glass formed lines of figures.

"What you did," Rita told her, voice strong with encouragement, "was access the comm. With this machine, you can learn everything you need. It will teach you—even while you sleep."

Rita put another headset on her own head. "Welcome to a new life, kid. Today, you're learning the alphabet."

Susan's mind whirled as she walked past the hatch of the AT. "I'm going to get my things," she added, turning to Rita. "I don't have much, just a few things." She shrugged.

"All right," Rita nodded. "Uh, look. You'll have plenty of time to learn on the way to Sirius. Uh, you might have a . . . um, you know, young man or something. We're not leaving for another day or so. Take your time. Say goodbye. Hell, you might even want out."

"Thank you, Rita." She smiled and shocked herself. A smile? A real unforced smile?

She walked through the dark streets, alphabet running through her mind. With it, words were built. Different letters for different sounds. How right Sarsa had been. A new life lay just beyond her fingertips. What other wonders did the comm hide? A machine? Really? Not a strange sort of God?

Lost in thoughts, she didn't notice when Willy Red Hawk Horsecapture's soft feet whispered behind her. Her first start came as his thick arms wrapped around her—a hard hand clapped to her mouth.

"Got her!" Horsecapture laughed as Ramon ghosted from behind a house, binding her thrashing limbs with a pigging string.

"And now, my friend," Ramon giggled, "we'll get rid of her forever. She has shamed me for the last time. I couldn't have done it without your help."

Horsecapture laughed. "You never know when I might need something in return, Ramon. One of these days I may need your—"

"Ask, my friend. Ask anytime. You know better than that."

"We'll have to kill her far from the Settlements," Horsecapture added. "It wouldn't do for someone to find her body before I leave for the stars. Not with the Patrol bringing new ways."

"Very well," Ramon agreed, "but she's just a woman. You know what they're worth."

CHAPTER VI

John Smith Iron Eyes blinked awake to the sound of water spattering onto the rocks. About him, Gessali Shelter lay like a quiet tomb except for the water cascading out of the gray mists outside. In the cold air, he shivered, hugging his blanket around him, aware of the dead fire beside him.

Over his head, hidden in the shadow of the overhanging rock, a spider effigy radiated its power. He blinked into the darkness, knowing the intricate details of the drawing by heart.

Leeta had changed under that sign. The frightened, perpetually cold anthropologist had found new strength through Spider. She had hauled John Smith Iron Eyes—wounded and dying from a Santos bullet—into Gessali Camp. She had taken coup from the man she'd killed, thrown the rotting corpses of the dead out into the storm. Here, she'd grown into a warrior woman, committing herself to the People . . . and Spider.

Here, John Smith Iron Eyes had fallen in love with her.

Iron Eyes bit back his pain. "And now you've taken her from me as you have taken every woman I cared for." His eyes narrowed. "You may be God, Spider, but why do you torment me? Must your purposes and mine always lie at odds? Must I always curse your acts? Must you always destroy those I love?"

He pulled himself upright, banging his little finger in the process and wincing. The first joint he'd cut off after Jenny's death, leaving the tip of his finger buried in a cairn of rocks high in the Bear Mountains. Now, the second joint, too, lay buried in a high place—and with it the pain of Leeta's death. The practice of leaving a piece of the body soothed the soul, making grief bearable, a palpable symbol of the hurt and loss.

The act of lifting his finger for inspection triggered the burning itch of the healing shoulder wound dealt him by Big Man.

"Ah, Leeta," he whispered, feeling her presence in the rock womb of Gessali Camp. "Now, I go to the stars to live your dream. See. See around you? The People live. We have won this time." He glanced up at the soot-stained darkness overhead. "Or until Spider turns on us again."

He drew his lungs full of the damp storm, looking out beyond the gaping maw of Gessali Camp. The musty odor of rain and mud and fresh vegetation filled his nostrils. Beyond the drip-line, the air lay heavy and gray, cut by ethereal streamers of rain, the rock of the canyon water-shiny, rivulets already forming.

Iron Eyes' black mare stood, rain-slick, head down, grazing in the subdued morning light, harvesting the rich forage along the slopes below the rock shelter.

"Leeta, be with me," he whispered dully, as if he could draw tendrils of her soul from the very rocks, cloak himself in her memory.

For long moments, he sat, back stooped, heavy shoulders hanging as he looked out into the rain. His thoughts drifted with the sense of the place, remembering scenes of Leeta against the light of the fire, remembering her hands on his fevered body. He shivered at the recollection of the violent burn of the whiskey she'd used to sterilize his wound. Yes, she was here, all around him.

The shrill whistle barely penetrated the clouds at first, growing continually, filling the canyon in a final piercing wail.

Iron Eyes cursed, getting to his feet and stamping into his boots before grabbing up the black's picket rope and pulling her close, calming her as the scream of the AT increased.

Outside, the rain twisted in odd patterns as the shrill noise deafened him. Iron Eyes winced as he watched the huge craft sink to a landing before the shelter, a wall of white hovering beyond the steep slope past the drip line. The obnoxious odor of the exhausts burned sharply in his nose. Deftly, the pilot planted a skid and the ramp dropped.

A marine in leisure dress trotted out, shading his eyes from the rain before making his way up the slippery slope and into the shadow of the rock.

"War Chief Iron Eyes?" he called somewhat uncertainly over the roar of the AT.

Iron Eyes nodded, and the man ran forward.

"You know," Iron Eyes told him shortly, "you shouldn't just run up to a warrior. Not all Romanans are friendly in the back country. Some would take your coup just to spite that AT for ruining their peace and quiet."

The young man gulped. "Yes, sir. Uh, the Colonel sent us down to find you. With the Colonel's respects, sir. He'd like to discuss the Sirian campaign. Says he needs your input."

Iron Eyes sighed. "Very well. I'll ride back to the Settlements and catch an AT there."

The private winced slightly. "Uh, sir, if you don't mind, I think the Colonel would like to see you soonest."

Iron Eyes nodded, resigned. "Then help me load the mare. She's been on ATs before. Doesn't like them—but she's a good horse. We can take time to drop her off in my corral, can't we?"

"I, uh, yes, sir. I'm sure we can."

Iron Eyes jammed the lead rope into the young man's unwilling hands and went about packing up. Curious about the star men. They could fly through the air without a second thought, but place a trained war horse's lead in their putty hands and they shivered in their boots!

In the dim rear of the shelter, he rolled his blankets, stuffing his personal possessions into his pack. For a second he stopped, looking around, irritated by the drowning whine of the AT.

"Until next time, Leeta. Spider and my People call. My life is no longer mine. I love you. Guard this place well." He looked up at the spider effigy drawn on the rock one last time and sprinted for the AT.

The black mare, eyes rolling, ears pricked, danced and snorted up the ramp, head back. Nostrils flared, she trembled under his hand as he tied her firmly.

"Tell the pilot no fancy stuff or he'll have that mare loose and mad," Iron Eyes instructed.

The private accessed comm, muttering under his breath.

The craft lifted, Iron Eyes staring out the blaster port at the dark mouth of Gessali Camp. An hour later—and horseless—he watched World drop away in storm and rain. The AT shot through the clouds into sunlight and the deeper and deeper blue of the heavens, the stars growing bright along with World's three small moons.

Bullet appeared, a bright white dot on the curve of the horizon. Behind her were the two Patrol battleships, *Brotherhood* and *Victory*. From this distance, the battle damage hardly showed.

"So long as I live," he muttered to himself, "I'll never cease to marvel at the sight." From the side, *Bullet* looked trim and long, marred by the huge sail which carried the AT comm tower. Large shield generators stuck out at angles along with sensor and transduction antennae. Here and there, black-lipped gashes were partly plated over in gray, the tiny dots of tugs swarming about the sections being repaired. As the AT lifted into a traffic pattern, the shape of *Bullet* loomed, the scalloped hull broadening with the slitted AT docks running down the length of the vessel above the vast bulk of the giant gimbaled reaction motors on either side of the vessel.

Only as the AT dropped did the huge bulk of *Bullet* fall into true perspective. Over a kilometer and a half long, the big ship seemed to swallow the AT as it settled into a dock.

Iron Eyes stood, ordering his things, looking longingly to where the mare had stood, only a pile of green manure now left on the deck. A private with a vacuum trotted forward as the docking clearance sounded and even that tie with reality disappeared.

"War Chief?" a young corporal called.

Iron Eyes shouldered his pack and rifle and followed the young woman down the ramp, past a heavy lock and into the endless white corridors. In the aftermath of the battle, the ship would never be the same. Here and there on bulkheads, the scrawly effigies of spiders and crosses had been drawn on hatches, comm terminals, and even overhead. *Bullet* had been changed, metamorphosed into something different. The corporal he followed wore a coup at her belt—a fact which had caused Damen Ree no little disturbance at first.

The corporal stopped, calling out, "War Chief Iron Eyes to see you, sir."

"Enter," Ree's voice came through the door comm and the portal slid open.

Iron Eyes walked into the Colonel's private quarters, swinging his pack and rifle down into a corner. He passed the familiar display of Romanan weapons decorating Ree's wall and found the Colonel seated in a plush body-conforming grav chair. Before him a holo of a world spun, cloudless, lights glittering across the topographically depicted continents.

"Sirius," Ree informed him, waving a hand at the holo. "That's what we're going to go . . . raid."

Iron Eyes nodded, stepping closer, fighting the urge to poke his finger through the image. Holography still awed him, like so much of the Directorate technology. It seemed magic, something from nothing. Still, he held himself back, acting as would befit the War Chief of the Romanans.

"And these lights out here in orbit?" Iron Eyes asked, indicating a string of regularly spaced spheres.

"Orbiting stations," Ree supplied. "Originally they were navigational controls, weather control, planetary comm, zero-g manufacturing, that sort of thing. Now they're being fitted out for planetary defense. That's not your worry. What we have to talk about is the planet."

"You look like you haven't slept in three weeks," Iron Eyes told him. "You're pushing yourself, Colonel."

Ree chuckled harshly, rubbing a callused hand over his pale face. "Yeah, I suppose. What did you do to your hand? Romanan funeral, isn't it? When we're done, I'll have med take a look at it."

Iron Eyes sighed, walking over to the dispenser, squinting. "Blue is coffee?" he asked, trying to remember.

"Yeah, punch it twice. I could use some, too."

Iron Eyes handed him the cup.

Ree continued. "You hear about the Santos kid? Got so carried away with the dispenser he emptied commissary for

an entire section. Stood there for hours pushing the button
until the corridor couldn't hold any more coffee cups!"

Iron Eyes laughed. "Your *Bullet* still baffles us. Too
much like magic. You have to think of it in their terms. So
many wonders all at once."

Ree sipped his hot coffee, smacking his lips. "Oh, I'm
amazed all right. They learn remarkably fast. Some can use
a sonic welder better than my techs now." Ree pointed at
the holo. "That's the immediate problem. How do you want
to coordinate this thing?"

Iron Eyes savored the coffee. Wonderful beverage that.
"As you just so aptly pointed out, my Romanans will have
trouble on Sirius. It's a technological world. We'll be at a
disadvantage."

Ree nodded soberly. "I hoped you'd see it that way."

Iron Eyes turned. "Let me put it this way. We Romanans
have a saying, 'The war chief who can't see as far as his
horse's hooves will never see victory.' You know what a
horse means to a warrior on World?"

Ree rubbed the back of his neck. "Yeah, the little things
make or break a raid."

"And a warrior must know his limitations and plan around
them or his horse herds will never grow."

"So, what do you Romanans want out of Sirius?" Ree
tilted his head to the side. "What are your terms?"

Iron Eyes crossed his arms. "We want education, medicine, the people necessary to bring us up from raiding to
producing. We wanted the stars. I don't know, I suppose
we'll see things we can't conceive of now. My People need
to know so much. We would catch up with the rest of
human technology. Make our own. Find our own stars."

"You know what that will cost you?" Ree lowered his
chin.

Iron Eyes nodded. "Leeta taught me a great deal. I
know. I think deep down inside, my People know. At the
same time, we want the stars. Spider sends us to learn, to
get the most out of life before he calls our souls back. The
Prophets know what it will cost. They have told us. We'll
pay the price."

"Yes," Ree mused. "Leeta would have told you all about
acculturation." He shook his head sadly. "I . . . I miss her.
No, don't look at me that way. She was one of the best
friends I ever had."

Ree got wearily to his feet. "You wouldn't understand,

but a Patrol Colonel has no friends. We've built a system of mutual throat-cutting, a constant struggle to get to the top—and stay there. Leeta treated me as an equal, spoke honestly to me, faced me as a man—not a potential target." He chuckled hollowly. "You know what that means to a man who's been alone all his life? For once I had someone I could talk to . . . confide in." He dropped his head. "I . . . I'll miss her."

Iron Eyes settled himself on a console. "Spider gave me a quick mind, Colonel. I think I can imagine."

Ree turned, studying him seriously. "And I can imagine what her loss means to you." He steepled his fingers, pacing slowly before the spinning holo of Sirius. "You and I, Iron Eyes, now we have the responsibility for all this. On your shoulders, and mine, rests the entire future of Romanan relations."

Iron Eyes studied the Colonel, wary. "I made my decision the day I killed your Major Reary. You know what I'd give for my People. So long as my honor is uncompromised, I'll do what I must."

Ree nodded, a restless smile on his lips. "I think we understand each other." A pause. "You know, we can't lose, you and I. I lose and they take my ship. You lose and they take your planet. Sirius isn't the only enemy we face."

Iron Eyes frowned pensively, fingering one of his braids as he drank the last of his coffee. "It isn't the way of Spider to make things easy. Very well, I've buried my grief, said my prayers and attended to my visions. Let's get to work, Colonel. Tell me about Sirius, tell me everything." He smiled wryly. "Like you, I don't like to lose."

Ree studied him. "You know, you're a sharp character, Iron Eyes. At first, I couldn't imagine what she saw in you."

Iron Eyes gave Ree a bloodless smile. "Nor I in you. Tell me about Sirius, and I'll tell you how to use Romanans to break it like a cracked egg."

Ree's eyes narrowed. "You know. I'm glad we're on the same side. God knows what we'll do to humanity, you and I."

"We're chosen by Spider." Iron Eyes punched the cup into the dispenser. "What we do to humanity is Spider's will."

Ree placed his hands on his hips, studying the holo. "That's reassuring."

Iron Eyes asked ironically, "Considering the pain Spider has dealt me, is it really?"

Ree just stared back, eyes dull.

* * *

Short, stocky, with a barrel chest and bowed legs, men teased Friday Garcia Yellow Legs because he didn't quite come up to an average warrior's shoulders. Women looked at him and giggled—none of which bothered Friday. He enjoyed himself—firmly believing Spider had made him this way to learn something of life. If he was different, then Spider had a use for his difference. With that in mind, he enjoyed the joke of his height—and had done everything he could to spread it around.

This night, however, Friday Garcia Yellow Legs had no thoughts of humor. At last—after four days of prayer, fasting, and thirst—he could feel the presence. He blinked owlishly in the night; a cool breeze caressed his hot body. To each side of the high pinnacle of rock he perched on, blackness fell away in dizzying depths.

"What do you wish?" The voice seemed born of the night wind.

"I have come to pray for strength and Power. I have come to call upon Spider to make me a warrior that I might bring him honor and speak his name," Friday sang his response.

"Who would do this?" the whispered voice asked.

"I am called Friday Garcia Yellow Legs." Friday pulled himself upright and nodded respectfully to the four cardinal directions.

"Strength is yours. I hear your prayer. Spider hears your prayer. Heed not the path of the Prophets for their way is not yours. Would you have stars tremble at your name? Would you have the love of people? Would you share your life with a woman? Would you have many children? What do you will for your destiny, Garcia Yellow Legs?"

Friday frowned. "I would have honor and bring greatness to my people. I would see them as powerful as the star men. I would see Spider's web strewn through the stars."

"Spider is already among the stars," the voice whispered softly.

"I would have the star men know his name," Friday amended. "I would be Spider's warrior."

"And if that duty destroyed what you held most dear? You would pay that price? That would be your free will?" the voice asked.

"Yes," Friday Garcia Yellow Legs whispered. "Yes, anything would be worth it."

"Your life?" The voice seemed to sigh.

"My life is Spider's."

"Go forth!" The voice commanded. *"Go among the stars and spin the web of Spider. Show the star men the way of Spider. You are His messenger. Take the word to the stars."*

At that, a twinkling light appeared before Friday's wide eyes. It winked, shimmered, and rose slowly into the night sky. Friday watched it climb, seeing it find a place among the myriad of stars—only to become uncertain which light was his when he finally blinked.

His dry throat stuck when he tried to swallow. Four days had passed since his last drink. Four days of singing, fasting, and praying. He'd forced himself to stay awake, suffering through the cold and the rains and the blistering sun. He'd watched, through flickering vision as the green plains spread toward the ocean. Now, after all his sacrifice and hunger and thirst, the vision had come.

Friday drew his blanket up around his shoulders—suddenly chilled to the bone. He got to his feet, placing his magic amulets in his pouch, and started threading his way down the mountain.

His vision had come—a spirit-helper had been sent to answer his prayers and songs. It was the way of the People. Spider had heard. Friday had been chosen. His life, he dedicated to Spider—God's tool to bring the word to the star men.

For the first time, Friday Garcia Yellow Legs began to wonder at Spider's price. Duty would destroy what he held most dear. What could that be? His clan? His people? His planet? What? A sudden chill swept through his body. Unbeknown to Friday Yellow Legs, he began to realize the age-old dilemma of men chosen by their God; the sudden uncertainty of treading on holy ground always made for itchy feet.

"No matter," he muttered under his breath. "I shall be honored, a great man among the stars. I shall help string Spider's web." He experienced a rush of euphoria. In spite of his hunger-weakened legs, he trotted down the path.

By the time Friday reached his horse, the euphoria had passed, replaced by a hollow sense of foreboding—dropped like a mantle on his shoulders. Friday drank from the stream, cool water soaking into desiccated tissues and renewing his life. Exhausted, he ate and slept.

The next morning, in a light drizzle, he pulled the picket

pin—checking to make sure the horse hadn't wanted for anything during his vision quest—and saddled the animal. He inspected his rifle and strapped on his knife. Munching on knife bush root bread, he turned the animal toward the Settlements.

He couldn't shake the sense of dread. Something lay just over the horizon of time . . . coming ever closer. He'd made a commitment; could he keep it? Awed by his convulsive feelings, he watched the third moon sink slowly into the sea as the dull glow of dawn silhouetted the Bear Mountains.

Around noon, Friday noticed the riders. He stopped, dropping from his saddle, and watched. Wary, the riders led a roan packing a dejected solitary figure. Friday could feel his heart beat dully in his body as he hushed his horse. Half-screened by knife bush, he checked his rifle by instinct, awaiting the riders. Odd that they kept glancing behind—as if worried about observation.

Ramon Luis Andojar! Friday frowned. A nutty old man. Never the same since the Santos had taken his coup so long ago. Behind him followed Willy Red Hawk Horsecapture. A young girl—ah, yes, Susan—and dressed in star clothing of all things! Relieved, he stepped into the saddle and rode out to meet them.

They saw him, stopping, bending heads close to mutter. Susan stiffened in fear.

"Greetings!" Old Ramon called.

"What have you here?" Friday asked, uncertainty growing. No good would come of this. Prophet blood ran strong in his family. He could sense the future even if he couldn't see it clearly.

"It is my niece," Ramon spat. "She has shamed me and run off to the star men. When she came home to get her things, I tied her up. I have promised to marry her off to a man. She would shame me by running off and breaking my word."

Friday looked the girl over. Well formed, pretty, almost bordering on beautiful, Susan had caught his eye before. Were it not for the frantic fear in her eyes, he would have smiled. Behind the terror sparked a glint of defiance Yellow Legs felt an admiration for. Who would Susan marry this far beyond the Settlements? Ramon hated the Santos.

"Who is the girl to marry?" Friday asked curiously, conscious of the haughty look Red Hawk Horsecapture gave him. He shifted narrowed eyes to the warrior. Horsecapture had four coups hanging from his belt. Friday's thoughts suddenly centered on his own vest which sported only two.

Ramon grinned wickedly. "She will marry Old Man Wattie." He said it with a sneer, leering as he saw Friday's reaction.

"Old Man Wattie?" Friday shook his head, incredulous. "That is *ridiculous*, Ramon!"

"*She has shamed me!*" Ramon shouted suddenly. "She has shamed her clan! She would go off among the stars to be a warrior!" His thin limbs shook with uncontrolled fury, eyes glittering with his disgust. "Imagine, a woman of the People trying to be a warrior! It is blasphemous! Does a man wear a dress?"

Friday considered it. A woman warrior? Another of Spider's jokes? A joke on the People's sensibilities? Why not?

"The star men have women warriors. Like Willy Red Hawk Horsecapture, I have fought at their side. Maybe it is wrong to keep our women penned up like so much livestock. There are new ways coming," Friday said reasonably. "When your anger cools, you would regret having given her to Wattie."

Ramon's old voice quavered. "*You* do not tell *me*—an elder—what I shall do, young man!" Friday could see a touch of madness tracing behind the old man's eyes.

"Nevertheless, you shall not give her to Wattie. Let John Smith Iron Eyes decide her fate." Friday tried to lower his voice. Sudden hope flashed in the girl's eyes.

"Iron Eyes has had enough say in this matter," Horsecapture interrupted. "You have said enough, too. Your mouth becomes offensive. Move, youngster, I would not waste time paddling your bottom."

Friday's scalp began to prickle. "Paddling?" he mused, as if to himself. "Offensive?" Eyes slitted, he looked at Horsecapture. "Wattie lives back there, behind you. I might have ignored it, Willy." A crooked smile crossed his lips. "Now I call you a liar!"

Friday remembered the vision. Chosen by Spider, he would not be defeated here. The feeling of wrongness rose in his chest. Pain shimmered ahead, somewhere over the horizon of time. If he let the girl go with Ramon, someone would pay in the end.

"*They go to kill me!*" she screamed. "Don't listen to— "

Horsecapture's hard hand slapped her, the smack loud in the morning air.

"Hysterical woman," he grunted, jaw tight as his eyes shifted to take in Friday's reaction. "You know how they are during that time of the month."

Friday bit off an acid remark. Desperation vied with fear in the girl's face, making his heart cry. Ramon Smith Andojar pushed past imperiously. Willy sneered as he rode by. Moving quickly, Friday whipped his knife from his belt and neatly slashed the lead rope in two. By the time Horsecapture had turned, Yellow Legs' rifle centered on the man's chest.

"We fought together, you and I," Friday whispered. "We are brothers. Do not force me to shoot you over a skinny woman. I can foretell trouble from all this. Perhaps—with luck—I can stop it. Who told the girl she could be a warrior?"

"Red Many Coups!" Susan cried out on her own. "She would kill Ramon if she knew what he is trying to do to me. She invited me to the stars!"

"And Iron Eyes would know." Friday nodded, conscious of the burning hatred he'd inspired in Horsecapture's eyes. "John Smith Iron Eyes is my War Chief," Friday added. "He saved us from the star men. Red Many Coups not only shamed you at Navel Camp, Horsecapture, she led us to *Bullet.* It would not be good to displease those chosen by Spider."

"Spider!" Ramon shouted, waving his thin arms. "What do *you* know of Spider? You flaunt the laws of God in my very face! It was Spider's will that men be different than women! Who will cook the food and bear the children? Who will care for our houses? Spider's wrath will fall on you! Women are weak! They are as animals! Do you see a warrior in *her?* If this one is not taught to be submissive, another will follow in her tracks. Where will it end, stupid child?" The old man glared at Friday.

"I'll *kill* you for this," Horsecapture added. "I will kill you for holding a rifle on me . . . and I will kill you for shaming Ramon, who is my friend. I call you an enemy of the People. I swear knife feud, Friday Garcia Yellow Legs." The warrior straightened in his saddle.

"Kill me three times? All in one speech? I look forward to you doing this, Horsecapture." Friday nodded, grinning at the thought even as his throat constricted. "Very well. You have sworn the knife feud. I will meet you. I would meet you . . . ah, yes! I set the date for a month from this day!"

The girl's eyes were wide now, appraising Friday Yellow Legs with wonder, admiration, and fear.

Horsecapture laughed. "You must set it sooner, *fool*! I will be long gone to Sirius by that time."

"And so will I," Yellow Legs nodded. "You and I will fight on *Bullet* to see which of us is chosen for the stars. Ramon, do you honor this knife feud?" Friday squinted at the old man.

"I do," Andojar grunted. "You have gone against the ways of the People. You have spit upon the customs of our fathers which were given to us by God. You are no good." Venom filled the old man's tone.

"Come, Susan," Friday said softly to the girl. "They will not bother you now. You are safe. Knife feud has been sworn." Friday kicked his gelding into motion as he cut the bonds on her wrists. "I am Friday Garcia Yellow Legs." He shot her a quick grin, aware of gloom lifting from his thoughts like mist in the sun. Happiness, hope, and something else he didn't exactly understand replaced his unease.

"You have sworn a knife feud with Willy Red Hawk Horsecapture," she said in amazement. "He is a very great warrior. You could be . . . I mean, are you sure you want to go through with this? What if Ramon is right? What if . . . if you are offending Spider? Perhaps you should let me escape, then . . . then go apologize to Willy. He would have to take back the . . . the blood oath."

Her concern touched him. He felt himself warming to this unusual woman. "Would you rather marry old Man Wattie?" he asked. "I have known Ramon a long time. He is not a bad man. Maybe a little crazy, but not bad. How could you have driven him to such desperation?"

She blushed, looking at the ground. "They say that I have no respect for my clan or family. My mother died bearing me. She was to marry my father when he returned from raiding the Santos for horses to make bride price. He . . . never returned. Mother was shamed; she never married. The young men do not . . . look in my direction. They think I would make . . . trouble."

"No!" Friday mocked. "Trouble? *You?*"

She hesitated. "It is not right that Willy Horsecapture should kill you because . . . because I disobey. I would go back rather than see you . . . see you die."

Friday groused to himself, perplexed by what her words implied. Cursed girl!

"Do you really think that Red Hawk will kill *me?*" he chided. He swelled his bandy chest, thumping his breastbone. Chin out, head back. *"I am Friday Garcia Yellow Legs!* It will take more than luck for him to beat me. I am just now returning from praying in the mountains. The spirit-helpers have shown me my destiny. I am not to die on the blade of Horsecapture's knife." He snorted his disgust at the thought.

"I can get away again," she said simply—evidently not believing it. "You couldn't win . . ." She bit her lip, wincing "I am not worth your life."

"That is for Spider to decide," Friday muttered sourly. Such a diplomat, this girl! "I think you don't believe that anyway." He saw the answer in her eyes: sudden defiance. "So why did you say that?"

"How *else* do you deal with men?" she demanded hotly. "If you don't cower before them . . . they beat you!" She tensed, as if waiting for a blow.

"Most women never seek beyond a man and children," Yellow Legs reminded. "Even as you can't see the greatest Spider warrior before your very—"

"If they don't, it is only because their dreams are beaten out of them. The People treat horses with more respect than women!" she snapped, black eyes flashing, color rising in her cheeks.

"It is no wonder Ramon wanted to marry you off to Old Man Wattie. Verily, Susan Smith Andojar, I think you have the spirit to be a warrior." He paused before adding caustically, "Why do I think I would be better off to take you back to Ramon?"

"I would expect no less from a man," she added coldly.

"I get the feeling you don't like me."

"It's not that I dislike you. It's only that you are a man. Men have . . . hurt me. A woman . . . a single woman . . . does not trust a man."

He frowned. "Then I have a month to show you that a man can be trusted. I would see your eyes shine for me one day. It will be a challenge. In the meantime, you can, um, help me train to beat Horsecapture."

"You would practice combat with a woman?" she asked incredulously.

"I think I'll enjoy your company during this last month of my life. Sure. If you are serious about this madness of yours, of course." Under his breath, he mumbled, "I *knew* something horrible was going to happen."

"What did you say?"

"Nothing," he grunted, working his mouth like something bitter lay in it.

A quick look over his shoulder proved that Ramon and Willy hadn't moved their horses. They were watching intently. Even over the distance, Friday could feel the hatred. No matter what front he showed the girl, the odds were that he would be killed or badly wounded by Horsecapture. There would be pain.

Susan waved a farewell to Friday as she climbed the ramp into the AT, saluting the guard. In Rita's quarters, the lieutenant's things were laid out. Tired, Susan stood in the center of the room, looking around.

Timidly, she pulled the seat loose as Rita had shown her. Uncovered, the black eye of the comm monitor stared at her. Heart beating, she placed the golden headset on her brow, watching the comm flicker to life. How did it do that?

She accessed the system, thoughts in a tumble and watched the alphabet form on the screen.

"So much to learn. So little time to do it. And now a man is going to die because of me." She couldn't keep her mind on the lesson. With the comm still feeding information into her brain, she didn't realize she'd fallen asleep.

CHAPTER VII

Susan Smith Andojar settled the heavy rifle against her shoulder, squinting down the long barrel, struggling to keep the front sighting blade from wavering as she aimed at the distant target.

"Easy, watch your breathing," Friday's voice encouraged. "Don't jerk the trigger. Keep your eyes open this time, don't blink. Jerk the shot, and you'll miss again."

Recoil pounded her cheekbone on the stock—pain lancing her shoulder. Concussion smashed her ears. Blinking, she peered at the target.

"Not bad," Friday grinned. "That shot landed within a

hand's breadth. You'll shoot better than Red Many Coups before you know it. Ramon's trembling in his boots already."

Susan worked her jaw, trying to equalize the pressure in her ears and stop the ringing sound. "Must it kick so hard?" she asked, rubbing a hand over her tender shoulder. She winced at the pain, imagining the wretched bruise.

Friday pulled down on the trigger guard, jacking out the spent case as the block lowered. He inserted another cartridge and closed the action, setting the safety. "Takes a big bullet to kill a bear. For men, a smaller bullet would do. This way one gun can serve both purposes. The important thing to remember is the gun must be steady. The kick comes after the bullet has left the barrel."

She nodded, closing her eyes, reviewing the exact sequence of events as she shot. She remembered the way the rifle felt, the anticipation of the shot. "Let me try one more. I think I can hit dead center."

Her shoulder cringed as she brought the rifle up. She positioned her arm the way Friday had shown her—the barrel resting on a solid support of bone. Breathing deeply, she settled the front blade on the target. For the moment, nothing existed except the target and the blade that was lined up with it. The rifle booted her unmercifully, rocking her off her heels and onto her side. She struggled to keep the gun from falling.

Friday—choking on laughter—caught the heavy rifle as she clawed her way upright.

"*Damn you*, did I hit it?"

"You all right?" he asked, typically male in his solicitousness.

"I'm fine!" she flared. "Answer me or . . . or I'll wrap that barrel around your head! I don't break *that* easily. You just shut . . . Why, I'll have you know *I* can take anything *you* can!"

Friday Yellow Legs nodded, obviously hurt, and peered out to where the target had been pinned to an arroyo cut-bank. "I can't see any new dirt around the target. I guess we'd better walk out and see."

She dusted herself off as she stood and followed along behind, chambering another of the cartridges and setting the safety. The little square of leather lay a good one hundred meters away.

As she got closer she could see the misses—darker patches where the heavy bullet had flung up the dirt. Friday bounded up the slope to let out a long low whistle. Whooping for joy he slid down with the leather in hand.

"Better keep that with you for a while." His toothy grin proclaimed victory. The little round hole smack in the center of the leather patch left her giddy with triumph.

"I think that will do for today," she agreed. "If I miss on a second attempt, it would make me nervous next time."

"Wish we could get a blaster for you to shoot."

"What are they like?" Susan looked down at Friday. She'd been appalled the first time she'd seen him on foot. He stood a good thirty centimeters shorter than she did.

"They don't kick like the rifle does." He winked at her playfully. "Just a constant push against your hand, not a violent jerk. Sights are wonderful. They magnify . . . see in the dark . . . tell you the range. You don't have to watch elevation because blaster bolts travel along line of sight. All range tells you is if the charge will work at that distance. Wonderful—"

"The Sirians will have blasters?" she asked.

Friday reached for his horse. "Yes. And battle armor, too. Bullets don't penetrate the stuff. Blaster fire does—but it can bounce off, too. It takes a center shot." He grinned. "Like your leather there."

Susan pulled herself into the saddle. "When are you going up to *Bullet*?"

"Tomorrow," Friday replied as he jumped and swung his leg over the cantle.

"Would you mind if I rode up with you?" she asked too quickly. She knew her face burned red. Suddenly angry she added, "Friday, you're the only friend I have! Red Many Coups is up there already. She came in last night and took the AT up. I . . . I stayed to shoot with you today. I don't have anyone to talk to! I . . . I'm scared Ramon will . . ."

He hesitated, eyes searching hers. She met the gaze, wondering at the same time why his expression touched her so.

"Sure." He added huskily, "Always nice to have someone along to make sure my hair's dry."

"Hair's dry?"

"Sure," his puckish features twisted in a smile. "Sometimes when I walk under a mud puddle, my hair gets wet."

"You're not *that* short!"

"I don't know." Eyes twinkled. "You're talking over my head right now."

She was forming a reply when something whupped past her ear. She started and turned to Friday. Heard the boom. Friday arched through the air, arms outstretched, eyes fearful, lips pulled back in a horrible snarl. No time to react, he hit her, spun her from the saddle and landed heavily on top of her. Frantic, she smashed at him viciously, trying to beat him off. Fear lent strength but still she was no match. He pinned her arms and threw her bodily into the lush grass.

"*Keep down!*" he hissed hotly.

Helpless, tense, Susan quivered, waiting for him to hurt her. Only his attention wasn't on her. She heard a ragged *hiss-thock* through the grass, followed by a hollow boom.

Her heart threatened to burst from her rib cage. As Friday loosened his grip, she tried to get up.

"*Stay down, damn it!*" he gritted. "Someone's *shooting* at us!"

The revelation stunned her. So that's what the whupping noise and the hiss through the grass had been? "I'm sorry," she whispered, heart really pounding now. Her bowels loosened in the age-old way of fear.

Friday slithered off her and began worming his way toward the horses which had walked off a couple of steps and stopped, throwing them curious looks.

She rolled onto her stomach and followed, mimicking his manner of crawling. She heard a whiz-splat and as the report boomed in the distance—saw the furrow the slug slashed in the ground where she had been sprawled—and shivered.

At the sound of the shot, Friday jumped to his feet, reached his horse, and pulled the rifle from the scabbard. Susan heard the meaty *SPLAT* of a bullet striking flesh.

Friday dropped as the horse bucked, squealed shrilly, and collapsed.

"*Bastard!*" Friday screamed at the silent hillside. Susan pulled her way into the shelter of the dead horse, feeling warm blood spread from under the dying animal.

"Too bad we only have one rifle," Susan offered.

"And one horse. Only thing is . . . how many enemies do we have out there?" Friday hawked, then spat for emphasis.

"What . . . what now?" she asked, digging her way into the soft dirt, wincing as she found a patch of bayonet grass.

"He's up there." Friday pointed a finger and pulled himself under one of the horse's legs. Carefully, he looked over the neck. "Take off your shirt."

"What?" Susan threw his squirming legs a look of disbelief. "What are you—"

"Take off your shirt and push it out behind the horse. He may take a shot at it. If there's ground jump . . . from the muzzle blast . . . maybe I can spot him," the muffled voice came back.

Taking care to keep down, Susan pulled off her shirt. Admiring the fabric—the like of which she had never thought to own—she balled it up in a wad and tossed it behind the animal's hindquarters. An instant whiz-splat preceded a boom. On impulse, Susan yipped a cry.

"I'm all right!" she hissed. "See anything?"

For an answer, Friday's rifle banged in the still air. "He's up in the rocks. What made you holler? You scared the bejeesus out of me."

"I don't know," she mused. "Just thought it might give us an edge. You know, he might think I'm wounded."

"Huh, just might." Friday shouted his next words. "You killed a *woman*! May Spider rot your testicles from your body! May maggots live in the genitals of your children! *I WILL KILL YOU FOR THAT!*"

Friday came sliding back under the horse's leg. He bit his lip, frowning, hesitant. "Can you . . . Hell! Crawl under the leg. Take the rifle. Place the gun over the horse's neck for a rest. There's an outcrop . . . the pile of rock at the top of the hill. Here are all of my cartridges. You see movement up there . . . shoot! If you get the chance, kill him. Fire, reload, count three seconds, and fire. Do that for six shots. After that, take your time. Don't run us out of ammunition."

"What are you going to do?" Fear tightened icy fingers around her gut.

"I'm going to sneak around and knife him." Friday grinned. "You wanted to be a warrior? What's it feel like?"

"I . . . I'm scared," she whispered, dropping her eyes, sucking a deep breath.

"That's part of it. Get up there and shoot. If we're lucky, he thinks you're dead." At that, he pushed her forward—helping her under the heavy foreleg. A bullet whupped over her head. Rattled, she shot too quickly—not having the rifle firmly against her shoulder. Dust puffed from below the rocks as she fought to blink back tears from the pain in her shoulder.

Remembering Friday's instructions, she reloaded, counted to three and shot again. The rifle, snugged against her shoulder, still hurt her. Reload, count, fire. Reload, count, fire. Chips flew from the rocks, pleasing her. Somewhere, she lost track of shots. The pile of brass cartridges began to dwindle.

Friday should have gotten away. A bullet made a splatting noise as it hit the horse's body. The report followed a half-second later.

With her eyes barely above the animal's neck, Susan studied the rocky position. A minute later, a bullet passed her head, batting her with the change of air pressure.

A giddy feeling ran down her limbs as she thought how close that bullet had come. For the first time, Susan lived with the realization that she could die. It would be so quick, one second she'd be there, squinting down the sights, the next she would be dead meat—just like the horse.

She settled the sights on the rock pile, finding a crevice through which she perceived movement. She swallowed, her throat dry. Her eyes seemed to water as she tried to center the blade on that dark fissure in the rock.

Just as she had when she took her practice shot, she willed everything out of her mind, seeking to concentrate. The shining blade rested in the notch of the rear sight. Hesitating between deep breaths, she felt her fingertip on the trigger.

She almost didn't hear the rifle go off—the recoil vague, only half-noticed in her concentration. A sharp curse erupted from the rocks as Susan jacked another cartridge into the chamber.

She waited. Nothing. The sun burned hot on her back. The breeze stroked softly along her hot cheek, the dirt a comforting security underneath her. Her perceptions were crystal clear, as if she were one with the world around her.

How long had it been? Friday seemed to have left only seconds ago. She counted the pile of cartridges. Three left, fifteen empty brass. Had she shot that many? Had it been five minutes? Twenty?

A rock rattled down the slope. Over the sight, a man lunged unsteadily to his feet. Automatically, Susan settled the blade on the staggering figure. Heart beating to a staccato tune, her blood raced. An adrenaline rush charged her as the quarry tried to scurry away.

The big rifle boomed and jumped in her hands, the barrel obscuring her view of the fleeing man. Susan fumbled the reloading as her eyes sought her enemy. She finally got the breech closed on another cartridge and settled the rifle, waiting for the target to reappear.

Nothing. Silence. Only the wind-teased grasses waved back and forth on the hillside. What to do? Wait? Holler for Friday? Get up and check that last shot? Her tongue stuck when she tried to swallow. Flies were coming to dip proboscises in the dead horse's blood. They lit and tickled her sweaty back, increasing her irritation.

"*Susan?*" It was Friday's voice. "It's all right. He's dead." Friday stood up to one side, waving frantically.

Relief sucked her empty as she picked up her shirt, glared at the bullet hole, and pulled it over her shoulders before she caught up her horse's reins. With the heavy rifle over her shoulder, she led the animal up the slope to where Friday stood. Awed at the sensations, the feelings, the reality of life. She lived!

The body lay almost hidden in the tall grass. Friday's grim face betrayed distaste as he studied the remains.

Hard black eyes met hers, affecting the thrill of life that played so lightly with her emotions. Friday's guttural voice surprised her. "He's yours. You killed him. You must take coup, warrior." Friday measured her as he handed her his big fighting knife.

When she reached for the knife, her hand trembled. The big blade hung heavily, awkwardly, cool against her fingers and palm. The trembling worsened and she took a deep breath, feeling numb, frightened, suddenly unsure of herself.

"*Your coup,*" Friday hissed, knobby finger pointing to the limp body.

Susan experienced a sudden desire to run away from this awful man and the grisly slumped mass before her.

"I don't want it," she whimpered.

"*Take it!*" Friday thundered at her. "It is the way of the People. You are no more than a woman who would play at being a man!" Scorn lashed her.

That deeply-seated inner strength railed at the tone in his voice. She shot a hot look of defiance at him and sank down on her knees, whispering, "I don't know how."

"Pull out hard on the hair so the scalp is stretched. Cut around it as you keep pulling. Any tissue that remains can be severed as you go." His voice sounded almost mechanical.

She looked then, noticing the wrappings, the lopsided head. "Oh, my God!"

At the touch of the hair, she jerked her hand back. Swallowing, she twisted her fingers in the dark strands and pulled. The head rolled limply and turned so she could see the face.

"The coup!" Friday growled, ripping the wrappings loose. "He broke the honor of his clan. He violated the knife feud. He is an animal without honor. He deserved death."

Susan shook as an unbidden portion of her mind forced her to steady the heavy knife over Ramon Luis Andojar's scalp. As if in a dream, she worked at the resisting flesh. To Susan, it took forever to carve the bloody trophy clean from the skull.

The thing dangled loose in her fingers. She stood, feeling the wind tug the hanging flesh. Turning, she glared hatred into Friday's eyes only to find understanding, sympathy, and most of all, respect.

"You are crying," he added softly. "Do not worry. I myself cried. You must cleanse yourself. Go to a high place and pray. Find your spirit-helper. Spider will hear your words. You are strong. I thought . . . thought you would break. You will walk with honor among the stars."

Without warning her stomach heaved. Again and again she vomited into the grass. Gasping, she straightened, leaning against Friday's arm. Spasmodically, her limbs shook. Knees weak, she gasped clean air. The bloody thing was clutched in her hand, the limp corpse lay before her. Flies buzzed around the ragged red patch of skull.

She nodded silently and reached for the arm Friday extended from her horse. He handed her Ramon's rifle and cartridge belt. Together they rode to claim Ramon's tethered mount.

Riding side by side, they turned back for the mountains— and a high place to pray. For an hour they could be seen as they made their way east, a man and a woman, each carrying a rifle.

The sun slanted to the west, falling ever closer to the ocean that lay beyond the rolling, grazing lands of the Romanans. As the shadows deepened, another rider worked his way up from the Settlements. He leaned over the neck of his horse, following the dim tracks in the deep grass— working out a fading trail. As he snaked his way up the knoll, Willy Red Hawk Horsecapture's mare blew nervously and sidestepped.

The warrior slid out of the saddle in one fluid motion, crouching, rifle gripped tightly. Hawklike eyes made out the flies circling the corpse. Willy crept carefully forward, reading the tale of the fight in the grass. When he came to the corpse, he rolled the body over with one toe, grunting at the identity of the victim.

Horsecapture straightened, peering toward the east and the mountains. He settled his rifle butt down in the grass before him, resting his hands on the muzzle. The time would come. A knife feud must be fought first. Then, who knows? Revenge might be his at any time.

"That's the last of them," John Smith Iron Eyes noted as he watched the monitor where the last of the ATs grappled with the lock, securing its 120 meter length to *Bullet*.

"Well, War Chief, we're off. Everything's finished." Rita Sarsa leaned back and crossed her arms. "Damn, who'd have ever thought we'd do it?" Her eyes clouded and she shook her head. "You know, Iron Eyes, we were crazier than loons to have tried this."

"Did we have any other choice?" Iron Eyes shrugged, watching as marines directed the unloading of the last Romanan warriors who'd shipped up. The dead ache left by Leeta's death made an empty hole under his heart. He nodded to those he knew as they passed. The expressions of disbelief on the faces of the new men were almost comic.

"Friday Garcia Yellow Legs!" Iron Eyes called to the short man who stepped out of the AT's hatch. Behind the sawed off warrior came a— No! But it was indeed the Romanan girl. Dressed in ship's clothing, she walked proudly, her black hair tied back in a braid. A rifle filled her hands and a long fighting knife stuck garishly out of her belt. Iron Eyes blinked and shook his head. Coup hung from her belt.

"John Smith Iron Eyes," Friday greeted, eyes flashing with merriment. "It is good to be aboard. We almost missed the last AT. Thought I'd have to ride up clinging by my fingernails!"

Rita's head cocked. "Here I thought you'd run out on me and you've been turning yourself into a warrior."

Susan Smith Andojar met Rita's eyes with confidence. "I just returned from my vision quest. Ramon broke . . . I . . .

needed time to purify myself. I am ready for Sirius, Red Many Coups."

"You have taken a lot on your shoulders, woman," Iron Eyes said softly. "I worry at the effect you will have on my men." She looked so sure of herself now, stronger, harder. Yes, she might make a warrior. His heart tightened.

"She killed a man who violated knife feud." Friday explained stiffly. "She killed a man who would have killed her."

"Who? Ramon?" Rita asked, glancing nervously at Iron Eyes.

Susan replied with controlled passion, "He ambushed us and tried to kill us after he swore honor to Friday Garcia Yellow Legs. I shot him." The pride in the girl's voice grated.

"Your uncle?" Iron Eyes whispered. "You lived in his household."

"He tried to kill the girl!" Friday's face turned grim. "It is a new time, John. We are going to the stars. The star men have women warriors. They have Red Many Coups. They *had* Leeta Dobra." Friday didn't stop at the pain it caused Iron Eyes. The little man placed fists on his hips and glared up. "Spider brings us new ways. If Susan goes . . . I go. Choose, War Chief."

"Susan!" Rita interrupted, voice sharp, eyes on John Smith. "You are assigned as my personal aide. Get your things moved to my quarters. You've a lot to do. You don't speak a word of Standard, you can't read, you don't know the first thing about equipment. Hop to it, double time! Yellow Legs, see that she gets there. I want you on my staff, too."

A voice deep inside Rita insisted, *There will be trouble from this.*

Comm ordered, "Lieutenant Rita Sarsa and John Smith Iron Eyes. Report to the Colonel in the conference room."

Iron Eyes promptly turned on his heel and strode off down the companionway, muscles tense in his back. Rita followed hot on his heels as they made the lift. Once inside, the doors closed, she looked up at Iron Eyes' stiff face.

"So what is it?" Rita demanded, squinting. "You knew things like this were going to happen. What in hell's wrong with that girl going off to space?"

Iron Eyes maintained his stolid expression. Finally he said, "We face enough turmoil without stirring up more. It's not right."

"Right, how?" Rita shook her head, "It didn't seem to bother you when Leeta took charge of stymieing the Directorate. You were right there backing her up. You don't mind me ordering your warriors about. What is it? Come on, John. You're not being yourself!"

He didn't raise his voice. "Spider gave us a way to live. Gave each of us certain things to do. Men make war . . . women tend houses and raise our young. You are from the stars. Your ways are . . . different. The People—"

"Jesus!" Rita breathed. "You're smarter than that, Iron Eyes. By your same logic, Spider sent the star men to the People for something. Spider originally had you and the Santos killing each other right and left—like rats or something! If Susan can't become a soldier because of Spider . . . Ah, hell, what's the damn difference? Huh?"

How could he tell her what his fears were? That it wasn't Susan; it was him.

The lift stopped and the door shot open. Refusing to answer, Iron Eyes led the way to the conference room. The door slid open and he entered, dropping into a seat, trying to ignore Rita as she slid in beside him. Captain Neal Iverson followed after them.

"Won't talk about it, huh?" Rita grumbled, face red, eyes slitted. "That's answer enough!"

Iron Eyes ground his teeth, jaw tight.

Coffee and tea appeared from dispensers. Colonel Damen Ree entered and saluted before dropping his square muscular body into the seat at the head of the table.

"To order," Ree said almost as an afterthought. "First and foremost, the Romanan warriors are all aboard and we are accelerating from orbit. *Brotherhood* and *Victory* are ahead of us by about three hours and heading for jump. The members of the scientific staff who have chosen to remain are on planet along with Doctor Szchinzki Montaldo who will oversee representation of the Romanan toron interests. Marty Bruk and Bella Vola will continue anthropological studies from base camp. Chem and his people are leaving by Fast Transport for university. Any questions?"

Colonel Ree searched the various faces. He continued, "Very well, we haven't really had a chance to sit down and iron out a lot of the difficulties we've faced in the past six months. We've been too damn busy. In short, ladies and gentlemen, this is a war council. None of us are leaving here until we rebuild this command."

Captain Iverson saluted and stood, back stiff, eyes ahead. "With the Colonel's pardon, sir." Tall and blond, he looked the part of a brave young officer.

Damen Ree motioned in his direction. "At ease, Neal. I'm dispensing with formality for the purpose of this meeting. I need all of you to be brutally honest. Sit down and tell me what's on your mind."

Iverson dropped back into his chair. "Colonel, if I can be blunt, we've got to do something with the Romanans. They may fight like crazy, but they present a discipline problem for my men. In a lot of ways, having them aboard is like having a bunch of children loose in a candy factory. They're into everything and my officers can't tell them no."

Ree shot a glance at Iron Eyes. "Before I broach my ideas on that, let me congratulate Major Neal Iverson on his promotion. I would similarly like to congratulate Major Rita Sarsa on hers." Ree's eyes cataloged reactions. Looks of surprise and shock appeared around the table.

Ree silenced the babble of voices with a raised hand. "I realize some of you may feel slighted at the moment. I am not trying to anger anyone by jumping Rita from lieutenant to major." Ree's hard face tightened. "You see, Rita, *you* are responsible for the Romanans. At the same time, I am appointing John Smith Iron Eyes as Rita's second in command. How you divide up the responsibilities is up to you—just so it works."

Nods of dawning comprehension bobbed along the table.

"Ah, you understand," Ree seemed satisfied. "None of you knows the Romanans better than Major Sarsa. At the same time, Neal steps in to fill the shoes of Major Reary. In the event of my . . . uh, death, command will devolve on his shoulders. I dare say, Neal, you have my every confidence."

A round of restrained applause followed.

Grimly, Ree added, "We have an awesome task, people. We must teach the Romanans to be a functioning part of this ship. At the same time, so much is so different. I don't know if any of you have given any thought to the changes which have befallen us.

"Consider, if you will, the Patrol has shed its own blood. In doing so, we have all become outlaws." Ree's eyes hardened. "Do you really think they will let us keep this ship after the Sirian unrest is quelled?"

Voices muttered. Captain Moshe Rashid asked, "Colonel, what can they do? I didn't mind shooting back when *Brotherhood* tried to kill us. Uh, self defense and all."

As the noise level rose, Rita stood in spite of the informal nature of the conference. "Let me see if I can put this in perspective," she began. Green eyes searched out each of the officers. "When we made the choice to disobey the Directorate, we made the jump, people. We can't go back now.

"Insofar as the Patrol itself is concerned, they need us for the moment. Think now. How about after the Sirians have been put down? I'm willing to wager two months' pay we get a rash of transfer orders. When they have the crew scattered, we each get retired . . . or worse, sometime during annual physicals, each of us will be slightly, um, 'reoriented' by a psych team.

"One thing we can accept as done is that Damen will be relieved of command on some pretext or another and retired with all kinds of wonderful honors. Do any of you really believe that Neal or anyone else from this crew will be placed in command of *Bullet* by the Directorate?

"Look people, we're considered a threat to the Directorate. They think we're dangerous. We revolted once and we might do it again. They can no longer predict our behavior." She paused, tracing her fingers absently over the table-top. "Personally, I've given up too much to be sent back to rot on a station in retirement. Or be brain-zapped by some smiling bastard in a white coat."

"Sarsa, damn you! I curse the day you ran into my reactor room with that rabble," Major Glick, the chief engineer said angrily. He looked around. "At the same time, Rita's right—and we all know it. They won't let us alone. Can't. Think about the ramifications within the Patrol. A ship of the line disobeyed orders and—"

"But they were *stupid* orders!" Captain Adam Chung pointed out. "We couldn't destroy that whole planet! What the hell do they think we are? Murderers? Burning people like . . . like . . ."

Ree bit off a chuckle, remembering Chung's willingness to shoot down Romanans in the beginning. Now he had a Spider stenciled on his uniform.

"No, we couldn't," Glick agreed. "But it doesn't matter what the humanitarian concerns were. The fact remains that we, all of us, disobeyed an order sent straight from the Director himself. If you were in control of the Patrol, how would you react?" Glick raised his eyebrows and leaned back, jaw forward.

In his hesitating Standard, Iron Eyes began, "Among my People, we have groups who split off all the time. Many years ago after the *Nicholai Romanan* landed from the stars, we were all one People. The Gritas and the White Eagles were displeased with the way the settlement was run. They moved into the mountains to have their own God and Prophets. From Spiders . . . as well as from the Santos . . . others left . . . left to live as they wanted. Why do the star people fear making their own groups?" He spread his hands. "Is that not what we have done by mixing the clans of Spiders, Santos, and *Bullet*? Made something new?"

Ree nodded, replying, "With the establishment of the Directorate, warfare stopped. The fear now is that by diversifying we may again go to war."

"Fine by me," Moshe Rashid grunted. He looked around, seeing some agreeing, others frowning. "Well, what have we been trained for? What did the jug heads—"

"To *protect*!" Ree growled. "To keep men from killing each other."

"And what has it cost us?" Rita asked suddenly. "Damen, what has the race accomplished in the last two hundred years? I've done a little research, trying to understand what we've become. The Confederacy was an age of heroes. When we see, or read, or sleep-stim for leisure, all the stories are centered on the era of the Confederacy when people were bigger than life, right?

"Our technology is Confederate. Hasn't changed . . . except to decline through time. We're stagnating! And worse, degenerating. We think of the old Brotherhood ships as being magic! They weren't just sophisticated computers we can't build anymore. That's only one example. Think about it! There are others. How many people travel anymore? Our populations die where they were born."

Iron Eyes studied Ree. "We have heard from many here, Colonel. What of yourself? I respect you. You lead with honor. What do you think we should do?"

Colonel Ree sipped his coffee and frowned as if trying to put his thoughts together. "I've known most of you for twenty years. Long time. In that time, we've seen some remarkable things out here. I've fought you—or backed you—on matters of policy and I've watched each of you grow even as you've watched me.

"Like each and every one of you, I've dedicated my life to the Patrol. I have perhaps another forty years of service before I get to the point where I'm too senile to be trusted with the command of *Bullet*. Yes, in addition to Rita's argument, we've lost the medical ability to prolong our lives, too."

"This ship is my life." Ree's face had become wooden. "I don't like the thought of . . . dying on some station or planet where I can't move about. They'll do that to me. Don't think there's any question about it.

"So what can we do?" Ree asked, eyes searching the faces about him. "I can make only a suggestion, friends. As of the moment that Skor Robinson asked us to kill the Romanan planet, our duty changed. Just one of those things. For that matter, from the moment that first GCI picked up radio communication from the Romanans, the Directorate changed."

Ree hesitated, seeing anticipation in the eyes of his officers. "I think," he paused again, monitoring reactions, "that the best thing for us to do is to continue our patrols as before."

"I don't understand?" Chung looked puzzled. "What if Headquarters won't let us? How do we . . ."

Colonel Damen Ree sipped his coffee. "Could they stop us?" he asked. In the pregnant silence, no one said anything. "We are dedicated to protecting Far Side. Further, after the fight off Atlantis no one will want to tangle with us. I don't know about the rest of you, but I take my oath seriously. I promised to serve the people. In the event the Patrol would prefer to serve itself, I must side with the intent of my obligations."

Silence.

Neal Iverson nodded his understanding. "The only change would be that we no longer take orders from the Patrol."

"Selected orders," Ree corrected. "For example, if the Patrol asked us to administer relief to a damaged station, we would. If they requested that we send them Major Neal Iverson for discipline," he chuckled, "we wouldn't."

"How about spare parts, replacements, supplies, things like that?" Rashid asked.

"If we based at Atlantis, would the Romanans supply us with toron, warriors, food, and raw materials?" Ree asked Iron Eyes.

The War Chief laughed. "Of course! The young men would feel very poorly if they couldn't travel the stars like their fathers."

"We could also advertise to university for ambitious graduates who have skills we need," Rita added. "There are ways to circumvent the Directorate's policy."

"And for wages, we could charge for transportation and protection," Chung said thoughtfully.

Major Glick nodded. "There are very few things which we can't manufacture ourselves. The raw materials are all around us. Toron would be the hang-up but there's more than we'll ever use on Atlantis. The rest we can always trade for things we can't make."

"I motion then that we declare ourselves independent after the Sirian adventure. Shall we put it to a vote?" Iverson looked around.

Ree let his eyes rest on each of their faces. "Ladies and gentlemen, what shall it be?"

The result was a unanimous decision. As of that moment, *Bullet* had committed total treason. Robinson would have to kill them now.

"One last thing," the Colonel said softly. "What we have decided must not go beyond this room for the time being. You understand? There will be plenty of time for our declaration of independence in the future. In the meantime, lay your groundwork for that day."

CHAPTER VIII

"What do you mean? *A knife feud? On my ship?*" Damen Ree paced restlessly, smacking his fist into his palm. *"ON MY SHIP?"*

Friday Garcia Yellow Legs stood stiffly, head thrown back, stolid face like cast bronze. Thick, muscle-corded arms crossed tightly over his chest, accenting the two coups hanging from his vest. Legs braced, he missed nothing, black eyes shifting from face to face.

John Smith Iron Eyes sighed and rubbed a hand over his visage. "You knew, Friday. Yet you came along—joined a war party—knowing blood feud would have to be honored by Willy Red Hawk Horsecapture."

"No, War Chief," Friday grunted, flinty eyes narrowing. "*He* came along knowing it was blood feud."

"Same thing," Rita grumbled. "I oughta break both of you in two. You could ride to Sirius in med units—or the brig!"

"It's stopped!" Ree turned from where he'd paused to stare up at the display of Romanan weapons hanging on his wall. "That's all there is to it. I'm in command of this ship—*it's stopped!*"

Rita looked nervously at Iron Eyes.

"It will not be so simple," John added *sotto voce*. "For you to stop the knife feud will anger the warriors. Break their morale for the fighting on Sirius. The People will lose heart."

Ree's blunt face tightened. He poked a stiff finger in Yellow Legs' direction. "You can order him to retract it, can't you?"

John Smith Iron Eyes nodded. "I can."

Friday Garcia Yellow Legs began to tremble, face contorting blackly as his jaws clamped shut.

"But I would not recommend it, Colonel. I would not like to dishonor Friday Garcia Yellow Legs. To do so would insult him and Horsecapture." Iron Eyes spread his arms helplessly. "They are both responsible for bringing feud on a war party. When Friday told me, it seemed stupid. Perhaps Spider plays with us, tricks us again. But you do have another way out."

"I'm all ears," Ree grunted.

Iron Eyes frowned, looking at the Colonel. He blinked. "All ears?" Head tilted he looked at Ree's ears. "I don't . . . uh . . ."

"It's a figure of speech," Rita muttered wryly. "You need more time on the language tapes, War Chief. The Colonel means he's ready for advice."

"Ah! I see. Yes, well, Colonel. Let them fight it out. To do so is a simple thing. Honor will be upheld, the Romanans will adore you, morale will soar, the problem will be settled, and the loser is dumped out an air lock. In the meantime, no other knife feud will be sworn since we are on the war trail. You will have no more trouble until we come back from Sirius."

"Loser goes out the air lock, huh?" Ree locked his fingers behind him, head back, eyes closed as he pursued his options. "Yeah, might do it," he breathed. "We'll see if we can talk Horsecapture out of it first. We can do that, can't we?"

"Yes," Friday agreed. "I would accept *mutual* withdrawal of knife feud for the benefit of the Sirian raid. There is honor in that."

Ree's smile held no humor. "Honor, huh, Friday? You know, that's one of the things I appreciated about you people, still have honor. Didn't know it could be so damn convoluted."

"What's this all about?" Rita scowled in distaste. "What started it?"

Friday smiled shyly. "I caught Ramon and Willy taking Susan Smith Andojar out to kill her."

Iron Eyes winced, placing a palm to his forehead. "That girl! I *told* you she would be trouble."

"Doesn't anyone human design computers anymore?" Corporal Hans Yeager muttered, back cricked until it hurt as he squirmed his arm through a maze of master boards deep in the guts of the comm. Major Sarsa's system needed an upgrade—he'd gotten the job. Straining, his fingers snapped the K deck fasteners loose.

"Feel like a monkey screwing a football," he gritted, slithering out of the comm.

When she walked in, Hans stood up quickly to salute—figuring it was the Major.

"You don't need salute to me." The wrong voice stumbled, awkward, accented to beat hell—and obviously not the Major's.

Hans peered out from under his hand and encountered black eyes, a heart-shaped face which surrounded a firm, straight nose, and full red lips. The girl's hair gleamed, thick, raven-black, and hanging in a lustrous braid over one shoulder. Not only that, he'd never seen her before.

"You're Romanan!" Hans guessed.

"That am I." She nodded happily and gave him a grin. "You do here . . . uh, what?"

Hans blushed. "Why I . . . I'm just putting in a new board for the Major's comm. Since she got promoted, she'll need more power for this unit." Hans felt himself coloring. Had he ever seen such a beautiful woman? *Not in this lifetime.*

The girl gave him a ravishing smile and went over to a chair, placed a headset on her brow, and dropped into whatever she was studying. Hans continued his upgrade, checking each and every circuit four or five times so he could sneak peeks over his shoulder at the enticing female concentrating at her comm.

Finally the girl got up and went into the toilet. Hans waited until she emerged, buttoned up the board, and dropped his testing device into its carry case. "Uh," he stumbled over the words, "I guess this is about done here."

The girl nodded, paying attention. His fluster grew.

"Well, uh, maybe I'd . . . I'd better be going." Hans smiled too quickly. *I'm making an ass of myself—again.* "Yep, I guess I'd . . . better." He smacked his hands together, grinning, bouncing on energy-charged toes.

Her smile ravished him once more, virtually stopping his heart.

"Where will you go?" she asked, eyes half-closed, brow furrowed as she studied the pronunciation.

"Why, uh, to the mess . . . for a cup of coffee . . . I suppose." Hans blinked, tongue-tied.

"I enjoy coffee," she said, still concentrating. Her eyes widened. "I said that well?"

"Gee, uh, yeah . . . that's great." Hans laughed. "You speak very well. You're just learning?"

"I started the language tapes in my sleep days ago two." She grinned. "I learn Standard fast."

Hans felt himself warm to her eager expression. "You do real good for two days." He hesitated, suddenly nervous. "Hey, you busy? I mean . . . I'd be happy to share a . . . cup of coffee with you. If you don't . . . uh . . . mind." He swallowed hard—loud. *What did I just do?* Hans gritted his teeth, awaiting rejection.

The girl's smile broadened. "You will talk Standard with . . . with me?"

"Well, I . . . yeah," Hans staggered, feeling himself blush. "Yeah, I'll talk Standard with you all you want. Sure."

"I with you go." The girl turned and opened her wardrobe compartment. Hastily, she drew out a belt with a big Romanan knife and whipped it about her narrow waist. She turned to Hans and smiled. "Ready! I be . . . uh, am Susan Smith Andojar."

"Corporal Hans Yeager." He palmed the door. As she followed him out, he noticed the coup. *Easy boy, keep the smile on your face! Lordy! This delicate looking wisp of a girl* killed *a man.*

"My pleasure to meet you," she said with a slight bow and offered her hand.

He shook it nervously and her eyes narrowed. "Something wrong is?" she had come to a stop in the hall.

"Well . . . uh, you see . . ." He rubbed his hands together, trying to grin. At that moment Lieutenant Ara Breeze rounded a corner of the companionway and pulled to a stop—mouth open. A wry grin beginning to curl on sardonic lips.

Put Marla in my bed, did they? Made a damn fool out of me? Anger clamped on Hans' heart. *She may kill me—cut my hair of my head—but none of them other assholes has a Romanan date!*

"No," Hans forced his voice even. "Not a thing." He offered his arm and Susan took it. With a swagger, Hans paraded past Breeze, whistling merrily.

"I thought your . . . um, mind . . . yes, mind had changed." He caught the evaluative glance from the corner of her eye.

"Uh . . . well, I . . . you know, never met a Romanan woman before . . . face to face that is. I mean, well, I saw your coup. I'd heard women didn't take coups. I'd heard you were just, well, noncombatants." He felt himself blushing.

Her expression narrowed with hostility. "You no approve?"

He shook his head in genuine negation. "Not at all. Uh, I mean . . . I'm glad that a girl with a coup would go and get coffee with me. Uh, in Romanan, I guess I'd say you did me honor. Only I don't know the words."

"Honor?" Her eyes danced as she grinned at him. She translated and helped him with the pronunciation. In the gun deck mess, eyes followed them to their table.

He decided on coffee. "You want anything different? I'd be pleased to buy you whatever you wanted."

"Really?" Her eyes glowed. "You would get for me a . . . a lemonade?"

Hans felt flushed with excitement as he seated himself next to the girl, almost afraid to look at her. She seemed so very beautiful—and he couldn't keep his eyes from straying to the shocked faces around them. Yep, so much for *his* reputation as a boob!

Giorj Hambrei stood on the bridge of the *Hiram Lazar* and nodded to himself as the monitors showed the ship's bright purple blaster bolts lancing into the moon. Dust, detritus, and steam boiled off the surface so many kilometers below.

He yawned, tired, showing the strain of the heavy g, the long hours.

Giorj's stature fell below the median for a Sirian man. Thin—literally skin on bone—his weight, too, placed below normal. It was his coloration—or rather the lack of it—that drew attention to him. He was a washed-out gray man, without skin tones, his hair thin and dull against his scalp. Pale eyes stared out of a face so expressionless, some thought it dead. In a very real way, radiation had left it so.

"Magnificent!" Ngen Van Chow breathed from his seat in the command chair. Around him, the bridge of the *Hiram Lazar* blinked and displayed data. Several officers bent over various comms monitoring energy production, shield draw, and systems functions.

"It took some doing," Giorj replied, gray face expressionless. Only his movements betrayed his satisfaction. "The information was there all along. Curse the Brotherhood for writing in that damnable code—but we were able to get the general idea from the diagrams. There are no blasters within the Directorate to compare with these. At the same time, our shields are now doubly augmented—even pulling a full blaster load.

"We can handle any three line ships they send at us. The Patrol has nothing comparable. Cease fire," he ordered, and the violet light vanished, leaving only the vortex of dust and rock that spewed from the dead surface far below.

"Why not?" Ngen Van Chow murmured as he leaned on his elbow.

"Dry rot within the Directorate," Giorj said matter-of-factly. "The Patrol has no possible competition. As a result, their weaponry is little more than adequate. My task was to excel their maximum. The hardest part was locating the information. The Brotherhood records are still on Frontier."

"The Brotherhood still exists?" Ngen looked startled. He began chewing his lip.

"Of course." Giorj nodded, his mind half on the readouts from the computer. "Rotted like everything else. They don't really know what they have. The Grand Master may, but he's a senile fool. I met him while I was there. Entropy is the legacy of the Directorate."

"Too bad we can't get all their information." Ngen shifted

his eyes to Giorj. *What a jewel you are, my engineer! Brilliance comes in such strange packages!*

"When we destroy the Patrol and roll the Directorate back, we can have it all." Giorj studied the final results of his test and smiled his satisfaction. "It's only a matter of time, Ngen," the engineer added tonelessly. He turned and looked at the First Citizen, bony arms crossed on his chest.

"We have perhaps three months before the Patrol line ships arrive. Is that enough? And what is the status of the rest of the fleet?" Ngen mused, his mind half on Frontier and the files stored there.

"By the time the Patrol is within striking distance, we will have *Helk* and *Dastar* ready for combat with the same potential as *Hiram Lazar*. I think with their entire fleet, they might have a chance to destroy us. With anything less," he shrugged, "we should be able to stand them off and destroy most of the Patrol."

Ngen shook his head slowly, baffled. "The thought that such an advanced physics has been ignored for so long amazes me. Why didn't the Directorate make use of it? Their ignorance will destroy them now. I can't imagine . . ."

Giorj seemed nonplussed. "It would have been dangerous to dig up Brotherhood secrets. Allusions to them would have fired interest in their philosophy. Their thirst for knowledge would stir unrest among the ignorant within the Directorate. A population stupid as sheep is easier to control than one which thinks and questions."

Ngen looked up, still partly lost in his thoughts. "What have we been doing these last three hundred years? Where would we be today had our ancestors not discredited the Brotherhood and established the Directorate in place of the Confederacy? Just imagine . . . What miracles would be ours had the people been seekers instead of brainless beasts?"

Giorj blinked lifelessly. "It matters not what might have been, First Citizen. The arena for concern is what will be . . ."

"How true," Ngen admitted from a long way away. "Perhaps we can strangle the Directorate and at the same time destroy these barbarian Romanans they bring with them." He laughed. "Imagine, Stone Age warriors . . . against *our* Home Legions? The marines I would worry about. But these cow herders? Fodder for our men. Stupid targets to be—"

"They need not even be allowed to land, you know. The satellite defense system should be able to destroy each and every one of the ATs." Giorj allowed his eyes to almost close.

Ngen bounded to his feet and began to pace. "No! I think it wise to let some through. We need to destroy them on the planet—"

"They will cause substantial damage. It means lives, First Citizen." Giorj pulled a cup of coffee from a dispenser and sipped.

"And lives, my good Giorj, will make martyrs for Sirius. Martyrs drive the people harder than any threat by government. The corpses of my fellow citizens will bring home the fact that we are fighting for our lives. Keep in mind that those who have nothing to lose, those who think themselves already dead, they make the *finest* soldiers."

"So there will be another bombing before the Patrol arrives?" Giorj asked after a long pause.

"Production of war machinery is dropping off. From the curves, it will begin to sag significantly by the middle of next month. I can't allow that. As a result, we will experience another act of Directorate retaliation . . . um, how about Saturday morning?" Ngen smiled.

Giorj moved back to the ship's controls. "Men seem such an irrational lot. It pleases me to no end that you do so well with them, First Citizen." He ran thin white fingers over the comm console, voice wistful. "Engineering, on the other hand, is rational. Clean, without moral dilemma. Do as you will with your herd, Ngen. Shape them as you wish. Simply leave me the freedom to experiment and I shall . . . shall say nothing about your methods with flesh and blood."

Ngen nodded slowly, mind drawn once more to the secrets the Brotherhood had stashed away in their wonderful computers. So much had been lost. Just where would humanity have gone had it not been for the Directorate? *First I must destroy my rivals. Then comes the Patrol. Behind them the Directorate lies helpless—a sheep whose throat is exposed to the wolf. Thereafter, only one question remains: Where will I take our future?*

Willy Red Hawk Horsecapture glared hotly into the lean faces surrounding him. "*I* care nothing for what John Smith Iron Eyes says. He is no longer of the People. This girl . . . this Susan Smith Andojar . . . has shamed us all. She has shamed the Smith clan and the Andojar clan. She is without honor. She acts like she has no relatives," he spit out the worst insult among the People.

"We are all learning different things." José Grita White Eagle, the Santos War Chief, shrugged his shoulders. "I study under a woman warrior. Why should not our own People let the women who wish go to the stars? Does it hurt our children? Perhaps not. Perhaps a woman who has seen battle will bring stronger blood to a warrior's offspring?"

Occasional grunts of assent echoed among the men where they hunched on stacked bunks or sat at tables, cleaning rifles, sharpening knives, listening politely.

"She killed her uncle!" Horsecapture shouted. "Doesn't that fact bother you? *Murdered* the man who *fed* her! She sees not the men of the People. She walks the halls with star men. Spreads her legs like a slave woman!" His lips curled in disgust as he paced, seeing anger lighting other eyes.

"You would accuse Red Many Coups of the same?" asked Toby Garcia Andojar. "She slept with Philip Smith Iron Eyes. She loved him. Maybe Susan loves this corporal or perhaps she loves Friday Garcia Yellow Legs? I think it is none of my business. And she is of my clan. I do not worry too much about her. Old Ramon was a little odd in his head. You make—"

"Bah! Women belong home!" Ray Smith spat, gesturing angrily.

Horsecapture stood in the center of the room, shoulders flexed, fists clenched, head down as he looked from face to face. When he spoke, his voice was low. "We are losing our way. Spider came to our grandfathers' grandfathers. He was nailed to a cross of wood . . . *nailed*, eh? That we would be free, never be slaves of men like the Sobyets again.

"When Henry Garcia took him down from the cross, Spider gave men the great *laws of the People*. He told men how they should live to be strong. He told women how they should live. That's right, *He* told them! Here . . . in this ship . . . we have no high place where we can pray to Spider. The Prophets did not come with us on this journey. Why . . . eh? They stay among the People." His voice dropped to a penetrating hiss. "It is no wonder that you are turning from Spider."

"Willy Red Hawk Horsecapture is *right*!" Sam Yellow Legs Iron Eyes stood up from his bunk. He worked his lips—an old man with a face scarred from many fights with

the Santos. A more recent scar had been left by a blaster
when he'd fought the marines.

"We lose our way, Spider's way!" His old voice trembled.
"I see you young men walking around talking of . . . of
capacitors, eh? Wavelengths? Photon density . . . red shift
. . . quanta? And there's other words I do not know. Do I
hear you pray to Spider? Huh? Tell me? How often do you
call upon your spirit-helpers to guide you? Fools, do you
think your spirit-helpers are only for battle? *They are for
every day of your lives!*" He paused to wipe away the spittle
at the corner of his mouth. "You are as children. You forget
who you are . . . and play at a new game as boys instead of
men."

Silence filled the room as eyes dropped to muscular brown
hands. Some shifted, uneasy in their new star clothing.
Others pursed their lips—shamed.

"We don't pray enough," someone whispered in the brooding silence.

"I pray every day!" The strong voice rang out in the
room. Eyes shifted to the pressure hatch. Friday Yellow
Legs Garcia stood there, defiant, arms crossed, haughty.

"And I, too." John Smith Iron Eyes pushed past the
bantam warrior, striding into the room, eyes flashing.

"Who do you pray to?" Sam Iron Eyes demanded, voice
as dry as the Bear Mountains in fall.

"To Spider, my Grandfather," John Smith Iron Eyes said
softly, eyes properly downcast before an elder.

Colonel Damen Ree entered after the rest. "What of
me?" he asked curiously. "I, too, have come to pray to
Spider. Does it matter that I am not of the People, Grandfather?" Ree—commander of his ship—refused to lower his
eyes.

"I know not," Sam grumbled, raising his hands in frustration. "I see only that things are not . . . not right. The
People are not as they used to be. I no longer know Spider's
will. There are no Prophets here to teach us. They stay on
World . . . with the People. Perhaps I was wrong to come
here." His old eyes looked searchingly into Damen Ree's.

"Grandfather," Ree addressed the old warrior sincerely,
"You may send a message to the Prophets at your leisure.
This offer I make out of respect for your wisdom. Lead the
young men. It would not be good that they lose the way of
Spider. I have read from the books that Leeta Dobra had. I
have read of what happens to People who lose themselves.

It would harm your young ones. I leave the discretion of making such calls to you. You are wise, teach them." Ree bowed formally.

Sam's eyes gleamed again, sharpening as he noted renewed respect in the way others looked at him. He opened his mouth, gratitude on his tongue, but Horsecapture cut him off.

"Words as smooth as a woman's!"

Ree looked like he'd been struck. His eyes slitted, face reddening, he turned on his heels, dropping to a crouch.

"What would you do different?" John Smith Iron Eyes asked, trying to defuse the situation. "Would you take the warriors back to World? Would you turn down a chance at coup? Would you dishonor your—"

"I would make sure the People do not lose their way!" Horsecapture growled. "Why did you come here, Iron Eyes? To water the blood of warriors with weak words?"

Iron Eyes stiffened.

Ree spoke, voice clipped by tight jaws. "I brought Friday Garcia Yellow Legs here to see if I could stop the knife feud which you have planned to fight tonight. I understand that it is permissible for me to try and work out a compromise."

Horsecapture whirled to face Yellow Legs. "You are a coward? You would not fight me?" He broke into peals of laughter, the muscles under his bronze skin jumped tight as he pointed at Friday. "You are a worm. May maggots rot your testicles!"

Friday's face went ashen. "I came to see if there was a way of dealing with you as a man instead of a rock slug. I was wrong."

"Jesus!" Ree exploded, throwing up his hands and turning away.

"I think there is no way of making a peaceful solution out of this," Iron Eyes said evenly.

Damen Ree took a quick breath and turned to Iron Eyes. "I can order this stopped. My options include putting them both in the brig."

"Do it, star man!" Horsecapture sneered. "You are a worm like Yellow—"

Ree moved like lightning. He flipped in the air, neatly hammering Horsecapture to the floor, dropping on him like a ton of neutrons.

Muscular forearm across Horsecapture's throat, Ree gritted, *"Damn you! That's enough!"* He swallowed hard, trembling with anger as he glared hotly into Horsecapture's crazed black eyes. "I am *your* commanding officer so long as you are on this ship! You EVER raise your voice to me again—I'll break your damn neck!"

Then Ree was back on his feet, glaring at the shocked faces. "Anyone else want a piece of me? I command this vessel." He jammed a thumb at his chest. "I do so by right, like a War Chief. If you don't like the way things are, if you won't take my order, tell me now!"

"He is the War Chief," Iron Eyes reminded. "He leads this raid."

Sam Yellow Legs nodded, a smile on his old lips. "Horsecapture has acted without honor. No man insults his war chief." His face betrayed confusion. "Colonel? Why didn't you kill him? It was your right—your honor?"

"A good leader doesn't destroy a strong warrior, does he?" Ree lifted an eyebrow, aware of Horsecapture sitting up, gasping, a hand to his throat.

Yips of agreement burst out as warriors raised their rifles and knives.

"Good work, Colonel," Iron Eyes whispered. "You have won them."

"Want to withdraw knife feud?" Ree bent hot eyes on Horsecapture.

"Now it is *my* honor! I'll kill him!" came the gritty reply as Willy fingered his neck, face twisted in hatred.

Friday Garcia Yellow Legs nodded slowly. "It must be finished, Colonel. There is a corruption deep within Willy Red Hawk Horsecapture. It has been decided by Spider. If he would settle it peacefully, I would, too. I do not wish—"

"The corruption," Horsecapture hissed, "is in you, short freak of the People. It is you who . . . who turn your back from the ways of your fathers. Dip your spear into that abomination of a girl who has . . . has murdered her uncle. Throws shit upon the name of her clan . . . and shames us all!"

Friday Garcia Yellow Legs fought valiantly to keep from throwing himself at Horsecapture. Eyes narrowed throughout the room. Ree settled into a combat stance ready to bring either of them down.

"It will be blood." Iron Eyes' wooden voice cut the tension. "Friday, come away from here. You have your chance tonight. Spider will choose between the two of you." He placed a firm hand on the young man's shoulder and backed him from the room, corded muscle rippling under the soft leather clothing.

Ree followed, head shaking as he muttered under his breath. He looked up. "John, what if I ordered them to stop this nonsense? What would happen?"

Iron Eyes paused, thoughtful. "Like we decided earlier. It would hurt. It would make it seem that Red Hawk is right. Many would believe that we are turning away from Spider."

Ree laughed sourly, a sudden light coming to his face. He smacked fist into palm. "What the hell! Go ahead, kill each other. You fight with knives, right?" His eyes twinkled with relief. "Friday, I hope you cut that bastard into little pieces." At that the Colonel pushed past, headed for the bridge, a look of anticipation about him.

Two marines walking toward them stopped and stared—realizing who Yellow Legs was. They whispered to each other, engrossing themselves in a study of the wall as Friday passed.

"It would seem that I have become a source of entertainment," Friday grumbled with a bitter laugh. "Short freak of the people? Me?"

"You've been thinking about this fight?" Iron Eyes wondered.

"Sure have," Friday nodded. "First I cut him down to size, then I worry about what to do with the rest of him!"

CHAPTER IX

On Range, the citizens' council has formulated a petition for further information on the Romanan policies. New Zion requests elaboration on our actions regarding Atlantis. The Terran Defense League would like us to respond to charges of genocide. We have actually had riots on Star's End, calling for the dismissal of the Directorate link to their world. Directorate Coordinator Fidor Roch on Antares V reports sedition in the domes. Derogatory graffiti is appearing on the walls. Tierbault Station, with their long history of tradition, notes that the young have formed grievance committees and clamor for attention and redress. In Solacris a riot was suppressed only by the most desperate measures. . . . Navtov's report continued.

Enough. Skor sent through the comm. *I can review the data myself. Your continued listing of every center of social unrest is no longer—*

We have a Directorate-wide problem! And it's growing! Navtov insisted. *Doctor Dobra's broadcast has acted like yeast in a sugar solution! Ferment arises throughout space. This goes totally beyond prediction! How can we—*

Silence! An Roque's thunderous presence resounded through the Gi-net. *The entire problem defies rationality. The Directorate staggers under the presence of this broadcast. Ngen Van Chow adds fuel to the flames, stirring the conflagration started by the Dobra broadcast with his own. What is his purpose? His actions are illogical.*

Skor sent a plea for silence through the system. *The Prophet has been right all along. We are out of touch. Our actions to subdue these perturbations have been ineffective. Logic no longer has anything to do with social control.*

Navtov criticized, *Then if you have the answer, lead us! From your vast stores of human lore, how do we cope with the current crisis? Even the Sirian rebels are making this Damen Ree and his rebellious pirates into heroes! Even the Sirians! Now Van Chow tells all human space to destroy the Gi-net, remove the single factor which has given the species peace and security all these years. Irrationality! Insanity!*

Skor waited him out. *The Prophet is right. We have lost our ability to control information. The lesson, so long repressed, has been spread like your hypothetical fungus.*

Roque added, *In the end, as soon as the Sirians are returned to normalcy, this Ree and his Romanans must be destroyed.*

Agreed, Navtov replied. *I suggest we lay our plans to that effect. The Sirians will take a day or two to subjugate. Thereafter, the pirate Ree will be outnumbered by loyal Patrol forces. His Romanans can be effectively eliminated on the ground by the marines. The damage may thus be contained on an interdicted world. No more information will be passed into human space.*

Wait, Skor cautioned. *I'm not sure it will be that easy. I am calling back three of the Patrol ships.*

I thought we decided to use the entire Patrol to put down

the Sirian revolt? Roque reminded. *That way, there would be no chance of Ree escaping to—*

Logic, Skor reminded, *would lead you to think that. At the same time, let us remember, logic has fled. No, I have learned from the Prophet, Chester Armijo Garcia. In this case, perhaps prudence would dictate leaving a portion of the fleet in reserve. Suppose a different revolt erupts on Desseret or Outback? The chances of—*

Illogical! Roque continued obstinately.

So was the Dobra broadcast," Skor reminded. *Directors, the universe has changed. Now we must adapt—if we can. The people are seeking something they hadn't realized they were missing until Dobra and Van Chow reminded them. I see black days ahead. And Directors,* Skor added sincerely, *we must accept that there is a chance we might not win.*

Impossible! Roque crowed intractably.

Skor cut the connection. He refocused his attention on the backlog of administrative details which had amassed during the conversation, while with another level of his mind he continued to consider the current crisis.

Impossible? His heart began to thump in his fragile rib cage. Once, perhaps, he might have shared Roque's beliefs. Then he had met Chester and realized what the Romanans could do. With that thought, he summoned the Prophet.

Chester rode into the blue room on the grav chair, his expression as inscrutably pleasant as ever.

Skor reviewed the tapes of the unrest brewing throughout the Directorate, showing them to the Prophet. "Tell me, Prophet, what do these people seek that we cannot provide for them?"

Chester smiled—that warmth in his eyes forever left Skor unsettled. "Would you learn, Director?"

"Would I have called you otherwise?" Skor snapped, realizing his voice had grown stronger, less awkward with use.

"You can provide total mental and physical security, Director," Chester continued in his knowing voice. "But what of the other human need? Think. What part of a human must eat, but not of bread? Drink, but not of wine? Feel, without fingers? Search, without looking? Call, without a voice? Act, without a—"

"Enough!" Skor snapped. "Again, you mock me!"

Chester shook his head. "A Prophet can never mock. Do you know what this is?" He held up a common headset.

Skor glared.

"Ah! I see you would call it a headset." Chester sighed, studying the golden circlet, running his fingers lovingly over the smooth metal. "No, Director, it is a window. A delightful window which has led me into other worlds, human history, music, art, literature, and—"

"You have not answered my questions!" Skor hissed, feeling trapped by this enigmatic man who seemed to know so much with so small a brain.

"Indeed," Chester agreed amiably. "But through delay, your interest is piqued. You will think on my answer more. What you cannot provide is a soul. Indeed, soul. That which is nourished not of bread, drinks not of wine—"

"Enough! I heard. I have never seen a soul, Prophet. I—"

"Nor have you seen an idea in its raw form," Chester told him. "Nevertheless, your problems revolve around that fundamental human need—to nourish the soul. Provide a solution to that, and your Directorate will fall back into your hands. Only be warned. It will never be the same."

"And you know how to do this?" Skor demanded. Seeing Chester's serene nod, he added, "Tell me!"

Chester Armijo Garcia shook his head sadly. "No, Director. That discovery must be yours. Were I to tell you, I would go mad and you would have learned nothing."

"You will tell me!" Skor ordered.

Chester filled his lungs and exhaled. "Have you ever read the ancient plays by Euripides?"

"No, I have not! *Tell me!*"

Chester's warm eyes regarded him, curiously tender. "Oh. I had hoped we might discuss them. Delightful plays. Some of the earliest recorded theater, quite sophisticated in the portrayal of—"

"You will not tell me?"

"No. But I would talk about ancient plays, they are most remarkable in the thematic uses of—"

"Get out!"

"Susan?" Hans' voice caught her off guard. She lifted the headset from her brow after saving the mathematics problem she was working on.

"Come in, Hans. The hatch will pass you." She turned in the comm chair, watching as he entered. He smiled hesitantly, stopping just inside the hatch, hands fluttering at his sides.

"Uh, I waited until I knew the Major was with Colonel Ree." He looked around nervously. "Bet my butt would get slung three ways from tomorrow if Rita found me here."

His awe amused her. "No, not if you came to visit me. Sit down. Cup of coffee? Anything else? Help yourself to the dispenser."

He stood awkwardly—as if he hadn't heard—eyes everywhere but on her.

"Something's wrong?" Susan asked, frowning. "What is it, Hans?"

He took a deep breath. "Uh, there's a strange rumor running around the gun deck . . ." He dropped his eyes. "Hey, by the way, did you know your Standard is a lot better?"

"That doesn't have anything to do with the gun deck," Susan reminded, an uneasy tightness building in her gut.

"Uh, no," he agreed, running his fingers through his blond hair.

"Damn!" she exploded. "Sit down, Hans! You're practically bouncing. The Major's not going to scalp you for being here. You're visiting me." She raised her hands helplessly.

Hans nodded, fidgeting, and sat. "Uh . . . I mean, how are the lessons coming?" He seemed genuinely interested.

Susan sighed and stood, walking to the dispenser for a cup of tea. Absently, she shook her head. "I . . . I honestly don't know." At his baffled look, she added. "Um, think of it like . . . like having machine parts dumped into a ship's hold. Any part you pick up you can name. But you don't know what fits where—or even what machine it comes from— let alone what it does." She sipped the tea. "That's what sleep stim and all the hours in front of the comm are doing to my head. Thoughts. Bits of information . . . all jumbled together."

"Can I help?" he asked automatically, genuinely concerned. "I mean, that's horrible. Maybe I could help you put it all . . ." He caught himself, suddenly worried. Abashed, he looked down to where he played with his fingers.

"You want to tell me what's bothering you?" Susan asked softly, leaning her chin on the back of the chair.

He chewed his lips for a second. "You know this Friday Garcia Yellow Legs? The one fighting Horsecapture?" His face puckered uncertainly.

She nodded, now wary.

"Well . . . uh, there's talk on the gun deck." Hans rubbed the back of his neck. He blurted, "People are saying the fight is over you."

Susan closed her eyes, feeling the color drain from her face. "That's . . . that's right, Hans. They're . . ." She looked up to see him leaving.

"Hans?" she called, getting to her feet. "*Hans?*" But he was gone, the hatch whispering shut behind him. She watched the portal seal, a curious hollowness in her chest.

For long minutes she fought the urge to run after him, find him, force him to tell her. Angry, thoughts drifting from Friday to Hans, she deliberately turned back to the comm. Sternly, she picked up her headset and placed it on her forehead—willing herself to work on mathematics.

She'd only been at her studies for an hour when Friday's voice brought her upright. She experienced a feeling of foolishness as she rushed for the hatch.

He stood there, smiling uncertainly. "Guess what?"

"What?" she gasped. "Horsecapture called off the feud!"

"Wrong!" Friday chortled, hopping lithely through the door.

Susan frowned, "Then . . . what?"

"Well, it's like this, I just got the latest odds on the knife feud. Three to one . . . in favor of Horsecapture."

"Oh, no."

"Oh, no, is right!" Friday assented, gnomelike face tense. "I know better."

She took his hand, looking down into his twinkling eyes. The wretched hollowness left by Hans began to expand. This man would die for her. Here he stood, the hint of a laugh ghosting around his broad lips. She realized then just how much she cared for him, how much he'd placed in jeopardy for her sake.

"Sure," Friday continued, nonplussed. "He's twice as big as me, right? So all I got to do is cut him in half, see. Then it's only two to one!"

Susan closed her eyes, hugging him close. "Friday Garcia Yellow Legs, you're . . . you're impossible!"

"That's what my mother said when I was born. She thought she'd always been faithful to my father."

"*Friday!*" she cried, the tightness growing within. Her eyes dropped as she pushed him away, her heart tearing.

"Listen, there's still time. Go apologize to Horsecapture. I'm . . . not worth your life. He'll cut you to—"

"Hush," he whispered, hugging her close, mock humor vanishing. He touched her tenderly, fingers stroking lightly through her long hair. "Hush, now. No such thing will happen. Besides, I've got to see how you make out. I made some bets that you'd become the greatest Spider warrior of all—got *great* odds against you. I'll make a fortune and I want to be around to spend it—with you."

Heart pounding, she looked into his eyes, seeing the softness there, the vulnerability. What if he died? A realization of how much he'd come to mean to her began to penetrate her worry. Their lips met, the kiss warm on her mouth.

His eyes glowed, a bittersweet longing vying with his tension. "I've hoped for that," he mumbled happily. "I'll die fulfilled."

"Oh, Friday . . ." she began, but he kissed her again. A miserable ache began to grow inside. "Please, don't. Not for me. I . . . I couldn't stand it if you . . ."

"Shhhh! Major's gone to talk to Iron Eyes. Won't be back for a couple hours. We have time to . . . talk. Go for a walk. Whatever you want."

She nodded, fighting a throttled sensation in her throat, wanting to wrap him inside of her where he'd be safe. She kept him pulled tight against her straining breasts, feeling the curious tingle of desire.

They kissed again, her breathing coming short, the feel of his hands reassuring, causing a flutter deep inside. For long minutes, the tingle built. Warmth replaced the endless confusion. A honey glow spread from her hips to her thighs, tickling her toes. She arched into him, pressing close, his kisses demanding more from her lips.

He pulled back, searching her face intently. "You know where this will end up?"

She nodded, a flush spreading through her.

"Um, I don't want you from guilt." He winced. "Oh, what a poor liar I am!"

She fought a giggle as he made hungry noises, nibbling at her flesh. He looked up again, serious. "You're sure, Susan?"

She nodded, blood beginning to race. Her eyes drifted closed as his fingers moved lightly on her skin. She trembled as he lifted her blouse over her head, feeling the pants loosen and fall about her ankles. With sure fingers she undid his war shirt, driven by her need. Her breathing came as ragged gasps, fingers frantic on his body, exploring the hard muscle of his chest and shoulders while he kissed her.

Her fingers dropped, finding his hard manhood. "Oh, Friday," she choked on her desire. "I've never . . . never done this . . ."

His mouth moved on her breast, teasing the nipple hard. Lungs heaving, she led him to the narrow bunk, barely aware of the soft fabric against her back. His skin burned hot on hers as he lowered himself, powerful muscles rippling. She pulled him to her.

In Rita's quarters, John Smith Iron Eyes settled himself at a monitor and waited expectantly. To his surprise, Rita handed him a glass of scotch.

"What about the Sirians?" he asked, frowning. "You said you wanted to show me some data."

Rita flipped hair out of her collar and settled back into one of the chairs. "Were you this blockheaded around Doc?"

"I don't understand." Iron Eyes leaned forward, elbows on knees.

"Friday wanted to be alone with Susan, War Chief," Rita remarked snidely. "I had to tell you something to drag you away from him."

Iron Eyes thought about it for a second, then shook his head, his face lighting with amusement. "Blockheaded? Yes, I suppose so. No, I don't think of things like that. You suppose it's a fatal flaw?"

Rita laughed easily. "Only when you have to deal with personal matters. Funny about you . . . you've always been behind the eight ball, Iron Eyes. I don't think you ever learned how people work—except in warfare."

He ran his tongue over his lips, nodding. "Guess not." He paused. "I know how to deal with Friday in war . . . but in love?" His eyes narrowed in concentration. "On the other hand, maybe she'll marry him and stop this woman warrior nonsense!"

"Star rot!" Rita snapped irritably, sinking deeper into the chair and studying him over the rim of her scotch glass. "Why, Iron Eyes? What is it really that bothers you? And don't tell me it's about Spider making men one way and women another. It's inside you. Something personal."

He chewed his lip in silence for a bit, a dark scowl marking his brow. "I, well, think of it like this," he said unevenly. "Women to us—Romanans, that is—are mothers. The . . . the strength of the People, if you will. A man, a warrior, well, he's replaceable. Kill one man, another takes his place. If a lot of men die, there are more wives married to one man. But kill one woman and you deny the tribe three or four children. A woman is the future. A man is nothing, experimental, expendable. If only one man is left alive he can assure the future—even if he's a little busy in the process. If only one woman lives . . . the People die."

"One bull to the herd?" she asked caustically.

"I don't think you can call—"

"Star shine," she grumbled. Rita cocked her head. "You given any thought about what's gonna happen when your warriors come marching home from Sirius with their 'wives'? All those Sirian women will have ideas like Susan's—and mine. No second fiddle to any man, War Chief. No meek, ignorant, cowed, eyes-to-the-ground submission. How are the warriors like old Sam Yellow Legs gonna take that? Beat them all to death? Not much value in a female slave if she's dead, huh?"

Iron Eyes rubbed a callused hand over his face. "No, there's no honor in beating a woman to death. I mean . . . Oh, Spider take it, we're going to change, Rita. There's no way around it. New ideas . . . Well, I guess we just wait and see what happens." He narrowed one eye into a disgusted squint. "You and Leeta . . . both trouble."

"So?" she challenged. "What about Susan?"

He spread his arms. "She's here, isn't she?"

"But you don't approve."

"Hell, no! I . . ." He filled his lungs, looking away. "Maybe I'll learn. A lifetime of beliefs don't just fade like morning mist in the Bear Mountains."

She smiled wryly at him. "No, but at least you've admitted there might be another way. Give her a chance. If I can cram enough information into the kid's head, maybe she'll make it."

"Maybe?"

"John, you know what she's up against? In five months we'll be landing on Sirius and she's going head first into combat on a world of which she has no comprehension. Oh, sure, the pysch machines can give her the dry information. But it's like . . . like putting an encyclopedia in your brain. It still takes a native intelligence to learn how to use it right, to keep from being overwhelmed by all the mountains of discrete bits of data.''

"And you think she can?"

"I'm betting the bank roll, John. I, well, it can break a person—overwhelm them because their mind's different—and don't you tell her, either. She's got enough to worry about. But sometimes . . . well, the machine overlays memories. Occasionally a person can't deal with what they've lost. They, um, go a little crazy. Identity shock."

Iron Eyes nodded. "This machine. It's like the psych?"

Rita nodded. "Now you know why I'm scared. Some Romanans, those with Prophet blood, go real berserk under psych. Susan reacts well, I don't think there's any problem with—"

"Ah!" Iron Eyes nodded. "That's why the techs were taking all those tests when we adjusted the combat simulators to the warriors. You had to change them so we didn't go berserk when the machines interacted with our minds."

Rita pursed her lips. "That's right. We've learned a lot about how to work around Romanan neurophysiology. It'll save a lot of lives when we hit Sirius. Susan, on the other hand, is getting a double dose. She demonstrates remarkable tolerance for the teaching machine."

He sighed, gaze drifting around his quarters. "When we hit Sirius? Rita, I . . . Well, it won't be as easy as we think. I just have a . . . a feeling, Rita. Call it a warrior's premonition. I see all the optimism around me, but it's . . . false. Here I am, surrounded by all this technology—but I *know* war. That's what I did—led men into war. Something deep in my bones tells me Sirius will be more horrible than any of us—"

"Come on! You know what sort of power the Patrol has. How can one planet converting a couple of GCIs stand against us? I mean, we're going in with the whole fleet! Sirians aren't warriors, they're—"

"Anyone will fight when they have nothing left to lose." Iron Eyes lifted a tanned hand. "No, there's something else. My Romanans and I, we're at a disadvantage here. Raiding a high tech world? What traps could a clever man make for a barbarian? How do I even explain just how big an arcology is to a Santos warrior who gapes at the Settlements?"

Rita brooded over her drink for several minutes. "I don't want to scoff, but think about it. Once the Patrol takes control of the skies, we'll have the ability to call down strikes against the Sirian strong points. Demoralize them from above. The ATs will give us superior mobility. If the Romanans get in trouble, we'll be able to shunt marines in to cover for their—"

"No," Iron Eyes growled. "That's not good for Romanan honor or morale. No, we've got to take our own ground—do our own work—or we'd best call it off now. My people have to bear their own burdens on Sirius. If we assume anything different, it'll be disastrous for—"

"What could go wrong?" Rita demanded skeptically. "The Patrol comes in in force and the planet crumbles. It's always worked that . . . What are you looking at me like that for?"

He reached over and placed a sun-browned hand on her pale one. "Rita," he added soberly, "Trust me. You and your Patrol, you have a lot of practice with 'policing' your Directorate. Me? I have a lot of practice making war. I have learned one iron rule when it comes to war."

"And that is?"

"You can predict nothing. True, you can plan, but nothing ever works according to plan." He smiled. "My cousin Chester is a Prophet. Philip was almost a Prophet. My grandfather's brother was a Prophet. It doesn't run strong in me; I can still sense trouble at Sirius. Things will not work the way we want them to. No, I can see the question in your eyes. I can't tell you how it will go wrong, it just will."

"You talked to Ree about this?"

Iron Eyes shrugged. "He's a Romanan at heart. We've talked. He listens, and nods, and thinks. Then he worries about what I've said and we discuss potential trouble. Any kind we can think of. For that attitude, I've come to respect him a great deal. I have finally met a commander I can trust and subordinate myself to."

She looked up, green eyes wide. "I guess . . . that . . . well, takes a lot to admit, doesn't it?"

The corners of his lips curled. Gently he said, "Yes, more than you could ever know." He shifted uneasily in the chair. "And to admit it to you, well, that takes some respect and trust too."

Rita opened her mouth, saying nothing, a sudden vulnerability in her eyes. For long moments they looked at each other.

"Thanks for the trust," she whispered finally. "I . . . I'll try and live up to it."

He chuckled quietly. "Oh, I think you will. And I . . .

perhaps . . . well, when this is all over. . . . Well, maybe you and Ree will let me stay with *Bullet*? Take me to other worlds so I can see and learn? I . . . I'm not sure I can go back to raiding Santos for a living."

She laughed. "Damen will keep you. You and he seem to get along. And as for me?" Her voice lowered. "I'd like it if you stayed. We see eye to eye, you and me. No one else could understand about Philip and . . . and . . ." She looked away.

Iron Eyes tightened his grip on her hand, letting his warm flesh say everything.

"I'm on the last of the scotch. In a half hour, Friday has to fight Horsecapture." She sounded weary. "Here's to the Patrol." She downed the strong drink. "And the way of Spider."

"Here's to warfare and blood, for whatever it teaches." Iron Eyes gulped his and started for the door.

"Willy Red Hawk Horsecapture is seeking status by a campaign to return to the old ways." Rita stared up at the ceiling panels. "A bit early for that. Nativistic movements and revitalization brouhahas generally come later."

"What?" Friday looked up from where he was working out with the combat robot, moving easily, warming up. Iron Eyes watched from the side, eyes critical.

"I got it out of some of Doc's old books." Rita shook her head. "There are ways in which people try and get back to their original culture, reconstruct the good old mythical past. The Romanans haven't lost enough to worry about it yet. Horsecapture's just ahead of the game."

Susan moved over to sit next to Friday and hold his hand as he left the training floor and sprawled on a bench. "Will you win?" Her eyes glowed with a deep warmth that irritated Rita.

Friday laughed. "I hope so. I've got too much to do. My idea of a good time isn't having Horsecapture's knife stuck into my guts. If he needs more hair for his vest—he can carve it off Sirian heads! As to mine, my skull sunburns too easy—thank you. Besides, short as I am, I can't afford to lose anymore of me. Do that too often and one of these days . . . I'll up and disappear."

"You'll win," Rita added, nodding her head. Susan's doe eyes continued to grate on a raw nerve. *Damn it, she's fawning!*

"You're sure?" Susan asked. "He's fighting because of . . . It's my honor that caused all of this." Her eyes had taken on a haggard look. "Perhaps I should go talk to Willy. Perhaps if he killed me—took coup—it would all be finished."

Rita's eyes narrowed to slits.

Friday straightened at the tone of her voice. He turned her by the shoulders. "I called for knife feud. No man should sell his clanswoman to Old Man Wattie. I never liked Horsecapture anyway. He's always—"

"It's not worth your life!" Susan shook her head doggedly.

"I don't think he can lose," Rita reminded, hardness tightening in her chest. *Come on, kid, buck up. Don't you dare let me down. You go emotional and mushy . . . and you're dead meat.*

"Why not?" Iron Eyes asked. "Death can come to anyone. Spider might have decided to take Friday today. Perhaps he has learned what is necessary in this life."

"I can think of many things I would like to learn all of a sudden," Friday declared solemnly. "I think maybe I need to know much much more! Like what tomorrow looks like!" He cupped his lips, head tilted up. "You hear that, Spider? I will *never ever* know enough!"

Rita ignored him, saying to Iron Eyes, "Friday's about the best of the Romanans when it comes to hand-to-hand combat. I've had him working overtime on the combat machines. He can't take me yet, but give him another six months of training and he could run me ragged. I've fought Horsecapture. I know for a fact he spends more time bragging than working."

Susan clutched Friday's hand tightly, desperation in her eyes. "There is still accident. A foot can slip, sweat can drip into your eyes at the wrong time. Luck can never be discounted. So many things . . ."

"Little one," Friday laughed warmly, "I'll be fine. Don't worry about me."

Rita swallowed her irritation. *Hell, the kid just made love for the first time. Why should I care if she fawns over her man? Yeah, yeah, I know. 'Cause if she ain't perfect, she's gonna sink herself. Damn it! Why can't God be more fair to women?* Rita ground her teeth. *And what if Horsecapture kills Friday—and Susan breaks under it. Then what?*

"It's time," Iron Eyes said.

Rita looked up to see Willy Red Hawk Horsecapture walking into the gym. He reeked of insolence, arms swinging by his sides. From the other door came Colonel Ree and several med techs with antigrav-borne med units towed behind.

Susan's face turned ashen, a frantic desperation in her eyes.

Crap! You look half-broken now, girl! What if you can't take it? Why am I afraid she'll break? Worry chewed at Rita's heart as Friday grinned at Horsecapture.

Giorj Hambrei ran a test sequence through his monitors. The holo readout told him the field generators were sufficient for the First Citizen's specs. He shut the system down, looking around Ngen's private quarters. Every square inch had been padded. No sharp corners remained. Facilities had been recessed. Now Ngen had ordered a restraining field around his bed.

Curious about what the refined psych machine might be for, Giorj wondered if the First Citizen had trouble dreaming. He studied the medical psych machine he'd installed in the wall above the bed. What possible need did Ngen Van Chow have for implanted fantasies?

Giorj's expression didn't change as he clapped his sensor on his tool belt. What Ngen did or didn't do made no difference as long as his own mother received her medical treatments and he received unlimited materials for his work.

He passed the hatch, double-checking the complicated security system, and made his way to the shuttle locks. Subject to Ngen's orders, no guard had been posted. Leona Magill had arrived an hour before. She and Ngen had a full agenda to discuss.

Giorj entered the lock, crossed to Leona's shuttle and climbed into the restricted bridge. He studied the comm, carefully undid molding, and nodded. With quick fingers, he unfastened two of the command boards and began the modifications Ngen had ordered.

The gunner's seat conformed to the curves of his body as Hans slouched in the half-dark of the abandoned gun deck. The big blaster made a good retreat. He bit his lip, frowning, wrestling with his topsy-turvy emotions. Of course he was in love with her! What the hell did he expect? No other woman on the ship could touch her perfect beauty! That long black hair, those deep heart-reflecting eyes, the youthful vigor in her skin, it all returned to haunt him.

Now, another man fought for her honor! Hans closed his eyes, locked in misery. She'd never look twice at him now. What chance did a lowly corporal computer whiz have against a Romanan warrior with coups? A warrior who'd risk his life for her, no less?

Hans glanced at his chronometer. The fight would be shown all over the ship. Every pair of eyes that could be spared would be locked on a monitor. Every pair of eyes except for Hans Yeager's, that is.

In the half-dark of the gun deck, he crossed his arms, leaning back in the gunner's chair, imagining the frightful power of the blaster. In his mind, he pictured himself sighting, monitoring the huge gun, as *Bullet* fought for life. Only his skill with the weapon kept the ship—and Susan—from instant fiery death.

The fantasy wore thin. Hans checked the time again. Soon now. He hadn't been able to stay in the gun room—not with Breeze and the rest. They hadn't started ribbing him yet. It was coming, how two Romanan warriors were fighting over his girl.

"God," Hans whispered. "Why am I always so miserable?" What could he do?

Nothing.

Less than a minute until they'd scheduled the fight to begin. His feet jiggled in the stirrups as he scowled at the dead holo sights. He kept crossing and recrossing his arms. Unbidden, his hands jerked up and down, absently feeling the fabric of his uniform. He *couldn't* sit still.

Irritated he crawled down, walking nervously along the deck. What the hell, just a peek at the monitor. That wouldn't hurt anything.

Besides, what if this Friday Yellow Legs character lost? What then? What would happen to Susan? He hardly realized he'd broken into a run. Which monitor? Not the gun decks! Anywhere but there. He wouldn't give Breeze that much satisfaction!

He slid around the corner in time to see the two men coming together on an overhead monitor. Patrol techs watched, open mouthed, eyes wide. Which was Yellow Legs? Couldn't be that little guy. Hans studied the big man, noting the evil leer on his face, the swinging coups on his vest. Something inside tightened. That figure of evil? He was Susan's champion?

CHAPTER X

Ree marched out into the center of the gym and glared at Horsecapture. "I *don't* like the idea of knife feud on *my* ship." He was certain that every monitor on *Bullet* had an audience glued to it. "This is contrary to every regulation in the Patrol. It's barbaric, cruel, and vicious—but I swore I would uphold the ways of the People. If this is Spider's way . . . so be it."

Ree turned to the monitor, face tight. "Be it known that Willy Red Hawk Horsecapture is charged with insubordination. He insulted the Colonel in command of this vessel and his superior officer and War Chief, John Smith Iron Eyes. At my discretion he was left at liberty until this matter could be settled. I want every Romanan on this ship to know that I will not tolerate any other behavior than the respect due to a War Chief." Ree scowled at the pickup. "Let it begin."

He walked to Rita's side. "It's a goddamn Roman circus on my ship!" Anger bubbled and boiled inside of him. He'd been smarting ever since that son of a bitch Horsecapture had said he spoke like a woman. So he'd taken him down? The man's tone and insolence kept Ree stewing in rage.

"What's worse, I talked myself into a corner!" Ree rocked back and forth on his heels. "I told them I'd make sure the Romanan ways were upheld. How in hell did I end up in a mess like this? What did I do to—"

"Easy, Damen. It'll all work out." Rita grinned. "The ship is in the jump. Nothing can go wrong. Besides," she added, humor flicking at her lips, "they're *only* knives."

Ree stopped short. His grin formed slowly. "Yeah, only knives." He shot a quick glance at the med teams waiting along the white walls of the gym. "Friday and Horsecapture don't have the slightest idea. . . ."

Across the gym, Susan placed a hand on Friday's shoulder. "You still have time to get out of this. Tell—tell Horsecapture you withdraw the feud."

"Would you?" Friday asked, a thin smile darting lines around his lips.

She lowered her eyes and shook her head slowly.

"I must get ready." Friday winked conspiratorially and walked off to be by himself.

From where Susan sat, she could see his mouth moving as he sang the song given him by his spirit-helper. Horsecapture motioned, catching her attention. He leered at her, mouth working in unspoken promises. The four coups on his vest spoke eloquently of his prowess . . . and Friday had never fought a knife feud in his life.

Yellow Legs stripped off his shirt. On supple legs, he walked out into the center of the lock, knife held low. "You, Willy Red Hawk Horsecapture, are a profanity upon your kinsmen. You are a curse to Spider."

Horsecapture laughed as he crouched over his blade. "You know not your People. You act as if you had no kinship with men!" Cutting with a rapid backhand, he moved in a blur.

Friday bounced away, leaping out of reach, unable to riposte as Horsecapture—enjoying his extra long reach—struck again and again. The big man laughed wickedly as Friday twisted and scuttled.

"*Fight!*" Horsecapture cried, voice tight with anticipation. He grimaced, slashing, his eyes dancing with the promise of death.

Friday moved lightly, Willy's shining blade passing close to his flesh. Face contorted, breathing rapidly, he spun, ducked, dodged, and twisted.

"Nice footwork on Friday's part." Susan heard Ree mumble to himself. Friday Yellow Legs suffered a physical disadvantage. Within Horsecapture's means lay the ability to reach out in a stop-hit maneuver Friday couldn't counter.

Silence permeated the room but for the shuffling of feet and the panting of the two fighters. Friday went in low, caught Horsecapture's blade from beneath and flicked it up—drawing first blood as he creased the big man's side.

Horsecapture recovered and slashed Friday's shoulder as he twisted away.

"Why doesn't he use any combat tricks?" Rita asked Iron Eyes. "He should have been able to kick that knife hand silly a couple of times now. He's just fencing!"

As if Friday heard, he sprang into the air and stabbed out with a blinding kick. Horsecapture took the blow on his shoulder. The fleshy snap of breaking bone caused Iron Eyes to wince.

Horsecapture began backpedaling, facial muscles set in pain. Sudden desperation glimmered in his hot black eyes. Warily, Friday Yellow Legs followed.

Friday danced in, blade flicking at Horsecapture's body. Again, the longer reach kept Friday from anything more damaging than nicks in his adversary's arm or leg. Even so, the useless arm threw Horsecapture off balance.

The move came suddenly. Horsecapture flipped the knife underhanded. Fast as the desperate move was, Friday twisted—unable to avoid the blade entirely. It caught him low in the belly, the point lodging in the medial area of the ilium.

Susan yipped in fear and clapped a hand over her mouth.

Horsecapture closed, thinking to kick at Friday's head. As Willy's foot went back, the little man lunged, heedless of the tearing metal lodged in his body. They grappled, straining, mingled blood smearing their hot bodies.

Friday threw himself violently to the side. With all his power, he drove his blade upward, point ripping through Horsecapture's hard belly muscles, spilling intestines and offal.

Horsecapture screamed horribly until the point ruptured his diaphragm. They reeled apart, wavering, before collapsing to the padded deck. Streaming blood mingled in a growing pool. An acrid odor of gut juices leaking from severed intestines hung stinking in the air.

As the med teams ran forward, Friday struggled to his feet, gnome-face flickering from pain and effort. One hand held the knife sticking so rudely out of his groin. He let go of it long enough to carve the coup from Horsecapture's head, raise it above his own, and sing his war song.

The meds stopped, white-faced at the sight. Susan fought the light-headed sensation that possessed her. Blinking against the world that started to turn gray around her, she turned to Rita and buried her head in the woman's shoulder, biting her lips until blood came to keep from crying out her fear and horror.

"I've killed him!" she heard herself repeating in a daze.

"Here!" Sarsa's voice was as hard as steel. "Straighten up, damn you." Bitter scorn laced her voice. "He'll be fine. I think the meds can save that bastard Horsecapture, too."

Susan blinked, eyes burning with unshed tears. "What?"

She turned, disbelieving. The meds already had Horsecapture on an antigrav and were rushing him toward the hospital.

"Hell, yes," Rita growled. "You don't think Ree would let them kill each other, do you? Might have been different with blasters—but unless one of those fools cut the other one's head off, the meds can patch them up. I'd wager Horsecapture won't be on his feet for a while though."

"This is true?" Iron Eyes asked suddenly, his suspicious gaze shifting to Ree.

"Damn right," Ree admitted smugly, biting the end off one of his Terran cigars.

"Then you could have saved Major Reary when I knifed her," Iron Eyes accused.

Ree nodded easily. "Could have. She betrayed me." The Colonel looked up, lips twisted sourly. "Don't like people who betray me. Right now . . . I need loyalty. Reary would have always hated me afterward. Sure, you and Rita caused me grief, too, but we're committed to the same thing. You two don't . . . uh, threaten my position." Ree watched as Friday Yellow Legs, face contorted with pain, passed by on an antigrav. Susan followed behind, twisting her hands.

Rita's ice-green eyes tightened. "I wonder if I made a mistake with that girl?" she asked, bitter and sarcastic.

Ree puffed his cigar with satisfaction, seeing the deck crew already at work cleaning up the blood and stinking brown goo. "Why?" he demanded. "Thought you liked her."

Iron Eyes turned flintlike eyes on her. "I told you a Romanan girl would be trouble."

Rita shifted her eyes from one man to the other. "Yeah, well, I don't . . . I just don't know if she's got the guts to stand the gaff in the long run. She's too emotional. Gets wound up with her heart instead of using her brain. That'll kill her someday."

"She's young," Ree said absently. He turned his angular features on Rita. "I'm sure after she's had you chew on her butt a couple of times, she'll toughen up. There're men who come to the service that are worse raw material than that gal."

Ree squinted, seeing no change in Rita's hard face. "Come on, Major! You're not using your head. She's what, eighteen? Twenty at the most? How much did you have going for you at that age? Think about it." Ree grinned, punched Rita playfully in the shoulder, and left, walking off jauntily.

"Well? How about it?" She looked defiantly at Iron Eyes.

"You know how I feel about her." The War Chief's eyes didn't waver.

"Yeah, I know how you feel about her." Rita added, voice clipped, defensive. "I just don't know why." At that she shouldered her way through the hatch.

Susan palmed the hatch and entered the Major's quarters. Sarsa, knees up, lay on her bunk, eyes almost closed, a comm headset on her brow.

Susan opened out her bunk and sagged wearily onto the hard mattress. Desperately tired, she pulled off her clothing and adjusted the temperature.

"Where you been?" Rita studied her through slitted eyes.

"Hospital."

"How's he doing?"

"He's fine. Slept most of the afternoon. The meds say he'll be up and about within a week. Horsecapture is . . . is still iffy. The internal damage was more difficult to repair. The meds say he'd normally have about a thirty percent chance. For a Romanan? They don't know. Might be sixty percent."

"So he slept all afternoon?" Rita straightened, placing the headset in its holder. "You finish your tactics tables?"

Susan lowered her eyes. "No, I guess I didn't." Frantic, she looked up. "I was too worried about Friday. What if he would have died while I was doing tables?"

"I would assume you'd have gone to the funeral," Rita said coolly. "From now on, there will be no excuses. Assignments will be completed at the end of each day." A pause—then she exploded, *"Damn it, girl!"* A hard fist pounded the console. "You're coming from a world that doesn't even have a written language. You have fifteen years of learning to catch up on within a month! You're about to—"

"I thought I was doing very good, Major," Susan couldn't force herself to meet those hostile eyes.

"You bet your ass you are, sweetie! But keep in mind, within a month you've got to put your little tail on the line. There's a whole planet full of Sirians who are going to try to kill you. Dead! Understand that? There will be no time for worry about Yellow Legs . . . or anyone else for that matter. Your life is in your own hands."

Susan swallowed, nodding.

"For example, let's say your squad is working through a suburban area. You receive a heavy barrage of blaster fire from an AT. Where do you go for cover?"

Susan thought it over for a second. "Why, the closest structure I suppose."

"You're dead twice." Sarsa's voice went cold. "First, you took too long to think it out. Second, you dive for the powerlead access tubes. Those are the tunnels where they string power cable, optics and comm leads. They're also twenty feet underground."

"I've never heard of a power access tube," Susan defended, conscious of the anger lacing her Major's voice.

"That's exactly my point." Rita stood up. "Get some sleep. You have a new schedule tomorrow. I want all the tactics completed. And I want you to begin familiarizing yourself with Sirius. Everything. From Soviet colonial history up to garbage recycling, I want you to know it." At that she spun on her heel and left the room.

Susan sat in shock for several minutes. Her heart battered against her ribs. Nerves and hunger gnawed at her stomach. Feeling miserable, foolish, and scared, she ordered a quick meal from the dispenser and settled herself at comm. Hell with Rita—she'd finish the damn tables! Taking two stim-tabs with her coffee, she accessed the tactics tables she'd been working on and began to manipulate them.

"I'll show her," Susan rasped to herself, chafing at the injustice of it. *"By God, I'll show her!"*

Iron Eyes had never gotten used to the way starship doorways worked. He knew he could set the palm lock to his own hand and control access to his room. What was there to steal? Better yet, on this ship, who'd steal it? Used to Romanan ways, anyone who desired could enter at any time.

"Iron Eyes?" the door comm announced.

"Yes?" He pulled himself upright on his bunk, sorting out a reality different from the dream he'd been sharing with his black mare, now so many hundred million klicks behind.

"It's Rita. You asleep?"

"Come in." The lights had come on—another marvel of these starfaring men. Automatic light, electricity, fusion power, everything so different, and no time to learn it all. In so many ways, John Smith Iron Eyes—the greatest of the

Spider warriors and duly appointed War Chief of the Romanans—felt like a helpless child.

Rita ducked through the door as it slid open. Her quick eyes caught him blinking sleepily. "Hell," she muttered, "go back to bed. It's not that God almighty important."

"Wait. Sit down. What's wrong?" Strain pulled tight around her eyes. She'd been like that since Philip had been killed.

Without a second's hesitation, Rita flopped into one of the chairs. Head bent back to an impossible angle, she rubbed her eyes and gasped for a deep breath. "Damn it, John, I'm falling apart. I don't know what's wrong with me. The kid just came in, plain tuckered, worried sick about Yellow Legs, and I gave her a full charge.

"One moment, I think she's the greatest godsend to come along since I started this silly career . . . the next I think she's all thumbs. I expect her to be perfect all the time, and I know she can't. By Spider, do you know how much that girl has to learn? She's got every strike in the book against her . . . but I believe she can do it."

"You wish me to tell you different?" Iron Eyes asked, fetching two cups of coffee from the dispenser, knowing full well how confusing the ship was to Susan. Had he not known better, he himself would have believed the ship's powers magical.

Rita accepted the cup. "No, I know she can do it. The Colonel hit the nail on the head this afternoon. When I was her age, I was a . . . a damn wreck. She's miles beyond the fool I was then. I made it this far, why can't I give her a break?" Rita sipped the coffee.

"You have become harder since Philip died, Red Many Coups. You are still forging yourself into something tougher," Iron Eyes decided as he stuffed the thick muscles of his body into the cramped bunk. "I think you demand too much of yourself—and other people. Philip is dead. Quit punishing yourself for it."

Rita laughed. "You know, you'd think life would be for something besides guts, blood, and calluses. God, I've just doubled the girl's workload. I told her to learn all she can so she doesn't get her butt shot off on Sirius."

"Maybe that's your trouble. . . ." He cocked his head. "You see her as you were once. Wide-eyed? Ready to run off and swing the galaxy by its tail?" He arched an eyebrow. "You worry about her getting killed. Is it . . ." He bit his lip, black eyes unforgiving. ". . . that you've realized you care? That you can be hurt again?"

Rita nodded slowly, looking completely drained. "Yeah, maybe I do see her that way." She paused. "I never thought of it like that."

"As you say, life should be more than being tough. She should be at home, raising a family. She looks like my little sister did." Iron Eyes smiled, lost in memories.

Rita looked over, a frown creasing her forehead. "My God, I never thought of you having a sister. It's hard to think of you . . . invincible Iron Eyes . . . as even having a family."

He shrugged, eyes reflecting the drift of his mind. He looked up uncomfortably. "It is difficult to remain soft on World."

"And your sister?" Rita asked. "What was she like? Did she have other men's hair hanging all over her?"

He shook his head, amused. The carved lines of his face smoothed slightly. "She was just fun. She and Jenny were best friends. Always after me for something. You know . . . constant pranks. Couldn't seat myself on my blanket for dinner without checking it for a blade of bayonet grass first.

"She was young, vivacious, with bright eyes and glowing cheeks. I think she was the most beautiful girl in the whole world." He fell silent, a tightness pinching his face.

"What happened to her?"

"She was bringing in the cattle one night when Raiders hit. We never caught up with them to avenge her. They tried to steal her for a wife. She fought back so desperately she endangered the raid. When they were through, they shot her in the back of the head and left her. It was almost two weeks before we found her body. Summer then. The maggots had been at her for a long time."

Rita closed her eyes in the silence. For long minutes they sipped at their coffee.

"There's got to be a reason." She straightened her arm and ran a hand along the firm flesh.

"We've had that discussion before."

"I know, I just keep thinking we'll be able to do something about it one of these days." She looked up, green eyes pensive. "I think I've figured out why you dislike Susan so much."

"I don't dislike Susan," Iron Eyes looked his irritation at her. "I just . . ."

"You wish she wasn't here," Rita countered.

"I wish Horsecapture wasn't here, too." He raised a challenging eyebrow.

"You're afraid you'll get attached to her. That's it, isn't it? Anyone you've ever been fond of has died horribly." Rita pursed her lips.

"That's foolish," he muttered, shaking his head. "That's just . . ."

"You accused me of the same thing," she pointed out. "Hell, for all I know you might . . . might be right."

He shook his head adamantly. "It's a cultural difference. We're not used to seeing our women involved in warfare. All our lives, we're taught to protect our women and our families. Now, Susan goes off to war. What if all our women go off to war? Who raises the children?"

"Who raises ours?" she countered. "Not all men ride off to be warriors . . . even in your society. Similarly, not all women want the stars and blood and violence. No, now don't look at me like that. You know it. People are different."

"But that urge is—"

"Bullshit!" she cut him off.

His soft eyes raised. "If I didn't think you'd break my neck, I'd strangle you."

Her laughter flowed free, genuine. "If you ever decide to, I— I'm not sure I could stop you."

"I think you feel better."

She nodded quickly. "You balance things for me. It's odd, you're the only friend I've got anymore. Since the promotion, I'm not just one of the crew. I seem to . . . I'm someone to either be wary of or try to influence. I can't even find a sparring partner in the gym." Her voice went soft. "Thanks."

Eyes twinkling, he studied her, admiring the catlike strength in her body, noting the subtle female curves. The color of her hair had always fascinated him. She was a striking woman, her body balanced, perfectly proportioned. She walked with poised grace, the hallmark of a superb athlete.

"Feel free to stop by whenever you need it." He forced the smile to cover his thoughts. They had been tense since Leeta and Philip's deaths. Pain lurked just under the surface. They stepped softly around feelings, careful to keep from stirring those waters.

Her sigh exploded as a grunt. "Might be more often than

not. I don't have that old devil-may-care attitude. I feel old."

"I would think you'd be too busy chasing off the men. I heard you used to be the belle of the ship." It slipped out. Curious, he waited for a reaction.

She laughed. "Maybe I was. Since I got rank I haven't heard a word from any of them."

"Perhaps someone will cease being foolish." He smiled gently, inoffensively, wondering at his own interest.

"Maybe." Her smile faded. "He'd have to be the right one. I'm not sure I . . . It's just that . . . You know, Philip is a tough act to follow." She got to her feet and hesitated. "Damn, I don't want to go back and face Susan. I'd like to just escape somewhere. This ship needs a camp site and a couple dozen horses."

Distant longing grew in her eyes.

"Here." He pulled out a second bunk he never used. "Drop yourself in there."

She looked at the bunk thoughtfully, lips pursed. "I . . . What the hell, it might be a good idea. But I . . ."

"What?"

"Oh, nothing." She shook her head and sighed absently.

"I'd rather we talked. We're all we've got. No one else would understand where we came from . . . who we are." He cocked his head.

Her face reflected struggle. "Well, I just want to be . . . to be held for a while. Nothing else, Iron Eyes." She closed her eyes. "It would simply be nice to know that in the entire universe there's another warm human body."

"I think I understand," he answered. "Come, lie down next to me. I won't hurt you."

"Iron Eyes, what would I do without you," she whispered in resignation as he lay down and wrapped his arms around her. Within minutes her breathing betrayed sleep.

For long hours he held her, his eyes probing the darkness, thinking.

Leona Magill's first inkling that anything was wrong came when the shuttle's course changed. She frowned and activated the manual controls. Nothing. No response.

Then a second shuttle entered the range of her screens. Accessing comm, she hailed the oncoming craft.

No response.

A quick check of the system proved her comm was dead.

Worse, she had dropped around the planet, out of line of sight from *Helk* where she'd been occupied with the new shields.

Frantic, she tore into the control console. The black box shouldn't have been there. She traced leads spliced into the computer and comm. She looked it over carefully and noted the energy pack that hooked into the black box with a tiny silver wire. Detonator. She'd need special tools to bypass, otherwise it would destroy the cockpit controls.

Cursing, she looked up at the monitor to see the second shuttle closing. Patrol? Had they pulled this elaborate scheme to trap her? Desperate, she pulled her blaster and hauled herself down the tunnel to the main shuttle deck.

It had to be the Patrol. Damn them! Skor Robinson wouldn't have the pleasure of taking her alive. To hell with their pyschological reorientation! Leona Magill would rather be dead than turned into a sweet, satisfied, Directorate maniken.

A clank and bang echoed as the other shuttle matched hers. She felt the tremors through the hull. Her eyes went to the lock. The gauge indicated a slight drop in pressure. The hatch undogged and swung open.

Leona crouched behind a seat and settled the blaster on the lock, finger tense on the trigger.

"Leona?" the voice called pleasantly.

She frowned. "*Ngen?* That you? What the hell's going on here?"

"Hang on, I'll be right out." Van Chow's voice carried a note of relief.

"My controls have been tampered with," she told him crossly. "I'm in no mood for games. You part of this?"

"Oh, there's an explanation," he called out cheerily, appearing in the lock, a benevolent smile on his lips. His eyes opened wide at the sight of the blaster. "Remember me? I'm on your side."

She stood carefully, still alert. "Why are you here? How did you know I would be in trouble?"

"You couldn't hear?" Ngen crossed his arms and leaned against the lock. "It wouldn't make any difference anyway."

"Hear what?" she asked, frown deepening. The blaster still centered on his belly.

He noted her aim hadn't wavered. "You always were . . . um, shall we say, perceptive? I'm answering your distress call."

The pleasant tone in his voice kept her off balance. "*You* sabotaged my controls? But . . . why?"

He pushed off the wall in the zero g and somersaulted over a chair back, still far out of reach. "But of course." He nodded. "Time is running out though. We only have another couple of minutes to make an easy orbit to *Hiram Lazar.*"

A fear began to build under her heart. Blood pumped hard in her veins and her mouth was going dry. "What are you talking about? Tell me, Ngen. Tell me . . . or I'll shoot you down."

He chuckled happily, dark eyes glowing with an unnatural excitement. "Oh, I knew you wouldn't come of your own free will, Leona darling."

"I'm not your darling! Not now or ever, you foul . . ." she hissed, fear growing stronger. Vision seemed to blur and she blinked; a slight tremble shook her body.

Ngen's smile widened. "This will be most pleasant, Leona. I've always wondered what sensations you could provide a man."

The shuttle seemed to shift under her feet. Desperate, she held her aim and triggered the blaster, bracing for the recoil. Nothing! Again and again she triggered the weapon as the insides of the shuttle grew hazy. Her stomach heaved suddenly and she vomited a stream across the deck.

Vaguely, she saw Ngen duck to one side and push toward her. "Splendid!" Ngen chortled as he took her now unresisting arm. "You would have killed me just that quick. You will be delightful, dear one. Of course I had to slip a dead charge into your blaster. Giorj took care of that detail at the same time he, shall we say, adjusted, your controls."

"Whaaaa. . . ." She struggled to make her mouth function. "Whaaaa. . . ."

"What did I do to you?" he asked as he pulled her through the lock and cycled his own system. Like so much clay, he dragged her into his ship, his smile sweetly innocent. "Quite simply, dearest Leona, I gassed you."

She watched stupidly as he pulled the small tubes and plugs from his nose. They'd been perfectly hidden in his mustache.

"Oh, I could have waited until you were out before I entered." His cheek twitched in a curious tick. "It wouldn't have brought me the exhilaration of knowing you could kill me so easily. I'll enjoy you so much more this way."

He strapped her into a chair, happy, whistling. Struggling to concentrate, she turned her head enough to watch him climb into the cockpit. She experienced a muzzy sensation of acceleration. Time dilated.

Later, Ngen climbed down and Leona realized gravity had returned. He lifted her easily over his shoulder and strode to the lock. She absently recognized the interior of *Hiram Lazar*. They passed no one in the empty corridors.

Ngen passed through a hatch and into a room decorated with the finest of Sirian furniture. Dim lights changed from light orange to yellow to green.

Ngen dropped her on the bed, bound her arms and legs with police restraints and accessed comm. "We're back, Giorj. What were the results?"

"Superb," the pale engineer began, the words garbling in her ears.

Ngen nodded easily, a slight smile at the corners of his mouth. His eyes were a study in concentration. After a time he said, "I'll come to the bridge to address the masses. After all, this is a terrible setback."

He turned as the monitor went blank. "Dearest, Leona. I have to address our fellow citizens. They are most distraught at your unfortunate demise. In this time of great sorrow they look for leadership. Fear not, dearest one. I shall return to fulfill you. Besides, you will be much more delightful when your faculties return." At that he stood up smartly and left the room.

In the silence, Leona tried to think. People upset? At her demise? None of it made sense. Her mind slipped off the subject, numbly awkward. A gray cloud of unconsciousness settled over her.

Leona found temporary refuge in a dream. She reveled in the security of her father's house. Wide vistas of gray-black rock scintillated under the glare of the blue star that shone upon the mining world of Atlas IV. Beyond the dome stretched rolling mounds of rock and methane ice.

She stretched lithely in the comfort of her home, even as she remembered that it was long gone. She tried to turn, but couldn't. Angered, she fought and came awake, looking into a holo of a star field. She yawned and tried to stretch her arms. The bonds were tight. She simply couldn't move.

"What the . . ." She blinked hard and tried to pull free. At the same time her eyes cataloged the strange surround-

ings. Ngen? But that, too, was a dream, just like her father's house had been.

She pulled her head up and looked down at her naked
body. Craning her neck, she could see the police restraints.
It wasn't a dream. She remembered having been clothed.
Her blaster! She strained to lift her head as high as possible.
The room was bare.

"Help me!" she screamed at the top of her lungs. "Help!
Please, help me!"

Nothing. Only the ever present silence.

"Let me loose, damn you, Ngen Van Chow!"

Twenty minutes passed before he entered, his smile as
pleasant as always. "Damn you, you bastard!" she spat at
him. "Let me out of this now!" She glared at him, aware of
her vulnerability.

Ngen seated himself casually on the bed, letting his eyes
rove over her warm flesh. "I've wondered about what you
looked like under all that provincial garb you like to affect.
I had no idea you were so smooth and tempting." His voice
cooed at her.

"What are you . . . you . . . doing?" she asked brokenly
as he began to stroke her. She squirmed frantically. The
bonds tightened.

"I'm going to teach you enjoyment," he whispered as he
pulled out of his shirt and dropped his pants.

Wide-eyed, she stared at his naked body. "You're mad!
This is rape! *Ngen, you're mad!*"

"No, dearest Leona. I'm not mad." He settled himself
next to her again. "I have to dispose of you. You are
causing too many problems. You see, I don't trust your
judgment anymore. The People need a new martyr—a leader
dead for the cause. You're perfect. Your dedication to the
revolution is lauded by all the union and worker coalitions.
Right now, they're parading through the streets with your
portrait, singing their little songs. Tomorrow they'll produce
twice as much as today."

She shivered as he bent over her. Whimpering, she tried
to back away. "What . . . what are you g-going to d-do with
me?"

He looked up, surprised. "Why, bring you pleasure, dearest
Leona."

"I . . . I . . . mean after," she tried to keep her voice
level, unable to meet his eyes.

He laughed gaily. "Dearest woman! I will bring you ecstasy again and again. So long as you bring me pleasure, I will keep you in the finest of health. An equitable bargain, don't you agree?" His head dropped again.

Her voice had gone hoarse. "You mean the people think I'm . . . *I'm dead?*"

He moved his head up to her neck, kissing her, nibbling lightly at her skin. She tried to pull away, but he pinned her in place. "But of course, my alabaster beauty. Your shuttle burned on reentry. It would seem the Directorate would do anything to strike out at us. For the moment, they're attempting to eliminate the leadership of the revolution."

"So I will never leave here alive?" The words were cold in her mouth.

"It would prove an embarrassment." His regret sounded sincere. "You wouldn't want to disappoint the people. They're reveling in the tragedy of the occasion."

"*You are a monster!*" she hissed, fear and shame consuming her as his hand crept between her spread legs. She flinched at his touch.

"And you are a virgin," he said matter of factly. "How did you ever manage that? And you in your late twenties!"

She turned her head away, fighting for control.

He promptly backed off, leaving her shivering on the bed. Half-crazed she stared up in disbelief. Sudden hope welled in her throat. Could it be that . . . that he'd let her go now?

He made himself a drink and sat by the bed sipping it, seeming to ignore her. At last he looked over. "Better now?" He smiled and set the drink down, reaching for a curious headset on the wall, placing it lightly about her brows.

"Relax," he said softly. "We have plenty of time and I don't want you tense. The headset will help."

He dropped his head down. She flinched at the feel of his tongue. Gritting her teeth, she tried to fight. Twisting her body only seemed to make it worse. A warm flush filled her, the psych machine spinning images in her mind. Horrified, she realized her body was beginning to respond to his caresses.

"See," he crooned happily, "you're learning pleasure."

She screamed, bladder and bowels evacuating as he lowered himself onto her.

CHAPTER XI

"The important thing is that you listen and learn. Strategy is the game plan for any operation." Rita explained, tapping her fingers into her palm as they hurried down a long white hall. "You have to know the strategy because as soon as the fight starts, something goes wrong. Call it the first rule of war. If you don't know what the game plan called for, you can't anticipate changes in tactics without screwing things up even worse."

Susan nodded, trying to assimilate the whirlwind of ideas Major Sarsa bombarded her with. They turned down a companionway at a dogtrot. Fighting off a yawn, blinking her eyes, she tried repeating each of Rita's words mentally.

The hatch swung open as Rita slowed and Susan ducked in at her heels; she ran headlong into a wall of noise and confusion. Everyone was talking—shouting over others—the war room a roar of sound. Every square inch of wall space glowed with multicolored monitors displaying tables, graphs, and figures or holos of Sirius, cities, or battle class ships.

Susan swallowed nervously, looked around at the ranking officers, and stuck to Rita's heels. She could see Moshe Rashid and Iron Eyes poring over a surface map. Moshe pointed at something and Iron Eyes nodded, face lined with concentration.

"Ten'*shun!*" boomed out. Each of the milling bodies jerked up straight, sentences cut off in mid-word.

Having been briefed, Susan stood like a ramrod and kept her head back. From the corner of her eye, she saw Colonel Ree enter with a swinging stride, snap a salute, and order, "At ease." The stiff figures broke and shuffled to the table amid murmurs of continued conversation.

Rita found a seat and slid into it, her mind on whatever her comm headset was feeding her. Susan took her place behind Rita's chair. Iron Eyes slid his solid mass in next to Rita, still conversing quietly with Moshe.

"You have the preliminary estimates," Ree began, stand-

ing at the head of the table, eyes gleaming and arms crossed.
"Most of you are more than familiar with the procedure.
The only element which differs from standard training is the
deployment of the Romanans and how they will react to a
battle situation."

Iron Eyes narrowed his eyes to predatory slits.

A holo of the largest continent on Sirius formed. Susan
recognized it as Ekrania, the seat of the Sirian industrial
district.

The holo expanded. "Here," lights glowed, "are the known
satellite defenses. These are small manned stations mount-
ing blaster and laser cannon. They will provide the hottest
moments for the AT operations. Moshe?" Ree's eyes shifted.

Captain Moshe Rashid stood, clearing his throat. "The
ATs will break off within twenty minutes of maximum engagement range. From our estimates, we can achieve enough
dispersion to avoid drawing concentrated defensive fire and
we'll go in dead to lessen the chances of observation and
tracking. From our intelligence, we think they've underestimated AT maneuverability and speed.

"On the first pass by the planet we'll use the gravity well
to shed delta V. At the same time we can locate and tag any
satellite defenses. On the second pass, we take those stations out and decelerate for planetary penetration.

"Team one, consisting of the marines and Romanans
from *Bullet*, will deploy in all the major urban areas of
Ekrania. By breaking the industrial back of the planet, we
destroy logistical support to the Rebels and deal them a
severe psychological blow. Teams two and three from
Brotherhood and *Victory* will attend to the other continents."

Ree interrupted. "Iron Eyes, do your people understand
just how to initiate this?" Lines tightened at the sides of his
thin-lipped mouth.

John stood, eyes those of a chained hawk. "I think we do,
Colonel. Each of my groups has seen the comm-generated
scenarios. With the exception of the novelty of the planet,
we are simply overlaying sophistication to normal raiding
behavior."

Ree fingered his chin. "We've seen your Romanans in
action, War Chief." Ree cocked his bullet head. "We have
orders to make Sirius an example. Can your men strike
terror into the civilian populace? The Directors are counting
on dramatic effect."

Iron Eyes' lips twisted wryly. "Colonel, I'm not sure Skor Robinson realizes what he's unleashing against the Sirians."

Tory Yarovitch, the liaison from *Victory*, stood to be recognized. She looked hesitantly at Iron Eyes. "Some of us have reservations about using Romanans against Ekrania. Mr., uh, Iron Eyes, we're concerned about the reactions of your troops when they run up against a force armed with modern tactics and weapons. If you'll excuse me, sir, how do we know they won't bolt?" Tory sat, dark face reflecting skepticism.

In the silence, Iron Eyes looked thoughtfully to Ree. "Colonel, you have personally fought the People. Would you care to make a comment on Romanan courage?"

Ree leaned forward, staring at the two liaisons from the other ships. *"They don't break!"* he snapped. "Using rifles against ATs they didn't break. When we tried to impose military law on Atlantis, they didn't give an inch."

Yarovitch shook her head vehemently. "But what about offensive combat on another world? I can see a desperate defense when losing means everything . . . but what about an offensive action where families and private property are not involved? We're just not—"

"Then I can explain." Iron Eyes gave her an earnest look. "Have you read of our religion? No? You must understand that we do not fear death. Those who die bravely in service of Spider are richly rewarded. Among your people, the future is unknown, what lies beyond the grave is unknown. Our Prophets have taught us to live with the future. We know death will exist in many different forms. Our Holy Old Ones foresee our deaths. Our decisions affect when and how we will die. But we all know we cannot escape it. Our orientation is . . . different than yours."

Tory seemed unconvinced. "Religion doesn't interest me. I look for motivation."

Iron Eyes paused to think for a moment before nodding in satisfaction. "Very well, I'll give you a motivation you can understand. On my planet, we obtain women, horses, honor, status, rank, prestige, or what have you by our raiding. The greatest disgrace is to go home poor.

"These men, my Romanans, are staking their lives that they will go home heroes. My World, Atlantis to you, has no fine clothing. No comm units. No aircars, No reactors. Only one, six hundred-year-old electrical generator. We would have aircraft. Space ships like this one. We would have a hospital and paved roads and industries. We will get them from the Sirians. Those who go home will be rich, powerful men. They will take the wealth of the stars with them. Their names will be sung by their clans and their enemies' clans. What could drive a man harder? Do you—"

Tory shook her head. "*Barbaric!* And the Directors went along with this . . . this *idea?*"

Susan tensed, oblivious to everything else as her attention riveted on Tory's face.

"They have their own Romanan Prophet," Rita explained with a cool grin.

"Enough," Ree said mildly, raising his hand. "Let's proceed under the assumption Romanans will fight."

Chuckles came from Ree's officers. They knew.

The Colonel's face went tight. "Iron Eyes, your orders are to allow your men free reign. We are here to crush rebellion before it destablizes an entire sector of space. They can destroy, loot, rape, and plunder where they will so long as no organized resistance remains on the ground. Is that understood?"

Iron Eyes grinned in satisfaction. "Yes, Colonel."

Rita stood. "Regarding the Romanans, Colonel. I suggest a marine tech be assigned to each group. In putting this thing together, it has become obvious that while the Romanans learn quickly, they can still get into trouble. For instance, what would happen if a Romanan unthinkingly turned a blaster on a power plant? How would they recognize it? The antimatter detonation would destroy half the planet!"

"Good point," Ree agreed. "Moshe, attend to that."

Major Neal Iverson stood. "Colonel, can we count on any ground support from the population?"

Ree shook his head slowly. "The man running the show on Sirius is one Ngen Van Chow. A rather colorful character, he grew up on the docks. The couple of times they charged him with violations of the law, he was never proved guilty. In retrospect, they should have psyched him out of general principal.

"In addition to all the bombings the Directorate has been blamed for, we're now accused of having eliminated a leader of the revolutionary party, one Leona Magill, who coordinated the technical aspects of the revolt. In summation, publicity has been so well adapted to the situation the entire planet is up in arms. Those who wavered toward the Directorate are now firmly in favor of the revolution. Conservatives have either capitulated or been imprisoned."

"So it's more serious than we expected," Neal frowned as he thought. "What about the skies? How does that look? Long range intelligence wrong about that, too?"

Ree's face tightened. "Yes." The room was silent. "We originally thought they might be able to get *Hiram Lazar* refitted to put up a resistance. Our agents on the planet report that somehow they got hold of enough toron to outfit *Helk* and *Dastar* as well."

He turned to a screen. The image of a boxy cargo ship formed. Violet threads spun from its dark gray sides.

"This holo of *Hiram Lazar* was taken from the observatory station. As you can see, the ship is operational. Further, spectrometry reports the blasters are similar to those used by the Brotherhood several centuries ago."

A silent gasp rose from the seated officers.

"Sir?" Adam Chung stood. "Is it possible that . . . that these are Brotherhood ships? Could *they* be making a comeback?" Faces had become grim, to Susan's eyes, frightened. She made a note to herself to look up the Brotherhood.

"No," Ree shook his head positively. "As much as they were maligned at the end of the Confederacy, they would never have used the population as diabolically as Ngen Van Chow appears to. This is their technology . . . not their handiwork."

A visible tremor of relief went through the officers. Only Rita and Iron eyes seemed unaffected.

"As a result," Ree continued, "we have no idea about how we will be received. As to control of the skies, well, who knows? Based on the evidence provided, *Defiance*, *Miliken*, and *Toreon* have been dispatched. They have coordinated and while we head insystem from jump at twenty gravities, they will enter at thirty. We should arrive at the same time. Six to three. Those are the odds. We should be able to handle them—no matter how powerful their blasters."

Someone whispered, "Jesus!"

"Quite a fleet," Ree said soberly. "This has gotten too far out of hand. No matter what the Directorate does on Sirius, the repercussions will rock all of civilization."

Rita leaned back. "I've been reading some of Doc's, er, Leeta Dobra's books. Throughout our history as a species, it seems that certain societies reach a maximum density, if you will. When that point is attained, nothing anyone can do will hold them together."

Her eyes glowed. "The Directors are incredibly intelligent. They've been bred specifically for the single task of balancing human society. The Sumerians, the Assyrians, the Hittites, the Babylonians, the Greeks, the Romans, Byzantium, the English Empire, the Soviets, and the Confederacy all fell when they reached critical mass. Each of those societies decayed internally and then a catalyst set off a social reaction."

Rita took a deep breath. "I wonder if, in our case, the catalyst is composed of Romanans?"

Haunted eyes stared at her across the table.

"Chester Armijo Garcia told Skor Robinson that without the Romanans, the Directorate would be destroyed within six months. Three of those have passed," Ree reminded. "Romanans have—"

"You place too much emphasis on these barbarians," Tory Yarovitch said condescendingly.

Ree didn't deign to answer. Neither did any of his officers. Susan ground her teeth. Fool! What did she think a Prophet was? An ignorant savage?

"Iron Eyes?" Iverson asked, blond complexion crinkled with thought. "What have your people got that makes you such a key in all this? How do . . . I mean, your effect on the Sirians won't hold a candle to having their three warships shot out of space and a total blockade enforced."

Iron Eyes didn't change his expression as he spread his callused hands. "I don't know, Major. Our destiny lies with Spider. We are no more than His tools."

Tory smirked, lighting fire to something foul under Susan's heart.

"Any other questions?" Ree asked. Seeing none, he dismissed the meeting. Immediately, everyone rose, chattering at once. Rita made a beeline for Tory Yarovitch.

"A moment, Captain Yarovitch."

Tory turned, expression veiled. "Yes, Major?"

"Just for your information, I'll bet my Romanans have the Sirians in retreat faster than *Victory's* marines." Rita grinned. "Five thousand credits says I'm right."

"Five thou . . ." Tory's mouth fell open. "That's a year's salary!"

"That's how sure I am. You in . . . or out?"

"In!" Tory gasped, coloring with pleasure.

"Susan," Rita turned. "Please see the word is passed."

"Yes, Major." Susan, haggard from loss of sleep, grinned

sheepishly. "They're going to love this. I'll bet they don't leave a building standing! So many coups will be taken that you'll need an aircar to haul them all." The anger inside turned to glee.

"Think so?" Tory turned her attention to Susan. "I take it you don't have a very high opinion of our marines."

"Not at all, ma'am," Susan shook her head, not liking Yarovitch or the hot smirk on her lips. "You see, Rita has made it a matter of honor. The warriors will view this like knife feud."

"Knife feud?" Tory asked with a curious laugh. "And that is?" An eyebrow lifted.

"A duel to the death among individuals whose honor is at stake." Susan said.

"How delightfully rich." Tory turned to Rita. "I see why you keep one on your staff. Wonderful amusement! Duels, indeed! Quaint!"

Susan's blood stirred.

"Susan, don't—" Rita's hand caught her shoulder.

"*You bitch!*" Her exhausted mind didn't stop her in time. "I'd gut you myself!"

"*Susan!*" Rita's voice pierced the anger like a whip. "Damn you! Not here! Not now!"

"Really!" Tory laughed. "Gut me? That thin stick of a woman? I'll bet she still eats her meat raw."

Susan chuckled sourly. "I'm sorry, Major Sarsa. She's been, as you say, a pain in the ass all through the meeting. If she were not a coward, I'd swear knife feud and teach her humility."

An audience had grown. Iron Eyes came pushing through the crowd, Ree hot on his tail.

"I'll play your game," Tory leered, laughing at the absurdity of it. "Let's do your knife feud!" Her voice hung heavy with scorn. "Do I have to kill a spider first? Hmm? Make black magic so I win? Perhaps I sacrifice a virgin at midnight?"

Rita's quick action saved Susan from connecting with a well-aimed kick. While Captain Tory Yarovitch ungracefully tripped out of the way, Rita and Iron Eyes muscled a howling Susan to the floor.

"*Ten'shut!*" Major Iverson bellowed at the top of his lungs. Officers came to order, including Rita. Iron Eyes dragged Susan to her feet, growling threats in her ear.

"What the hell *is* this?" Colonel Ree demanded, eyes narrowed, face reddening.

Tory faced Ree and saluted. "I was insulted and attacked, sir. That . . . *being* . . . insulted my person and rank and challenged me to a knife combat. She then attempted to assault me."

"It is knife feud," Susan growled to herself, adrenaline draining from her body. "She had no right to drag Spider's name through the dirt!"

"*Bastard God!*" Tory spat.

Everyone in the room stiffened. Only steel-banded arms kept a struggling Susan from Yarovitch's throat.

As if he'd swallowed a live fish, Ree croaked, "Knife feud?" He turned to Rita who'd kept silent. "You in on this, too, Major?"

In a voice that cut she replied, "Only to the extent that I bet the Captain my Romanans would have Ekrania before her marines cracked that easy nut ben Ahmad gave them, sir." She saluted crisply.

"Iron Eyes!" Ree snapped. "You're War Chief. Tell me, what's correct in this situation? I can't have the Romanans in an uproar over knife feud . . . and I can't have visiting officers insulted in *my* war room!"

"The knife feud is withdrawn," Iron Eyes said through gritted teeth. His glittering eyes never left Tory's; but the words obviously cost him. As Susan Smith Andojar's eyes widened he added in stilted Romanan. "You would be a warrior, *woman*. This *is* a war trail. By law, I withdraw knife feud."

Susan swallowed hard, nodding. She turned to Captain Yarovitch and repeated the withdrawal in Standard, eyes slitted in hate. She threw a salute to Ree and Sarsa and stalked out of the room.

"Captain," Ree's tone was deadly as he studied Yarovitch. "These Romanans take their honor and their God very seriously. *I* take their honor and their God seriously. In the future, would you accord my people such respect as you would me? I, in turn, shall see that they respect your position and your authority on my ship." He ended with a bow and turned, beckoning Rita to follow. A red-faced Yarovitch glared after them, fists clenched at her side.

"Major," Ree began, "why did Susan Smith Andojar threaten the Captain?"

"I don't know, sir."

Ree fingered his chin. "During the conference, I . . . uh,

noticed she was practically weaving on her feet. She was either drunk or exhausted. Which?''

"I don't know, sir. I doubt she was drunk. Her only true vice seems to be lemonade."

"Lemonade?" Ree glanced up quizzically, slightly off balance.

"They don't have lemons on World, sir. It's still a novelty for the Romanans."

"Sounds harmless enough," Ree remarked. "I must assume then that she was tired. Is she working herself to death . . . or playing too hard?"

Rita let herself glower at Ree for all of a second. "I am attempting to ensure the girl is properly educated. Her schedule is rigorous to make up for deficiencies in her training."

Ree grunted, frown-lines compressed. "Romanan women are still at the bottom of the heap. I know you, Rita. You're a fighter. You've seen an injustice among your chosen prodigies. You'll kill to change it." He stifled her protest with a lifted hand. "She's a bright, motivated young lady, Major. Give her some credit. She'll do all—"

"If she fails, she'll fail for all the Romanan women," Rita protested hotly. "The men will take the story back. She can't be anything less than perfect!" She emphasized that with a clenched fist. "You know what young girls are fated for on that planet. They're chattel! Slaves to clan, family, children, and warriors. Prizes from raiding, personal whores to the—"

Ree's jaw thrust out. "And what if I hadn't been lucky and had Iron Eyes to get her out of that knife feud? Tory would have killed her. Yarovitch isn't a . . a Romanan. She'd have cut Susan so the meds couldn't patch her up again. Tory's a *professional*."

"There's always a risk," Rita growled, defensively.

"Don't make more risk." Ree shot back. "I like the kid. I admire the guts she has to take on her people . . . and you, too." He jammed a finger into her chest. "Ease up on her, Sarsa! Or, by God, I'll land on you like a ton of neutrons!"

"Yes, sir!" Rita snapped to attention and saluted. Glancing around the room, she forced herself to leave with decorum.

It took another hour before Ree could pull Iron Eyes away from Moshe's battle map. "What's eating Sarsa?" he asked. "Something about Susan is ripping her apart."

"Susan should have stayed with her People." Iron Eyes'
face stiffened into a mask.

"Not you, too," Ree said in frustration. "What is it about
that girl?" He took a breath. "She's all right. She's trying
too hard, but she's all right. I've watched her, John. She
worships two people on this ship—you and Rita. At the
same time you both beat her down. And every time you
think you've dumped enough on her to stop her, she comes
up for more. What does it take?" Ree ended with his jaw
muscles in tight bands.

Iron Eyes said nothing.

"Oh, hell." Ree, raised his hands in defeat. "Go back to
what you were doing. Just think about it." Mystified, he
searched for the coffee dispenser.

Susan blinked back hot tears as she stamped down the
companionway. From the heat in her face, she knew shame
branded her expression. At the door to her quarters, she
stopped.

Drained and beaten, stubborn pride wouldn't let her quit.
Damn!

Why did it all have to be so hard? Her mind didn't belong
to her anymore. It had become some *thing* else. Susan
Smith Andojar was more than a collection of facts strung
together in a random sequence. Who was she? Slamming
her fist against the door, she trotted frantically down the
corridor.

Hans was sleeping soundly in his bunk when she entered.
Dropping down next to him, she carefully shook his shoulder instead of blasting him bodily from the bunk as she
wished to do.

"Huh?" he mumbled, looking up stupidly. His eyes focused and he started wide awake. "Susan? What, uh, are,
uh. . . ." His mouth bobbed a couple of times, but no words
came out. He looked nervously around, catching the curious
stares from across the gun room, and blushed bright red.

Susan hissed, "Hans, I've got to talk to someone. You're
the only friend I can turn to. Friday's on duty . . . and I'm
not . . . not sure he'd understand. Can we go somewhere?"
She glanced around at the ring of male eyes staring her way.

"Uh, yeah, sure." He pulled himself up and drew his
uniform on. She vaguely noted how flustered he was.

They ended up in one of the observation blisters off the
gun deck. Susan dropped into a heap behind a spectrometer

and fought to put her mind in order. Thought was confusion. In defeat she dropped her head into her hands.

"You look completely shot, Susan," Hans mumbled, baffled, unsure of how to proceed. "Where have you been? I haven't seen you for weeks."

"Rita upgraded my duty after Friday got cut in that knife feud. I haven't had time to do anything but study." She looked down at her hands, moving the fingers slowly.

"I saw you there. Rumor had it that, uh, Yellow Legs was your, uh, boyfriend." He tried to smile, but his lips just twitched, panic in his eyes.

"He's. . . ." She ended with a shrug. "I don't know what he is. He kept me alive. Fought for my honor. Helped me become what I am today, whoever that is."

"What do you mean?" he cried, perplexed, forgetting his nervousness. "You know exactly who you are. I know who you are. You're Susan!"

"Who's Susan?" she demanded. "There are things I can't remember!" She held up her hand. "See this scar? I know how I got it. I mean, I know I know—but I don't anymore."

He exhaled, understanding. "Ah, you've been on the teaching machines too long."

"So?"

"So, nothing comes free. Sleep stim, constant use of the headset can do that. Think of it like this. Ever since they mapped the brain, it's been possible to teach it. I mean, consider how you learn. You see something, that stimulates the optic nerve and part of your brain reorders. The synapses realign to form the memory. The teaching machine through comm does the same thing only without the interface of your own senses. Instead, an electromagnetic pattern is superimposed over random synapses. Presto, instant memory."

"So why can't I remember getting this scar?"

"You can—but you can't. Part of the synaptic order has been overlaid." He frowned. "You see, the comm headset picks up the greatest number of random synapses and overlays. Too much too quick and it begins selectively removing what seem to be the most trivial memories. Why trivial? They're used the least, the synapses begin to look random."

"Oh, great," Susan moaned. "Not only am I nutty, I'm losing me!"

"No, you can't. I mean not unless they use the big psych machines. Teaching doesn't affect thought, personality, cognitive ability, or behavior . . . only memories, sometimes, when the brain doesn't have time to sort itself out and learn the new systems implanted in the thought processes. We only use a small part of our brain."

"And that's why I'm learning so fast?" She propped her chin. "Instant genius . . . all for a few paltry memories. No wonder I'm going crazy!"

"Crazy?"

"I just came from the war room. I tried to start a knife feud with the *Victory* liaison officer! I work from the time I get up to the time I go to sleep. I don't see you, I don't see Friday, I don't see anyone but the images that God-rotted machine puts in my head!" She felt herself losing control and bit her finger, hoping the pain would give her a centering point to keep her from bawling like a calf.

Hans moved over and put an arm around her, hugging her close. "Here, relax. You're all right. Remember me, Corporal Hans Yeager? I'm the man who can fix anything. I've never worked on a Romanan girl before. I don't guess the circuits are too tough to figure."

He stopped suddenly and chuckled out loud at himself. "Who the hell am I trying to kid? I'm the laughing stock of five decks!"

His sarcastic voice made her look up. "Why?"

Suddenly embarrassed, he withdrew his arms. "Aw, uh, you see, I got a deal going with Tony in comm. I've got stats on every girl in the ship." He stood up and faced away from her, head down. "The only problem is I can't get the nerve to ask one out. Every time I try, I get all self-conscious and I can't talk. You know, like the day in the Major's quarters."

"I had lemonade with you," Susan reminded, puzzled. "I was glad to talk to you. I thought you sounded fine—better than me."

He nodded, facing her, a curious grin on his face. "That's just it. You didn't know what a jerk I was making of myself. Maybe that's why it was all right."

"You don't talk badly now."

He paused, brow creased. "No, I guess not. But that's because . . . because you're in trouble. I'm trying to help you—so why are we talking about me?"

"Maybe we both found our own level." Susan gasped out a sigh. "I can't do anything right for either the Major or Iron Eyes. I don't know what I'm doing anymore. Now you tell me my mind isn't all my mind anymore? I'm not sure I can make it, Hans. You know what that means? Back to World to be married off by my clan, then pregnant and stuck like a bug in a jar."

He dropped down next to her again. "So, what's wrong? Where do you think you're failing?"

"I can't learn enough quick enough. And after what you just told me, do I want to? Sometimes Rita tells me about other women, like Doc Dobra, who . . . What's wrong?"

Hans had stiffened. "I knew Doctor Dobra. In fact I had her on the wrong end of a blaster one fine day that I'd rather forget."

"She's almost a saint to Rita and Iron Eyes. I only saw her a couple of times when she came to the settlements. What was she like?"

Hans laughed nervously. "One tough lady! You know, she was real different before she got kidnapped by the Santos. Then that day we found her—almost got her killed cause we thought she was just another Romanan—we, uh, sorry about that." He blushed.

"Go on."

"Well, she was smart. You know, she outfoxed Captain Helstead, the Colonel, and the Romanans to boot. Rita trained the troops, but Doc was the brains." Hans nodded to himself.

"Yeah, the brains. She always thought things through. She'd think about what the Colonel wanted to hear, and that's what she'd give him. Did the same for the Romanans. All that time she ferried Iron Eyes around on our AT, we never even had a hint she was soft on him. Amazing lady."

"Did she know Brotherhood tricks?" Susan asked quickly.

"Brotherhood? No, I don't think so. How'd you hear about the Brotherhood? They're almost legendary. I think most of the stuff on them is under security seal."

"Security seal?" Susan mused. "What I'd give to get into that. I just thought they were a political faction in the Confederacy. Why does everyone treat them with such awe?"

Hans looked around warily before he leaned closer. "They were more than just a political faction. Their ships were almost magical. Their technology was superb—beyond anything we have today. They didn't even hold a seat in the Confederacy, but when they spoke, whole sectors jumped."

"So they had a special power? I wonder what it . . ." Susan lost herself in thought. "I guess I'll just check the records and—"

"Good luck," Hans laughed nervously. "It would be security sealed, remember? Excuse me, but for a lady who just learned how to read a month ago, you aren't up to security seals. Try and access those files and every red light on the bridge will be flashing!"

"Who can get me into them? The Colonel?" Her mind worked again and—for the first time—she had a definite problem. Some of the thousands of facts she had been cramming her head with gave her a clue as to its importance.

"Maybe." Hans squinted, lost in thought. "I don't even know what might be hidden in comm. They might not have programmed anything into the ship's system. At the same time, *Bullet* herself is over three hundred years old. There's no telling what might be buried in the deep banks."

"I suppose I'd trigger something by trying to learn that from my unit." She felt better.

"Sure enough. You don't have the background. I'm not even sure I could get in . . . and I have years of that sort of stuff under my belt. I . . . What are you thinking? Oh, no! Huh-uh! Susan, that stuff's off limits!" He shook his head slowly, looking furtively around the gun deck again.

Fired, eyes alight, she added, "Hans, consider, that might be it! You *could* do it!"

"It might be a royal bust, too," he moaned. "A bust from corporal to . . . brig rat!"

She gave him what she hoped was her most ravishing smile. "Hans, you say that you don't know how to deal with women, right? How about we trade? I'll teach you to never fear another woman for the rest of your life and you teach me how to break into computers!" She clapped her hands happily.

He took a deep breath, puffing out his cheeks as he exhaled. "Me being a bachelor forever would be a bunch better than spending a half-day at a court-martial, especially *mine*!"

"Hans," Susan said slyly, taking his arm and leaning intimately up against him. "No one would rib you in the gun room again. Would you rather see me wash out? Won't you help me learn why the Brotherhood was so powerful?"

"I just don't know," he muttered half to himself, shivering at her touch.

"Look, I know I'm no beauty, but—"

He interrupted with an explosion, "Are you *kidding*! Half the men on this ship would love to get close to you. They just think Friday Yellow Legs has a prior claim! My God, Susan, you're the most beautiful woman on the ship even ragged out like you are now!"

She gave him a disbelieving squint. "You're sweet, Hans, but I'm not fooled that easily. I know I . . ."

"Ever notice how the men watch you when you go down the hall? Ever notice how many smile at you? Open hatches? Help you pick up in the gym?"

"Yes, but—" caught off guard, she stumbled. "I . . . I thought they were just . . . just polite."

"There's another reason for it," he told her earnestly. "And it's not because you're the only Romanan woman on board either."

"Then why are you turning me down? Do we have a deal?" she challenged.

"What about Friday?" he asked, suddenly skeptical. "Nobody on the crew wants to tangle with him after that knife feud. I like my guts where they are, thanks. Horsecapture hasn't set foot out of the hospital and won't until after we reach Sirius. Maybe knives aren't that dangerous, but who needs the pain?"

"What about Friday?" she repeated, pulling back a little so she could see his eyes. "He's my friend. I love him a great deal for what he did to help me and I'm forever in his debt. That doesn't mean he owns me.

"You're my friend, too. Maybe you weren't there when I took my first coup. You're here now. I want to go after another trophy . . . and sure there's risk in that, Hans. Risk is part of the game. Spider thrives on risk. That's how men and women learn. Take a risk with me. There might be great honor—"

"There might be great disaster, too," he grumbled.

"That makes the honor greater." She frowned. "Are all Directorate men as cautious as you?"

"I'm not cautious." Hans said stiffly. "I can do anything any other man would do. You'd almost think I was a coward!"

"Aw," she smiled suddenly as a piece clicked into place. "Then of course you will help me. Only a coward could refuse."

"You just bet I will, I'll. . . ." Hans Yeager turned a bright shade of red. His silence was short. "Oh, hell, you're smart enough we just might get away with it.

"Why the Brotherhood?" He pushed her back, trying to see behind her eyes. "You're obsessed with them now where

fifteen minutes ago you were drowning in defeat. Why are
they so important?"

She pursed her lips, watching him intently. "I'm not sure
I should tell you."

"Hey, we're in this together," he reminded, frown
deepening.

"If you sink me, I sink you," she said, nodding. "Very
well, the agents have pictures of the biggest Sirian warship.
From the holos it looks like they have a peculiar blaster.
The intelligence officers think it's based on a Brotherhood
model."

"Susan, I . . . I was born on Frontier." Seeing her blank
stare, he continued, "That was the home planet of the
Brotherhood. To us, the wonders of their inventions aren't
myths. They're a lost heritage. If Sirius possesses a Brotherhood blaster—or even a poor copy—*Bullet* is in real trouble."

CHAPTER XII

Chester Armijo Garcia looked up from his reading seconds
before the holo images formed before him. He nodded
pleasantly and gave particular attention to Skor Robinson.
The Directors' bulging heads would never cease to amaze him.

"The Sirians have a new weapon," Skor began without
ceremony.

"You refer to the blaster." Chester nodded, lips in a
continuous smile.

Semri Navtov—little pig eyes hostile—snapped, "Why did
you not tell us?"

"It would be cliche to say that you did not ask; but the
truth is that many things cannot be foretold. Remember the
cusps, Directors. The future is a maze. Think of a forest of
trees with branches interwoven with vines linking each into
an impenetrable mass.

"Imagine now a diagram of one of those trees. Place yourself at the tip of a root. That is your birth in the past.
If you travel up the roots, one path joining another, eventually
you will come to the trunk which represents the present.

Looking up from the trunk, there are many major branches reaching out in all directions. The branches are the future. Choose one and the only options are branches on that limb. Each choice of a branch is a cusp. Or, will you take a vine to a completely different tree? Can I know in advance which choice you will make? Can I guess which leaf is your destiny?

"No." Chester smiled benignly, smoothing the fine Arcturian cloth on his chest. "That is free will. Spider—God—does not bias free will. I have told you before that Spider guards it jealously. Would I attempt to see your leaf, my mind would lose itself so deeply in the branches that I could never retrace my path to you. It is the madness of which I so often speak. If God does not bias free will, should I?"

"Your words are offensive," An Roque offered flatly. Chester could sense the Director's hatred of him. The unreasoning force of the emotion made him pause, feeling pity for the man.

"Would you have me lie?" Chester asked humbly. "I shall tell you all I can so long as it does not endanger my sanity or compromise my integrity. Save us the breath, gentlemen, I can see your threats coming. They are worthless. Kill me if you wish. Death is nothing. It lies on all sides of us, distracted by one cusp, enticed by another.

"At the same time, inspect your motives and learn of yourselves. I understand there have been riots in university. The Gulag Sector smuggling has increased. You are uncertain what the offer Respit extends to the Romanans means. You see confusion all around you. You are under pressure. What do you learn of yourselves?"

Skor's eyes were half closed. "Prophet, we are in need. Teach us."

"He will teach us death!" Roque stated viperously. "I should have him dispatched!"

Chester interrupted by raising his hands in a placating movement. "Director Roque, you are becoming irrational . . . gigged by your loss of control over Respit. You would regret a loss of emotional control. Beware emotions, Director, your kind are not used to them. Emotions are one of the strongest forces in the universe. Tamed, they can lead you to greatness—unleashed they can lead you to foolish, deplorable destruction."

Rogue's entire balloonlike head slowly turned red.

"Roque!" Robinson hissed, atrophied vocal chords straining. Judging by their eyes, Robinson and Navtov were in frantic communication through their intricate computer links.

Finally, Roque closed his eyes, took a deep breath that expanded his fragile rib cage and exhaled. After minutes of silence, he opened his eyes again to look daggers at Chester.

"Director," Chester bowed. "Consider what just happened. Consider how close you came to losing yourself to blind rage. Think objectively about the ramifications of the emotions you have just experienced. Where would they have led you? What changes would you have dealt society?" His voice soothed, eyes unwavering.

Roque's face quivered violently before his holo blinked out.

Robinson and Navtov closed their eyes to communicate. Skor recovered first, opening his little blue eyes to study Chester. Navtov followed a second later.

"You play with danger," Robinson's voice sounded squeaky. "Do not bait him. By a hair's breadth we avoided disaster."

Chester inclined his head. "It was a cusp, Directors. An Roque is the least human of your kind. I am a teacher and you yourself implored me to teach. I have shown him the rudiments of a weapon common to all people. A weapon you yourselves possess but understand poorly.

"Your kind have been taught to govern dispassionately, objectively, in total alienation from the true lives of humanity. You live sequestered here. Your dealings with people are through a comm link and are deciphered by the Gi-net. You have no understanding of the motivations of human beings."

"But Roque's reaction was . . . was illogical." Navtov protested. "For whole minutes he acted completely irrational, driven by his desire to destroy you! To do so, he would have disrupted the entire course of civilization! Is this becoming an age of madness?"

"No, Director Navtov," Chester shook his head slightly. "I needed to teach you the bounds of emotion. Ngen Van Chow, Damen Ree, the Romanans, and the Sirians are all motivated in the same manner Roque was a moment ago. We are not entering an age of madness—though it may appear so to you. We are on the verge of an age of passion."

"Passion?" Skor asked. "Emotion? Is it not the same?"

"Are bricks and walls the same?" Chester countered. "Passion is emotion channeled . . . as a wall is composed of stacked bricks. Do you see what I—"

"And men's lives are driven by such passions?" Navtov's scratchy voice echoed with his disbelief.

"The farther men get from life, Director, the less they
know of passion." Chester managed a slight shrug. "Your
Directorate has attempted to isolate people from themselves
and the basic drives they were bred to experience. You
yourselves have no concept of emotion. Love, hate, jealousy, guilt, envy, revenge, justice, freedom, status, power,
and other base drives are not rational—but they wield more
power than raw intellect."

"Why do you tell us this?" Skor asked. "What are your
driving motives? Are you on our side in this conflict with
the Sirians? Or do you have goals for your own Romanans?"

"My motive is to educate, Director." Chester nodded
easily, peaceful features radiating serenity. "I have no passions. I have only future running into past like a stream.
Were I to rage, would it make any difference to Spider?
Were I to plot, would my soul change its properties? Were I
to accumulate riches, would I find greater truth than Deity?

"No, I have need of nothing more. I have no need even
for life itself. This body is but a husk—like yours—to be
discarded."

"Then why live?" Navtov's cardboard voice betrayed
skepticism.

"Have you learned anything from me, Skor Robinson?
Have you, Semri Navtov?" Chester asked in a gentle voice.

"You have taught me discord," Robinson's voice stretched
tight.

"I have taught you life," Chester corrected. "Life is experience, not a series of academic puzzles interpreted by your
Gi-net computers. Your lives are meaningless to yourselves,
Directors. Look to your souls. You are convinced you have
none, that souls are not rational. At the same time, you
once thought emotion was beyond the pall of your exalted
existences. I have at least taught you that while you would
deny your humanity, you *are* still human. Perhaps I am not
so wrong about your souls."

"Do you seek converts for your Spider God?" Navtov's
voice hinted at scorn.

Chester gave him a benevolent look. "God—whether you
call him Spider or not—needs no converts. The soul is of
God, how could it be converted? Can you turn a fish into a
bird? You create a paradox by trying to convert God into
God."

"Then your actions are futile," Robinson said as he squinted
his little eyes triumphantly. "It makes no difference what we

learn, our souls are God and God is soul. As you yourself said, passion is pointless."

"Not at all," Chester returned. "You are aware of God today. Five months ago, your life was sterile, Skor. You floated above the Gi-net and solved complicated problems. You devised and manipulated the lives of millions within a self-imposed vacuum. Today, you wonder about right and wrong, good and evil, pain and pleasure. Your soul harvests the fruits of what you learn and, in so doing, so does God."

"Why must God learn?" Navtov asked. "There should be no greater quality in the universe than God!"

"Quite correct," Chester agreed, a trace of enthusiasm in his voice. "At the same time, Spider created the universe and it must serve a purpose. To be a Prophet is to see the universe as the environment of Spider. Each soul is a bit of Deity. When your physical life is over, would you send that spark of God we call soul back to Deity dull and meaningless? Would you not rather send it back gleaming with revelation."

"Am I to understand that we are God's senses?" Navtov asked. "Is that what you teach?"

"Indeed, we are the sight, sound, smell, touch, pain, and pleasure of Deity. What do you feel of life? What have you to contribute? Systems? The matrix algebra of economics? Rationality? You are knowledge without substance. You are sterile. To question is to feel. Where is your revelation?"

"Do these revelations help us defeat the Sirian Rebels?" Navtov asked.

Chester shook his head ever so slightly, beatific smile unchanged. "No."

"Then what good do we derive from them?" Robinson asked.

"You have missed my point, Director. It matters not who wins in the upcoming struggle. Suffice it to say that your universe shall not perish in civil war as it would have without the Romanans. I am here for *your* benefit—not the Directorate's. Think of my words. If you have no more use for me, send me away. A Prophet may always find those in search of knowledge. There are always humans who would learn."

"You are a constant source of irritation," Navtov's voice came, lifelessly. "I would like to know your worth."

Chester's manner remained mild. "A teacher is a constant irritation; and the worth of a man is God."

"And the blaster we originally wished to know about?" Skor reminded. "Will you tell us how it will affect our fleet?"

"It will be a decisive factor," Chester said easily. "The blaster is the center of several cusps which will play a major role in the future. Free will is at play. Final victory by Directorate forces is in doubt depending on the cusps. Ngen Van Chow, Damen Ree, Susan Andojar, Friday Yellow Legs, Rita Sarsa, and others are standing on the trunk of the tree; they are looking out over the branches. I know not which limbs they will choose."

"Bah!" Navtov interrupted.

"I do know that neither side foresees the actual consequences of their actions. Each sees a future which will not be. Your educated predictions, Colonel Ree's strategies, Van Chow's confidence, and hopes on both sides are brutally erroneous.

"Remember the lesson you have learned today. Study the effects of passion, for within hours, the fleets will meet and the age of passion will be unleashed on the Directorate. Let each of you think on what emotion is and how passion can change the perceived value of life. Passion is a key to knowledge. It is the way of Spider."

Chester bowed humbly, closing his eyes, remaining oblivious despite the questions hurled at him by both Robinson and Navtov. After several minutes of increased agitation, they flicked off their holos. Chester looked at the now blank wall, nodded with a light smile, and continued his study of Jean Paul Sartre.

Damen Ree twisted, his foot lashing out.

Iron Eyes caught it, grunting with effort and wheeling, slamming Ree to the mat, dropping, his forearm across the Colonel's throat. Ree bucked, curled, and got a bent knee between them. With an explosive bellow, he pried Iron Eyes off, tucking and rolling away, slamming vicious fists to Iron Eyes' gut.

They broke apart, panting, sweat streaming down their flushed faces, eyes gleaming. Iron Eyes leaped, planted a foot and drove into Ree, pounding the smaller man into the wall through sheer momentum. Ree spun in his grasp, battering the War Chief's chest and stomach with all his might before back-heeling him, driving the Romanan to the mat, fingers pointed in a dart at Iron Eyes' throat.

"You're . . . dead!" Ree gasped, swallowing hard, fighting for breath.

A slow grin spread over Iron Eyes' broad face. "But I'm
getting better. At first you and Rita could kill me all the
time."

Ree rolled off the bigger man, flopping on his back on the
cool mat. "Ohhhh!" he moaned. "I'm not as . . . young as I
. . . used to be. Yeah, you're better all right. Won't be long
and you'll outclass me."

Iron Eyes sat up, bracing himself on his wide-flung knees,
head down. "This body armor. You could have killed me a
couple of times but for it. I can feel the bruises already."

"You're not the only one." Ree puffed and sat up, un-
buckling the form-fitting armor. "You know, since you've
come aboard, I'm getting right fit again. Can't get anyone
else to spar with. Have to use the combat robot."

Iron Eyes heard the loneliness in the Colonel's voice and
nodded. The hand-to-hand practice had become a ritual for
both of them in the off hours.

"How's the reading coming?" Ree asked.

"Slow," Iron Eyes grunted. "I caught an allusion to teaching old dogs new tricks. I think I spent too long sniffing
after Santos horses and coups, not enough time listening to
the Old Ones. Maybe my brain isn't made for letters. But
. . . but I promised Leeta."

Ree winced and stood up, offering the Romanan a hand
up to his feet. "Old dogs and new tricks." He paused
thoughtfully, wiping at the sweat running down his thick
neck. "And it looks like Ngen's got some to teach, too."

Iron Eyes stripped off the body armor. "You're worried
about these blasters?"

Ree lifted a shoulder. "You bet I'm worried. Any commander worth his weight in hydrogen worries about what he
doesn't understand. When it comes to combat, I don't like
surprises."

"And the Brotherhood?"

"The Brotherhood," Ree snorted, combat armor slung
over his shoulder. "Things get blown out of proportion over
time. You know, turned into legend. But in a D-shell,
here's the story. Six hundred years ago, the Brotherhood—
like your ancestors—proved to be a thorn in the Soviets'
side. Like all the rest of the dissidents, they got deported.
Soviets sent them to Frontier figuring they could expend
their energy on the bullbears and the hostile climate. That

they did, and at the same time, they established the foremost underground university in space.

"Like all good empires, the Soviets got rich and fat and lazy and their army stagnated and they suffered sybaritic rot. On Frontier, the Brotherhood struck the sparks for the Confederate revolution. The Brotherhood continued to be on the forefront of human development for the next three hundred years. Their philosophy was that you didn't need guns to maintain control—just be smarter than the other guy. And were they ever! Ships that thought, you know, had their own brains. Developed medicine to heights we can only dream of. Opened whole new sectors of space, controlled piracy, taught the best and brightest to—"

"Yet they are gone," Iron Eyes mused.

"Yeah," Ree stepped into the shower, letting the water cascade over him. "Seems they underestimated humanity's ability to bear a grudge. Anyhow, when things got rough because of Sirian and Arpeggian pressure, they just up and left rather than have their people harassed or provoke a war."

"And you don't know where they went?" Iron Eyes frowned.

"Nope. Only that they left human space at the dawn of the Directorate. They cleaned up right down to the last comm holo, packed it all in their fleet, and jumped out. No telling where. For years that was a big mystery. Then—as with all things—time softened the effects, people lost interest. The Directorate buried the knowledge from all but a few."

"But Ngen has found something," Iron Eyes reminded. He tensed as the force fields slid over his skin, drying him. He leaned on his arms over the partition. "You're worried, Damen. That worries me. What am I taking my people into? I don't know the ropes here, but if I was on World, on a raid, I'd call my medicine bad, run for home, and await a better day."

Ree slapped a palm on the dryer. "Yeah, I wish we could do that." He motioned around him. "This ship is already strained. Sure, we patched things up—but they're still patches, damn it. We need a refitting after the mauling *Victory* gave us. We need time to train your people to fill in for casualties and defections. We're not full strength."

Iron Eyes scratched under his chin. "But we don't have much of a choice, do we. Spider's way is before us. Those who will not take it will find no glory."

Ree pulled his uniform over his head, snugging the equipment belt about his waist. "Warriors never really have much choice, do they? I think we'll . . . Hell! I don't know what kind of mess we're spacing into, John. I wish we had a Prophet with us."

Iron Eyes dressed in his new Patrol uniform—so much lighter than leather—and fingered the Spider effigy Rita had embossed on the fabric. He flipped his braids over his thick shoulders, stretching his arms to settle the light fabric. "The Prophets are highly overrated. If you had one, he'd just drive you crazy asking you questions and giving you ambiguous answers. Prophets do not make a man sleep well at night. For us normal humans, the future is not a place to meddle with. Horror is there. You don't want to know your destiny—your coming tragedies."

Ree frowned pensively. "Maybe not, but, John, keep in mind it could all fall apart down there. So much can go wrong in war—like that lucky shot Maya made over World. Hell, you've been on the ground in a fight, you know. This operation has too many unknowns. Untried troops, unknown Sirian capabilities, unsure leadership, political intrigue. Hell, the Patrol could turn on us at the last instant. You might be thinking about what to do if Spider tricks us all in the end."

Iron Eyes slapped him on the shoulder. "Don't worry, my friend. I've dealt with Spider before. I've seen uncertain futures."

"Yeah, but Sirius is a strange world. A whole different horse raid . . . if you know what I mean."

Iron Eyes winked. "Spider will guard us. I have to go back to my reading lesson."

"Suppose Spider looks the other way?" Ree insisted.

"Then I do things different." Iron Eyes hesitated. "Colonel. Don't worry about it. Any war chief must adapt by the moment. If we get down there and Sirius turns the tables, we'll just follow our noses. But most of all, I don't like to lose. No Romanan ever does. Keeps us strong."

Ree fingered his chin as the War Chief padded down the white corridor. "I hope we're strong enough."

Hans blinked his eyes, wishing it didn't take all his concentration just to stay awake. "We don't have much time left, you know," he grunted. He and Susan had been buried under the guts of *Bullet's* comm for almost two days.

Just when they were wondering how they would ever manage to get the time to conduct a serious study of the ship's computers, Rita had walked in and suddenly—if resentfully—granted Susan a reprieve from her studies. She'd told her to take a couple of days off and relax.

Had anyone noticed, Corporal Hans Yeager put in for—and received—two days of personal time to "conduct further study on advanced computer maintenance."

Forty-three hours later—with a stack of empty food packets piled in a corner and a container of personal waste sealed next to it—they hadn't made much progress.

"Try Captain's code access," Hans finally suggested, peering at the readout on the portable monitor. "Back in the old days, ships were commanded by captains, not colonels."

Instantly, Susan's monitor blinked out a series of characters. "What's this?"

Hans maneuvered himself around her body in the narrow crawlspace. They'd invaded a restricted area of the ship; but only in the event of a major computer failure would anyone unbolt the inspection cover and climb over the conduit, powerleads, and vacuum ducts to where they hid.

"Jesus!" Hans breathed. "That's it! All we have to do is figure out the authorization. I wonder . . ."

"Do you think they'd have anything under Brotherhood?" Susan asked. "If this is as old as you think, maybe it wasn't security sealed." She entered it.

"Impossible. They . . ." Instantly the monitor began processing information.

"Oh, really?" she asked smugly, afraid to take her eyes from the screen to grin her triumph.

"This stuff isn't even confidential!" Hans erupted in astonishment.

"Let's see. Technology," Susan guessed as she accessed another portion of the system. Facts and figures glowed green. "This mean anything to you?"

Hans crawled up next to her, aware of her odor and how her body felt next to his bare arm. Dragging his attention away from the girl, he began studying the subcategories. "Let's take weaponry," he decided. "That damn blaster brought us here in the first place."

He accessed the information and watched as several diagrams and schematics formed on the screens. "Real different from the ones we use," he mused. "Lordy, no wonder, look at that! Each of those big ones uses a huge strip of hyperconductor."

"What's that?"

"Well, to us it's an expensive, difficult to manufacture alloy. Superconductor will pass an electron without resistance, right? Well, hyperconductor goes a step beyond, it repulses the electron, pushing it along, but only in a certain direction and within certain capacities.

"Now, take the blaster. The powerlead going into the blaster provides energy, right? Hyperconductor surrounds the bare end of the powerlead and the heavy-element core which acts as the ammunition. When the powerlead is energized, the field generated through the hyperconductor disrupts the forces which give an atom integrity in the heavy-element core. When the atom destabilizes, you get a violent reaction with a certain charge. The hyperconductor is excited by that reaction, and with a like charge, forces the atomic debris away, which is down the blaster barrel. Gravitic fields restrict the output and allow us to give it a narrow focus. That's the purpose of the rings around the gun tubes."

"So if they have so much hyperconductor, they produce more power?"

"Basically, but at the same time, there's something here I don't understand. See this structure. It's listed as a Fujiki Amplifier. I wonder what that does?"

"Why don't we have more hyperconductor?"

"Easy," Hans muttered and shrugged, eyes trying to piece out what the Fujiki Amplifier did. "The stuff is very difficult to manufacture. At the same time, without it, atomic fields are difficult to manipulate without huge machinery and tremendous power production. Unless you can separate and change the color and spin of strong-force leptons, manipulation is impossible.

"The result is that the Directorate channeled all the hyperconductor into grav plates for stations, power units for antimatter reactors, subspace transductors, and all the other amenities of modern civilization. They probably stripped the Patrol ships to the bone for any excess hyperconductor for civilian use."

Susan shook her head. "I guess I don't understand why they didn't put more effort into manufacturing more."

"To get the metamorphosed crystals necessary, you have to mine dead stars. I think you can begin to see the technical problems associated with that!" He chewed his thumb, puzzling at the diagram.

"But I learned that those heavy crystals are shot out of dying stars, too," she reminded. "Supernovas aren't always normal. Odd things happen with that much gravity and energy. Bits get blown out. There are always accidents."

"Yeah, and the loose stuff has been carefully raked out of human space over the last six hundred years," Hans reminded. "Why do you think they formed the Directorate? To ensure that things like hyperconductor and toron were utilized to the greatest efficiency for all concerned."

"Sure," she growled. "And they should have been sending probes out to find more of the stuff. Besides weapons, what else have they cut to a bare minimum? You know, I keep reading that space is an open resource base, but somehow, the Directorate has produced shortages." She gave him a thoughtful look. "Makes you wonder."

Hans lowered his eyes. "No," his voice was hoarse. "I know how they did it. You'll see, too, when you get to Sirius. The Directorate controls society. Deviants are sent in for psych reorientation. From childhood on, the rest are trained to do as they are instructed for the common good. Thoughts about the outside or other worlds are disruptive. The golden rule in the Directorate is that personal ambition and gain mean someone else must suffer for your good fortune. Would you deprive me to have more hyperconductor?"

"A whole species of sheep!" She twisted her face in disgust and disbelief.

"They don't think so. They consider themselves a civilization of 'civilized' men and women. Uh, enlightened. Living without risk, or danger. You don't have guilt if you don't disadvantage anyone.

"Okay, there are always deviants. The range of human behavior has all kinds of odd throwbacks. They take them straight to psych. The ones who won't react to the psych treatment are killed or locked up for the purpose of study. After three hundred years, the science is pretty well developed. How do you think they made your teaching machine?"

"God," Susan whispered. "Our Romanans will murder them on the ground. We'll throw the entire culture into shock. They'll literally believe we're fire-breathing demons straight from hell."

Hans nodded, making a mental connection. "I'll bet that's just the effect the Directorate wants you to make. You're all a living, breathing lesson to the Sirians or anyone else who wants to revolt. 'Look here! These are human animals! Would you be like them? Don't make waves. Follow directions. Trust in the nature of the Directors. If you don't, *you* will end up like this.' "

"So what happened to all you good Patrol soldiers?" Susan asked. "I don't notice too many sheep on *Bullet*. When I watched this ship fight *Brotherhood* and *Victory*, it was frightening. The people around me were scared, too."

Hans gave her a wry grin. "In the first place, we aren't normal. A few who have the mental ability to crack a strict university education, or the ones who are militarily oriented and can be controlled, are sent to the Patrol. Skor and his cronies needed some sort of police, just in case. Within limits, the Patrol allows individuality."

"I've seen a lot of ambition on this ship," she pointed out, eyes on his, waiting.

"We've all been to Atlantis. We fought your Romanans and our people died fighting against the Directorate." His voice went low, eyes far away. "We saw who and what your people were. We . . . learned from you."

Hans swallowed dryly. "Early in the pacification, I . . . I remember looking down a blaster at a man who'd just had his leg blown off." He shook his head, drawing a breath. "Lord, that must have hurt! The guy didn't know a blaster bolt from a rock. Still, he kept dragging himself toward where he'd dropped his rifle. I couldn't do anything but watch.

"Don't you understand? He was dead, Susan! Dead. Just a matter of time. He should have . . . should have stopped and made his peace with himself. He kept pulling himself along with those fingers.

"He got to that rifle and rolled over, I looked into his eyes and he was victorious! He grinned as he shot me! He whooped with victory! Thought he'd killed me, taken me with him." Swallowing again, Hans shook his head as if he still didn't believe it.

"So what happened?" Susan demanded, gripping his shoulder.

Hans forced himself from the memory. "Wheeler blew his head off. I was fine. *Bullet* hit my combat armor. The important thing is that we respected you. We wanted to be like you. We saw something noble, something that made us proud! We can't go back now."

Susan nodded. "We ought to think about getting out of

here. I've recorded all these codes. I can recall it on my own comp unit. Here, check my work. Make sure I didn't botch anything."

Hans reran the copy just to be sure. He noted uneasily that Susan had taken every file on the Brotherhood. A lot of it was security coded, but it all took. There was just enough storage left to run the accessing programs.

"That's it. You've got everything in the ship's banks. I'll bet the Colonel doesn't even know it's here. Wait what's this?" Hans pulled up the program. "What the . . ." He scanned it, excitement growing. "The Brotherhood isn't dead." Hans looked up. "They're out there. Somewhere. Out beyond human space, doing something. Gone for centuries! No wonder the Directorate tried to quash all the information. Wow!"

"We could go find them," Susan breathed.

"What would we find?" Hans felt a cold premonition. "Maybe their power has increased and grown to the point they're like gods. Maybe they would make slaves of humanity."

"And the Directorate didn't?" she snorted.

"Jesus!" His eyes were skimming the readout. "*Bullet* was one of the ships that escorted them from Frontier. The tone isn't hostile at all! Look at this! The Captain of *Bullet* wished them luck and godspeed. The Patrol and the Brotherhood were allies. My god, we've been told they were fiends—enemies of mankind!"

"Be that as it may, in less than an hour you've got to be on duty and I have to be back at my lessons." Susan's enthusiasm deflated. "By the hallowed name of Spider, why am I always so damn tired?"

Hans went about disconnecting the portable units with his usual efficiency. At the same time, his thoughts whirled with the gravity of the things they had discovered locked in *Bullet's* deep banks.

"I'll bet no one's accessed that information in three hundred years," he muttered in awe. "If that got out, it would turn the Directorate on its ear. If Skor was worried about the Romanans getting loose, imagine the impact if the Brotherhood showed up in one of their superships one bright afternoon!"

Susan stuffed the depleted food packets into a sack and carefully picked up the honey bucket. She shot Hans a quick glance, remembering how embarrassed he'd been the first time she'd used it. His bright red flush had grown worse when he'd finally been forced to evacuate himself. Well,

Hans had no more illusions about femininity. Her ties to biological reality were as firm as his.

"All right," Hans whispered as he undid the fastening to the inspection panel. "Let's just hope no one's in the corridor. I'm not sure I can explain all this." He wiped sweaty hands on grimy breeches.

"Wait," Susan whispered quickly. "If we do get caught, they might check my unit. They'd get that Brotherhood stuff right off the bat."

"Let me see," Hans reached for the device and looked it over. He nodded, grinned, and bent over his case. Pulling out a couple of instruments, he undid the back of the unit and frowned. He smiled again as he quickly joined two thin boards together and resealed the cover.

Powering the unit up, he placed the headset on his brow. From his own unit he fed information into Susan's. His smile flashed victory as he handed her the headset. "Think of a code word no one else could ever guess. Don't tell me, I don't want to know."

She nodded and looked at him curiously. "Now what?"

"Turn it off. You've got a complete Directorate history text and two logic games which will access to anyone. All you need to do is access your code word and the rest will show up. If you ever clear the banks completely, you'll have twice the storage."

"And I can't erase it by accident?"

"Not unless you use that code first."

She nodded, turned off the lighting unit, and crawled out the hatch right into disaster.

"Halt!" the sharp cry came. Susan jumped down and turned to see Major Neal Iverson advancing with a drawn blaster.

CHAPTER XIII

"Uh-oh," Hans groaned, seeming to shrink even as he stood rigidly at attention.

Guilt crept up her cheeks.

Iverson approached, eyes flashing. "You'd better have a hell of a good explanation for this, Corporal!"

Fighting to swallow, Han's managed an "uh" that was barely a gasp. With more force he stuttered, "N-No excuse, sir. J-Just showing the lady . . . advanced c-computer repair."

Hans' control was failing. Would he break? She'd heard of the psych interrogation. They'd have it out of him some-how or another that he'd been into security sealed data.

She took a deep breath. "It's all right, Hans. I guess it's no use now."

Hans gave her a desperate look. Iverson saw it and tilted his head, eyes darting from one smudged face to another.

"You can't tell anyone, Major." Susan pleaded desper-ately. "Yellow Legs would swear knife feud. Hans and I . . . well . . . I mean there wasn't any other place. There's no privacy—"

"Susan!" Hans yipped. "No! What are you doing?" His mouth dropped in shocked surprise.

She turned to face him. "Look! All right, so the Major knows. Maybe it won't go any further. If he drags us in for questioning, the story will go all over the ship. Then where would we be? Friday would . . . It would mean knife feud . . . and you know that in spite of Iron Eyes and the war code, Friday would kill you! That would turn the Romanans and marines wild!" She shot her arms out imploringly. "We *have* to trust the Major!"

Hans seemed to have trouble breathing. "I . . . I . . . suppose . . . well . . . uh . . ." He colored bright red. "Oh, Susan, what will people say?"

Iverson's eyes betrayed a deep-felt amusement although he kept his face stiff as cast bronze. "Corporal! To be frank, I'm shocked. To use a computer access for a liaison is a major breach of regulations. What do you think I should do with you?"

"I . . . I don't know, sir," Hans said meekly, shooting a pleading look at Susan.

"Young lady," Iverson turned to Susan. "You are not under my authority; however, I assure you, Major Sarsa will hear about this. Any discipline will be up to her. I suppose, knowing the Major, you're probably the worse off for that. May I see your computer?"

She handed it to him, eyes downcast, adopting the slouched posture she had used before Ramon.

Iverson ran the programs on the unit and a slight twist of a smile curled his lips. He handed the unit back. "You'd better be on your way, young lady." He made a gesture of dismissal.

As Susan shuffled down the hall, she overheard Iverson begin his verbal assault on Hans. "Corporal Yeager, I don't believe this! Of all the horny bastards on this ship, I thought you were a zero! Now *this*—and with *that* number! You know the policy on sex, *mister*! What you do on your own is your business, but when you disappear into a restricted part of the ship for the purpose of. . . ."

The hall cut it off and she allowed herself a sly grin. Rita, she could handle. Friday Garcia Yellow Legs would learn somehow. A challenge, that. What would she do? His male pride would need some massaging and preparation.

Susan shook her head as she sent the lift flying for her deck. In the meantime, poor Hans! Whether he liked it or not, he would never again be an object of ridicule.

She suffered a quick twinge of guilt as she leaned against the side of the lift, the precious comp unit under her arm. Hans had been a gentleman. Not so much in his behavior, but in the deeper quality of honesty, virtue, and nobility. Worse, he'd been horrified, unable to believe she would even consider staining her reputation rather than admit to having tampered with the ship! It made her giggle.

As the lift stopped she paused before stepping out, a sudden frown on her brow. Why did Hans' reaction touch her so? She puzzled at it. Remembering the look of shock on his face, her insides warmed. She'd become almost dreamy when she reached her quarters.

Rita lay asleep on her bunk. Susan set the comp unit on her bed and settled down to think.

She shook her head slowly. She'd taken the only logical option, providing Major Iverson with exactly the story he wanted to hear. His mind had leaped at the plausibility of the situation. Her boyfriend having a reputation as a knife-duelist, how better to avoid a confrontation than diddling Friday's girl where no one would possibly suspect.

Iverson would have the accessway checked for tampering, of course, but Hans had been skillful. They would find no evidence. Susan dropped the honey bucket and food sack into the converter. Postcoital evidence would logically be considered to be in there. Shucking her dirty clothing, she ditched the garment in the converter, too.

She showered quickly and employed a douche in the off chance a suspicious someone might run a med check. On the sly, she borrowed Rita's spermaticide and applied it.

Reclothed, hair pulled back, she walked over and sat down next to Sarsa's bunk.

"Rita?" she called softly. "I need to talk to you. I've done a terrible thing."

Sarsa's eyes opened. She pulled herself to a sitting position. " 'Bout time you got back. Where in hell you been? I'd have thought . . . Hey? You okay?"

Susan dropped her eyes and tried to fake a blush. Maybe she succeeded because the major put a hand on her shoulder. "What is it?" she sounded motherly.

Susan kept her eyes lowered and poured out a story of how she and Hans had wanted to be with each other for so long. How when she got two whole days they grabbed the opportunity. How they were afraid of Friday's reaction. How Iverson had caught them and he might do something terrible to Hans.

Then Susan made her gamble. She looked up at Rita defiantly. "Look, Major, I know it was my fault. At the same time I don't make any excuses. I was a virgin when I came to this ship. A whole new universe is opening up before me. I care a great deal about Friday . . . but I want a chance to explore.

"Major Sarsa," comm announced tonelessly. "Respond please."

Rita slipped her headset on, listening. "I understand. Your information corresponds with what she's told me. I'll handle it." A pause. "Yeah, I don't think it's all that serious either." Another pause. "Well, let me see what else she's got to say. Yeah, thanks for the call, Neal. I'll be getting back to you." She took the headset off, racking it neatly.

"That was Major Iverson. He's wondering whether to gut Hans and hang him out to dry or just slap his tallywacker."

"Tallywacker?"

"Never mind."

"It wasn't his fault," Susan insisted. "I don't know what you'll do to me. I suppose you could break me if you wanted. Ship me back to Atlantis. That would be about the worst. Let Andojar clan marry me off to some . . . some cattle breeder." She met the piercing green eyes with her own defiance.

When Rita didn't say anything, Susan continued. "I knew the risks. Iverson just happened to be passing by when Hans opened the inspection cover. I'm only hoping he'll keep it under his hat. If Friday finds out . . . Well, you know, it will be . . . difficult."

Rita surprised her. "Are you smart enough to keep from getting knocked up?"

Susan shot her an impish grin. "Um, Major, I used yours."

Rita laughed, and stood up to stretch. She chuckled, rubbing her freckled arms. Pulling a cup of coffee from the dispenser, Rita leaned against the bulkhead, a devilish look on her face. "You know, warrior woman, if turning Romanan women loose is going to create a whole army of trouble like you, I'm not sure the Directorate can handle it."

Susan threw up her hands. "Why can't I have the freedom other women do? I feel like I'm under a . . . a microscope! I want to have a little adventure in my life. I want to know men—and I mean that in more ways than one. I feel . . . trapped."

Rita nodded slowly. "Can I ask a question? I guess you don't need to answer it if you don't want." At Susan's nod she continued, "Why Hans? What did you ever see in . . ."

"He's a gentleman," Susan said positively. "He's a sweet, kind man." As an afterthought, she added, "Not only that, he isn't threatening. Um, I, uh. . . ."

Rita nodded her understanding. Then she laughed. "God! I feel like a mother . . . and I'm not much older than you."

"I'd rather have you feel like my friend," Susan kept her voice even with just a hint of underlying challenge. "I made it this far without a mother."

Rita grinned her appreciation. "You know, I've felt real odd about you. Maybe, way down deep, you represent what I never had." She dropped her eyes. "I wanted a family once. Didn't work out. Maybe I saw you as the fulfillment of that need I thought I'd killed so long ago." Hurt hid there.

Susan knew she flushed. "I'm honored by that, Rita. Maybe you've represented too much of an ideal. I thought you were perfect, made of iron, invincible, the acme of efficiency and professionalism. Maybe I haven't seen you as quite human." There was a slightly embarrassed silence. "Can I ask a question?"

Rita smiled and dropped into her bunk, eyes softening and warm—if a bit nervous. "Sure."

Susan marveled at the change, a bit taken aback—leery of the vulnerability she saw in this new Rita Sarsa. "Since we're on the topic of men—what are you going to do about Iron Eyes?"

Rita's eyes widened. "Iron Eyes?"

"You both care about each other a great deal." Susan
didn't let her eyes leave Rita's. The major's brow flinched
as she lost herself in thought.

Finally, Rita shrugged. "I don't know. We don't see each
other as lovers. I don't know what our relationship is. There's
too much pain behind us. We buried our loves long ago.
Spider dealt us a tough hand to play." She ended with her
shoulders hunched. "I never thought about him and myself
in those terms. At least, not consciously."

"If you need to talk about it sometime . . ."

"All right," Rita whispered, eyes shining. "And in the
meantime, don't worry about Major Iverson. I'll handle him—
and Friday, too, if need be. You look pretty worn out. Hans
must have more to his makeup than I thought." Her grin
went wicked. "If he's that good . . . and you get tired of him
. . . maybe I'll look him up."

"He'd like that," Susan lied, knowing Hans would faint.

"If you're late to your studies tomorrow, I guess I can
make an allowance." Rita gave her a ribald wink and turned
out the light.

Susan pulled her clothes off in the dark and settled her
tired body into the bunk. She let herself have one big,
triumphant grin. The immortal Doctor Leeta Dobra couldn't
have done any better than Susan Smith Andojar!

"And look! Not even a scar!" Friday had his pants half down
pointing to the smooth skin of his groin.

"For a little guy, how'd you get such big testicles? Cut
'em off a horse?" Patan Smith grunted.

Friday gave him a hard, squinty look and pulled his pants
up. "You think my balls is big, you ought to see the other
thing when it . . . Aw, no sense in making you guys feel
jealous. You see, that's the advantage of being short. While
the rest of you grew up I kept myself short so other things
could grow out when they—"

"Uh-huh," Toby Garcia Andojar called from his comm.
He looked bored. He took his headset off and rubbed the
red mark it left in his temple. "Forgot how nice life was
without you, Friday." He waved at the comm. "Now, all we
got to do is sit and play holo games with these machines. I
don't know. I'm not sure the way to coup is through any
machine."

"I heard the warriors were grumbling," Friday admitted.
"Heard there was talk things weren't good."

Willy Grita nodded. "I have taken many coups! I had the largest horse herd in my village. I didn't learn from any machine!" he spit the word.

"So, why do we do this?" Sam Yellow Legs wondered. "This isn't war! It's a picture in the mind."

Friday frowned. "I don't think the War Chief would have us do this if there wasn't a reason. Be patient. It will make—"

"Huh!" Grita snorted. "Why should I—"

"You need the machines. We all do," Iron Eyes called from the hatch. They turned to see his thick bulk blocking the door. He stepped in, adding, "You can't see it, but you've all learned from these pictures in your mind."

"How do you know?" Sam Yellow Legs called. "We got three thousand warriors on this ship!"

Iron Eyes swung a monitor chair from the wall and settled himself. "Something called statistics." He raised his hands, indicating his lack of comprehension. "I'm not sure how it works. Something with numbers. But each of you, think back. Remember all the times the simulation killed you? It doesn't happen as often anymore, does it?"

Reesh pulled his own headset off, scowling at the monitor that went dark before him. "Yeah, but then who'd ever heard of a street? Of course, we don't get killed. It's like . . . like a raid, but it isn't. No fire in the blood when you see it all in your head. No sensation, can't feel the gun in your hand. It ain't . . . ain't real!"

"How did you die in the last simulation, Reesh?"

The Warrior's brow lined and his lips pursed. "There was this black loglike thing. Powerlead. I didn't have any place to put my knife, so I stuck it into the log. I'd do that with a pole tree at home!"

Friday cried, "You know how much electricity runs through a powerlead? You crazy Spider son of a—"

"But you won't stick your knife into a powerlead when we get to Sirius, will you?" Iron Eyes suggested amiably.

"Well, now I—"

"But it ain't real!" Sam insisted stubbornly.

Iron Eyes stretched out his legs. "It's not supposed to be. Think, there are two levels to war. One is the way you think. The other is the way you move and act. A good warrior has to think and act. We, the People, the Spiders and Santos, know how to think and act war on World. We're good at it. So it's not the acting we need right now.

Sirius is going to be deadly in ways we can't see yet. For now, we gotta learn to think. We do that—and when the time comes, we'll act right, too."

"These magic things," Sam Yellow Legs indicated the screen, "They real? I mean all them big things flying around in the air? They got stuff like that?"

"And I don't see no horses!" Patan complained. "Can't imagine no people getting around without horses. And there's no plants, no grass, nothing familiar. The holo machines show places where there ain't no dirt! That the way it really is? All them big houses and places?"

Iron Eyes crossed his arms. "That's the way it is. That's why the time on the machines is so important. Think of the dumb things, the times you got mad because you were run over by a cargo truck or got trapped because you didn't know what a grav-tube was. All those mistakes were made in your heads—not on Sirius. Wish we'd had machines like that to teach the kids back home to steal horses!"

"Aw," Willy Grita called out from across the room, "even with the machines, you Spiders couldn't steal the bones out of a horse's skeleton!"

"We'll steal Sirius blind while you're still thinking up jokes to tell!" Toby Andojar called back.

"I'm tired of machines and pictures in my head," Ray Smith growled, arms crossing over his chest. "I don't do this no more."

"That's what I came to see about," Iron Eyes told him. "We've got to use the machines. We've got to learn."

Grita shifted his gaze to Iron Eyes. "So, War Chief, tell me, who scores highest on these machines? Spiders? Or Santos?"

Iron Eyes drew a deep breath, wincing. "It hurts my soul. These statistics show the Santos are better at city war than Spiders."

"Ain't no Santos better than me!" Ray Smith cried. Pandemonium broke loose, Spiders howling while Santos yipped and cheered.

Iron Eyes waved them down. "Do not think it is a won battle! The Santos don't have all the coups in this game! I think, if the Spiders will work a little harder, they can catch up. If the Santos start bragging, patting each other on the back and snickering about the poor Spiders, they will wake up one morning behind."

"How do we know who is ahead?" Felix White Eagle demanded. A ground swell of supporting cries rose.

Iron Eyes waved them down again. "I will post it each morning. You can see then, see how close the competition for coups is. Then, when it is all finished and we have beaten the Sirians, we will count real coups."

The warriors pondered that. With gleaming eyes, they sized each other up, the old rivalries evident.

"Post the scores," old Sam Yellow Legs called. "Let's see who is ahead by the time we get to Sirius!"

"And Ray," Iron Eyes called, getting to his feet. "Your score was the worst this morning."

Ray Smith dropped his eyes, shifting uncomfortably in his seat. "It won't be from now on!"

Iron Eyes nodded, a slight smile on his thin lips. "I thought that would be the way it turned out." Heads bent to the machines, fierce scowls of concentration lining their faces as they fought Sirians in their minds.

Friday saw his chance and followed Iron Eyes out into the corridor. "John?"

The War Chief turned.

"Um, I tried to get a call through to Susan. Comm couldn't locate her." Friday cocked his head. "I mean, as I understand it, comm can find anyone on the ship. I thought she'd be there when I got out of med. Seems like that would have been the least she could have done."

Iron Eyes lifted his shoulders. "Don't ask me about Susan. You heard she got in trouble with one of the Patrol liaisons? Rita told me she told Susan to take two days off." Iron Eyes grinned. "From the look of her last time I saw her, she'd have been smart to go sleep for those two days."

Friday screwed his face into a scowl. "Yeah, that must be it. She'd been hitting it pretty hard as it was. I remember the hours she was keeping."

Iron Eyes clapped him on the shoulder. "Don't worry about her. She has enough trouble in her for two. She'll come give you your share."

Friday chuckled. "Yeah, I suppose so."

"You're feeling okay?" Iron Eyes shook his head. "Still can't believe this Patrol medicine. That wound should have sent you straight to Spider."

"Not even a scar!" Friday cried. "Want to see?" He had his pants halfway down pointing when two female marines rounded the corner, stopping dead in their tracks.

Friday froze in mid-point, face going ashen.

The women stared, wide-eyed and giggling. "Bragging?" one asked casually as they passed.

Friday gulped and yanked at his pants, the soft material ripping loudly in the process.

Iron Eyes bit his tongue to keep a straight face and looked down to where Friday glowed sunrise red, fists knotted in torn fabric. "On second thought, you don't need Susan. You do fine on your own."

Skor Robinson shifted in the eternal blue haze. *Directors, you have all reviewed Ngen Van Chow's latest broadcast. Again, damage is done. The extent of his influence on the people cannot be measured at this time. Nevertheless, we must accept that traditional methods of social control can no longer be expected to have any appreciable effect.*

Roque interjected, *There have been riots at university! Looting and murder have occurred on Bazaar. The Gi-net complex on Saggitarius III has been sabotaged. People have been killed in social protest! KILLED! Not for three hundred years have riots occurred in public places! Social structure has developed a friable edge. We are seeing order crumble!*

Navtov sent, *Indeed, Director, I am in total agreement. The Romanan Prophet warned of this. Passion, he called it. Yes, that is what we are seeing. Somehow Ngen is touching this atavistic passion latent in the species. That an emotional plea can defy rational thought is beyond comprehension. How do the masses expect freedom without Direction? I support my point with the following information.*

Skor considered the reams of data Natvov sent him, shunting most of it back. *Assistant Director Navtov, you do not need to convince me. I am not the one instigating the current social ferment. Indeed, you need to convince the billions of people out there who are beginning to find a heroic aspect to this Van Chow's character!*

And in the pirate, Ree, and his filthy Romanan animals, Navtov reminded. *The people are too engrossed by the Dobra broadcast. They dwell on it, dream of it, almost worship the image they have of these illiterate savages.*

Roque's input consisted of: *Let us begin a campaign of our own. I shall commence responding to Ngen Van Chow's charges, providing incontrovertible proof that Ngen's system would necessarily imply disorder and social turbulence.*

Skor considered the logical framework of the argument Roque began to flesh out through the system, gigabytes of data unfolding in waves of mathematical and algebraic sequence. How could a rational person argue with that?

At the same time, he couldn't help but wonder at Chester Armijo Garcia's curious preoccupation with the soul. Did he, Skor Robinson—the most powerful figure in the Directorate—truly have a soul? How would mountains of data soothe humans seeking a soul? Just what was a soul? Skor fretted, trying to put all of his mind to work on the problem, frustrated by the result.

Navtov was saying, *Very good, Assistant Director Roque! I believe with the dissemination of your political proofs, humanity shall regain its sanity. How could anyone argue in the face of such massive evidence? Perhaps, Assistant Director, you have saved us all!*

Yes, perhaps he had after all. What good could an ancient concept like a soul be in a modern world? Having excoriated religion from the social body, there could only be pain in returning to the errors of the past. Soul? Indeed! A fantasy of the unthinking masses.

As Director, Skor input, *I congratulate you on your program of proper propaganda. By all means, send it out at once. Let us see what fruit your data bears. Indeed, humanity may owe you an enormous debt.*

For a moment, Skor thought about consulting the Romanan Prophet, but then, the results of Roque's political thesis were self-evident, incontrovertible. No one could deny Roque's logical countering of Ngen's emotional claims. Now that the Sirian revolt could be discredited, all that remained was to disarm the pirate, Damen Ree, and his hooligan warship. Of course, the Romanans could be dealt with independently as long as *Bullet* had been neutralized first.

The comm called for attention. Susan shunted her program to the side and accepted the call, seeing Hans' face form on the monitor.

"You court-martialed? Or just blacklisted as a ravisher of young Romanan women?" she greeted, winking saucily.

Hans swallowed hard. "Got double duty. Somehow, I didn't get busted." His eyes darted back and forth and his mouth worked. "Listen, about what we . . . uh, you know, discussed in such detail. I think I ought to take it to the Colonel. It might be important. You know, about the Fujiki thing?"

Susan frowned. "What about the security seal?"

Hans rolled his eyes. "Yeah, that's the only snag. You know what they'd do to a lowly corporal who showed up with a classified secret?" He clamped his eyes shut. "But we don't know enough! I mean, what if the Sirians have that blaster? It might mean the difference between life and death for a lot of people. Look, I helped glue this bucket of air back together after last time. I know what shape the hull is in."

"Then tell them!" Susan gasped.

"But it's security sealed!" Hans cried. "I mean, I can't just walk up and say, oh, by the way, when you thought I was screwing Susan in the computer access, we were really involved in lifting State secrets out of top secret files! Sure, Susan. I like my body like it is—not all exploded like it will be when Ree throws me out the lock for high treason!"

"Then don't tell them."

"But . . . but . . . it could be important!" Hans cried out, anguished.

"Well . . ." Susan leaned forward, chewing on her thumb. "Couldn't . . . couldn't you leave a note somewhere? You know . . . like where it would be found by Iverson . . . or Ree . . . or someone?"

Hans looked at her glumly. "Uh, Susan, you might be greased neutrinos when it comes to lying your way out of a tight fix, but when it comes to how to deal with a technological problem, you'd hang yourself within minutes."

"Hans, I'm not a . . . a . . ."

"Yes, you are." He gave her a solicitous look. "Say the information appears as an anonymous entry to Ree's comm. He sees what's involved and calls Tony on the carpet, demanding where the information could have come from. Anthony jumps to the Colonel's tune, finds the lost Brotherhood files hidden away deep in the guts of the system, right?"

"Right." Susan winced.

"Uh-huh, and the next question is who has accessed the system? The comm log will show that no one used a terminal to gain access. So, what's left?" Hans' grin became a rictus. "Someone plugged an unauthorized terminal into the main housing. Now, who do you think the last unauthorized people to have access to the—"

"I see the problem." She rubbed her brow. "So, if you tell, we're caught. Treason, huh? That's a word I could have gone a long time without learning."

Hans stared miserably into the comm. "I've got to get back to work. I just wanted to talk to you."

Susan searched her mind frantically. "Don't do anything yet. Just sit on it for a bit. Let's see what happens. Rita seems to think that with six Patrol ships, we'll come out of the jump and blast the Sirians into plasma without any muss or fuss. If we do, the problem is solved."

Hans reluctantly nodded his agreement. "All right. I'll keep mum for the time being. I don't feel good about—"

"Hans?" she called softly.

"Huh?"

"Thank you. Just for being you, I mean. You're pretty special."

His mouth opened. "You mean . . . mean that?"

She nodded. "Yes, I do. You're, well, I don't know what I'd do without you. I need your . . . Well, you know. You're my best friend."

She could see him perk up, eyes brightening. "You know, you're about the best thing to—"

"*Corporal Yeager!*" someone shouted in the background. "What the hell do you think you're—" Hans disappeared in a dead connection. Susan giggled softly to herself, thinking.

Ngen Van Chow laughed and slapped his thigh. "Oh, this is rich!"

Giorj Hambrei peered up from the guts of the fire control computer he was modifying. Originally, it had supervised mining lasers; now—with new programming and faster responses—it would deliver death to the Patrol. "Rich, First Citizen?"

The smile plastered on Ngen's wide face seemed incongruous with the somber brooding master of Sirius Giorj had grown accustomed to. Ngen's black hair contrasted with the white of the bridge. Such a curious man, Giorj thought yet again.

"Rich indeed, Engineer!" Ngen hooted. "The Directorate responds! Oh, and how they did it! They have been broadcasting nonstop now for minutes on end. Go. Look for yourself!" Ngen waved a limp hand toward the comm.

Giorj carefully set the board he worked on to the side and stood, walking over to the comm, placing a headset on his brow. The amount of information pouring into the computer proved truly staggering. Even more outrageous, the information continued to stream in, and continued, and continued.

"There!" Ngen cried, clapping his hands. "They have just overloaded the ship's storage capacity!"

Giorj lifted the headset from his brow and paused, thoughtfully watching the comm monitor. "Don't they realize that no one could assimilate all that?"

Ngen hissed his amusement. "Of course not! Giorj, they have no comprehension of . . . of reality! They think to rebut our broadcasts with hard data? They only dig their graves deeper. How would you respond to this? Hmm?" Ngen stopped in mid-sentence. "Oh, never mind. You're not all human either."

The First Citizen dismissed Giorj from his mind and bent over the comm, placing a call to Pika Vitr.

Not all human? The thought continued to drift through Giorj's mind as he returned to the fire control computer, mechanically picking up the board and resuming his duties. *Not all human?* Patiently he continued his work, curious as to why Ngen's flippant comment hurt him so.

Behind him, Ngen crowed, ". . . so abstract and convoluted, no one could follow it! The average man will find it meaningless. What? Of course! Don't you see? We're hurting them! If we weren't stimulating all of human space, they wouldn't be responding! No, we must increase our broadcast output. Sting them harder, stir the pot to a full boil. They couldn't have handed us a better means either! I'll turn this against them. Just wait . . ."

Giorj bit his thin gray lip, wondering about his mother on the planet below. Did Ngen consider her a human being? Did he consider anyone else human?

He sighed, thankful for the cool, elegant simplicity of his machines.

CHAPTER XIV

"Cut! Thrust! Parry! Duck!" Sarsa shouted rapid-fire. Susan fought for air and snapped her head to whip the sweat from her brow before it dripped, stinging, into her eyes.

"I'll die of old age before you knife me," Rita growled,

settling herself into a fighting stance again. "Watch your grip on that knife!"

Susan barely had time to regrip the knife as Rita jumped, thrusting in a brutal, low, disemboweling move. Susan blocked it, sprang back and countered with a savage cut to the head. Rita ducked under it, tucked, and rolled, kicking the knife from Susan's hand.

Unarmed, she faced Rita, knife hand numb and tingling. Rita settled into her stance, advancing and circling. Her hand flashed like a streak. Susan ducked, twisted, and chopped down with a doubled elbow into Sarsa's ribs.

The Major grunted, stunned, as the air whooshed from her body. Susan jacked her body sideways in the air, curling an arm around Rita's shoulder and slamming her to the mat. As Sarsa tried to roll away, Susan pinned her neck with a knee.

"How's that?" Susan wheezed, frantically sucking breath into her oxygen-starved body.

"Check . . . my right . . . hand," Rita managed before she broke into a fit of coughing.

Susan glanced down and froze, the knife tip pressed firmly against the body armor at her side, just under the ribs. Without the armor, the keen point would have been through her liver, lower right lung lobe, and into her heart.

Nodding in defeat, she sighed and stood, skin shimmering with sweat, breasts heaving as she tried to catch her breath. Rita remained on the mat, hacking and trying to breathe.

"You all right?" Susan asked, extending a hand down.

Rita nodded and took the hand, rolling to her feet as Susan pulled. Her face strained into a mask of pain. "You know, kid," Rita groaned, leaning on the younger woman, "the body armor takes a lot of the energy out of the blow. If we'd been going for real, you'd a had me with that rib shot."

"I thought I lost," Susan said through gasps, looking her confusion at Rita.

"Ouch," Rita's face pinched as she stretched. "I'm not as young as I used to be. God, I hurt. No, you'd have had me. I made a mistake. Thought you were more clumsy than you really are."

"I guess the sleep synch helped." Susan reached down and picked up her knife. She slipped the heavy blade into her belt. "Go again?" she forced herself to ask, body hanging limp as she tried to summon the energy.

"Not with this lady," Rita muttered, her expression an agony of hurt and exhaustion. "I haven't had a workout like that since . . . since before *Bullet* was called to Atlantis. I'm out of shape."

"Thank God!" Susan grunted in agreement. Shaking her tingling hand, she began to strip the battle armor off her body. The shower seemed pure heaven, but she started at the sight of the red bruise on Rita's side.

"Maybe you'd better get down to med."

Rita coughed again and shook her head. "I'll be fine, squirt. Didn't know you had that much punch locked away."

"I was desperate, I didn't want to . . . to lose again," Susan cried, experiencing guilt as the bluing patch held her attention.

"That's how you win, kid." Rita nodded, wincing. "Desperation brings success. Takes risks to win. You've got to be audacious; if not, you're a sheep."

"I'm taking you to med," Susan decided, chewing the insides of her cheeks.

"Like hell!"

"You're going. If not by force then as . . . as a personal favor to me. I'm not going to be able to study unless I know you won't keel over in a meeting." Susan dried off and put both hands on Rita's shoulders, looking deeply into her eyes.

"All right," Rita cried helplessly, raising an arm in defeat. "Anything to get you off my back!"

They almost didn't make it. Rita started out briskly, muttering under her breath; she faded quickly. By the time they made the hospital, Rita had bent double, clutching her middle and shuffling.

The first tinges of panic nibbled at Susan as the med techs grabbed Rita out of her arms and hustled her into one of the huge machines. Rita looked over from where her head poked out and winked.

Susan took a deep breath and began pacing. On impulse, she called Iron Eyes. "I'm with Rita down at the hospital—" She stared into a blank set as he left at a run.

Worried, she took a moment to reassess. Life had settled back into routine after the incident with Hans. Susan attacked her studies with a passion and she chipped away at the Brotherhood secret codes in her spare time. At night, her body was hooked to the sleepsynch which taught her combat, her mind reacting in a dream state while her muscles responded in twitches, teaching the neural circuits.

Her training engrossed her twenty-four hours a day with compressed periods of computer-controlled deep sleep. The long strings of facts the teaching machines had planted in her brain began to form patterns now. At times she would have a brilliant insight that made sense of meaningless trivia.

Six months of constant training had drained her. She'd learned so much and comprehended so little! She remembered Maria Yellow Legs Andojar and the hopeless nature of her existence; worse now that her husband was dead: Susan's responsibility.

"But what have I lost?" she whispered to herself. "How much of me is still me?" She couldn't shake Hans' description of how the machine overlaid synaptic patterns in her head. Curiously empty, she fingered the scar on her hand, trying to remember, finding nothing.

"What happened?" Iron Eyes' terse voice shattered her thoughts.

"I think I broke Rita's ribs during knife practice."

"You?" he breathed incredulously. "Are you sure she wasn't hurt before?"

Susan shook her head, a flash of anger competing with concern. She opened her mouth to vent her feelings but clamped her lips tightly. Couldn't he ever take her seriously? Damn him! Sexist bastard. What did Rita see in him anyway? How in hell had he ever gotten along with Doctor Dobra?

Iron Eyes searched until he could see Rita's icy stare. His lips twisted suddenly into a sheepish grin and before Susan's eyes, Iron Eyes wilted.

"You all right?" he called out softly, afraid to get in the way of the techs.

Rita's eyebrows raised helplessly, expressing humor at her deplorable situation.

"What happened, Susan?" Iron Eyes asked, voice gentle. "Didn't you use precautions?"

The hollow vulnerability awed her. Could *this* be the same Iron Eyes?

"I just couldn't stand to lose again, John," She used his first name on impulse. "She'd kicked the knife away and I had to get her before she rubbed my nose in it one more

time. There was nothing left to lose so I followed an instinct
and hit . . ."

"Nothing left to lose," he mused, lost in his own thoughts.
"I'd forgotten that. I once had nothing left to lose. Or so I
thought. Odd, how you can think that until . . . well, you
lose something you didn't know you had."

"Leeta?" Susan asked cautiously. "And now you're worried about Rita?"

Hard eyes looked at her, lips firmly pinched.

"Oh, come on," Susan snapped. "Rita is fine. I didn't hit
her *that* hard. If the meds can fix blaster burns, and damage
like Friday inflicted on Horsecapture, a simple internal rup-
ture will be a piece of cake. This isn't World." She met his
anger head-on. "How do you think I feel? I did it to her. *I
love her too, you know!*"

A faint spark glimmered behind his black eyes. Anything
he was about to say sidetracked as a med approached.

The woman nodded evenly. "She'll be fine. Lost a little
blood from a puncture to her liver. Broke two ribs—a
fragment of which caused the problem. The bleeding is
stopped, and we've got electro-stim on the ribs and trauma-
tized tissue. She'll be out of here in twenty hours."

"We're to engage the Sirians in thirty," Iron Eyes reminded. "Will she be ready for that?" Tension lurked in his
voice. Could that be a tremble in his hand?

"Probably," the med said with a nod. "We could release
her in fifteen hours." He waved around the unit, "As you
can see, there's not much else to do here. Further, if she
were a junior grade officer, we would; but the Major is
slated for combat and landing on the planet. As a result,
we'd prefer to send her out completely fit. She can attend to
briefings and meetings through a comm link from here."

"Thank God," Susan whispered to herself. She looked
over to where Rita now slept—the med unit having taken
charge of her body. Exhausted, Susan plodded back to her
quarters and buried herself in the endless studies.

The voice fit into her dreams. She was waiting for Hans to
build a Fujiki device on the blaster. Susan kept watch as
Hans wrapped a thick cable around the top of the blaster.

"Susan?" Friday's voice called.

"He can't find us here!" she cried, seeing Hans' frightened eyes.

"Susan Smith Andojar? It's Friday. Open up!" An emotional note lay deep in the base voice.

"Run!" she urged Hans. He simply shrugged and returned to winding his cable around the blaster.

Susan turned and started awake. Blinking, she shook her head and sat up. She had elected to forgo sleep stim that night. A mistake?

"Susan, this is your last chance. If you don't want to talk to me, *say so!*" Friday's voice thundered from outside the door.

"*Friday!* Wait! I was asleep!" she pleaded, grabbing her clothing from the floor. Bad practice on a warship; the luxury of a night without Rita had been too tempting.

She fought her way into the uniform and ran for the door, pulling her hair back, rubbing her eyes. She palmed the door and stepped back as Friday walked in, face like a mask.

Susan felt herself shiver with premonition. "What's wrong? Oh, my God! *Not Rita!*" she cried suddenly. "She's all right, isn't she?"

"She's fine," Friday said firmly. "I came to talk to you."

"What is it?" But she knew. Friday looked ready for battle, broad shoulders drawn back, eyes hard. His whole body was tensed, muscles rippled along his short torso.

"I have heard of Hans Yeager. It is said that you and he were together in an air duct for two days. Is this so?" His voice was steel.

On the verge of breaking out in shivers, she fought the need to escape from his accusing eyes.

To gain time, she turned away and pressed for a cup of coffee. "You want any?" she asked wearily.

"No."

"I suppose it wouldn't do me any good to plead innocence." She had her control back when she turned to meet his hot gaze.

"No." His expression didn't change although he somehow seemed to withdraw. "I should kill him . . . and maybe you."

"Why?" she demanded, setting the coffee down and moving closer to look into his fiery eyes. "I'm *not* your wife. We had no agreements. Not only that, Hans and I did nothing wrong! If you hurt him, Friday Garcia Yellow Legs, I'll . . . I'll kill you!"

The corners of his mouth twitched. He spun on his heels to leave, something violent gleaming in his eyes.

"Wait!" she ordered. He barely hesitated. "I don't need this from you. I love you, Friday. You're one of my best friends. Hans is one of my best friends! I need you to come back, sit down, and let me talk to you. I . . . just . . ."

He stopped, hand hovering over the door plate. "Why, warrior? What have we to say to each other?"

She picked up the coffee and settled herself into her bunk. "I earned the right to speak. You took a chance on me when my honor was at question. Perhaps it is at question again. When I was desperate, you were there. I want to tell you who I have become . . . and why."

"Do I care who you—"

"I think you're more than a simple man. I think you're a very smart, perceptive man. Are you strong enough to cover your emotions with logic and hear me out?" She watched him through half-lidded eyes.

Friday walked to the dispenser, back to her, fingers fumbling with a cup. An undisciplined part of her brain wondered if that was why the Patrol put the things in cabins in the first place.

"I will listen," he said as he came back with a cup of coffee. Like a caged lion, he eased into the chair, coffee unnoticed in his hand, flintlike eyes on hers.

She nodded, pleased with that much cooperation. "You can believe it or not, but Hans and I did not make love. It wouldn't be any of your business if we did . . . just like our relationship is none of Hans'."

One corner of his mouth turned up. A neutral expression. He said nothing.

"Beyond that, I'm not the same girl who stared with dreamy eyes at the sky back on World. So much has changed in my life, Friday . . . just like yours has. All of us will change. We can't help it. Hans is helping me grow . . . like you did."

"Then let him help you," Friday grunted. "I'm sorry I couldn't have helped you more. Maybe you would have stayed with me. Maybe my heart would have been big enough for . . ."

Susan closed her eyes and drew a deep breath, hearing the pain in his voice. "It is, Friday. Your heart is just *fine*. I don't want you to leave my life. At the same time . . . I'm not ready to be your wife. Maybe I was wrong that day I loved you. But it . . . it felt right and I wouldn't trade that afternoon for—"

"Do you know that I love you?" Friday asked, voice brittle. *"I would marry you!"* He clenched a fist.

"And you'd make a fine husband!" She heard the sincerity: it scared her. "I think of you as a special man in a lot of ways . . . but I'm not ready to marry. Perhaps when I am, you won't want me. I can't marry you and . . . and then demand my own rights. It would place too much strain on our relationship. . . ." she ended in a whisper.

"You think I could hate you?" he asked, genuinely puzzled.

"If I were your wife . . . yes." She nodded soberly, realizing how far beyond him her education had taken her. Nevertheless, he gave her direction and he had a quality she craved. He understood life with the undiluted reality of the warrior who looked out at a hard, brutal world without pretension.

He stood, sipping at his coffee, trying to do something with the nervous energy bundled in his body.

"Married, you would want to care for me. You would want me to fit into the traditional mold of a woman of the People. How would you feel if you wanted a child immediately and I didn't? What if I wanted to go to Arcturus and you wanted to go back to World? Suppose I'm promoted—become an officer in the Patrol—and I want to stay on this ship? Would you stay with me?"

His grin spread. "You know, you fascinate me, Susan. I—I hate you for it . . . but you draw me to you like a fly to blood."

His eyes were on her, measuring, questioning. "You're a poor excuse for a good humble woman. At the same time, your body makes mine ache. I dream of you through the night. I see your face before me during training. Perhaps it is Spider dangling my happiness from a thread of his web to tease me. Perhaps if I knew I could have you for my obedient wife, I'd tire of you . . . throw you out. Why do you torment me this way?" He raised his hands and let them fall.

She laughed, feeling the subtle change in Friday's manner. "I don't torment you, Friday Yellow Legs. It's all in your mind. I think you're a . . . a dreamer. The shortest man among the People, you have to reach higher than any of the others. I think you wish for greater heights than anyone. Unless you pursue a dream you are unhappy."

"Do you like being thought of as a dream?" he asked, a half smile on his lips.

"I do," she agreed, face lighting. "It means I'm desirable and exotic. So long as I remain mysterious . . . above your reach . . . you'll continue to want me."

"Call me fool," he noted too lightly, voice picking up a trace of banter. She'd plucked a nerve—though he might not even recognize his unease. It attracted her, making her remember that afternoon he had taken her. An internal heat mounted.

"Why do you play a buffoon, Friday? You always play for fun. Your pranks are legendary. You're driven to joke— even when you do it at risk of your life. Yet I remember the knife feud. I was the difference. You fought for me."

"I fought for honor," he muttered. "Partly for yours . . . partly for mine." Jumpy again, he paced the narrow quarters, coffee forgotten in his hand. "Say you're right. Say I reach for stars when my feet are in the mud. Isn't that a noble goal? A better way . . ."

"I wouldn't love you if you weren't such a dreamer, Friday. You could have rescued me from an army of Ramons and I would owe you . . . but not love you. Don't look at me like that! I *do* love you, Friday. For who you are . . . and what you dream. You're the future of the People. You're dream and reality . . . all mixed into one." She watched him pensively, lips pursed.

"So you love me, and won't pledge your life to mine?" He raised an eyebrow, skeptical.

"I love you so much . . . I wouldn't *dare* marry you." Her voice made it clear. "That isn't a puzzle. No, I see what you're thinking. I'd rather be your friend in freedom than your enemy in marriage. You'd want to reach beyond me . . . and I beyond you. Spider has taught us to want and desire. I couldn't let you beat me, Friday."

His eyes flashed appreciation. "Then how do I live with my desire for you? Huh? How do I deal with this jealousy for a man you say you also love? How could I live if he was to marry you? Perhaps I should go ahead and kill him? Get him out of—"

"I won't marry him! By Spider, Yellow Legs! Hans is a very special man . . . but not one I could marry." She frowned as she thought. "Like you, he's considered a joker, a fool. Like you, he's changed because of me. If you could see beyond your disjointed male nose, you'd like him. Like you, he is very efficient at what he does. Unlike you, he doesn't have that warrior streak to bear him up under serious stress. He's never been tried."

"I won't kill him," Friday decided dryly. "If you like him and he makes you happy, keep him. Spider plays me for a fool—like always. I am a cuckold without right. Wait a minute! Did I *really* just tell the woman I love to love another man?" He shook his head. "For anyone but you, I would split him from brisket to . . ."

She watched his lean body as it moved—a trim athletic gracefulness. She stood, sighing, and walked over to him.

"Thank you," she whispered, putting her arms around his neck. She kissed him lightly on the lips. His arms slipped around her waist. The fire built.

"He might have been tougher than Horsecapture," Friday decided. "I'm a coward at heart."

She shuddered as his muscular body pressed against her. Her tender breasts flattened against his chest. His arms made her secure. She could feel him harden, stirring her.

"I've missed you," she whispered. "I've dreamed of you."

"Dreamed how?" A teasing smile danced on his lips.

"I'll show you," she whispered. She kissed him passionately on the mouth, pulling him close and taking a shuddering breath.

His body trembled as he lifted her from the floor and settled her on the bunk. His fingers were frantic as he pulled at her clothing, tasting her on his tongue, letting his frantic need drive him.

She gasped with pleasure as she opened herself to him.

"I love you," he whispered fiercely.

Susan drew a quick breath, a fleeting memory of Hans formed, and she suffered a curious twinge. Then Friday's demanding body became her reality.

Leona Magill, hollowed-eyed, gasped weakly for air as Ngen Van Chow stood and yawned mightily, stretching his arms and shoulders. She looked up at him woodenly. Didn't he ever tire?

"Ah, my ice queen, you see, I no longer need the pysch to make you respond. Now your body has learned. I need only caress you." He ran a finger down her leg, causing her to tremble.

Her traitorous body had once again responded. Was there nothing she could do? She turned her head away.

She closed her eyes, disgusted with herself—and him. If

only she could end it. A single tear welled at the corner of her eye and staggered its way down her cheek, tracing laterally along the crow's-feet her tightly clamped eyelids formed.

She'd tried. Nothing lethal remained in the room. No length of cloth or wire to hang herself with. No depth of water in which she could place her nostrils. Thick padding lined every wall. The power outlets were impossible to access. She found nothing sharp enough to cut or pierce her body. She'd tried starvation. Then he'd forced a drug down her resisting throat which made her eat—forcing her to hate herself that much more.

"Ah, delightful, dear Leona." He stepped into the shower and rinsed off. "You are indeed a passionate young thing. See how well I keep my promises? I need but run my finger across your skin and your body cries for me.

"I'd rather be a street whore," she hissed.

"See! The fear is gone, my flower. I knew it would be so. Life isn't meant for fear. It's for pleasure, sweet one. I revel as I hold your precious body, knowing that your keen mind is helpless to resist the sensations I create."

"I'd kill you," she gasped through gritted teeth.

He laughed lightly. "Oh, my gay rose, that makes you so much more fulfilling." He paused. "I know it must grieve you, but I have to leave you for a while, sweet one. The Patrol is coming. They will be within range in a couple of hours."

"If there is justice in the universe, I pray . . . I pray they blast you and this hell-gotten ship into infinity!" she rasped, fearing to look at him. Knowing she would see his well-muscled body gleaming in the light. Oh, yes, he'd planned this room perfectly.

"Is that any way to talk to a man who leaves you yearning for his return? Where would you ever find my equal, dear luscious fruit?" his voice chided her intimately.

"In hell!"

"There," he said with concern. She winced as she felt his body sink down next to her. "I try so hard for you, Leona." His hand settled on her hip and she shivered, fighting to keep her body still, fighting to pull away from him—and managing. She cramped against the wall till there was no more retreating.

"Let me refresh your innocent mind," he murmured, leaning across the bed. His fingertips barely touched her flesh as they glided down her spine. "You want me again, don't you, angel of love?" The gentle whisper prodded her with its sensuous tones.

"No!" She shook her head vigorously. "*Oh, God, no!*" But her body began to respond. Her breasts became tender, her nipples tightened erect. This time she had no excuse; the machine had taught her too well. Stimulus-response, the old psychological nightmare in new guise no matter how her frightened brain howled in silent anguish.

"Ah, I see. You do wish me to stay. Your body betrays what your mind would mislead me to believe." He slowly withdrew. "You almost tempt me again."

She shuddered, fighting with herself, hating herself more with every second. "Leave," she muttered, voice flat. "Just go."

He asked solicitously, "Dear one? I detect a note of discord in your velvet voice." He sounded so genuinely distressed.

She turned to look at his fine features. "You are foul, Ngen. I doubt that in all of human history there has been a man so depraved as you. You're twisted, sick. The filthiest thing on two feet!"

His eyes expressed a slight pain. "Have I given you filth, dear one? What do you desire that I have not given you?"

She breathed, "Death."

He chuckled happily. "Death, flower? My, I have no intention of neglecting you to that point. On the contrary, I would have more time with you, if anything."

Leona looked up in horror and saw the truth in his eyes. "Oh, God!" She felt faint.

"Magnificent!" he cried gleefully. "You find so much joy from my desire that you swoon?"

She shook her head, slowly. This man had destroyed her, shattered her, beaten her into total submission.

Frantically, she gathered herself and leaped at him, scratching, biting, striking out and kicking, seeking desperately to harm him, to mar his smirking abomination of a face.

Ngen caught her deftly, smoothly circling her wrists in his strong hands. He ducked his head under hers and bit the side of her neck until she gasped in pain, straining his body against hers.

Savagely, he bent her back over the bed, crashing his body down on top of hers. "Oh, yes!" he gasped, mouth seeking hers, hands trapping her under him. "Oh, indeed, yes. My magnificent Leona, this is superb!"

"Bastard animal!" she screamed, fear growing and vying with hatred and self-loathing. *"Damn you to hell, bastard!"*

He ripped the clothes from his body and she cried as she felt him, hot against her flesh. She screamed again, half-insane with shame and disgust as he took her savagely.

He left her limp, wallowing in her own mental filth. She screamed to deaf walls, drowning in self-disgust. More than dead, less than alive, Leona Magill gasped out her last despair. Her final will to resist crumbled, draining away from the numb shell of her mind.

A human had died.

Ngen emerged from his retreat euphoric. Energetic, charged, ready to meet the threat of the Patrol ships entering Sirian space, he walked with new spirit. That last bout with Leona had cleared his mind, providing him with an unclouded optimism.

He cocked his head and frowned. Why did such vigorous activity make him feel so refreshed and at ease when within hours he would face defeat? Leona had given him back his perspective. He could anticipate the fight now. He mastered his impatience, waiting for the Patrol ships to come to him.

He swung onto the bridge and dropped eagerly into his control chair. Giorj Hambrei looked up from the comm and shot him a curious, evaluative stare. "We have less than two hours to maximum range, First Citizen. Do you anticipate a change in our status?"

Ngen looked around the bridge. There were five other officers present—the cream of Sirius' spacefarers. His smile went stiff for Giorj. The engineer had delicately given him a way out. They could still run, avoid the danger, the potential for disaster.

Face radiant, he shook his head in a definite no. "We'll take them," Ngen grinned. "We are destiny, gentlemen. The Directorate must be shown that men and freedom cannot be stopped. I have faith in you . . . and the principles of our cause."

"You look most confident, First Citizen," Giorj observed, pale eyes on Ngen, gray face expressionless.

Yes, Giorj, I am well aware you have the yacht stocked and ready to go. Good man. Indeed, you have done marvels with the craft. All I need is a small head start. Your handi-work did the rest. But I shall win today. I can feel it!

"Let us say that I have had a good omen, gentlemen. There is victory in the very air! I have faith." He ended with a satisfied smile. Giorj nodded, a curious reservation in his flat eyes.

Too bad about Giorj. The man had been sterilized, rendered impotent by a radiation accident years ago while working on Ngen's smuggling craft.

Well, perhaps he would give Leona to Giorj—a symbolic gift—when she became too broken to be amusing. It would put him in his place despite his one weakness: an aging mother who depended on full med to live.

"I place more faith in Brotherhood technology than in omen, First Citizen." Giorj didn't turn from his instruments. "Our weapons and shielding . . ."

Ngen checked the monitors. "Why Giorj, there are only six of them! I believe we shall do fine. The best projections I can make show us destroying them all. The worst case scenarios show us losing *Dastar* or *Helk*, but not both. Correct?"

"That is what the computers predict, First Citizen," Giorj said without enthusiasm. "Do you have any additional instructions for the planetary defense stations? They can commence AT destruction—"

"No! Let them land the Romanans—the ATs with drawings on the side. Make sure the gunners know those are to be let through. We shall destroy them on the ground." Ngen steepled his fingers.

"Very well, sir." Giorj's fingers flew over the comm panel. Brow furrowed, he contacted the satellites through the headset.

Leona had worried about the Romanans. Ngen amused himself over that. Everything about Leona amused him—down to the last look he'd seen in her dull eyes. Victory! He'd broken her completely—shattered her will and identity. A bursting warmth spread through his chest. As he had broken her, so would he break the Patrol—then the Directorate seat of Arcturus.

Arcturus, the ring of stations circling the red star was symbolic in more ways than one. Since the days of the Soviet, this had been the seat of power. Never had a single man ruled from Arcturus. *Not until Ngen Van Chow!* he added to himself.

Leona provided but a trifling victory. There would be others—greater than Leona—who had farther to fall. Too bad there were no female Directors at present.

He frowned. What would one of them be like. They had no conception of sex. Could an expert on the human body, like Ngen, build a desire within a Director?

How far could he take mankind? What glories awaited his engineers when they broke into those sealed Brotherhood data banks on Frontier? The potential excited him physically. He would push back the frontiers of human knowledge. He would thrust the colonies of mankind deeper into the unknown. A torch, he would bring light to the benighted masses of humanity. The age of darkness passed away before them. Revitalization had arrived—and he, Ngen, would be the impetus. As he drew vitality from those he broke, so would humanity draw from him!

"The Patrol ships are test firing their guns, First Citizen," Giorj called.

"Excellent!" Ngen, narrowed his eyes. "Message to fleet, Engineer. Test weapons at will. Gunnery officer, I want a three second burst from each gun."

"Weapons fired, sir." The gunnery officer didn't take his eyes from the board.

"That ought to give them a big surprise," Ngen remarked. "They'll be reading the spectrographs and wondering. I hope the news travels fast. I do, indeed. Tonight, gentlemen, we shall land at Sirius space port. We shall march our prisoners to the auditorium and we shall execute the Patrol leaders who do not swear fealty to me."

"And the Romanans!" Ngen hooted, "Perhaps we shall reinstitute the ancient tradition of gladiatorial games! It may take a couple of days to round them all up, but we shall have an abundance of them."

"And then?" Giorj looked up.

"And then," Ngen smiled, relishing a fleeting thought of Leona's weeping, limp body on the bed. "And then I break Arcturus and we execute the Directors. From there, gentlemen, we shall sweep out over all of known space until we have made every many, woman, and child citizens of our society!"

Idly he wondered if there would be any spirited women among the Patrol captives. After all, Leona would have to be replaced soon.

CHAPTER XV

Susan waited patiently, fingers interlaced. She'd managed to tie into *Bullet's* comm problem-solving capabilities and let the system work on those horribly frustrating Brotherhood codes. While the ship's computers poked and pried, she reviewed the historical data from an unrestricted file.

The Brotherhood itself had a fascinating history. The actual roots of the organization were buried in antiquity, dating to the earliest of Earth's cultures. After constant persecution by various churches and governments, the Soviets had deported the whole lot to Frontier—figuring they would tame the bullbears and inclement weather or die.

The Brotherhood had led the revolt against the Soviets and established the Confederacy which initiated a period of over two hundred years of human expansion among the stars.

Susan sat back and frowned at the images the headset formed in her mind. The constant problems of violence, piracy, and social ferment had taken their toll in the end. Sirius and Arpeggio led the cause in which the Confederacy was finally supplanted. Sirius first proposed the Directors and the Gi-net. Sirian and Arpeggian pressure had led the way in establishing them.

When public opinion turned against them; when Brotherhood agents found on the street were mobbed and killed; when Frontier was threatened with destruction; the Brotherhood packed up and left. By then the Directorate had been established and the departure created no stir. The legendary Brotherhood vanished—spaced to no one knew where.

And in its place? Susan scowled to herself. *Stagnation!* The Directorate had rotted to the point where it couldn't even manage the conquest of her primitive planet; no matter that the Romanans had the advantage of the Prophets and a rogue battleship.

And what of the future? What role could her people play in that? The People, following and loving their Spider God, would find the worlds of the Directorate occupied by the human equivalent of sheep. Her lips twisted in a nasty smile. Not even Susan Smith Andojar would like to see the results of a Romanan raid on a world like Range or Earth.

Susan screamed as something grabbed at her side. She shot out of the chair, clawing for the knife at her waist. The image from the headset snapped out as she ripped it from her brow and spun, dropping into a crouch, knife point low, ready to thrust.

"Not bad, squirt!" Rita chuckled, jumping back, fists on her hips.

Susan pressed a hand against her chest, gasping in deep breaths. "*Damn you, Rita!* You scared the life right out of me. Don't do that! I might have cut you!" She forced her heart back into her chest and wondered if molar marks were on it.

Eyes twinkling, Rita laughed. "Just wanted to check your reactions. Thought maybe you'd gotten soft and slow while I was rotting in that miserable med unit."

"How are you?" Susan asked, feeling guilty. She searched out her headset and shut down the program.

"Fit as can be." Rita shrugged, digging into her personal gear and packing a war bag.

"Where are you going?" Susan asked curiously, watching the belt with Rita's coups being slung around the redhead's trim waist.

"I have to be in planning meetings for hours, kid." Rita threw her a look of disgust. "I'm not sure that once the deployment starts I'll be able to get back and put together a kit. If I do it now, I'm sure to get it into the AT. In fact, I want you to deliver this to number 22. That'll be our lander."

Susan swallowed hard. "This is really it," she breathed. "Hadn't sunk in until now. We're really going on a raid!"

"Got that right, squirt. You need to assemble with the rest in four hours. Make your way to Dock 22. You're going down with me. On the ground, we meet up with Iron Eyes as soon as a perimeter is established. We take the spaceport first. That cuts off their shuttle traffic. From there, we expand through the capital city of Ekrania and then provide support for the other Romanan units."

"What about Horsecapture?" Susan asked suddenly.

Rita smiled. "He's still in hospital—sputtering mad, I might add. He might take it, but Doc Hardy says his guts aren't quite knitted yet. A hard bounce could blow him right open again."

"I'll bet that tears it," Susan laughed. "His hair growing back yet?"

"Friday took a big hunk. Horsecapture should have a new scalp within a week or two." Rita straightened and took a quick study of her quarters. "I guess that's about it. Be sure the rifle is aboard. We'll be using blasters—but it can't hurt to have them for backup."

"Five hours," Susan's face flushed. She looked up. "Am I ready? Do I know enough? Do you think I can do it?"

Rita shrugged. "Kid, you're never ready. You've had the raw data dumped in your brain. It's up to you to put it together. You've studied tactics. You're proficient with a knife, rifle, blaster, and hand to hand. As to whether you can do it, that's up to you. You don't know until the air around your head crackles with blaster bolts and you have to carry out your part of the fight. I learned on Atlantis, maybe you did, too, when you took that first coup. How did you feel then?"

"Scared enough to foul my pants," Susan whispered, remembering. "It was afterward that I felt wonderful. There was a light-headed feeling, everything seemed to be clearer to me. I could smell things. I was aware. I could—"

"It will be like that in about ten hours, kid." She hesitated. "Almost forgot. You gave it your best shot, Susan. You pushed yourself. You crammed years of education into the last six months. I couldn't have done it. I think you've earned these." She pulled Susan's armor from the rack, sticking two corporal's stars on the sleeve. "Congratulations, kid."

"But those are—"

"Damn right. Someone's got to shame those men into winning!" Rita chuckled and slapped her on the shoulder.

Susan blinked and shook her head, trying to believe.

Rita turned for the hatch and stopped, a sober light in her green eyes. "Uh, take care of yourself down there. Do an old lady a favor. Don't take any risks you don't have to. Keep your head down . . . and think. And there's one other thing . . ." Rita paused.

"What's that?" Susan demanded. "You're hesitating, that's not like you."

Rita dropped into a bunk, eyes glittering. "You know you're a very beautiful young woman. You know what hap-

pens to women prisoners? They . . . Well, think about it.
Keep in mind that unless he kills you . . . you'll live through
it. It will probably hurt. Some gals . . . um, break. Some
don't. You're only marked for life if you want to be."

Susan swallowed, tight inside.

Rita pointed a finger, green eyes like ice. "Now, pay
attention. If a man gets you down and he's on top of you,
stick with it. Let him reach climax. They lose their concentration then. That's when you move. Dig your fingers as
deeply as you can between his eyes next to the nose. The
bones in there are called the lacrimals, they're very thin and
delicate. Squeeze with everything you've got, and believe
me, you'll have plenty. Those little bones will shatter and
he'll be blind and disabled with pain. Kill him with a quick
kick to the throat. Similarly, if you can get a grip on his
testicles, rip 'em right off his damn body!"

Susan's expression tightened. "Women on World live
with rape, Major. It isn't unknown for a girl to kill a man
who captures her. We're not that delicate. I'll get any man
who does that to me. One way or another, I'll cut him and
leave him to live with it. He can dream of knives for the rest
of his life."

"Right," Sarsa nodded. "That's the attitude. Good luck,
Susan. Come back alive. Fill your belt with coups and show
those sexist Romanan bastards!" She punched Susan lightly
in the side.

"You, too, Major."

"Yeah, don't be late for assembly. You forget that kit bag
of mine and I'll have your cute ass on a platter." Rita
grinned, saluted, and left.

Susan sat silently, eyes on the gleaming stars, thoughts
on Sirius, on how she would react. They were the old
thoughts of soldiers everywhere who wait on destiny. The
shade of death slipped around the back of her consciousness—
ever present, but never tangible. The black shadow demanded recognition but wavered just beyond belief. Susan
looked up at the chronometer and learned a brutal reality of
war. The toughest thing was to simply sit and wait and
think.

She forced herself to get up and pack her own kit. She
didn't have much. The rifle and the cartridges for it were set
out. Her coup belt went about her waist and she absently
ran her fingers through Ramon's hair, seeking to draw strength
from it. Her clothes consisted of one change and her battle

armor, slightly dank from the smell of her sweat. She had forgotten to wash it after she'd hurt Rita.

With all her packing, she'd used up no more than ten minutes. She cleaned her rifle—then did it again for another twenty minutes.

Hans called to let her know he'd been assigned to a Romanan unit as a technical adviser. Orders told him to report to AT21 for the descent. He seemed rested and nervous. She smiled, sent him her love, and signed off when he needed to attend to his duties. Another eight minutes gone.

Time dragged. She watched a holo on one of the monitors. She ate continuously and drank what must have been gallons of coffee. Finally, the clock began counting down toward assembly time. She'd be a half hour early—but it beat waiting. Taking a deep breath, she stood, looked around the tiny room that had been her quarters, and wondered if she'd ever see it again.

The bunk seemed to hold the outline of her and Friday. The ghost of her virginity lay there, silent, and sadly sweet. Would she ever see him again?

Here, she had encountered another world, learned a new language and how to read it. Here she had grown from a young girl into a woman.

"At how much cost?" she wondered, thinking of all the headset must have blotted out to give her so much so quickly.

She ran long fingers over the panel Hans had so laboriously checked and rechecked while he screwed up the nerve to ask her for coffee. The ghost of his uncertain words haunted her along with his flushed smile and pleading blue eyes.

Uneasy at what she considered foolishness, she reached for her precious comp unit still hooked into comm. She picked up the headset—her constant companion—and accessed the file to check it before she disconnected—a routine habit. To her surprise, the program had accessed.

She ran the file—all technical data on Brotherhood politics, names, lists of ships, estimates of manpower and access codes for Patrol emergencies. Shocked, her mind went numb at the material. The wealth of a vanished civilization!

"Attention!" comm squawked. "All personnel will assemble at battle stations. ATs will prepare to disembark within one hour. This is first call. Please report to stations."

Susan looked up. Her half hour had vanished. Frantically, she saved the file and the access code and stuffed the comp into her pack. Where time had dragged, she now knew she'd be late. Fumbling in her haste, she gathered up both kits, slung the rifles over her shoulder and made a last check of the room. Neat, tidy, nothing but her headset looked out of place. Struggling under her burden, she racked her headset and palmed the door.

Dock 22 roiled with orderly confusion. *Bullet's* crew had more non-drill practice than any other Patrol ship in space. Even so, men and women ran back and forth, rushing equipment and crates in and out of the gaping ramps.

Susan lugged her kits to the ramp, skipping around an antigrav loading a big plastic crate. She located the hatch officer and reported.

"One kit only, Corporal," the man said, noting her arrival to comm. "That's the rules."

"I've only got one kit," Susan protested. "If you want, you throw that one out, uh, Corporal Naguchi." Susan squinted at the name and rank stenciled on his battle armor. "That's Major Sarsa's. She'd want to know who ordered it left behind."

Naguchi's eyes slid to the kit. He saw the ID and waved quickly, swallowing. "Give the Major my compliments." He promptly lost himself in something else.

Susan made her way into the crowded, jostling guts of the AT. The blaster techs were making a final check of the relays. People shoved past her. The very air seemed to beat with the sound of excited voices, shuffling feet, and adrenaline. The roar of activity created a dull cadence that should have been louder. A bristling tension crackled, tangible, part of the atmosphere reminding her that within hours, AT22 would be fighting for its very life—and hers.

Pushing past shoulders and elbows she found the assault deck filled with Romanans and occasional marines. She hesitated, unsure, and moved to one side of the hatch. Looking over the sea of faces, there were men she'd known in the Settlements and many strangers. Spider and Santos warriors mingled, laughed softly, and traded jokes, puns, or brags.

A phenomenal adventure, the likes of which they could only have dreamed, she knew their experience lacked reality. They had no idea of the risk they would run as AT22 tried to evade the satellite defenses. They didn't know that they might die in a fireball long before they reached atmosphere. They didn't understand decompression. They didn't know they might end up falling thousands of meters to their death. They didn't know what defenses they would find on the ground—if they made it that far.

A two-edged sword, this education. Had Rita not made her pry into the nature of space warfare, she herself would have been just as happy-go-lucky as her fellow countrymen, expecting to pull off a raid on a new, rich planet. They hadn't quite figured out that if their ATs were shot up, if *Bullet* were blown out of space, they had no way home.

Susan dragged her kits to the assault benches—stowing hers the way Rita had shown her—and racked her rifle. Next to it rested a shoulder blaster. She immediately field stripped it and checked the charges. The deadly weapon was ready. She checked the crash harness, suddenly aware that someone had figured out who she was.

Like a ripple of water, men nudged their partners and pointed, watching, muttering to themselves. With nothing to look at but the bulkhead or the Romanan warriors, Susan took the bulkhead—tense as a wound spring. Her bladder and colon began to beg for attention. Unstrapping, she stood—amazed at the nervous energy in her legs—and made for the toilet.

When the door closed behind her, she experienced instant relief. She slipped her battle armor open and squatted on the freefall toilet, amazed at the pressure of bladder and gut. Her hands shook. Her breathing came too fast. The air seemed stuffy and she wondered why she had come so damned early.

"Five minutes to disembarkation," comm announced. It chattered on about several things and as Susan was rehitching her armor, she started, remembering Rita's kit.

Susan fastened her crotch and checked her appearance. Opening the door she grabbed Rita's kit and moved forward. Her way to the bridge wound through corridors of bustling marines. Moving past sweating bodies she heard men and women joking ribaldly, making out wills, leaving prized dice and sex holos to each other.

At the bridge a marine barred her way with a blaster. "Name, rank, and business," he demanded, tension in his face.

"Corporal Susan Smith Andojar!" She snapped a salute. "I have Major Sarsa's kit."

"Enter," the marine said mechanically as he snapped to attention and shouldered his blaster.

Susan gingerly stepped through the big pressure hatch and onto the bridge. Here, too, an electric energy pulsed. Men and women ran through instrument checks and called code sequences to each other. Some were sitting in command chairs, eyes closed, headsets demanding all their concentration.

"Susan!" Rita shouted from the other side where she bent over a monitor with the captain.

She made her way over, eyes trying to take in everything, wondering if the men and women who peered at monitors and ran checks would be clever enough to keep the fragile craft from a fiery death.

"Major!" Susan stiffened and saluted.

"That my kit?" Rita demanded half-absorbed with the monitor.

"Yes, ma'am," Susan called out proudly.

"How do the boys in the back look? They worried?"

"They don't even know what's happening, Major. They think everything's peaches and cream. To them this is as simple as making planetfall on World. They haven't figured out the Sirians will be shooting."

Rita took enough time from the monitor to grin her confidence to Susan. She caught a glimpse of Iron Eyes on the screen. Not here?

Noting Susan's surprise, Rita shrugged. "Hell, don't think we'd put all our officers in one ship, do you? This way someone in the know will get through.

"In the meantime, get back below. I want you back there with those apes. If things get rough, be where they can see you. There's too much pride in those boys to allow them to break if a woman is holding her own. I'm counting on you. Remember, you can give orders. If you need to enforce them, use your blaster. Shoot to disable."

Rita grabbed a marker from the table and quickly drew a Spider effigy on the armor. "Gives you luck, kid. Don't forget your prayers and medicine before you jump out the hatch. The monitor will show you our objective on the way down. Take care." At that Rita turned her back and bent over the monitor, talking hurriedly to Iron Eyes.

Susan saluted her backside and started off in a daze.

In the assault room, Susan pulled her packs from under the bench and restowed them at the front of the room.

Marines were entering, moving about with the Romanans. The Patrol marines saluted her on sight. The Romanans just looked, wide-eyed, shook their heads, and whispered behind their hands.

A blaring klaxon rang through the white corridors and metal clanged, vibrating the deck plates.

"Attention. To your places. We are underway. Combat conditions. Attend to decompression gear."

Susan automatically swung her helmet over her head, and made sure the warriors near her had theirs fitted right. She tightened the straps to her armor, snugging the fit. They were committed. Gravity dropped off to nothingness until the grav plates compensated; but for that brief instant, Susan felt herself falling. Her stomach lurched and she heard the chuckles the men used to cover their dismay.

Committed. The word echoed in her head. Surrounded by her men and the Patrol marines—and locked within herself. It was the same for everyone, she realized. The slight rasping of air being drawn in and pushed out of her lungs; the beat of her heart; the throb of her pulse became her world. The dimly lit assault bay filled her universe.

Bulkhead loomed before her eyes. A thin sheet of graphitic metal between her and open space. She looked around, seeing the shining white of battle armor. The marines were locked into their own thoughts, eyes staring blankly. The Romanans—now unsettled by the strangeness—looked to each other, banter cut off by the unaccustomed helmets, white battle armor painted in curious designs to reflect their spirit power.

White armor. White walls. White world. White reality. She realized her mouth had gone dry, and running her tongue over her teeth, forced a swallow. White armor, so that if she got blown out into space and didn't get instantly fried by a blaster, they had a better chance of seeing her. White could be spotted in the stark light of space. The color provided a little protection since it reflected light instead of absorbing it.

She flexed her fingers, acutely aware how incredibly complicated and delicate that hand was. With nothing left to do, she sat and waited in the reduced gravity, moving her fingers, rubbing her fingertips together under the battle armor to savor the sensation.

A sudden pressure pushed her to one side. Evasive action! They were under attack. How long since they had dropped from *Bullet*? A half hour? An hour? Three? Time lost itself in the stress and the fear. Her bladder demanded relief. Her bowels were feeling loose and runny. Her heart beat a rhythm of fear.

They went weightless again. Her warriors looked uneasy. They *were* hers. These men had grown up under the same sun. What were they all doing out here so far from World? At what instant would they suddenly die in a mass of released energy over a world they had never seen?

Susan wished she could cry out. She could do nothing. Her fate hovered beyond her control, hovered at the fingertips of the AT's pilot; in the aim of the targeting computers and the gunners; in the sighting mechanisms of the planetary defenses. A man she didn't know, from a world she'd never seen, would press a firing stud and a thread of purple light would flicker across space. He would never know he had killed Susan Smith Andojar.

Remembering Rita's words, Susan began to sing the song her medicine had told her would bring her faith and strength and courage. She heard herself pray to Spider, promising to spread his way through the universe. Again, the AT jolted and g pressed her into the seat, then threw her against the straps that bound her in.

"Attention." Rita's voice spoke calmly. "We're on our way down." The lights dimmed suddenly as the blasters drew power. At least AT22 fought back.

A picture formed on the big monitor. "This is the objective." A square white structure. "Take coup off any Sirians you find within. Wreck any equipment. Your technical advisers have informed us that anything is fair game. This is the comm center for the Ekrania spaceport. Destroy it and they can't talk to anyone."

Susan saw heads nodding and the warriors were now grinning to each other. Some fingered coups through their combat armor.

"Don't get too far apart," Rita warned. "War Chiefs, keep your men together. Don't worry, there will be more than enough riches for all. When we take the building, a new objective will be given. Remember, it has become a matter of honor with *Victory* that we will not surrender."

Susan could see wolfish eyes gleaming behind helmets. Romanans were muttering at even the idea of surrender. The AT was buffeted and jerked. She could hear the roar through her helmet. A harsh vibration shook her seat and almost blurred her vision.

"We have less than a minute to landing. When the AT comes to a complete stop, hit your releases, grab your blasters and head for that white building. Good luck!" Rita's voice flicked off.

The lights dimmed again and again as the blasters poured out death and destruction. Susan imagined aircraft flinging themselves desperately at the AT. She could see streaks of black smoke as attackers were hit and destroyed. She could imagine the bolts of light that laced the ground, searching for defensive fire and silencing the positions.

In spite of her fear, she realized she was now living the other side of the fight she had witnessed so long ago over World. Long ago? It seemed to have been an eternity—a different life.

Her stomach dropped out from underneath her. Frightened, she gripped the seat firmly. Had they been hit? Were the engines out? Were they falling to their deaths even now? The AT bucked in the air and Susan fought to keep her stomach from voiding. Her fear grew as she wondered what it was going to be like if the ship split open—the eternal fall to her death.

Air would rush around her plunging body, the ground spinning, looming ever closer as she screamed hoarsely, weightless, wondering if she would feel the impact.

G jammed her into the seat. Pressure increased. She closed her eyes, took a deep breath, and shot one last look around the deck. The warriors sat frozen with fear.

The AT leveled off and the force that felt like a thousand gs, the pressure that had been pushing her into her seat, lifted. The lights dimmed again and again. The AT pulled her backward as it settled. Gravity returned and a warning blared.

Susan hit the release and sprang to her feet, ripping her helmet off. "Come on!" she shouted as she tore the blaster from the wall. "You! Warriors! You going to let a woman take the first coup?"

Heads turned in her direction and expressions hardened. Susan sprinted for the ramp as the lights flickered. The AT's heavy blasters poured fire around the ship in a covering barrage.

"Will you be cowards?" she taunted a group of men who sat huddled, eyes wide, hands frozen on the releases. Her

mockery brought them boiling to their feet, grabbing for
blasters.

At a run, Susan headed down the ramp into an evening
sun that threatened to blind her after the dimness of the
ship. The fear fled as her feet hit hard ground. She turned,
squinting in the light. The building stood before her, threads
of violet spinning from gaps blown in the walls.

A blaster bolt from the AT poured into the edifice, blowing a huge chunk of wall out in a burst of rock, plaster, and
dust, exposing floors and dividers. People ran.

Sprinting, Susan headed for the building, hand blaster
heavy in her arms.

Something crackled by her ear and she heard a man
behind her scream. She whooped out her war cry and began
singing to her Power. Calling Spider's name, she clambered
over the rubble in the breached wall and, from reflex, blew
an oncoming man in half with a precise shot. She stopped
only long enough to reach down with her knife and cut the
bloody coup from the victim's head.

She'd done it! Taken the first coup! Laughing insanely,
she waved the bloody trophy over her head, spinning it to
fling the gore away. With trembling fingers, she wove it into
her belt.

A chant of "Spider! Spider! Spider!" rose on the air as
the Romanans screamed and shot into the building. Whooping,
singing, shouting, and yelling, they charged into the place,
lacing the air with blaster bolts.

The building didn't even slow them. From the top of a
crumbling wall, Susan looked out over the spaceport and
watched ATs settling like giant bugs, ramps dropping and
hordes of shooting Romanans and marines rushing out into
the dying light of Sirius.

"Corporal Susan Smith Andojar," her belt comm crackled.

"Here," she answered, peering through the smoke.

"Susan, take as many men as you can and head down that
boulevard in front of you. We note a large force of Sirians
headed this way. They don't have battle armor; but they
appear to be armed. Take care, kid. Keep in touch. Let us
know your situation. Out."

"Roger." Susan slung her blaster over her shoulder. Most
of her men were scrambling around inside the building,
looking in awe at the sputtering, smoking equipment.

"Anyone for coups and Spider's Honor?" she called. "Red
Many Coups says a group of Sirians are coming down the

road out there. Let's go meet them." She spun on her heel, trotting out the wrecked door into the twilight.

"Keep an eye on what or who you're shooting at," she called. "When the light gets too bad, don't forget your night goggles."

Her ragtag band greeted the night with songs, wild laughter, insults, and good-natured mutterings about a Romanan woman who took first coup. Susan grinned wryly. As after the shooting with Ramon, she enjoyed a kind of euphoria. Her nose told her the air here hung heavy and moist with a slight stink.

Low buildings lined either side of the boulevard. Automatically, men were spreading out along the flanks, muttering at the strangeness. Chagrined, she knew she should have ordered that on her own. She began thinking of tactics.

"Split up," she called suddenly. "We're dumber than harvesters to trot down the road. Half of you, take that side. The others along there. Spider keep you!" She ran off to use the cover of the buildings.

Blaster fire snapped out of the evening. Men dressed in something dark came running down the road. Blue blaster bolts flickered.

Susan dropped to one knee, studying her IR sight picture. One by one, she shot them down, aware that her Romanans—marksmen from youth—were devastating the Sirian formation. Within minutes, they broke, fleeing into the night.

"Not much guts," a Santos muttered disgustedly. "They never even closed."

"Come on," another cried gleefully, "I have coups waiting there." Romanans rushed forward screaming, waving long knives.

To Susan, the night lost coherency. She kept a small patrol together and pushed out into the city. Sirians were fleeing madly before the Romanan wave.

She remembered shooting down aircars, dodging blaster bolts, forming her little command to assault Sirian roadblocks, firing at aircraft, and vigorous hand-to-hand combat. Rushes of ecstasy followed weary periods of exhaustion. Absolute terror swung crazily into mindless hilarity.

And horror lingered, like the Sirian man, crawling on his hands and knees, crying piteously for mercy, his skull a mass of coagulated blood where the scalp had been ripped off.

She'd gaped at the figure of a child, leg burned off,

shrieking in agony and fear as a Romanan swooped down on her with a big fighting knife to take a coup. Fire and death traced the night.

She'd laughed at the sight of three Romanans trotting alongside an antigrav loaded to a toppling mound with clothing, appliances, pictures, metal, weapons, and five screaming girls. The men were bickering among themselves over the spoils while around them lay untouched wealth.

They broke into buildings where huddled masses of humanity howled hoarsely as she played a light on fear-crazed faces. A world of sheep, they cowered before her, frozen with terror, frightened to the point their bladders and bowels loosened and fouled them. She choked on disgust.

A fleeting image: warriors held a struggling woman to the ground as they ripped off their battle armor and threw their hard bodies on her smooth one. Susan had watched, mildly revolted by the Romanan right of combat. The woman didn't even fight back. Had she, Susan might have saved her.

She remembered the old woman—hair so white no one would have stooped to taking coup—pleading frantically for the life of her son as a Romanan cut him apart joint by joint. The warrior's laughter seemed macabre as the man screamed his horror. Susan remembered the way the captive's head jerked as she blew it off his body. She'd told the warrior, "Kill quickly or don't foul yourself with their blood. Spider is shamed!" He'd slunk away, nodding, while the old woman clutched the bloody mass to her sunken chest.

Explosions ripped the huge brooding buildings of Sirius—many of them, Susan knew, built six hundred years ago. As the light of day crept around the eastern sky, she looked out through a veil of hanging smoke. The wide empty streets were littered with bodies, wreckage, piles of personal items dropped by fugitives or stumbling, victorious Romanans.

Five remained from her original command, the others lost somewhere, wandered away, or gone to find better amusements.

"Major Sarsa," Susan croaked hoarsely into her comm. "Corporal Andojar here." She blinked wearily, wondering at the grit in her eyes. She and her men sagged against a low mortared wall, bone tired, armor spattered with blood, stained with smoke and charred in places from near misses. Faces grimy and soot-blackened, the tracks of tears and crow's-feet stood out like the whites of their eyes.

I am tired of war. I want to go home. Susan closed her eyes and took a ragged breath of stinking air.

"Susan, that you?" Iron Eyes responded. "Are you all right?"

"Fine, John. We're about six K from the spaceport. Not much activity beyond this position. Warriors strung out behind us. We're running out of gas up here. Worn out. What do you want us to do?"

"Come on back, Susan. We'll send a couple of recon parties up your way. The Sirians are regrouping in the outskirts of the city. We have an AT keeping track of them and a couple of observation points set up to watch their movement. We desperately need to reorganize. I think Rita could use your help."

"Roger, we're on the way. Um, listen . . . if you have a chance . . . send an aircar down Union Avenue. We'd appreciate it." She slipped the comm back into her belt and forced her companions to their feet.

In all of Susan's memory, she couldn't remember being so tired. Her belt must have weighed thirty pounds from the scalps dangling there, dripping blood down her legs. Inside, Susan suffered a slight shame. They had all been so easy. The People back on World would never understand how little such a coup meant.

Bodies became more frequent as they made their way down the road. Buildings burned here and there, aircars lay piled up—wrecked. So much devastation.

"Car!" Bull Wing Reesh cried and dove for cover. Susan's Romanans melted into the curves and angles of a building.

"Hans!" Susan called, recognizing the aircar, now decked with Spider's effigies. "How are things going?" she asked as she flopped into the seat.

On impulse, she kissed him solidly on the lips, wishing they could go somewhere to be alone, to hold each other and talk. Maybe he could give all the horrors and exultations meaning. The stinking of burning flesh filled her nose. She wanted to wash the blood from her face and hair—and sleep.

"Glad to hear you were alive," Hans grinned, not even nervous at her attention. "We'd best get back. I don't know what the score is, but Rita and Moshe are plenty worried."

"We've been cutting them apart like butter," Susan protested. "God! I never knew it would be like this. They're sheep, Hans! They won't stand! They crawl, they plead, they beg! Doesn't humanity have any pride anymore? Don't they have any courage? Is this what the Directorate has bred?"

Hans' expression soured. His eyes showed his concern. "There's no word from *Bullet*."

"Oh." Involuntarily, she looked up, searching the lightly clouded skies. An unaccustomed tightness grew in her chest.

CHAPTER XVI

John Smith Iron Eyes watched as the last of the battle plans came together.

"Any questions?" Ree asked, bent at the hips to lean over the holo depiction of Ekrania. Given his posture, he looked like a Romanan bear about to snatch a yearling calf.

"You all know your objectives?" Ree's hard blue eyes searched faces. "Dismissed, then. And people, good luck!"

The meeting broke up, Iron Eyes still studying the layout of Ekrania, trying to burn the details of the city into his mind one last time, wondering what it would be like down there.

He looked up at the feel of a hand on his shoulder. "Well, War Chief, what do you think?"

Iron Eyes straightened, looking down into Ree's eyes. "I think it's a long way from Gessali Camp. I wonder if Leeta had any idea?"

Damen Ree shook his head. "No, my friend, I don't think she did—and part of this is her making. If anyone foresaw, it was the Prophets."

". . . And they never tell," Iron Eyes gave him a bitter smile. "I'd better be getting to my AT."

Ree nodded. "And I'm headed for the bridge. If everything goes well, we'll have the skies locked up tight. We should be able to provide tactical supporting fire from orbit if you need it."

"We'll see," Iron Eyes lifted his shoulder. "I've never had the advantage of such things in a raid before." He grinned. "Would have scared the horses."

Ree chuckled. "Yeah, guess so. At that same time, that worries me. This is an industrial world. So much could go wrong. Your people are still . . ."

"Ignorant savages?"

"Yeah, but I'm too much of a diplomat to say it."

Iron Eyes filled his lungs and sighed. "If we get in too much of a mess, we'll try and withdraw, find a wild place and regroup, maybe work our way in from the fringes. My people might be more effective that way."

"There's not many 'wild places' down there. Originally, Sirius was a terraforming project. The Soviets did some wild things—cracking the CO_2 cycle open, stimulating the greenhouse effect, and introducing Earth-normal plants. The first couple of hundred years were, uh, interesting for the Sirians." Ree frowned. "Maybe they got something funny in their genes as a result of the bio-engineering. Been troublemakers ever since."

Iron Eyes cocked his head. "Cee oh two? Greenhouse?"

"Never mind. If we live through this, you can catch up on terraforming."

"The hardest part is going to be keeping control of my people through belt comms. They're used to having a war chief within shouting distance. Again, maybe we'll have to adapt. Give a trusted man an objective and he can take the responsibility. So much could go wrong."

"You've given it some thought." Ree rubbed his chin, brow lined.

"I don't like losing," Iron Eyes reminded. "Nor do I like Maya and Arish behind my back. These other Patrol, I don't know them at all. They haven't had the benefit of being exposed to the truths of Spider. Like Raiders in the night, we can't tell their tribe."

Ree nodded, jaw muscles jumping. "I'll keep an eye on them as soon as we disable the Sirian fleet."

Iron Eyes smiled, placing both hands on Damen's shoulders and shaking him gently. "I have no doubts, Colonel. Until next time."

Ree clasped Iron Eyes in a tight grip. "Take care, my friend. Watch yourself down there. I'd hate to go back to sparring with the combat robot—even if you've gotten to beating me recently."

Iron Eyes laughed and turned for the door. He waved one last time, leaving Damen Ree, chin down, thoughtfully staring at the holo map.

AT21 proved to be a knot of confusion as Iron Eyes made his way to the bridge, checked in, and donned his combat armor. Immediately, he patched through to Rita, checking on crew status, calming unruly warriors. Time contracted.

"All hands, combat conditions!" The klaxon shrilled. Tied into comm, Iron Eyes barely realized they'd disembarked from *Bullet*. The chattering of his Romanans filled his ears as he answered questions, reviewed assault schedules, and reminded his warriors of objectives.

Strapped in, he felt the AT shuddering, turning, g forcing him into his seat. The lights dimmed as the fire control called out targets. In the corner of his eye, the flare and death of an orbiting gun platform registered briefly.

"All right, warriors," he called into the comm. "On the screen you should be seeing the shuttle maintenance building. Willy Grita, you take your party and raid it. Your tech will tell you which machines to shoot up. Patan, your party attacks this building. This is the administrative office. Gut it."

The AT barely jolted as it set down. "Go!"

Iron Eyes watched the confusion, wincing slightly as the Romanans got lined out, stumbled over each other in confusion, and finally went boiling down the ramp.

"Oh well, it was their first try," he remarked ruefully. "At least no one got killed." He followed their paths via the bridge monitors.

So this was another planet? It seemed so . . . artificial. In every direction, endless flatness spread to the nearest buildings—a world of gray angles and sterility, nothing living. The buildings, still on screens, looked like the holo projections they'd trained in. No surprises there. The only difference he could perceive from his command chair came from a harder pull of gravity than that experienced aboard *Bullet*. Other ATs were settling now, dropping ramps, disgorging marines and Romanans.

"War Chief?" Rita's voice came over the comm.

"Here. We're down. My warriors just charged off to glory and coup." He leaned back, seeing blaster fire seeking his running warriors. A curious emptiness built in his gut. He should be out there, running with them, not sitting here like an old man guarding a corral.

"We're down, too. My people are taking the comm building. Looks like the space port is ours. Their ground troops weren't up to the ATs. They broke and ran first thing. Time to start setting up logistics and operations," Rita told him. The task continued throughout the day. Night fell on a macabre scene, the red glow of fires silhouetting the irregular outlines of buildings in black.

Through the screens, he observed his teams as they moved out into the city. He kept watch through the fish-eye cameras of recon drones, informing his people of knots of resistance, helping them navigate through the endless streets. One stroke of luck, the Romanans took to radio command like ducks to water, trusting his assessment of the situation.

The coordination of AT air support baffled him at first. Only when he began using the air strikes like light cavalry did it all fall into place. Incredible! He could hit any fortified position from the air, keep his people out of major fields of fire, and see which way the Sirians retreated and how many there were.

"Look!" Shig Gulanan, the AT's captain called, pointing. In the overhead monitors, brilliant streaks of purple and violet seared the sky. "The Colonel's taking on Ngen Van Chow. Won't be long now and Sirius will crack like an egg."

Already strings of Romanans were staggering in bearing the loot they'd accumulated. Fighting in the city had begun to slow, his warriors slowly running out of energy. Studying the situation, Iron Eyes turned to establishing his people in defensive positions. As another couple of hours passed, he'd sent the relief forward to spell the warriors, using marines with their greater understanding of urban warfare to buttress his green raiders.

"Iron Eyes?" Rita called through the system.

"Here."

"Could you come to AT22? I'd like to review what we've accomplished so far."

"Sure." He lifted the headset from his brow, rubbing his temples. "Damn thing's still magic! How in Spider's web can a strip of metal read a man's thoughts?"

He stepped out into the night, curious at the odor of Sirius. The place reeked, a pungent sting to the air. Fumy, that was the word. The air seemed heavier, damp and acrid from smoke and burning chemicals. Altogether, the sensation proved most unpleasant. The material of the spaceport—concrete they'd called it—felt firm under his feet. About him, the city of Ekrania rose awesomely, now illuminated by the wildfires set by blasters and combat.

The sky glowed eerily. Iron Eyes looked up, realizing the

clouds didn't reflect moonlight, only the lights of the city and the baleful fires that ravaged the huge buildings. Violet light had ceased to lance the heavens.

Curiously, in the patch of black sky he could see, there were very few stars. Nothing like the view from space. Instead, the night sky lent him a feeling of somberness, of dark threat.

"So I have come to stand on another world," he whispered, hearing the distant sounds of concussions, the tinkling of glass and metal as some structure exploded. He closed his eyes, carried away by the realization, trying to feel the planet around him, pick up a sense of its soul.

The warm breeze caressed his cheek, the reek of the place never far from being a conscious irritant. Among all the smells, so many new and unknown, he could find no trace of vegetation, no mustiness of damp dirt. He missed the warm scent of manure, the gentle incense of polewood smoke. Instead, Sirius tried to sting him with its air.

The unease grew within him. "A planet with no soul will be no good for my People." He opened his eyes, scanning the area for danger while he cradled the blaster in his arms and continued toward Rita's craft.

AT22 whined, systems ready for quick action. Iron Eyes saluted the guard and bound up the ramp. Inside, he blinked in the sudden bright lights. A bustle of activity greeted him.

Passing the bridge hatch, he noticed Rita, eyes glued to a monitor. Crouching next to her, he asked, "What's happening?"

Rita shook her head, mouth working, jaw muscles jumping. "I don't know. The fighting in orbit's stopped, we should have had an all clear from the Colonel. Hard to say though, something might have botched up the comm dishes. Maybe a hit took out the antennae? Something's wrong."

Iron Eyes filled his lungs and sighed. "Maybe Spider is ready to test us, Major."

"Don't even say that in jest!" She took time to study him, green eyes cool with worry. "You know what it means if there's trouble?"

Iron Eyes lifted a slab of shoulder. "Rita, if it's Spider's will, I can die here as well as any place else. Spider will call my soul back. But I would rather my bones rot on World, given the choice."

She turned back to the screen. "You may not have that option."

Iron Eyes stood slowly, slapping his armor. "Yeah, well, we'll see. I keep telling you, I don't like to lose."

"I'll remember that," she said, still worried as she sent yet another query to the silent black skies.

Colonel Damen Ree stood on the bridge, eyes on the monitors. "Disembark," he ordered. At his word, each of the ATs drifted outward, stabilizing with their attitude jets before they shot away—white lances against gray-black star fields.

"May Spider keep you all," Ree whispered reverently as he watched them, aware of the spider effigy Leeta Dobra had drawn on the overhead plates of the bridge during another battle not so long ago.

Sirius gleamed, a target of mayhem and destruction. Behind and slightly to port, the double star of Sirius flickered in its emissions, causing the planet ahead to vary in intensity as the reflections bounced off the blue and white planet.

"Battery test," Ree growled, eyes on the readouts. Each of the big blasters shot threads of light out into the darkness.

"Report, sir," the weapons officer called. "One hundred percent response."

"Well done, and my compliments to the crews," Ree replied. Not half bad for a ship that had suffered the loss of an entire gun deck only four months ago—a mark of his crew's efficiency.

Comm alerted him to an incoming inter-ship. The images of Arish Amahanandras and Maya ben Ahmad formed. He greeted, "We've deployed our ATs. *Bullet* is on schedule."

Maya grinned, "We've got most of ours off, Damen. Arish, here, has had a couple of problems. Some of their makeshift repairs are giving *Brotherhood's* engineering fits."

"Serious?" Damen asked, an eyebrow shooting up. "Do I need to reorganize my ground crews to cover your deficiencies?" He tried to keep his voice even.

"We shall place our people on the planet exactly on schedule," Arish replied hotly.

"Damen," Maya shot a look of irritation his way. "We are still acting according to plan. Take your swing around the planet and bail us out if we're in trouble."

"Indeed, Maya. I'm betting you'll have destroyed him by the time I make my swing. That will enable me to cover either *Dastar* or *Helk* if the second group is muddled."

"Colonel!" the weapons officer interrupted. Damen turned.

Obviously his counterparts were receiving similar reports.
"*Hiram Lazar* is checking her weapons. Sir, the specs on
those blasters are considerably beyond our intelligence
estimates."

"You get that, Maya?" Damen asked.

"I did," she nodded, thinking hard. "I don't think this
will be as easy as we originally expected. In the event this
turns sour, one of us should survive to make a report. Run
for Arcturus to—"

"I think that is highly irregular!" Arish looked shocked.
"Seriously, you can't believe three converted cargo vessels
can be a . . . a match for six patrol ships of the line?" Her
head shook in disbelief.

"I suppose we won't know until we engage," Ree remarked with a shrug. "Good thinking, Maya. We'll just
take our chances. The last one with power to run, goes. I
won't expect to see you coming to my rescue if he's got
me." He ended with a chuckle.

"I might just to ruin your expectations!" Maya laughed.
"I'll transmit that to *Defiance*. She's liaison for our group."

"I'll keep the channel open." Ree turned away. "Course
correction. Take us out." He turned back to the comm.
"Colonels, I wish you good space, good fighting, and good
luck. May the honor of the Patrol keep us until we meet
again."

"Good luck, Damen." Maya inclined her head. It came as
no surprise that Arish said nothing. Did *Brotherhood* draw
bitches, or simply by chance have two commanders in a row
Ree couldn't stomach?

"Evacuate nonessential decks," Ree called to Iverson.

"Sir?" He looked up, baffled. "That's not part of the
procedure. If I may, sir, why?"

"Less mass for one thing, Neal. For another, if the decks
are evacuated, they can't explode under decompression like
last time. If there's no air, there's no fire control problems
. . . and we are short handed, Major." One corner of Ree's
mouth twisted in a wry smile while his eyes remained deadly
earnest.

"Yes, sir," Iverson said sharply and went about complying.
On the screens, lines of condensing atmosphere streamed
out in long white trails to mark *Bullet's* passage.

Ree took a deep breath and checked his combat suit. The
air supply and thermal units blinked green. Nothing to do
but wait and follow the descent of the ATs. They were zip-

ping back and forth on the monitor, darting about like flies, dropping like a plague toward the planet.

How good were the guns in those satellite bases? Did they have any idea about the maneuverability of the ATs? In the last four months, how much practice had they gotten with the fire control computers?

He rubbed his hand, remembering those brilliant violet blaster bolts arcing out of *Hiram Lazar*. Were *Bullet's* shields good enough to take that? Ree took a deep breath and felt his gut begin to heave. To quiet it, he drew a cup of coffee.

"Estimated time to maximum range?"

"One hour and three minutes, sir. *Victory* and *Brotherhood* will close within forty-five minutes."

Ree watched the screen, feeding potential tactical changes into the comm and considering the results. He let his mind become one with the ship, forecasting each of Ngen's moves, attempting to plot a counter measure. Time vanished.

Bullet slid around behind the planet, well above where *Helk* and *Dastar* were waiting for the incoming arcs of the Directorate's *Defiance*, *Miliken*, and *Toreon*. Ree watched them dropping into the gravity well, as *Bullet* cleared the planet. He hadn't seen the opening shots; but the two Patrol ships were closing on *Hiram Lazar*—pouring all their energy into the Sirian's shields.

Ree made a slight course correction and accelerated. From the way the Sirian shields were flaring, they would obviously hold. Ngen had done something to buttress his defense beyond expectations.

Four. Three. Two. One. Ree waited, letting *Bullet* close. Certain they couldn't miss, he ordered an open fire. Blaster bolts appeared between *Bullet* and her prey. The violet threads of light played on the defenses of *Hiram Lazar*, wavering through the spectrum as the shields began to absorb too much energy and waver.

Ree began to chuckle. Too easy! They had a sitting duck. He'd hoped Ngen would at least maneuver and make a short fight of it.

But just as he expected to see his enemy vanish in a brilliant flash, the deadly, brilliant violet threads snapped into existence around *Bullet*. The first salvo missed. Ngen had miscalculated *Bullet's* deceleration.

They didn't miss *Victory* or *Brotherhood*. Damen watched in awe as the powerful blasters smashed hole after hole into the Patrol shields. The threads of light that bound *Brotherhood* to her target flickered and went dead: guns out. *Hiram Lazar* had drawn the first blood. A second later, the shields dropped and *Brotherhood* lay unprotected. Searing white light flashed blindingly as Arish blew her antimatter in a desperate attempt to save the lives of her crew. She hurtled through space, a dead hulk.

Victory began to curve away, seeking distance so she could regroup with *Bullet*. Seeing Maya's change of course, he realized immediately that the blaster bolts settled on her were taking a deadly toll. Maya, to be sure, didn't go easily. She kept pouring everything she had into the Sirian ships.

"Can we get more power into those batteries?" Ree shouted. "We need everything we can get!"

"Only at the expense of the shields, Colonel," Iverson's voice snapped. No one had expected *Brotherhood* to fold so quickly.

Ree filled his lungs to give the order—but at that moment, *Hiram Lazar* found their range. Those terrible blasters locked onto *Bullet*.

"Overload!" Ree heard as he accelerated, praying the gunners could hold their target. He couldn't shake Ngen's blasters. He felt *Bullet* shudder and shake as the powerful Sirian guns raked her. Still, his gunners concentrated on the Rebel craft, pouring all they had into the unwavering rainbow-flaring shields of the *Hiram Lazar*.

Damen juggled the power from the shields to the drive to the blasters, playing each to its maximum, knowing the gunners were going mad with the fluctuating power in their cannons. By the skin of his teeth, he kept *Bullet* alive through that run, holding a total engagement longer than *Victory*, hoping in vain to wear a hole in that impenetrable shield.

"Out of range, sir," Neal reported needlessly.

Ree looked up at his bridge monitor, wiping tension-sweat from his brow. "Damage report!"

"Reactor stable, condition green. Helm condition green. Atmosphere green. Decks 7 and 8 gone, sir. All weapons operational. Locks 6, 15, and 19 out of commission. Section 3, decks 4 and 5 decompressing. Casualties unknown," Iverson called.

"By Spider," Ree wondered. "We had three ships pouring every erg into that guy and nothing happened!" He slammed a fist into the back of his command chair. *"Nothing happened, God damn it!"*

"Damen?" Maya called. He looked up to see her worried face form in holo. "We're hit pretty hard. I have power fluctuations in my starboard gun deck. Reactor's all right for now. *Brotherhood* is dead, no power readings at all. What the hell has he got in that thing? Two reactors?"

"Brotherhood technology, Maya," Ree whispered. "I don't know how, but that's what it reminds me of."

He looked up at the report from *Miliken*. The face of Toby Kuryaken formed. "We lost *Defiance* on the first pass. The two Sirians, *Helk* and *Dastar* hit her with a cross fire. Their blasters carved the ship into slag before she could pull out . . . the antimatter went. We've taken some damage. *Toreon* is still ninety percent."

Stoically, Damen made his report on their attack. "Suggestions?"

"Gang up and hit them one at a time," Maya shrugged. "The only advantage we've got is combined firepower. If Arish hadn't folded when she did, we'd have buckled his shields."

Ree checked his monitors. "They're moving, keeping each other in sight. I think that's out. Neal, how did the ATs do?"

"Fine, Colonel. We only lost one from *Victory*. The rest knocked out every single one of those satellite batteries on the way past."

Maya looked grim. "So our people have the planet. Van Chow has the orbit and controls the skies. Our people can't get off . . . and we can't get to them."

"What can we do?" Toby asked. "I'm of the opinion that another pass will do nothing more than lose us another couple of ships."

"I can't help but agree," Maya sounded like something had stuck in her throat.

"Form up," Ree decided. "Toby get up here and bring *Toreon* with you. Scattered like this, they can cut us apart one by one. This way we have the benefit of concentrated firepower if not shields."

"Seconded," Maya nodded, face a study in frustration.

"Then what?" Toby wondered. "We're the greatest military power in space! Here we sit, helpless, four to three!"

Damen rubbed his chin. "I propose we put our collective heads together, review the combat records, and see if we can't figure a way to outsmart him."

"That's not in the book." Yaisha Mendez's dark face formed on the monitor. *Toreon* had joined the conference.

"So? For the last couple of months, I've had to deal with a lot of situations that aren't in the book. We need to figure out how to make this work to our advantage, and it's obvious the standard tactics aren't going to turn the trick." Damen shot them a defiant look, demanding to know if they had a better idea.

"The book has answers for over three hundred years of problems," Mendez countered. "You can't just—"

"I'm with Damen," Maya agreed. "Besides, I need time to fix the damage to my ship. If I have to take that kind of a beating again, *Victory* will be swiss cheese."

"Neal?" Damen asked, "Is there any communication from Sarsa or any of the ground crews?"

"No, sir." Iverson shook his head. "From monitors, we can see substantial fighting taking place around the spaceport. I'd wager they don't have much time at the moment. We did get a landing signal. They all made it down safe."

"Send everything we've got so far to Arcturus, special code, Neal." Ree settled himself into his command chair, suddenly aware of his stone-cold coffee. A ring had formed around the edge of the cup. How long since he'd taken it?

"Hang on, Rita," Ree muttered, anxiety building. "God knows how long it will take, but we'll get you out of there some way. In the name of Spider, I promise that." He felt a depression he'd never experienced before. For the first time in his life, he doubted *Bullet's* ability to get him out alive.

CHAPTER XVII

Friday ducked around a corner, blaster gripped tightly against his chest. He gasped, lungs heaving, sweat trickling down the sides of his armor. Spider! Wasn't there a single part of this bear-cursed city that didn't consist of right angles? Couldn't Sirians build anything round or curved?

Blue blaster bolts hissed and crackled in the air beyond, exploding chunks of paneling from the bend in the corridor behind him.

"To think," Henry White Eagle called from across the way, "I never heard the word arcology before!"

"Doesn't this place ever stop?" A Santos behind Henry wondered. "We been ten kilometers already. Haysoos! It's the same Spider-cursed building!"

The Patrol tech slipped past close packed Romanan bodies. "What's the hang up?"

Friday jerked his head. "Down there. Bunch of Civil Guards got the corridor blocked off." Friday glanced over his shoulder. "How many ways could they work around us? Ambush us?"

The marine glanced at the panels overhead. "A bunch. Through the roof, from under the floor, maybe even cutting through apartment walls. We can't stay here. In a building, that's instant death. Gotta keep moving all the time. Anybody got a sonic grenade left?"

Two were passed along from hand to hand. The tech set them. "Now, when I throw these, two of you cover the corridor. The rest get past the hallway. If we split up, send two teams around the island of apartments in the center of this thing. We might get lucky."

"Whose bright idea was it to come in here?" a Spider wondered.

"Looked like a good place for loot and coup," Henry muttered. "How'd I know it'd be like this? I thought it'd be all hollow inside as big as it looked from out there on the street."

"I'll cover," Friday growled. "Never thought it would be like this! Whoever heard of fighting inside?"

"Not me, cousin," a Santos whispered. Cousin? Amazing the kinship ties that formed so far from one's World—and a reality they understood!

"Go!" The tech threw the grenades.

Friday started at the concussions, stepping out, draining his blaster as Henry stood at his shoulder. In the holocaust of smoke and detonations, a human screamed. An alarm howled loudly in the dust and debris. Behind them, armored feet pounded, passing the trap.

"That's the last!" the tech shouted, and he was running down the corridor.

Friday clipped another charge into his gun, staring at the shattered walls and twisted beams that formed out of the swirling smoke and destruction down the hallway.

"Spider!" he whispered, galloping off down the hallway behind his war party. They met two more patrols of Civil Guards—or else it was the same bunch twice. Both times the Sirians broke and fled.

"Damn!" Friday hissed. "They know the way around in here. We're just bumbling. We don't know enough! What if they set up an ambush, uh, traps in the floor or something?"

Henry shook his head. "You know, without that Patrol tech, we'd never have found our way out of—"

A door opened out of what seemed a solid wall behind them. The Civil Guard leveled his blaster, the charge taking Henry full in the back, blowing pieces of his body and armor all over the walls and floor.

Friday threw himself down, bringing his gun to bear, the bolt catching the Sirian square in the gut. Friday howled, charging to his feet, slipping on Henry's blood as he bulled through the door, bowling another Sirian over as he stepped to take his companion's place.

Screaming his fear, he flung himself into the middle of them, wild with a killing rage. The action became a blur of dark-clad bodies, the hollow pops of exploding flesh, and the stink of burned meat and hair. He remembered his gun going dead, and grabbing his fighting knife, kicking, thrusting, shrieking out of control as he exhausted his berserk fright in their densely packed bodies. Then the room seemed to jump, the floor buckled, and his body slammed into a mass of Sirians.

Dazed, he swallowed, smoke and stink making him gasp. His hand wouldn't move and he stared to where his fingers were still knotted around his knife hilt, the blade stuck in a dead man's ribs. He wrenched it loose, mind reeling drunkenly as he tried to stand.

He kicked a flopping body off his legs and it slid away to thud a second later. Puzzled, Friday stood slowly, blinking. A tremendous ringing shrilled in his ears. Sonic grenade. Someone had dropped it during the fight. Only his armor had saved him, his armor and a cushion of Sirian flesh. He looked at the hole the corpse had fallen into. Below were more mangled Sirian bodies. Electricity popped and crackled from a broken powerlead running through the blasted floor.

He clung to a half-destroyed wall and stared into a devastated household through its gaping holes, then made his way to the hall, finding it empty but for Henry's mangled body.

Aching in every bone and joint, he bent and picked up Henry's blaster, hobbling along, stumbling. An hour later, he swallowed hard, peeking around a corner. A grav lift—abandoned—beckoned.

Friday licked his lips, heart pounding. Around him the pastel colors of the arcology mocked him. Which way out? He gulped, sprinted for the grav tube and looked around. How did a fellow tell if it worked—or how? He turned, blasting a door, shouldering into the apartment. The place looked orderly, furniture placed around the spacious room.

Cautiously, he padded to the next room: food preparation. He could recognize the dispensers and appliances from the holo tapes. In the sleeping quarters, he found what he sought.

"You," he ordered in Standard. "Stand up."

Two young people, a blond man and a woman, stared, horrified, from where they huddled behind the bed. Slowly they stood, the man shaking his head, tears in his eyes, blubbering to Friday not to hurt them.

"Come!" Friday ordered.

They stood, frozen.

"I said, come!" Friday bellowed, feeling his fear, a tangible thing. To accent it, he blew a section out of the wall, exposing the apartment beyond. They came.

He checked the hallway before ducking out. "This way." They followed like sheep. At the grav lift, Friday indicated the controls. "Take me outside. Now! We all go together!"

The young man nodded, hand shaking as he tapped a button. He nodded to the lift. "I . . . It's okay. G-Go ahead."

"You first," Friday rasped, hating the delay, grabbing the girl's arm, feeling her trying to shrink away from his blood-streaked armor.

The young man nodded and stepped into open air. Friday dragged the girl after him, feeling his heart lurch as he placed a foot into seeming nothingness. Awed, he hovered there in air with the two Sirians. "Blessed Spider," he murmured, aware his voice quavered. They sank, the action without sensation.

"Here," the young man told him meekly, stepping out onto an open landing.

Friday yanked the girl after him, seeing a shattered doorway at street level. A Civil Guard looked over his shoulder from where he crouched behind a wraparound desk. Friday blew his head off, shoving the girl away and sprinting for the desk. A second man jumped out of a doorway, blue bolts crackling past Friday's head as he tumbled behind the desk. Above him, plastic and metal ruptured violently, spattering him with fragments.

On hands and knees, Friday made the desk corner, sneaking a quick look. The guard waited, blaster ready, an anxious look in his eyes.

"Spider lives!" Friday howled, whipping his weapon around the corner, sweeping the area. The bolt cut the man in two and Friday jolted to his feet, running like mad for the broken door.

Outside, the open sky over his head, he dived for a low wall of shrubbery along the arcology's side. He lay there, flat on his back, panting hoarsely until his heart slowed to a moderate beat.

He shook his head in disgust. "I don't think I'm gonna like this place!"

Warily, he took a look around, seeing the rising towers of the spaceport in the growing morning light. Nervous as a harvester in a bear run, he turned his tired feet that direction, skulking through the shadows, checking every dark doorway with his IR sight for an ambush before moving on.

"I have a report from the Civil Guard, sir." Giorj turned to look at Ngen.

The First Citizen leaned back in the command chair, elbow propped on knee, foot braced on a console. He studied the four Patrol ships, perplexed. What were they doing up there? They'd withdrawn, leaving their vulnerable surface positions wide open. Could the Patrol be composed of cowards?

"Sir?" Giorj reminded gently.

Ngen waved absently. "Put him on."

A face formed on the monitor. Grim, hard-lined, it betrayed a personality bitterly twisted by life. The man snapped to attention, waiting for Ngen to speak first.

"Report?" The First Citizen raised his hands helplessly.

"First Citizen," the man began nervously. "I know not how to tell you this, but Hell has been unleashed on our planet. Unspeakable horrors—which go beyond the understanding of an ordinary man—are visited upon us. Satan himself wreaks bloody disaster among the innocent . . ."

"What have you to report!" Ngen interrupted, irritation heavy in his tone. "Do you have the situation under control down there—or not?"

"We are trying, First Citizen!" The man almost pleaded, face going ashen. "We are regrouping the Civil Guard. We had no idea that we would have to deal with . . . with *animals!* Savage barbarians who cut the hair from men's heads. Wear it on their belts! They are . . . Men who kill a . . . a young child as easily as an armed opponent. Rape . . . rape our women in the streets! They know not the meaning of defeat! Sordid—"

"How long until you can contain the invaders, Praetor? Just tell me! Give me a time . . . and you had better be able to accomplish your objective. If you cannot, the Patrol marines will be the very least of your problems!"

"Yes, First Citizen," the Praetor said dejectedly. "We will have them contained within five—"

"Three!" Ngen interrupted. "Three days! Or you deal with me."

"Y-Yes, First Citizen."

"Send me records. I would see these Romanans in battle. It would also please me to see the marines in action. They should be outnumbered one hundred to one by our ground forces. Please see to it that appropriate records are sent up before the invaders are all destroyed."

"Yes, First Citizen," the Praetor moaned, nodding in resignation. "Anything else, First Citizen?"

"You might take some of these Romanans and marines prisoner. It would please me to have women . . . if you would, Praetor." Ngen smiled. "That is all."

"Yes, yes, of course, First Citizen." He saluted, looking as if he would rather have been ordered to levitate over boiling oil. The comm flicked off, leaving Ngen frowning.

"Giorj. How many of those ATs made it down?" Ngen turned, thinking quickly.

"We do not know, First Citizen. They managed to knock out all of the orbiting stations' defenses. Three have been completely decompressed with total loss of life. Two stations are still partially functional; without immediate medical aid, radiation exposure will kill survivors within days."

"Total casualties from the stations at present?" Ngen asked, dreading the answer.

"Sixty three thousand, nine hundred and some. The figure will rise as reports are processed." Giorj's unemotional voice betrayed nothing of his feelings.

"How did they hit us so hard?" Ngen wondered. "Those ATs were supposed to be sitting ducks."

"Evidently our intelligence was inaccurate. Standard Patrol combat instructions are to use ATs in ship to ship combat to secure landings after shields and hulls are breached.

The noses are designed specifically to penetrate hulls. None were deployed to attack us." Giorj cocked his head as if analyzing simple data. "I would presume that in force they overwhelmed the stations. Had they followed procedure, we would have destroyed the portion sent to board our fleet."

"Estimated number of landed troops?" Ngen thought quickly. *How bad could this be?*

"Standard complements of marines would allow the landing of six thousand from all of the Patrol ships. The unknown factor in this case is the extent of Romanan strength. Perhaps as many as another three thousand could have been transported by a ship the size of *Bullet* and landed by a complement of ATs.

"Nine thousand men?" Ngen mused. "We have over a half million men in arms. There should be no problem fighting these primitive vermin. We can overrun them by force of numbers alone."

"May I point out, First Citizen, there are also somewhere near one hundred and eighty ATs on the planet's surface. That gives them a tactical superiority that is difficult to overcome with poorly trained foot soldiers." Giorj kept his voice low to prevent the bridge officers from hearing his words.

"We need to hit them. Pinpoint the landing areas. Bombard them thoroughly as soon as you have them located," Ngen decided. He called surface maps up on comm and had the system reconstruct the landing of the ATs. It was an interesting tactical situation. He could shoot down at the ATs. They couldn't get back to their ships. The Patrol couldn't get down to them.

As long as he pinned them down, the surface troops couldn't move. But then, how did his fleet get far enough out of orbit to engage the Patrol? It took all three of his ships to cover the entire global surface.

"Hailing from the planet, sir." Giorj looked up. "Commercial frequency."

"Tell them we can't be bothered." Ngen grimaced distastefully.

"It is from the Union board, First Citizen."

"Very well," Ngen frowned. An image of a white-haired elder formed. He nodded respectfully.

"My compliments, Boardmember Pika Vitr." Ngen inclined his head. "Could you make this brief, we have four Patrol battleships left to destroy."

"Greetings, First Citizen. We hail your success against the Directorate tyrants with pleasure and admiration." Pika smiled his assurance. "Would you be so kind as to inform us of the schedule for ridding our cities of these Patrol vermin? Most especially, First Citizen, these psychotic Romanans. There is great concern here over when these beasts will be destroyed. They are less than human, First Citizen. In fact, I think it is a completely pathological society."

Ngen felt a slight chill deep within. "Would you mind elaborating, Boardmember? The Praetor has been in contact and informed me that he will have them under control within three days. They are simple primitives, are they not?"

"Observe," Pika said dryly.

The monitor formed a picture of three men in half suits of battle armor raping a young girl in the middle of the street. Then he saw a gleaming-eyed man with garish designs on his battle carapace running a knife through another man's hair. Fascinated, Ngen watched him rip the scalp off and whirl it around.

Yet another image formed, showing a formation of Home Guards moving forward with good discipline. Suddenly, blaster fire erupted from what seemed to be an empty street. The formation shot back, blowing out portions of buildings and scorching shrubbery. Each of the enemy blaster bolts seemed to find its target with uncanny efficiency. Within seconds, the formation broke, fleeing to the rear while Romanans appeared out of gaps in the pavement, bushes, from around the corners, and pounced gleefully on the dead.

Pika Vitr's face reformed. "There is more, First Citizen. These vile beasts not only desecrate the dead, they have little concept of property. They destroy what they cannot take with them. They are nothing more than brigands with the morals of dock scum!"

Ngen felt his gut tighten at the allusion to his own past, though obviously Pika was too distraught over the damage the Romanans were doing to Ekrania to realize what he'd said.

"We will deal with them as soon as possible, Boardmember," Ngen soothed. "We will be making strikes against their ATs and, similarly, we'll burn off any infestations of them. When you locate a concentration, please call in the coordinates and clear the Civil Guard from the area. We will sterilize it from space."

Pika smiled in deeply felt relief. "Bless you, First Citizen. These wretched demons are making it difficult to maintain morale. There are whispers among the people that it is better to flee on sight of these despicable vermin than have your hair hang from their belts.

"I greatly fear we will have to initiate a massive abortion program after it is all said and done. They are . . . Well, destroying the psychological integrity of our women. The men lose their capacity to think rationally when their wives are brutally raped. The psychological trauma is severe."

Ngen fingered his chin, as he chewed his lip.

"A most deplorable situation! They mutilate the men they take prisoner. Can these be human beings?" Pika cried out incredulously. He'd worked so hard to stay calm up to that point. "God has sent this insidious host against us for some reason! What have we done to merit such degradation and infamy? What did—"

"Here," Ngen soothed, while his gut twisted inside. "They will pay. I swear that to you on the soul of our martyred Leona Magill! They shall not avoid justice, Boardmember."

Pika was desperate, ready to believe.

"Now, I must set about clearing this situation up so we can get back to leading normal lives. Do call us with strike coordinates." Ngen bowed and signaled Giorj to cut the screen.

He'd always thought Pika a rock! How had a group of illiterate, rifle-bearing savages learned tactics so well? They had literally shot the living hell out of a perfectly organized and disciplined military formation. They had destroyed the iron control of Boardmember Pika Vitr—a man on the point of collapse. How did they strike such terror into otherwise intelligent, educated, authoritative men?

Ngen finally realized he was chewing his lip. If the Romanans weren't contained quickly, the morale of his people would erode like so much silt in a heavy rain. The orbital strikes would come down the second coordinates were called in. He'd shoot immediately. If sacred citizens died—it could be blamed on the Romanans.

Witnesses of atrocities and survivors of the rapes need not report to their families and friends. Such observances spread panic. And panic could defeat him just as quickly as a Patrol blaster. The thing to do would be to knock out the Romanan threat before it could spread to other areas. The savages were still close to their landing points. He had to act now.

"Concentrate all the ship's guns on the spaceport area. Blast everything, burn the sector down to bedrock." Ngen nodded to himself, that should take care of the capital. Then he would move on to other areas.

Giorj looked up, sallow face ashen. "Are you sure that would be a wise idea? There are thousands of . . ."

"I've heard enough!" Ngen snapped. *"Shoot!"*

Giorj took a deep breath, his normally emotionally-dead face oddly twisted. "Very well, First Citizen. Gunnery, all weapons to train on the Ekranian spaceport. Shoot until further notice." Giorj swallowed with difficulty, refusing to meet Ngen's fevered gaze.

Susan let her eyes play over the spaceport landing field. Sirian citizens packed it like the bleating animals they reminded her of. At the same time, they elicited a certain amount of pity as she thought of her days as Ramon's and Maria's virtual slave. Her escaped fate now awaited these cowering, crying figures. How many would have the strength to survive?

A little girl dressed in yellow hugged her mother's skirts, looking up with big eyes as Susan shot her a smile. The little girl grinned, lighting up at the sight of a friendly face. Her young eyes projected a deliberate curiosity.

"Wait," Susan ordered with a raised hand and Hans slowed the aircar and backed it up. The woman had picked up the little girl, backing away, feral fear in her eyes. Susan ordered, "Hold still!"

The woman stopped, panicked.

She looked at the little girl, seeing no fear, only wariness. "What is your name, little one?" Susan asked, voice soft.

"Mara," the little girl said, cheeks dimpling.

"Mara," Susan laughed. "Would you grow up to be a great warrior?"

"Like you?"

"Like me."

"Yes!" Mara cried to her mother's horror.

Susan glared at the cringing woman. "If anyone bothers you, tell them you are the property of Corporal Susan Smith Andojar. Understand?"

The woman nodded as Hans pulled away.

AT22 gleamed whitely in the morning light as Hans pulled up. Susan blinked burning eyes and saw that her five warriors had slept the whole way. Here the air stank worse than anywhere; clouds of black smoke hung low over burned-out aprons where the commerce of a planet had sent freighters to the stars in a better day.

Susan let Hans lift her out and for a fleeting moment, wished he would hold her forever, letting her sleep in his strong arms.

Her trembling, aching legs carried her up the ramp in pulled-muscle agony. She passed several marines in shining battle armor who saluted vigorously. They hadn't even been out of the AT. On the bridge, Susan gave her name and passed the hatch.

With some relief she noticed that while Rita's skin still glowed rosy pink, underneath, she, too, had been worn haggard.

"Reporting, Major." Susan saluted, weaving back and forth, struggling to keep her eyes focused. Things on the bridge kept getting fuzzy and almost spinning. Her legs shook, clattering the hard armor.

"Anything to report, Susan?" Iron Eyes asked as he looked up from comm.

"No, John," her voice sounded like gravel grinding on tin.

Rita's smirk showed her humor. "That's quite a bundle of fur on your belt. I take it you've truly found your calling in life. Sit down, Susan, you look like you're about to fall over."

She didn't remember dropping into the conforming command chair. The last thing she heard was Moshe's order. "Let's get out of here. The sooner we're away, the better. I don't like hanging around waiting to be shot at."

"The other ATs are positioned?" Rita's voice came through a gray fog.

"Yes. We've only got a skeleton crew here to guard the prisoners. A tech team is in the process of setting up a generator to build a field to contain them. Won't even need guards after that. . . ."

Susan slept.

"Hey!" A rough hand prodded her shoulder, dragging her up from bliss. "Wake up, kid. I think you'll want to see this." The excitement in Rita's voice made her force leaden eyelids open. Frowning, yawning, digging grimy fingers into her eyes, Susan looked up at the monitors.

Black clouds in the sky swirled in roiling circles around brilliant violet threads that hung in the air. Smoke, debris, flame, and explosion billowed up from the ground along with dust. Streamers of steam made a growing cloud that glimmered purple and flickered as the threads dimmed or brightened.

"What is that?" Susan asked, sitting up to see better, not comprehending the meaning of the spectacular light show partially blocked by the surrounding buildings.

"That," Rita said grimly, "is the spaceport. We pulled out twenty minutes ago. I'd imagine they didn't take the time to scan it."

"That field Moshe was talking about . . ." Susan struggled to make sense out of it. ". . . would that protect all those people?" She remembered Mara, whom she had fleeting hopes of seeing grow into a warrior. She'd seen the fire in those little eyes.

"No," Rita admitted hollowly. "They're dead, Susan. The irony is those aren't our blasters. Those are from *Hiram Lazar*. The bastard has just murdered his own people. Sure, he got maybe a hundred Romanans, too, but that's about all."

"All those people," Susan muttered to herself in disbelief. "There were thousands there." *Including a little girl in yellow who hadn't been afraid.*

"About five thousand," Iron Eyes said in wonderment. "So callous and hard. Are the star men always so heedless of the value of life? Do they have no sense of rightness?"

"We thought you Romanans were pretty mean and nasty," Moshe reminded, softly. "I don't think anyone could have anticipated this. Most of the captives were women brought in by your Romanans. They were all so young."

"They were to be wives," Iron Eyes added sadly. "They would have been taken back, married, and made one with the clans. There will be much violence now. The warriors will want the Sirians to pay for destroying what they have fought so hard for and taken with honor. I can't hold them back." He knotted a thick fist. "I won't! They'll leave this settlement in flames. They'll fear and hate the Sirians now. Before, they just despised them."

"Better move our combat teams as far from that concentrated fire as possible," Rita decided. She leaned over the comm talking in clipped tones.

Susan shook her head slowly, feeling her heart tear. The energy of the blasters diminished by two thirds as it penetrated the atmosphere. The focus of the beams would disperse rapidly as it collided with the gases. Warriors who had abandoned parts of their armor would receive terrible UV burns over most of their bodies.

The lights suddenly disappeared, changing the color of the destruction from purple to reddish yellow on the bottom as the flames boiled into black, impenetrable clouds. A rain squall formed where the blasters had lanced through the clouds. Something exploded in a mushroom of red-orange tinged with black wisps of smoke that curled into the fireball rising toward the darkening heavens.

"That cuts it,"Moshe Rashid declared. "The ATs are targets from now on." He turned, eyes pits of worry. "I think the work has really begun. We're no longer fighting a police action to clean up Sirius. If we don't win, we don't go home. If we don't go home, we all die here."

"What about *Bullet*?" Susan asked suddenly. "Hans said that you hadn't been able to make contact. What's wrong? Why didn't the Colonel destroy the ship that just shot?"

Rita took a deep breath and studied Susan coolly. "The Patrol lost two ships in the first fight. They didn't even scratch the Sirian fleet."

"I don't understand," Susan shook her head. "I thought the Patrol was the greatest power in the galaxy?"

Rita's laugh crackled, dry, bitter. "We were . . . until Ngen Van Chow converted those cargo ships up there. I think the balance of power changed very rapidly. You see, we got through to the Colonel a little while ago. We're the only thing keeping him from destruction. As long as we raise hell down here and draw fire from the Sirians, they can't go destroy what's left of the Patrol fleet.

"Kid, I hate to tell you this, but things are real desperate about now. I don't think it's going to get any better unless we can threaten this planet into surrender—in spite of those damn Sirian ships up there."

Susan frowned, trying to make sense of it with her sluggish mind. "Those Brotherhood blasters," she spoke her thoughts. "Too much hyperconductor and that Fujiki device. That's what gave them the power."

"What!" Moshe had listened absently until she mentioned the hyperconductor.

"Oh, something Hans and I dug up." Susan realized what she was saying and clamped a dirty hand to her mouth. Her guilty eyes shot from Moshe's intent expression to Rita's puzzlement to Iron Eyes' apathy.

"Tell me more, Susan," Moshe ordered tersely, getting to his feet, suddenly attentive. "Was this something you found on your raid last night?"

Susan took a deep breath and shook her head in defeat. It was out of the bag now. They'd really throw the book at Hans.

He had his hands on her shoulders. "Where did you hear this?" At Susan's defiance, Moshe rose. "Get Hans Yeager in here right now."

Susan throttled her urge to cry. Tired, worn out, emotionally drained from the last day, short on sleep—a little girl in yellow was dead—and now this.

Hans arrived, looking nervously about the bridge. Moshe motioned him over. Briefly he explained what Susan had said. Hans turned dead white and swallowed nervously.

"I won't tell them a thing, Hans," Susan said impulsively. She shifted her eyes to Moshe. "Look, it's all my fault. I found the stuff, I just asked Hans for an interpretation. He looked at the diagrams and explained about the hyperconductor. He didn't know what the Fujiki Amplifier did, and I don't either. Let him go—it's me you want." She stood up and sighed, handing her knife and blaster to Moshe. "Arrest me now."

"What in hell are you doing?" Rita demanded.

"I must be crazy," Hans chuckled, shaking his head. "Perhaps the key to this whole deadlock lies right here." He turned easily and tapped Susan's personal comp unit.

"What?" Rita asked, relieved by the lessening tension.

No one had a chance to explain. A violent explosion rocked the AT. Susan grabbed for her knife and blaster and scuttled to the rear of the bridge. She could hear the tearing of blaster fire coupled with rifle shots. Rita charged past her while Susan delivered covering fire from a hatch.

There was no telling how the Sirians had made it so close. Judging by the mass of fighters she could see, there were too many to stem. Was this death? She grimaced, blaster lacing fire into the darkly-clad figures.

CHAPTER XVIII

"What choices do we have?" Maya asked. "We could blow the whole planet apart . . . or lose it all. No matter what, we're stuck and so are our people down there. Ngen can pinpoint them, blow them apart, and then come for us!"

"We could always cut our losses," Toby reminded. "Blast the planet—and Ngen—with a cobalt warhead."

"Hell of a way to win a war," Ree growled. "No, that's out."

"How did this happen?" Yaisha Mendez exploded. "We can't blow a hole through Van Chow's shields because our blasters can't penetrate his shielding. On the other hand, we can bomb the planet with nuclear and antimatter and render it sterile. Overkill or underkill? Those are our options?"

"Wait," Ree mused, lifting a hand from where he stared absently into space. "There just might be another way. Have you thought about that?"

"Like what?" Maya wondered. "You know our capabilities as well as—"

"Like we're not just stuck with our existing arsenal." Ree straightened. "We've got a lot of sharp people at our disposal. The best brains we could recruit out of university for the last couple of decades, right? So let's have them think about it. Let's think about it ourselves. Maybe a gravity flux generator? Some sort of low yield projectiles?"

Maya chuckled ironically. "You know, Damen, I've come to really admire you over the last couple of months. You can cook up some of the most interesting schemes."

"Well," he waved her off, "it's an idea. Seems like that's the best we can do for the moment."

Toby Kuryaken added, "Ngen's people have *Brotherhood* in tow. It looks like the Sirians removed the survivors. God, what do you suppose he'll do to them?"

"The man just blasted his own spaceport. Killed his own people. What do you think?" Maya snapped. "I wouldn't wager but that he tries to use them as hostages against us."

"We can't bargain for them," Ree sighed, still staring into space, thinking hard. "Too much is at stake here."

"Not to mention the amount of intelligence Ngen's getting out of the ship." He sighed and shook his head. "If only there were some way of getting down there and blasting *Brotherhood* to plasma. No, now he knows what our strengths are, what our capacities consist of and how poorly off we are."

"Not to mention what he's pulled out of comm. I hope Arish had time to wipe as much as she could."

"Would she have thought of it?" Ree asked scathingly.

"They're still our people!" Yaisha cried. "Maybe we could put together some sort of rescue? We have responsibilities!"

Ree nodded. "Yes, I know. Now you have some idea of what I went through over Atlantis with the Romanan problem."

"Well, this isn't Atlantis!" Toby snapped. "I say cut our losses and sterilize the whole place. So we lose some marines and Romanans. I've seen the holos, they're barbaric! Savage . . ."

Maya waved them down. "Maybe so, but the Romanan marines sure seemed to have come through. They've routed every Sirian Civil and Home Guard force they've come across. They're suffering incredible casualties, but they don't seem to lose morale."

"How's your own ship?" Ree asked. "Drawings on the walls yet?"

Maya glared. "Hell, yes! How'd you know?"

"Spider has a habit of finding His way into a warrior's heart," Ree said evenly. "No, Maya, we won't lose. I just . . . just feel it. Not only that, I think I have an idea. I'll put Major Glick on it and see what he comes up with."

"You know," Maya said, eyes veiled, "I've been in touch with the Directors. Seems Ngen Van Chow is broadcasting Romanan atrocities all across space. If you do win, there might be a loud outcry for the removal of their, shall we say, social turbulence?"

Ree perked up. "Broadcasts! Of course!"

"What are you—"

"Van Chow would use Romanan barbarism against us?" Ree snapped his fingers. "Who's more barbaric? My warriors, with blasters and knives, or Ngen frying his own people at the spaceport?"

Maya's eyes slitted. "I think I see your point—but why?"

"Psychology. Ngen is using this war against the Directorate. It's time we used his actions against him."

Yaisha Mendez shook her head. "That is totally beyond any regulation in the book, Dam—"

"Neal!" Ree called over his shoulder. "Send the stuff on the Sirian attack. From now on, monitor his every move. Send anything you get that looks shifty."

"Yes, sir!"

"Damen!" Mendez gritted. "You are totally out of line! Of all the insubordinate . . . That's the responsibility of the Directors! You can't just take Directorate policy into your own hands and—"

"If you'll excuse me," Ree said, getting to his feet, "I think I've got an idea on how to whittle the odds a little more in our favor. I'll be in touch in another couple of hours and let you know if it will work." He cut the comm, trotting toward engineering.

"He's a danger," Yaisha Mendez declared.

"Perhaps," Maya admitted, staring at the monitor, chin resting in her palm. "At the same time, he's one sharp commander."

"If I'm not mistaken, Maya, he's gone rogue. Director Robinson refers to him as a pirate." Toby looked at her questioningly. "You can't seriously be thinking of supporting a . . . a rogue? An outlaw!"

Maya pushed herself up straight, elbows locking. "Skor called him a pirate?"

Toby's lips thinned. "What else? He disobeyed orders. Fired on you and Sheila. If that isn't piracy, what—"

"We fired on him first," Maya reminded dryly. "As to piracy, you know what that charge implies. You know what action the regulations require for—"

"You've seen the tapes," Yaisha pointed out. "These Romanans are a plague. Look to your own marines. You say you've got graffiti all over your ship! Your marines on the planet are decorated the same way. They're cutting human hair from their victims and wearing it like the barbarians. How can you condone that sort of—"

Maya thundered, "*Maybe they are!* What the hell, my people, working with Romanans, have taken three to four times the surface area your Patrol marines have! Hell, that's nothing. Arish's people have placed themselves under Iron Eyes and Rita Sarsa! They've . . . gone over. Your Patrol marines—"

"*Our* Patrol marines?" Toby slitted her eyes. "Very well, Maya, I ask you now. When this is over, are you loyal to the Directorate . . . or Damen Ree?"

Maya bit her lip, a hard glint in her eyes. "Loyal! Like I was over Atlantis when Damen would have killed us. No, I don't change sides, Toby. A little quirk of mine, you see. Something about honor."

Yaisha nodded slowly, as if making up her mind. "You know we might be ordered to destroy *Bullet* in the end. Civilization has to be maintained. We can't have Romanan chaos loose in a peaceful society. Think! Imagine what those butchers would do among Directorate citizens! We can't have that kind of role model for average citizens—there aren't enough psych machines to handle it!"

Maya lifted her chin, jaw muscles dancing. "I'd hate it . . . but maybe . . . if it comes to that, we'll have to turn on him. Orders and all." She slapped her hand on the table. "Yes, damn it! I'll stick with you. There, the cards are on the table. You know where I stand . . . and Spider help us."

She killed the comm conection and stood, arching her back, lips pressed together as she stretched. She looked over at the hatch, seeing the small black spider effigy a Romanan had drawn in defiance of orders—or had it been one of her own people?

"Damn it, Damen. I can't help it. If the order comes, well, I've sworn on my honor." She closed her eyes and shook her head. "And *I* swore by Spider? Me?"

Skor watched as Chester, hands clasped in his lap, watched a riot in Tarawa Station.

"You see?" Skor intoned. "The people are . . . are insane!"

"You shouldn't have released Roque's compendium of data refuting Ngen," Chester told him gently. "I thought of calling you about it, trying to get you to think the problem through, but you would have ignored me, sent me away for meddling."

"You knew! And you didn't tell us this would be a disaster?" Skor's mouth worked, opening and closing.

"Of course, I knew. Come, Director, you know better than that. It was a cusp. I have found myself dangerously close to fooling with the future as it is. No, the time was not right to tell you. Nor would my actions at the time have done any other good than to alienate you from me."

Skor hesitated a moment, a faint suggestion of a frown on his immense forehead. "Very well, teach me."

"I have told you already. Your perceptions of humanity are dangerously skewed. You have lost contact with your own roots. Think. You make the assumption that all men are rational beings—and to an extent they are. But can an ordinary man absorb the amount of data Roque assembled and sent? Indeed not, and as a result, the ordinary man can only feel affronted. That is the reaction Ngen played upon. He turned your work against you, pointing out your arrogance to the average person. He is most clever, this Ngen Van Chow. Most brilliant."

"You admire him?" Skor demanded.

"Oh, yes," Chester sighed. "Monster that he is, his ability to manipulate humans is most remarkable. Would that Spider could regain his soul. Nevertheless, I fear he shall do great damage." Chester cocked his head. "A fascinating dichotomy. Your kind, Skor, offers only a rational, logical future. Sterile. Ngen offers only an emotional, passionate future, also sterile. And, for the moment, humanity must chose between the two of you."

"Why can they not choose another approach?" Skor demanded. "They are rational beings. They—"

Chester raised his hand. "I see your entire argument in my head, Director. There is no need to tell me. The answer to your question, quite simply, is that they no longer have the ability to chose their own destinies. And why is that?"

Skor's eyes closed for a moment, his lips trembling as he thought. Finally, "I see. You think our policies have led to this. We did no wrong!"

"All administrations through all of human history have replied in exactly that manner, Skor." Chester smiled. "You did no wrong—but did you do right?"

"There have been no wars!" Skor's voice cracked with emotion. "There have been no starvations . . . plagues . . . political executions!"

"But the people have lost the ability to think . . . to care for themselves. You have taken their ability to adapt from them."

"Adaptation is change!" Skor defended. "Change rarely comes with predictability!"

"What is the major premise of anthropology?" Chester asked. "I assume you can access Leeta Dobra's Library. What do you see of humanity and adaptation?"

Skor looked up miserably. "I see the key to the success of the species, Prophet. Is it true then? Is mankind doomed to suffer?"

Chester smiled warmly. "That is the way of Spider, Director."

"But to have other than the Directorate is to have chaos!" Skor insisted. "An unpredictable life is not worth living! No, Prophet, I cannot accept your premise. Humanity has outgrown its savagery. We *will* have peace. No matter what the cost. You see the future? Tell me of the future you see with your Romanans loose in space? You've seen the holos of Romanans raping and killing on Sirius. Tell me the value of that suffering! You are wrong, and I shall see that you and your kind are stopped."

"Then we will be stopped. But do you not think the species would benefit from rational action combined with passion and emotion? That feeds the soul—"

"Combine the Directorate with such as Ngen Van Chow?" Skor cried, stricken. "That, Prophet, I will never accept!"

Skor's holo shimmered and disappeared.

Chester nodded briefly to himself before turning in his chair, playing Nikos Theodorakis' third symphony. And to think, such brilliance was ignored in the twentieth century.

"You will never accept? Ah, Director, you get more human by the day," he smiled, eyes softening as the music filled the room.

Susan clipped another charge into her blaster, bracing the weapon against her arm. She played the beam across the wave of yelling figures storming toward the AT, watching bodies convulse and explode. From the rear of the vessel could be heard shouts, screams, and explosions as blaster bolts ripped into men and metal.

"How did they get so close?" Rita demanded.

"Must have set down on a base," Moshe called. "Of all the rotten luck!"

The big blasters cut loose from the AT's side. The destruction was awesome and the Sirians broke, dropping back, seemingly leaping into nothingness as the big bolts hit them. Others scrambled into what seemed to be concrete molding.

"Underground installation!" Rita guessed. "No wonder we had room to set the ship down here."

As the Sirians retreated, a group of Romanans and marines boiled out after them. Taking advantage of the ATs' supporting fire they charged the Sirian rear.

"That's insanity!" Iron Eyes growled from where he huddled next to them, peering out of the smoking lock. "They'll be overwhelmed."

Susan felt her heart stop. "That's Friday in front! Look. You'll know him by that odd run of his. We've got to save him!" Susan leaped from the hatch as she spoke. Shouts and pleas were called from behind her. Heedless, she ignored Rita's order and ran on.

Concussion hit her like a steel bat. Lifted up and turned in the air—as if in slow motion—the universe twisted and whirled. She slammed to the ground with a bone-wrenching impact. Bits of earth and concrete rained down, beating on her unprotected head.

She tried to pull an agonized breath into her body. Nerves shrieked. Joints sizzled with hurt. She couldn't breathe—it was as if a huge weight had dropped on her chest. Worst of all, she couldn't move. Her numbed mind screamed, while her limbs remained unresponsive.

From nowhere, Hans crouched beside her, blaster crackling madly.

I'm dying. Doesn't hurt so badly after all. Odd. I don't fear. Dying isn't so bad. Her pleading eyes looked up into Hans' panic. He shot again and grabbed at her; hot fire made him resort to his blaster.

Susan struggled against a mental haze as she tried to scream at him to get back to cover—to save himself—that she was dead.

A bead of sweat ran gleaming down his flushed cheek as he frantically snapped another charge into the blaster. Face grim with purpose, he triggered the weapon, shooting from where he knelt next to her. The mad passion in his eyes touched her. His gritted teeth made the muscles along his jaw stand out. And, no, it wasn't sweat! It was a tear!

Rita dropped down next to her, the Major's big blaster humming while the bolts made a sound like velcro being ripped apart under amplification.

"Cover me!" Hans shouted, sweeping Susan into his arms. How odd. He had never seemed so strong!

The universe bounced crazily up and down as her head and body jerked to his awkward run. A blaster bolt hissed by her ear and blew a chunk out of the AT's whitish-gray ablative material.

Willing hands pulled her into the lock, Rita rolling in beside her. And Friday? She found she could roll her head. "Yellow Legs," she whispered. "Is Friday safe?" She gasped weakly for air, striving to fill her lungs.

Hans had grabbed up her hand, eyes warm, vulnerable,

and to Susan's sudden realization, so very sensuous. "I'll get him for you." The voice blurred, thick with regret and hurt.

"I'll be fine," Susan muttered, trying to sit up. To her surprise, nothing had been blown off. "What happened to me?"

"Big blaster bolt hit right next to you," Rita threw over her shoulder as she ran for the bridge. "We're getting out of here."

"Friday?" Susan whispered, face pinching from the sudden pain that racked every joint.

Hans jumped from the hatch. Grimly, Susan crawled to the lip of the big portal and stared out over the smoking ground before her. The hazy air made a light show of blue and violet, dust motes sparkling into infinity in the blaster bolts. Full out, Hans ran for a little knot of men huddled miserably behind a broken wall, pouring their fire into a position Susan couldn't see.

Hans broke most of the enfilading attack the Sirians had managed to put together, but in spite of the intensity of his sputtering blaster, some overran the Romanan position. Heroically, Friday and his men rose to meet them. Blasters fired point-blank. From where she lay, Susan helplessly watched the flash of knives, heard the screams of rage.

From behind, Hans charged down, clubbing and butt-stroking with his now empty blaster. She could see him hollering orders, pointing frantically at the AT. A little knot of Romanans broke and sprinted for the ship. Blaster bolts blew two men apart, scattering the pieces over the steaming ground.

The AT's heavy guns shot back, ripping into the Sirians unmercifully. Last out were Hans and Friday, running for their lives as blaster lines of death tried to pin them. Physically sick, Susan watched them, frozen at the sight.

Hans made the hatch just as the AT began to rise. He clutched the lip and pulled himself up. He swung in as the ground dropped away.

"Too high!" Friday screamed, a wry smile twisting his lips.

Hans flung himself out of the hatchway, hanging by his knees where they hooked around the pneumatic seal. "Jump! It's your last chance, man! *Jump! For God's sake!*" His fingers reached out.

Friday jumped with everything his short legs had. Hans

caught a wrist. The ground dropped ten meters, fifteen, twenty, more.

Friday got his other hand up, fingers locking in some loose plate. Fear glazed his eyes now. He shot a quick look over his shoulder at the ground so far below.

Susan could see the wrist, slowly pulling through Hans' grip. Hans—face contorted—reddened as he fought to hold Friday's weight.

"Help!" Susan screamed. "By Spider! Someone help us!" She pinned Hans' legs to keep him from slipping.

A concussion shook the AT. Friday jerked about like a rag doll. Inhumanly, Hans held on, the veins in his neck standing out, breath tearing from him in short gasps.

The light around them changed to brilliant violet.

"Close your eyes!" Hans ordered. "You'll go blind! That's blaster fire!"

The AT lurched. Hans slipped, pulled farther out of the hatch. Susan heard herself scream as she forced her agonized body to react. Hans now had only one foot wedged in the corner of the hatch.

Susan fought to pull them both back in. She could see the lip of the hatch cutting into Hans' skin. Violet light burned hot on her own skin.

"Help!" she screamed again. *"Help me!"* Her vocal chords were insignificant against the wind whipping past the hatch and the roaring of the blaster bolts that tried to seek out their craft.

Iron Eyes charged into the companionway, took in the situation, and dived to grab Hans' other foot.

"Save yourself!" Friday cried. "It is not worth two of us dying!"

"I've got you!" Hans grunted. "Hang on! This can't last forever."

"Your hand is slipping!" Friday tried to grin, desperation in his eyes. "I am proud to have known you, warrior. You are the brother of my soul. My coups are yours."

With the addition of Iron Eyes' tremendous strength, they pulled Hans up until his hips were inside the AT.

"Hang on, man!" Hans screamed. "Just a little more! They've got me!"

"They could turn off that light!" Friday decided, shouting against the wind. "My skin is burned from my body!"

"Keep your eyes away from it!" Hans ordered. "It will blind you to look at it."

With Susan pinning Hans' legs, Iron Eyes reached out and caught Friday's hand as it slipped from Hans' grasp. Hans caught at his other hand. Each bearing half the burden, they pulled the struggling warrior into the hatch.

Suddenly, g pitched them against the wall as Moshe fought to avoid blaster fire. "I'd have never held you through that," Hans gasped, trying to bend his fingers, wincing in pain.

Friday nodded, almost shaking, sucking in deep breaths, tenderly feeling where his skin had been burned by the UV from the blaster bolt. Blisters were rising along his neck. He looked out the hatch one last time and grinned at the ground so far below.

Susan sat there totally numb, fascinated by the look of Hans' face, one side pale and white, the other scorched red by the blaster bolt.

Iron Eyes chuckled and slapped them both on the back, rolling the hatch closed before he went forward.

"Why . . . why did you do that?" Friday asked at last. "You could have . . . been . . ." He absently rubbed the wrist the corporal had clung to.

Hans grinned weakly. "Soon as my heart gets out of my throat . . . I'll tell you."

Susan let herself slump, aware of the pain lancing her body. She'd never forget what she'd just witnessed. Friday, dangling over death as the Sirian landscape flashed below him. Hans, fighting desperately to overcome the pitching AT's gyrations to save a rival.

"I meant what I swore, Corporal Yeager," Friday added, grinning. "My coups are yours. You have done me honor. I pledge myself to your service."

Susan opened her weary eyes, noting solemnity in Friday's face. It had to hurt him. She thought back to the day he'd threatened to swear knife feud.

Hans shook his head. "I don't know about any of that. I don't know what's proper among your People." He paused, indicating Susan with a nod of his head. "She loves you. I couldn't let the man she loves be taken from her."

"What?" Susan demanded.

"Haven't you been taken to med yet?" Hans changed the subject, blushing red. "What if you're dying on us?"

"*Dying?*" Friday demanded; for the first time he noticed her battered, bloody appearance.

"Blaster bolt almost got her. We thought she was dead when she hit the ground. Come on, Susan. Let's get you to med—" pausing as the AT lurched horribly—"assuming we live that long."

She cried out when they picked her up. Teeth gritted, she fought tears and refused to let them carry her. Instead, she leaned on them and forced one foot after another down the companionway of the yawing, swaying AT.

As they made the med unit, the craft stabilized—safe for the moment at least. The med unit looked nightmarish, men and women laid out everywhere. Some were soaked in a yellow, jellylike stuff swabbed on stubs of arms and legs. Others had the material pasted over ribs where the flesh had been burned away. Some were hanging over the maw of death by a thread.

The tech got to her first, running a scanner over her body before slipping her into a med unit despite her protests. It was the same medicine she'd given Rita that day. Despairing, she looked out to see meds smearing stuff on Hans' and Friday's burns.

"Just shook up," the harried med told her. "Get out of here. Take a couple of days of rest and relaxation. You'll heal up just fine. In the meantime," he plopped a pill in her mouth, "this will keep the pain down. Remember, just because you don't feel it, doesn't mean you aren't hurt!"

She slid out and sat up as Rita's face formed on comm. "You all right, kid?"

"Yeah," Susan straightened and stood, feeling fire in every muscle of her body. "And I'm on my way up to kick your ass!"

"Good!" Rita laughed. "You don't know how close *Hiram Lazar* just came to cooking *your* ass with that blaster of theirs. We're not out of the woods yet. We're hovering over a densely populated area. If they keep shooting, they'll cook a lot of their own people. That bastard up there has already killed plenty trying to shoot us down.

"Come on up to the wardroom. We've got some strategy to work out." Rita's face disappeared.

Stiffly, almost gasping with each step, she went over to the two men sitting awkwardly against the wall—both of whom watched her with suddenly leery eyes.

"I've got to go," Susan said easily, wondering at the

sudden change in all their relationships. Friday seemed preoccupied with his thumbnail as he got up. Hans was staring
at the ceiling.

"You are all right?" Friday managed.

"Hans," she began, almost at a loss for words. "Thank
you. Out there, I mean. They'd have got me . . ."

He grinned and shook his head. "Call it even," Hans
mumbled, blushing.

She nodded, leaving them staring nervously at each other,
heading for the corridor, noting for the first time how grimy
the walls had become. She remembered them being sparkling clean.

And how did she feel? Susan chewed the inside of her
cheeks, blinking her eyes in tired frustration. She felt
half-dead. She could sort Hans and Friday out after she got
some sleep.

The situation doesn't look any too good for us," Rita
explained somberly. She turned, her expression pained. "We
could all die here."

Iron Eyes gave her a crooked grin. "Did you think
you would live forever? You should talk to a Prophet sometime."

She nodded. "Yeah, I know. I just don't like falling to a
bunch of civilized sheep." A short laugh. "Better a Santos
bullet on a horse raid, eh? More honor that way."

He placed a hand on her shoulder, turning her to face
him, looking down into her green eyes. "Spider hasn't pulled
us back yet."

Rita studied him, her mind racing. "But what do we do?
Without *Bullet*, and with Ngen controlling the skies . . .
Damn it! There's got to be a way!"

Iron Eyes patted her on the shoulder. "So we're trapped
here?" He walked over to stare at the monitor, seeing the
city drifting by below, a composite of shining angles, marred
here and there by columns of smoke. A conflagration raged
in the wreckage of the spaceport.

*And Ngen wastes his own people like a Raider burning
another's range? What sort of men are these Directorate
Sirians? What sort of civilization could have bred humans
without honor?*

Rita came to stand by his shoulder. "Yeah, we're trapped.
Unless the Colonel can pull a rabbit out of his hat."

He stared at her from the corner of his eye. "What's a rabbit . . . and what's it doing in his hat? I don't—"

"Never mind," she groaned. "Figure of speech."

"Still," he mused, pulling at one of the long braids hanging down over his chest. "Spider has made us for this. Somehow, someway, we'll make out." He raised his eyes to the heavens. "Ngen is up there, powerful, capable of destroying *Bullet*. We're down here, wild Romanans high on looting for the moment. But my People will tire, grow nervous at the strangeness once the battle flush has worn off. For now, they're mad. Ngen killed their captured wives, deprived them of the first night's spoil. I'm a war chief, how can I turn that to my favor?"

Rita nodded soberly. "All we have to do is tell them there's no way home."

Iron Eyes glared at the sultry heavens, mulling over what sort of man would kill his own women and children so callously. "Ngen, you don't realize it from your lofty heights, but down here, we've become a rock leech in your society! See what acids we'll let loose among your people. No, Sirian, the only way to stop a rock leech's poison is to cut the affected part off—quick. If you don't, there is no known cure!"

Rita's eyes glittered. "You know, I like that attitude. We just might be able to use it against him. Tell the warriors they're rock leeches? Why not?"

He winked at her. "Now, if we were on World, we could always steal the other guy's horses and ride home. How does a warrior steal a spaceship on Sirius?"

The laugh lines tightened at the corners of her eyes. "I wish . . . No, it's not that easy, War Chief. Not even for you." She shook her head. "Nope, what we've got is what you can see out there. Come on, let's go put our heads together and see if we can't figure a way out of this."

"But you don't have much hope," Iron Eyes observed.

She shook her head. "No, but we'll show the bastards how to die with honor, huh?"

CHAPTER XIX

The cramped wardroom was bustling with activity when Susan snuck in. She found a chair and slipped into it gratefully. She didn't realize she'd gone to sleep until she was painfully jabbed awake by the man next to her. She blinked, rubbing her eyes.

Rita was talking. "We need to make a determination of policy. We've managed to get occasional transmissions through to the Colonel. They're waiting in a high orbit, repairing damage, trying to think about what to do next."

Iron Eyes stood up, eyes playing over the haggard faces. Didn't the man ever tire? "Considering the options, Major Sarsa tells me you can't steal a starship to ride home in the way we steal horses on World." This comment broke the tension with a short wave of laughter. "I've talked over the situation with the Major. Given our present situation, I see one strategic advantage. We have the Sirian population hostage. I say we use it."

A captain from *Victory* shook his head. "That's barbaric. According to the rules of war, the innocent should not suffer."

There were nods around the room.

"That's not war," Rita replied. All eyes turned to her. "You've seen the reality out there. Why can't we use the population as hostages? Ngen himself burned thousands at the spaceport. Most of them were women and children. Read your history, ladies and gentlemen. Remember the Confederacy and the Soviets? The end justifies the means. So long as we delude ourselves into believing anything else . . . we're lost."

Susan searched each of the shocked faces. "That's right," she whispered under her breath.

Iron Eyes seemed to dominate the whole table. "We Romanans think a great deal of honor. We find our honor in winning an unwinnable situation. Spider is God. Spider tells us to struggle past hope. Spider has told us that death is better than subjugation. If we don't take this planet, what happens? The Patrol can't take the Sirian fleet because they can't outshoot their blasters. If the Patrol is destroyed, who's next? We sit on the eve of another Soviet style reign if Sirius wins."

"He's right." Rita Sarsa nodded. "The population is the only leverage we have. To date, our tactics have reflected piecemeal demonstrations of power. I think it's time we started to dominate."

"But the Patrol creed—" one man started.

"*Is crap!*" Iron Eyes thundered. "To hell with what you have been able to get away with during centuries of peace! Right now, right here, this very instant, we fight for our lives. Do you understand that? No one will come out of the stars and bail us out! Either we take this planet . . . by whatever means we've got . . or we die here!" Fire flickered behind the War Chief's eyes.

"I agree," Moshe said reasonably. "Part of Ngen Van Chow's success is the knowledge that the planet will back him up. If they don't provide him with a safe port and base, he's left with piracy as his only option. Raiding other—"

"Why won't he take it?" Iron Eyes demanded. "Raiding is a very good way of making a living."

"He wants more," Rita said softly. "Besides, piracy would only be a short-term solution until the Directorate could build better blasters. They'd get him in the end. No, he's got to sell himself to the people. To do that, he's got to turn Sirius into a model. Until we showed up, he—"

"But the destruction of *thousands*, perhaps *millions*, of lives are at stake!" one of the other captains cried.

"*Hell!*" Susan snorted, her mind catching glimmers of the illumination—or madness—that tinges the edges of consciousness when the brain is too fatigued. "They have a social responsibility . . . just like we do." She looked around dully. "After all, when you skin out the animal, the population is the objective of this whole campaign. Whoever ends up controlling the people wins the war. Do we . . . or does Ngen?"

"Any dissent?" Rita asked looking around. "That *is* the military objective when all the crap is stripped off it. We are here to squash a rebellion. The Sirians put Ngen Van Chow in power, only they can pull him down. What matters is that we get them to do it—not how!"

"And how do you propose to do this?" one of the captains asked. "We've always sworn to uphold—"

THE WAY OF SPIDER

"Fear," Susan hissed. "Sheep react only to fear. They shy from what they don't like or want." She lost herself in the memory of the huddled masses that first night of the raid.

Iron Eyes looked wolfishly at her. "Perhaps she is becoming a warrior after all?"

Susan glared.

Iron Eyes grinned. "They fear the Romanans. We don't play by the rules. We hurt them where it counts. The marines just demonstrate strength. We make them *fear*. Threaten their very understanding of reality. That terror is a weapon."

"I don't get it." Another captain was shaking her head. "I mean it's barbaric to . . . to . . ."

"I do," Rita said grimly. She looked at the woman who'd spoken. "The Patrol represents a known threat. We take over the planet and everything remains the same. Well, sure, different government. But no better or no worse than before the Independence Party took over. If on the other hand, the Romanans take over—what then?

The captain recoiled, horror in her eyes.

Susan laughed, wavering on the verge of unconsciousness. Iron Eyes studied each of the faces, his look predatory as his mind raced at the possibilities.

Rita continued, "You see, ladies and gentlemen, the Sirians have no conception of the Romanans. The future under barbarian rulership isn't just frightful, it's a horror come real. Let them think about it. Let their imaginations work. Let them see the evil alternative—"

"We're *not* evil!" Iron Eyes protested.

"No," Rita agreed, shaking her head. "But they don't know that."

Moshe looked annoyed. "Ngen Van Chow has been masterful at manipulating this whole world's psychology. He's managed to keep production up in spite of our projection of apathy. He did it by perfectly timed sabotage, martyrdom, and a host of other means. Surely, we can counter that."

"We can." Rita grinned happily. "As ranking officer here, I do hereby proclaim that those population centers which lay down their arms and submit to Patrol authority will be spared Romanan incursions. Those who do not will be turned over for Romanan rule." Rita looked very satisfied. "There, they have a choice to make; us, Ngen, or the Romanans."

The room broke into muttered discussion. Minutes later, the AT lurched, accelerated, then decelerated, pitching wildly.

"Bridge? Report!" Moshe ordered.

"Blaster fire, sir." The pilot's voice sounded cool. "We're evading. They seem to have picked us special—like they know we've got the command center here."

"Get us out of it!" Moshe ordered.

"Yes, sir. They seem to have trouble locking on, sir. They may have good space scan, but those converted cargo ships don't see so good through atmosphere."

"Just get us undercover." Moshe managed to keep his voice calm.

"Yes, sir." The pilot sounded oddly elated. The comm replied with a general warning. "Attention! All hands. Crash harness advised. Prepare to land hard."

People were strapping in all around Susan. She managed to get the job done, but her fingers felt thick.

The impact wasn't as bad as anticipated. From the rear came a muffled explosion.

"What the hell?" Rita asked as she struggled out of the webbing.

"Bridge, *report!*" Moshe demanded from comm.

"Sir," the pilot's voice was chipper. "I think we have them fooled. If their planet scanning capability is as poor as we think, they'll figure they hit us with that last shot. I ran us through a building and the aft blasters made it look good to the sky. They should consider us dead and gone."

"Is that in the book?" Moshe demanded.

"No, sir," the pilot sounded contrite, "I, uh, learned from a Romanan."

Someone laughed.

Rita stood. "I want to see some of you to work out details on governing this ball of mud. In the meantime, Iron Eyes, make sure we're secure in here. Take a party and round up any Sirians in this building.

"Susan, you and Hans to the bridge. Let's finish this Brotherhood blaster affair."

Hans, battle grimed and funny looking with the burn grease on his pinkened skin looked guilty as Rita beckoned him past the hatch.

"All right," she said, "let's hear it. Start from the beginning."

Susan wet her lips. "It was my fault. You remember the meeting where I would have sworn knife feud against Yarovitch?" The rest of the story spilled out, Susan too deathly tired to think.

Rita listened, frowning, chewing her thumb. In the end, she whistled softly. "No kidding? Holy Spider, we've got to get a line through to the Colonel. This might be what breaks it wide open. If Ree can upgrade *Bullet's* . . ." Rita looked around, suddenly self-conscious. "Kids, this is top secret, got it? No one must know. No one!"

Susan nodded.

Rita took her battered comp and turned to comm. Placing a headset on her brow, she opened a line to *Bullet*. "Colonel? Sarsa here. Secure this line as best you can. My favorite protégée has some information I'm patching through."

Rita indicated Susan needed to patch in. "It's uneven, kid, but I think we can get through."

Susan did, accessing her files, using her code word.

"Sending, Colonel," Rita added. After Susan's data drained, she added. "Did you get that?"

Rita looked up and winked. "That's all, kid. Take my quarters, get some rest. You look completely done in."

Hans followed her from the bridge, tired and spent himself. Susan looked up at him, yawning deeply. "Where's Friday?"

"Out on patrol with Iron Eyes. That maniac pilot ran us into a big warehouse full of exotic foods. I think I'll like this place."

"By Spider, I'm tired." She thought it took all her effort to nod her head.

"Come on, I've got a special bunk for you." He led her down a hall to Rita's small cabin. "It's all yours for twenty hours." Hans palmed the hatch.

"But where will Rita . . ."

"On the bridge. She's going to be busy as it is. Come on." He pulled her through the hatch entry.

Susan groaned as she leaned against the wall. Hans began undoing her battle armor, dropping the streaked, smudged, blood-spattered pieces to the floor. His elbows banged the close walls.

Susan looked up at the chronometer. "I've been up and at 'em for almost two days."

"I got a good sleep in between."

"I must look like washed-out hell."

"You're as beautiful as ever," Hans whispered, pulling the carapace from Susan's back.

"I stink," she said with a giggle. "I've smelled horses that were fresh air compared to me. I'm taking a shower."

Hans didn't even blush as she stripped in front of him and entered the small unit. Feeling at least a little alive, she dried and stepped out. Wearily, she dropped on the bunk and adjusted the controls.

Hans settled himself into the one little chair. She looked at him curiously, mind trying to play tricks on her. "Why did you do it?"

"What?"

"Friday. Me. You know you should have been killed out there ten times over."

"Spider was with me." Hans' lips curled. "I guess he likes fools." He sobered. "Besides, they would have wiped out all of them. You saw that flanking attack. It would have been Friday's death. I couldn't stand the thought. . . . would have hurt you terribly." He dropped his gaze to his hands, rubbing them tenderly back and forth as if remembering the feel of Friday's sweaty skin.

"You know I love you," she whispered. "You and Friday. I don't know what it would be like to live without either of you."

He didn't move, eyes focused on some infinite point beyond the bulkhead. Finally, he whispered hoarsely, "You go to sleep now, Susan. You're tired. It's affecting your mind."

She shook her head, seeing him struggle with his own concept of nobility. Her mind took her back to the look in his eyes when he rescued her and Friday. She saw the strength, the character, the resignation.

Forgetting her hurts, she stood and pulled him to his feet. He trembled as she undid his battle armor, fingers oddly supple in spite of her exhaustion.

"Susan?" he asked, as she peeled the undergarment from him. "Are you . . . sure? I mean . . . about Friday. . . ."

"I can't sleep, Hans. I'm too wound up. Besides, I need you now. I've wanted you for a long time. I just didn't really know it. You're the most—"

"But what does this mean?" he asked, reacting as her fingers traced the curve of his chest.

"It means I almost lost you today. We still might lose each other, you know. It would be wrong if one of us died and we hadn't . . . hadn't shared this. Our lives would be poorer for that." She pulled him down into the bunk with her.

"I've never been with a woman before," he said softly. "I'm a . . . I may not be any good."

"We have twenty hours to find out," she whispered, nibbling lightly on his ear.

"First Citizen!" Giorj's voice tugged at the edge of Ngen's consciousness. In his dream, a young Romanan girl with black hair lay writhing where she was bound before him. With an electronic whip he teased her firm body, changing the charge as he stimulated her, watching her moan to the visions the psych implanted in her mind.

"First Citizen? Please respond."

"Yes." The dream broke, leaving him flushed and excited.

"We have a Patrol broadcast, First Citizen. I think you should be apprised," Giorj's flat voice informed. "I have just returned from the captured ship. I was using their comm to monitor their communications. I think you should know that something was sent to *Bullet*. I couldn't get the data, but I know it has to do with Brotherhood information stored in *Bullet's* comm. Like Frontier, *Bullet* contains considerable data in her deep computer banks. Evidently, it's been there for centuries."

"What?" Ngen swung to his feet, wiping the sleep from his eyes. Leona's body lay next to his, still hot and sweaty from the exertion he had driven her to.

"I'm not sure, First Citizen. Suffice it to say, a Major Sarsa believes it could break the stalemate up here." Giorj's eyes glowed as he rubbed his fingers together. "What secrets could be hidden . . ." He shook his head. "If only I could get to that ship!"

"Giorj!" Ngen snapped. "How serious is this?"

The pale engineer shrugged. "We have no idea. Unfortunately, I had only begun my study of their comm. The technical data couldn't be retrieved and I didn't understand the recording commands at the time. I've given you the bulk of their conversation. At the same time, there has been another broadcast from the planet. I think you should see it."

A holo formed of a red-haired woman. Quite attractive. Then the hardness in those green eyes grabbed Ngen's attention. He saw challenge behind that stare. Challenge he instantly responded to. He ordered a copy of the holo stored.

"Citizens of Sirius," the deep contralto voice touched a chord within Ngen. "By military proclamation of the Directorate, any person or persons who does not willingly submit to the authority of the Directorate on this planet within ten hours will be considered hostile.

"Those areas remaining loyal to the Directorate will be protected by Patrol marines. Those areas which continue to support the policies of the outlawed Independence Party will be turned over to the Romanan nation for subjugation. Further, those areas granted to the Romanans will not be returned to Patrol jurisdiction after this planet has been subdued. It should be made clear that the Romanans are a separate political entity and are not bound by the laws, conventions, or compacts of Directorate space. They are political allies in name only. Those areas granted to them will remain theirs through perpetuity.

"The Romanans, we point out, have their own system of economics and distribution of resources. Some of you will be transported off-planet for the purpose of cattle herding, manufacturing rifles, knives, and harnesses, plowing fields, and cleaning corrals. Some of the women will be taken for the purposes of cooking, house cleaning, and nursing children. Those of richer families will be taken as wives of status. This should not deter you, ladies. The work load will be limited since the returning warriors are rich men. You will share your connubial duties with as many as seven other wives.

"Similarly, industry in the Romanan sectors will remain under Romanan control. They will determine wages, profits, and taxes on all production. The Patrol assumes that those deported to the Romanan home world will ensure that production meets their requirements. I believe you would refer to those individuals as hostages . . . were not the Romanans so kind and humanitarian in nature.

"Those areas seeking Patrol protection will be restored to normal conditions as soon as humanly possible. We realize that political machinations have led you to believe that death and destruction will be your lot under restored Directorate control. However, industry will be returned to normal and export will continue as before. Pending the settlement of our difficulties, GCI cargo ships are waiting to make the jump from Range, Zion, Earth, and other places where a surplus of food is building up. They, in turn, need generators, metals, and equipment manufactured here. There will be no penalties imposed by the Patrol if the leaders of the Independence Party are turned over to us.

"Citizens, you have ten hours. After that time—depending

on evidence of support—you will be either protected or granted to the Romanan forces. The decision is yours." The image disappeared.

Ngen frowned. A rather quick action on the part of the Patrol. He began chewing on his lip as his brow furrowed with thought. Things had not gone as anticipated. He'd hoped to blast the Patrol from the skies. Then the Civil Guard would destroy the Romanans and marines in hard fought ground action to temper their understanding of revolution.

The Patrol survived. The planet engaged in fierce ground combat; but his forces consistently got cut to ribbons making such small advances. Now this! How would the people react?

Ngen got up, dressed, and settled himself before the comm. "Giorj, prepare to send this. Planet-wide broadcast."

Ngen forced the lines of his face into a serious expression. "My fellow citizens! Oh, that such treachery could possibly be devised by the mind of man to fester in our reborn society. What the Patrol cannot do by force of weapons . . . they do instead by twisted words and lies!

"Remember our beloved Leona Magill? By treachery she forfeited her life. She died that you might live and," he paused, his eyes lighting, "may I add here, at the hands of that very same red-haired witch of the Patrol. Do any of you know her, citizens? If you do, bring such knowledge to me.

"Our agents identified her months ago. Vigorously, we pursued her to bring her to justice for her crimes! In vain, our security forces sought her that you might see the Directorate in its darkest truth!" He pounded a fist into his palm, eyes lighting with fanatical persuasion.

"This is but the *ultimate blasphemy!* That it would be *her* whom the Directorate beasts would send to try and draw you back into their fold! What does that tell us of the Directorate? Of the Patrol who would have you turn yourselves over to this witch of Hell? She who bombed your factories and murdered our glorious leader, Leona Magill? Who will follow? Who will listen?

"Not I, my brothers." He let his eyes burn into the comm pickup for a second. Then, in a gentler voice, "No . . . not I. We have given too much to turn our backs on those butchered by the Directorate. Should we surrender now, what do we say to the souls of those who died to bring us a living dream?" He stretched out his hands, imploring. "Could you tell any of the noble dead that we have *spurned their very graves?*"

Ngen let them have fifteen seconds to think of that. "Now they threaten us with barbarians! They claim that they would sell our families into slavery! What comes next? Do we want to see our daughters shipped off to be gutter whores to such animals as wear the hair of their victims about their waists? Do we want their unwashed, stinking bodies pressed against the pure clean flesh of young Sirian virtue?"

Ngen fired himself to a fever pitch. "Look at your children!" he cried passionately. "See your daughters taken and raped repeatedly in mass orgies! See their young bodies swell with devil-gotten spawn that defiles the name of human! See your sons, ripped from your strong hands and taught the evil passions of savagery! See them learn to drink the hot red blood of their victims! See them dancing under hair ripped from the heads of civilized men! See what you would do to them!"

Ngen allowed himself to settle back into his seat, face effecting a twitch as if he were fighting for control. "Citizens, the barbarians are men. Kill them in our streets. Kill them in the skies. Kill them in our houses and factories. They die but once. If we submit, we die a thousand times. I shall not quit. I am of your blood, born of your body. This battle for our future is mine until the death.

"If there be traitors among you, seek them out and treat them as they deserve. Nothing in our lives comes easily. Leona paid that supreme sacrifice that we might be free. She will never see the fruits of what we have wrought. I may never see those just rewards, nor may so many of you, my fellow citizens. Do we—who will not live—deny the dreams of others?"

"Remember that! Remember, too, if you can find that redheaded woman, I will offer one million credits, provided she is brought to me unharmed. Together, we will watch her trial. She will be an example for the entire galaxy that on Sirius, at least, justice exists!"

He shut the broadcast down and got Giorj's image. "I think that should take the energy out of their silly proclamation." Ngen smiled happily. "Was it a good performance?"

"Superb, First Citizen." Giorj bowed, something hesitant in his eyes.

"Yes, Giorj?" Ngen asked.

"Nothing, First Citizen. It is just that the Romanans are expanding toward my mother's house in Angla."

"She will be fine, Giorj," Ngen reassured him with a sincerity he didn't feel. If the Romanans took it . . . well, no telling how Giorj would react. "If things get rough, I promise I will personally order a patrol to evacuate her."

"Thank you, First Citizen." Giorj nodded.

"Oh, by the way," Ngen added, as if he'd just remembered. "Any sectors of the city which defect to the Patrol are to be burned. It will be a gentle reminder to the faithful that loyalty to the Party is of first importance; the official reason is that we are destroying counterrevolutionaries and Romanans."

Giorj entered the commands. "Very well, First Citizen. I am informing the gun control crews at this moment."

Ngen smiled happily, checked the position of the Patrol ships, and frowned. He would attend to them soon. But what did it mean that *Bullet* hid Brotherhood secrets? Just what was buried in her banks?

"Giorj?"

"Yes, First Citizen."

"When the Patrol makes the next move, concentrate our fire on *Bullet*. We need her—and this Brotherhood secret. You've studied the captured ship, you know her now, have you identified the weaknesses?"

"Yes, First Citizen."

"Good," Ngen added, eyes slitting. "To take the hero, Damen Ree, savior of Atlantis, would be a singular success, wouldn't it? A symbol of our power."

"Indeed, First Citizen." Giorj bowed, eyes still gleaming. Almost breathlessly, he added, "And I could get my hands on that technology!"

"Yes, Giorj," Ngen added smoothly. "*Bullet* will be yours. And tell any gunner who disables her, he will be rewarded amply. Any gunner, on the other hand, who hits the reactor, or destroys those computers, will be given to the Romanans before we destroy them."

"Yes, First Citizen."

"That will be all, Giorj." The comm went blank.

So the Patrol fought back, using the terror of the Romanans against his revolution. Ngen couldn't help but remember the terror in Pika Vitr's eyes as he showed the holos of the Romanans in action. "But then, I have taken countermeasures. Now we must wait and see."

He smiled at Leona, enjoying the glassy look of terror in her eyes.

But he passed by her and settled himself on a nearby bed next to a second woman. She glared, bound hand and foot. Smiling happily, he ran a finger around the puckering nipples and cooed easily, "Now you, too, will learn pleasure, my tall beauty. Yes, you will be a delight to break. All that power and command and self-assurance will do you no good in the end. I, Ngen Van Chow, will make your own body betray you. I will teach you to despise yourself, sweet jewel!"

Her eyes glinted hotly as she mumbled over the gag in her mouth. Oh, she'd kill him all right. Just a look at those muscular legs and arms showed him she'd kept in shape. The thought excited him.

"Yes, beloved dove, I see the hatred in your eyes." He smacked his lips. "But now, dearest love, the time has come to begin our lessons. You will cry for me. You will melt for me. All your power will become putty in my hands."

He carefully lowered the headset on her brow, and waited until her eyes went misty. Then he removed the gag from the woman's mouth and began kissing her neck and running his fingers along her sides. Colonel Arish Amahanandras tried to scream.

The ATs came in pairs, piercing whistles cracking the sky as they boomed overhead, blasters lacing the shining Sirian arcologies on the outskirts of Angla, one of the larger Ekranian manufacturing districts. In their wake, shattered glass and bent graphsteel twisted and smoldered, black clouds curling to the smoke-hazy sky.

"That should do it," Hans decided.

"Move up," Susan ordered. Flitting figures advanced up the wreckage-clogged street where the Civil Guard had bottled them. "Thank Spider for ATs."

"Keep your eyes on the windows," Friday reminded.

"Down!" Hans screamed. *"Sirians!"*

The ghosting Romanans ducked behind crashed cargo trucks, slipping into doorways and behind cracked, uprooted masonry, blasters ready.

"Hold your fire!" Susan ordered. "They've got a white flag. They're surrendering."

A steady stream, the broken Home Guards poured out of the huge bulk of the arcology, broken glass crunching under their boots, arms held high. Some wavered on their feet, dazed from the hell the ATs had unleashed. Others tried to stop leaking wounds. Some just stared numbly at the ground. The majority, however, shivered with fear, their terrified eyes searching the shadows.

"All right," Susan sighed, singling out Ray Smith and Patan Reesh. "You know the drill; get them back to our lines."

The Romanans sneered their disgust, rising, blasters ready, motioning the Sirians out away from the wreckage. Susan stood, knowing sixty Romanan rifles covered her.

Hans came in from the side as one of the Home Guards stepped forward, a commander's stripes on his arms. "We surrender! Don't hurt us! Don't mutilate us!"

Susan stopped before the man, taking a quick, uneasy glance at the cloudy sky. "You'll be fine. Romanans don't harm those who surrender. We just have problems respecting you."

A Spider chuckled from where he crouched under an overturned aircar.

The Sirian swallowed hard. "Well, what do you expect?" His eyes carried a frantic look. "We've seen the tapes. The ones Leeta Dobra sent from *Bullet*. We know about the Prophets. The stories are everywhere. How can we fight against you when you know the future? How can we plan when you know every move we make? You know in advance when you'll win! How can we stand against that?"

"The Prophets?" Susan wondered. "What do they—"

"*Yes!*" the Sirian commander cried. "Those men who see the future! How else could you beat us every time? Know our every weakness? You wouldn't have attacked unless you knew you'd win! We're helpless against that."

Susan laughed, slapping her knee. "How else, indeed? Know the power of Spider, Sirian. Now, get the hell out of here. We've got a planet to take!"

Reesh motioned the Sirians to begin moving, the long line straggling out of the sprawling wrecked building as the rest of her squad ran forward, taking up the positions the Sirians abandoned.

"Keep your eyes out for powerlead accesses!" Friday shouted, waving the rest ahead, looking nervously at the skies. Orbital attacks followed victories with unnerving frequency.

"Hans? Friday?" Susan called, moving under the shelter of a blasted conveyor tunnel. "What does this mean? What about this Prophet business?"

Friday gave her an impish grin. "Would you go to war against a man who sees the future?"

She shook her head. "No, but then, these people don't understand Prophets. A Prophet doesn't tell what he sees in the future; he'd go mad! Besides, we don't have a Prophet with us."

Hans waved them down. "No, but they don't know that. I think this is important." He lifted his belt comm. "Get me Major Sarsa!"

CHAPTER XX

Damen Ree studied the torpedo with interest. "You're sure it'll work?" he asked.

Major Glick lifted his hands helplessly. "I have no idea. It depends on what their engineering has come up with. I'd be willing to bet that they don't have much in the way of defensive gear. Devices for jamming systems like we built into this baby are rather sophisticated."

Ree rubbed his chin as he looked at the big metal basket. It was no more than a stasis field that surrounded an anti-matter generator. They'd scavenged most of *Bullet* to put the thing together. It filled the hold, taking up way too much space.

On the front of the thing a huge, perfectly drawn image of a spider in mid-jump had been painted, its legs outspread to seize its prey. The mouth gaped open, exposing two big poison-dripping fangs. Ree decided that if the artwork reflected the talent that went into the torpedo, they had a winner. If not, Spider would at least appreciate the effort.

"Comm, get me Colonel ben Ahmad." He looked up as the image formed. "We're ready, I guess. Do you want to review the operation again?"

Maya shook her head. "No, Damen. We'll make one run. Thirty g acceleration, drop through the gravity well, and climb out again on the other side. We hope your gizmo holds up and the rest of us take as much fire as possible since you've cannibalized to build the torpedo."

"Pray to Spider it works!" Ree muttered to himself, wishing he had a Prophet to give him one of those infuriating lessons.

"Any time, Damen," Maya replied.

"Let's go then." He shrugged. "Glick, get to engineering. You've got to hold this baby together for me." Ree looked at the ugly torpedo. "Lord, I hope that thing doesn't blow us apart when we turn it on."

"Me, too," Glick agreed as he trotted for the reactor room.

Ree caught a lift and rode to the bridge. On the status screens, he could see the rest of the fleet accelerating toward the planet. They formed up, *Victory* and *Toreon* first, then *Bullet* in the middle while *Miliken* took the tail position.

The rear would be the weakest link. *Miliken* would take the brunt of the fire if things went wrong. If things went right, the torpedo would take out one of the Sirian ships and the antimatter disruption would skew the targeting computers of the two remaining Sirian ships. One way, *Miliken* got off scot-free, the other, she would be lucky to make it back alive.

Nothing remained but to wait. Once set in motion, the ships could do little until the range closed. At their first movement, the Sirians had formed up. So much for any advantage of surprise. Ree hadn't counted on the Sirian officers being asleep anyway.

"Tony?" he called. "Anything on those hidden Brotherhood files from comm?"

"Yes, sir. They were there, just like Rita said. No one would have known that kind of information was buried in good old *Bullet*."

"Glick hasn't seen it yet?"

"No, sir. He's been too busy with the torpedo. So has all of engineering, for that matter."

Ree sucked in his lower lip. "First thing—provided we live through this—you send him a copy of that data, see if he can make anything out of it. Maybe some way to break Ngen's shielding."

"Yes, sir."

Damen drew his usual cup of coffee and sipped at it as he pulled on his combat armor. The normal checks felt routine— a time-honored tradition. From the screen, he could see the dead, lifeless bulk of *Brotherhood*. Idly, Ree wondered what had happened to the survivors. If Glick's reactor failed, they'd all know.

"Twenty minutes to maximum range, Colonel," Neal Iverson called from one side. "I have communication with the ground, sir. Major Sarsa confirms simultaneous ground strikes on all major Sirian strongholds. The ATs are in the air and shooting, sir. Ground teams are disrupting communications and sabotaging what they can."

"Good!" Ree nodded with satisfaction. "Let's hope they draw some of the attention away from us." He glanced up at the spider effigy drawn on the plating overhead. Compared to the one drawn on the torpedo, it wasn't much, but Leeta had drawn it, blessing the ship.

Ree sipped his coffee and stared at the monitors. So little time now. Almost there. On visual, the blasters of the Sirian fleet were piercing the atmosphere of the planet. Well, they'd take some of the heat off the joeys real soon. Unfortunately, it would fall on him and his precious *Bullet*. They'd weakened her to provide parts to build that second smaller reactor which made the torpedo so deadly. Generating and isolating antimatter still wasn't child's play!

"*Victory* and *Toreon* engaged, sir," Neal's calm voice came from the side. Ree watched those deadly Sirian blasters prodding the shields. The Patrol ships made a dazzling display of shifting multicolored light as the shields absorbed and deflected those deadly bolts.

They were still too far away, the blasters diffusing a lot of energy at that distance. When they got closer, things would get rough. The shield generators, already hot, would begin to overload. They would warp out of shape and hull plating would be exposed. Decks would be breached and decompress. Men would die.

At the same time, while the Sirians had little if any hope of poking holes in the Patrol at this distance, they would learn the acceleration and course of the Patrol ships, feed the data into their targeting computers, and be able to track their prey more efficiently.

"Engineering!" Ree called, "Keep on your toes. Get that torpedo outside."

"Yes, sir," a voice called back, "*Spider's Revenge* is outboard now, sir."

"*Spider's Revenge?*" Ree asked.

"Uh, that's what some of the techs called it, sir." The voice sounded apologetic.

"Let's hope it lives up to its name, technician."

Neal called out. "*Victory* is holed. I'm picking up gases from decompression of decks seven and eight. Ballistic computer is engaged. *Toreon* is overloading her front shields, but they're still holding."

"Hang in there!"

Violet shafts sought the weakened shields of *Bullet*. *Victory* shifted, taking the brunt of the fire, the telltale streamers of decompression following behind like a tail. Gases and vapors crystallized in the cold. Anything loose like coffee cups, papers, equipment, padding—or men—blew out the jagged holes in the hull to be left behind as the ship accelerated.

"Ten, nine, eight," Neal's voice began. Ree glued his gaze to the monitor showing the torpedo. "Three, two, one. We have release."

Eighty seconds away, Glick would throw the switch. If the jury-rigged reactor worked, if the Sirians didn't shoot the thing apart, if they considered it junk broken off or blown loose from their blaster hits, if they didn't jam the triggering device, *Bullet* might even the odds a little.

Damen Ree started, almost physically shaking as *Hiram Lazar* got *Bullet's* range. "Open fire!" Ree ordered. He balanced his reduced cannon, using fewer batteries at full power, the leads to many having been pulled out for use in the torpedo.

"*Spider's Revenge* is armed, Colonel," Glick's voice came tersely. "At least it didn't blow up when I flipped the switch."

"Damage control report, sir. All decks breached. Decks two and four decompressing." Neal's voice didn't carry so much as a tremor.

Ree shifted more power to the screens at the expense of the forward blasters. He could imagine the gunners cursing that decision.

"Oh, oh!" Neal called out. "They're shooting at the torpedo!"

"Course correction!" Ree called. He could see two of *Helk's* blasters seeking the torpedo. "Dive for *Helk*. All blasters, concentrate fire on *Helk*. Let's make those boys feel burned!"

Ree shifted his power, knowing he was overloading his banks.

He saw the shields fail at the same time Neal called it out.

That put more power into the blasters and for a brief moment, they had the joy of seeing *Helk*'s shield waver and collapse. A cloud of gas and debris boiled out of *Helk*'s hull before the blasters flickered and quit. They'd made one last good solid hit.

Naked, defenseless, Ree shuttled orders to helm. Nothing. *"Glick! What's happening?"*

"I'm losing the stasis, Colonel," Glick's voice was forced. "I'm shutting down to half power. It's that . . . or we blow the antimatter within minutes."

"Very well, engineer. Shut her down, we've got a lot of velocity, we're through for this round." Ree felt his gut wrench. Even as he thought it, he saw another blaster bolt searching them out.

"Spider," he muttered under his breath, hating the sour feeling in his gut. "If you are God, *make that torpedo work!*"

"Accelerate!" Ngen Van Chow ordered. "They're hurt badly. His weapons are out! His shields are down. He's cut power to almost nothing. *I want that ship!*"

"Request from *Helk* and *Dastar*, sir. They want to know if they should accompany. I might add on my own that *Helk* has sustained damage." Giorj looked up from his comm.

"Someone has to stay. My orders are that they concentrate on breaking up the Patrol advances on the ground." Ngen frowned, watching the other Patrol ships accelerating out of range. The tactic had worked. He'd stopped *Bullet*, Giorj's batteries crippling the ship.

Hiram Lazar moved out at twenty gravities. They should catch the Patrol ship within an hour and ten minutes.

"What if this is a trap?" Giorj asked.

"Then it is brilliantly executed!" Ngen chortled. "That ship engaged us the longest during the first fight. Did you notice where they placed her? She was in the middle, Giorj. They wanted her to be protected. They evidently hoped to hurt us enough to make that final ship safe in their formation.

"You see, they can concentrate firepower, but not shield strength. That's the tactical reality of space warfare." Ngen felt immensely pleased with himself. More so, now that he had a chance to take a damaged Patrol ship of the line. *Brotherhood* had been a gutted hulk when he got to her. This ship would be fixable and would have all its Brotherhood secrets intact.

Ngen began pacing the bridge, waiting as the Patrol ship slowly drew within range. "Now is the time to watch for tricks."

"Transmission from the Patrol vesse—" A blinding flash of light and radiation came from behind them.

"What was that?" Ngen demanded, seeing the filters on the monitors shifting in an attempt to compensate for the blast.

Giorj was rerunning the explosion on his screen, slowing it, studying the computer output. "Matter/antimatter reaction, First Citizen." He looked up, his face blank. "*Dastar* is no longer in orbit."

Ngen watched the monitors as the heavier radiation swept by. Indeed, only *Helk* remained where it had been shielded by the curvature of the atmosphere. Trying to raise *Helk*, static crackled on the speakers.

"Too much junk floating around as a result of that explosion. It will take a while for the hard debris to be blown out," Giorj declared.

Ngen closed his eyes, taking a deep breath. They'd cut his fleet by one third—bombed by an antimatter device he hadn't seen coming! Anger drifted into depression. He settled into his command chair and brooded at the monitor displaying the distance to the damaged Patrol ship.

"They took one of mine," he mumbled to himself. "I take one of theirs back!"

The slow minutes dragged at his soul. The Patrol ship seemed to grow so slowly on the screen. Pacing again, Ngen watched the bulk looming in the monitor. Along the scorched side of the battleship, he could read the faint letters BUL-LET P-8. *Bullet* was an old ship. She'd been in the Patrol for years. No wonder she carried Brotherhood secrets.

Now, up close, Ngen could make out the burn holes where his blasters had ripped into the ship. She had once been gleaming white, now she looked tattered, char running along the sides in streaks where she had accelerated while decompressing.

As he had noted with *Brotherhood*, this ship, too, had suffered battle damage prior to coming to Sirius. This ship, too, had been involved in the Atlantean fight. So not one but two were weakened before they arrived. How could Ngen Van Chow put that to work in his favor?

"Colonel Damen Ree," Ngen whispered. "The hero of Atlantis. Giorj, open a channel to the Colonel."

Visual established, the screen filled, and Ngen found himself looking into the familiar angular face of the Colonel he'd seen in the Dobra transmissions.

"Greetings, Colonel." Ngen smiled. "May I have the honor of your surrender?"

"You may not," Ree's crisply articulated words snapped out.

"It would be such a shame to destroy your ship and all your crew, Colonel. Surely, you must know that you have no defense. Is your starched honor worth all those lives?" Ngen assumed his pleading face.

"We think so," Ree gave him a fighting grin. "We don't give up, Ngen. We've learned that life is only acceptable on our terms, not someone else's."

"Very well." He turned away from the monitor. "Giorj, I think we have enough power to tow them. Magnetize that hull and let's pull them along.

"Colonel," Ngen bowed. "I don't have time for games. Right now I need you more as live hostages than as dead heroes. We'll worry about breaking you out of your shell when we have more time." He shut off the comm and looked at Giorj. "What could they possibly do to us, Engineer?"

Giorj's flat eyes didn't waver. "They might build up enough antimatter to trigger a reaction. Try the same trick they tried off Atlantis to save the Romanans."

"Can you stop it?"

"Of course. That is, I can if this ship's built on the same schematic as *Brotherhood*. I'll need the service of two blasters. It should take no longer than five minutes."

"They're yours." Ngen went back and settled himself in his chair. Giorj's surgery took less than three minutes. Atmosphere boiled out the holes he'd blown through *Bullet*. The battleship went dead.

"They no longer have powerleads capable of supplying them. The reactor is still operational, of course, but they'll need more lead material to utilize it." Giorj talked as he studied the printout on his system. "Hull's energized." He looked up and scanned his monitors. "Easy ahead, zero point two, Mister Helmsman."

Ngen nodded in satisfaction and they began plotting the quickest course back to Sirius. The screen dominated his thoughts and he chewed his lip, nervous at the proximity of a battleship that might be capable of dealing destruction.

Even so, Ree wouldn't gamble with the lives of his crew while he was at point-blank range against an undamaged ship, would he?

The other three Patrol ships had climbed back up, well out of range. Half their fleet had been destroyed while Ngen Van Chow had lost only a third of his and captured yet another battleship. The war in space was going superbly.

Damen Ree sat in the dim glow of the emergency lights and thought like he'd never thought before. The Sirians had him. Further, someone on that damned converted scow knew Patrol ships. Obviously, an engineer had gone over the wreck of *Brotherhood* with some competency.

"Line through to Maya, sir," Neal informed.

"Status, Damen?"

"We've got life support. The bastard destroyed most of the powerlead terminals—knew what he was doing. Watch out. Reactor is damped down to almost nothing. Other than that, we're right rosy. The crew and I are sitting around in battle armor, some in decompressed sections, waiting for what will be. From the computers Neal has determined we'll be locked into orbit within six hours. The magnetization of the hull isn't doing us any good either since it's making the computers a tad bit schizo."

"So what are you going to do?"

"Save *my* ship, Maya," Ree growled. "He'll take it when he blows it into atoms. Before that, we'll fight until we win, or we're dead, or we can rewire the reactor to take the bastard with us."

"Damen, just for the record . . ." Static buzzed ". . .you're one hell of a . . . and I'll miss your cussed hide. We'll be down to . . ." Lost it.

"If you can still hear me, Maya, thanks a lot. I always thought you were the best of the breed. In the event I don't see you again, thanks for everything. Take care of humanity for me." He sat, staring thoughtfully at the blank monitor. "She really was all right, you know."

"Good commander," Neal agreed, looking washed out in the pale red light.

"Yes, well, we've got one thing he doesn't have." Ree decided at last.

"I'm all ears," Neal looked up.

"I don't think he can board us and hold the ship. We're better at personal combat in zero g. We have the hand weapons and we know this ship inside and out. Neal, go to work. Get together with Glick. Figure out where they'd be most likely to break in and booby trap, mine, or defend every square inch. Let's make them come to us—the hard way!"

Neal's grim smile told him all he needed to know. The crew would back him. They wouldn't let *Bullet* down. The old girl's fate lay in good hands. Not only that, she'd killed one of the Sirians. Ree looked up at the spider on the overhead plates and, having nothing better to do, found a marker and began drawing one like it on his own combat armor.

"Now hear this," he called over the comm. "This is the Colonel. We're going to be boarded sometime soon. When it happens, remember the Romanans. They taught us the meaning of freedom and how to fight. Let's not let them down."

A cheer echoed from the decks that still held atmosphere. Patrol warriors and techs checked blasters, blocked companionways, rigged explosives, armored walls, and made ready.

On deck seven, beside a half-melted lock, Willy Red Hawk Horsecapture sat in the dark and shivered. No heat remained in his warren. Each time he got so cold that he started to feel hypothermia, the lock would spin toward the sun again and the temperature would climb to unbearable heights, drowning him in sweat. Then it would start all over again.

How long? A couple of hours? Already, he could see the planet below getting larger, fuller, more beautiful. Horsecapture checked his oxygen. The tank he'd carried out with him was still half full. Good, maybe ten hours left, if he didn't freeze first. He knew how much the cold periods sapped him, each worse than the one preceding it.

After an eternity, shivering with chill, Willy noted that one of the locks on the Sirian ship had opened. A small armored craft moved out and away from the *Hiram Lazar*. Willy readied himself and jumped. The time had come, now or never. Pray to Spider they listened before they shot. After all, what allegiance did Willy Red Hawk Horsecapture owe a man who called him insubordinate, flaunted the old ways, and had him jailed in that med unit for so long?

He would see his way to coup over that star colonel. Damen Ree's short hair would hang from his belt. Then—after the Sirians won—so would Friday Garcia Yellow Legs' and that miserable Susan's too—though he would keep her alive, her skull gleaming to remind her who her lord and master was.

As he crossed the gap in the hull he began falling. Panicked, out of his mind with fear, he kicked, thrashing in the zero g. He'd thought it would be like jumping; but the second he cleared the grav plate, his stomach flopped up into his throat and his ears lost the balance of up and down. He twisted, tumbling, helpless.

As his stomach voided into his faceplate, Willy Red Hawk Horsecapture screamed, choking on the watery vomit burning into his eyes and nose. He sucked for a breath of air, screaming as his stomach retched violently again. He sputtered and sucked another mouthful of vomit.

Ten minutes later, he didn't feel the clamp on his legs. He didn't realize he was being reeled into the little craft. Willy Red Hawk Horsecapture had suffocated on his own fluids.

Maya swallowed against the sourness in her stomach, one screen showing the battle raging around *Bullet*, the other her fellow commanders. Thank holy God, Ngen didn't have ATs. Ree had been holding out for a solid day now. Under high resolution, they could see the bodies floating around *Bullet*. Ngen s boats continued crisscrossing the space between *Hiram Lazar* and *Bullet*. How long until Ngen decided the price was too high and blasted the old ship of the line into slag?

"I, for one, am relieved," Toby's voice came over the comm.

"Indeed?" Maya asked dryly, shifting her glance to the comm monitor. "We're down to three ships. Or hadn't you noticed? Not only that, but our comrades are down there fighting and dying while we sit up here helpless to do more than lose our own ships. Haven't felt so impotent—"

"Comrades?" Toby snorted derision. "I had orders, Maya. If we took Sirius, Yaisha and I were to take *Bullet* and space the Romanans. The Directorate is too fragile for that kind—"

"You what?" Maya started to her feet. "You mean that balloon-headed freak broke his word? I heard him! He swore on his honor that—"

Yaisha stiffened. *"What* did you call the Director?"

"You heard me," Maya hissed. "He lied! I was there! I heard him! He gave his word—"

"To a pirate!" Yaisha growled. "Ree turned on the Directorate. He violated his oath, his word to honor the traditions of the Patrol! You can't possibly think he—"

"I damn well can," Maya told them coldly, glaring at both of them. "Oh, such a glorious service we have become! A two-bit Sirian hoodlum has destroyed half our fleet. Barbarians can conquer a planet the Patrol can't. Damen got the only score against the Sirian fleet and now he's down fighting for his life while the Director—along with his own colleagues—plans to cut his throat if he wins!" She spit on the deck under her feet. "That for the Director, Colonels."

Back straight, she stalked from the bridge, stopping only to stare for an instant at a spider effigy someone had painted on the bridge hatch.

"How do we surrender?" a fat Sirian man asked over the comm. "We can no longer war against your Prophets. Resistance is futile. When you know the future, what chance is there for us?" He spread his arms. "What do we do? How can we keep those barbarian Romanans from hurting us?"

Iron Eyes, leg propped on the console, fingered his chin. "If you would surrender . . . become one of us . . . draw a spider on your house. Under the symbol of God, you will be spared."

The man nodded in a flurry of shaking chins. He wrung his pudgy hands together. "And maybe when we surrender, you will tell us of the miracle of your God? Could . . . could we maybe talk with your Prophet who sees the future?"

"Maybe—after the war." Iron Eyes cocked his head. "But I can tell you now, Spider is no miracle. Spider is simply God, the Creator, that which makes the universe. You're part of God. Your soul is but a means for Spider to experience, to learn. You're part of His web."

The man blinked. "We're part of God? But the Directorate has always told us that God was a myth—an opiate of the ignorant masses. God is strife and pain and war."

Iron Eyes lifted his shoulder. "So? If I build a fire beneath you, you move. You change your life and better yourself. If I build a fire under you a second time, you get mad, you chase me away. You still change your world and, in the process, yourself. You have learned." He frowned. "No, I can't see the use of your Directorate. Where's the stimulation for new things? If you lie around and rot, grow fat, lazy, and do nothing new and important, what value is your soul to Spider?"

"But I—"

"Life has purpose!" Iron Eyes smacked a fist defiantly into a callused palm. "Live it, man! Go out, learn of yourself and your world! What would you have your soul take back to Spider when you die? Would you stand before God and say,

'My life was sterile but it sure was pleasant. I did nothing but eat and sleep and defecate and procreate.' And God will ask, 'But what have you learned about reality? About yourself which is myself?' What would you say then, Sirian?"

The man frowned, perplexed. He worked his mouth, licking his lips, staring down at his hands. "Well . . . I . . . I don't know. I never thought of it. I never did."

Iron Eyes smiled warmly. "You aren't dead yet, my friend. Paint your Spider on the wall of your house and think. There's nothing going on outside but war and death. You can maybe miss a little of that to devote some thought of your own life and soul, and what you would send to God if you could. Is a little war more important than that?"

The man nodded, an eagerness on his fleshy face. "Yes. Yes, I can think of that. You . . . you're Iron Eyes? The Romanan War Chief?"

"That's me."

"I, uh, recorded this. You . . . you wouldn't mind if I, well, showed it to some other friends?" He bit his lip, shoulders drooping a little. "I mean, you know, maybe it would explain about who you Romanans are. Why you . . . you know . . . are so fierce?"

Iron Eyes laughed, curiously amused. "I care not what you do with my words. Show them to whoever you will. The important thing is between you and Spider. Nothing else in life matters but how you feed and nourish your soul. What you would learn for God."

The man almost shook. "Thank you, War Chief. Thank you so much." Iron Eyes cut the connection, dropping his chin, thinking hard as he fingered his coups.

"Another one?" Rita asked, looking up from her seat at the AT controls.

"Yes." He squinted skeptically at the monitor which showed the warehouse around AT22. "These people are all starving their lives!" He paced back and forth. "There's no challenge here, nothing to make them learn, to better their lives, to try themselves and improve their souls! No wonder they're sheep! They've been *trained* to be sheep! Who's a greater abomination? Ngen Van Chow or Skor Robinson?"

Rita slipped the headset from her brow, rubbing her eyes, leaning back in the conforming cushions of the command chair. "I don't know. Why do you think Leeta and I went over to your side? We couldn't figure that out either." She studied him seriously. "John, what are you going to do when the war is over and they demand their Prophet?"

"I never told them we had a Prophet here." He spread his hands innocently. "What they choose to believe is their business."

"You aren't very convincing when you try and tell them we *don't* have a Prophet." One red eyebrow arched.

He grinned sheepishly. "So? It's a good thing for them to believe. Look how resistance is crumbling. Most of Ekrania is in our hands now. The story's spreading like wildfire through the remaining Sirian strongholds. More and more civic leaders—like that fat man—see hope in us and our magic. Who am I to discourage that?"

Rita smiled. "Well, you may not have a Prophet to give them, but, you know, they all want to talk to you. I'm starting to feel like a Gi-comm operator: a personal secretary! Maybe you ought to get a private to take your calls from now on instead of tying up a Major with your fan club."

"Fan club?"

"Like that fat man—and all the others fawning to get within fingering distance of your scarred hide. The ones who are starting to look to you as some sort of superhuman savior."

Iron Eyes laughed and took a deep breath. "Some of the prisoners were demanding that I let them join the Romanan forces. They say they want to take coup and march with the warriors." He shook his head. "I don't understand it."

She spun her headset in her fingers, looking up at the monitor absently. "It'll get worse, you know. It's a curious psychological response common to people who've lost everything. Your own ancestors did it on Earth when the Americans conquered them. They flocked to white ways, figuring to share the power. Obviously, if they were defeated so soundly, something had to be fatally wrong with their system and wondrously right with the victor's. They'll be calling your name in the streets soon."

Iron Eyes shrugged. "Maybe. In the meantime, perhaps we should bend our thoughts to the subjugation of Angla and the rest of the continent?"

"Wanna work again, huh?" Rita asked wryly. "I was afraid of that. Should have left you on World stealing horses. I had more free time then."

Friday Garcia Yellow Legs cast a suspicious look at John Smith Iron Eyes as he stepped into the huge room. Then he stopped dead in his tracks, gaping at the holo images on the walls. Before him stretched a vista from World: the Bear Mountains, pink granite so real he could imagine the feel of the stone but for the stink of Sirian air.

Iron Eyes grinned. "A bit of home."

Friday nodded. "Uh, you sent an AT to get me. What's up?"

"When we're done here, we'll send you back," Iron Eyes explained. "What we're doing is called propaganda. We've been canning something called commercials. Uh—like stories to sell things. Right now we're selling Romanans and unselling Ngen Van Chow."

Friday cocked his head. "You want to explain just what you mean by that?" He glanced nervously around at all the holo projectors and the gleaming-eyed techs.

Iron Eyes crossed his arms, face bland. "New ways. To put it in Romanan terms, you might say we're going to try and talk the Sirians into giving up their horses without a fight. Uh, talk them into laying down their weapons because Ngen is worse for them than we are."

Friday scuffed his boot toe on the fake dirt, seeing a green harvester and a bear perched on the far peaks. He blinked. "Hey," he pointed, "them animals wouldn't be—"

"It's art!"

"So? You snatched me out of a firefight. What do you need *me* for?"

Iron Eyes walked over and clapped Friday on the shoulder. "To sell Spider. Why, look at me. I'm rough and tough, big and mean and nasty. Now, Friday, who is the most unassuming man on all of World? Who tells the finest stories in all of the Settlements? Who has the quickest tongue of anybody? Who could talk a mother out of her baby's meal? Who has the greatest—"

Friday rolled his eyes. "Uh, I don't know about—"

"Sure you can!" Iron Eyes cried. "It's easy. I already did all the war stuff, showing how every time we took part of the city, Ngen blasted it to the ground. We already documented the destruction Ngen's inflicted on his own people. Used that violet blaster against him. I did the fierce part, but . . ."

He looked suddenly sheepish. "Well, you see, every five minutes I get a call. Some local leader wants a lecture on Spider. I don't have time to run the war anymore because I'm telling them about souls and Spider and Romanan ways. This fat guy called me and I got the idea—"

"I'm sure you're real good at that," Friday called over his shoulder, heading for the door. A thick hand landed on his shoulder, spinning him around to look into Iron Eyes' baleful glare.

"You'll be even better."

Friday swallowed hard.

His personal leather clothing appeared from his personal kit. His face twisted in a rictus as he shed charred armor and slipped into the soft leather. His throat dried and he croaked as the holo recorders settled on him. Iron Eyes beamed anticipation as Friday was positioned by Patrol techs in front of the Bear Mountain backdrop.

"I . . ." he gulped, seeing the lights go on. "I . . ." Invisible fingers locked on his throat. "I . . ."

"Hold it." Iron Eyes walked forward, anticipation sagging to a scowl. "Just talk! You know, like you were telling kids about Spider!"

Friday shook his head. "I'm not . . ."

Iron Eyes squinted. "Didn't I hear you tell me your medicine was to spread Spider's fame through the stars?"

"Well, I—"

"Didn't you tell me Spider gave you that power? That it scared you witless at what it would cost? That you promised Spider?"

Friday's thoughts swirled back to that day long ago on a mountaintop, a mountaintop like the one behind him. Unconsciously, his fingers traced the Spider effigy drawn in black on his war shirt.

What do you wish? the voice echoed in his mind. *Who would do this?*

Friday looked at John Smith Iron Eyes, nodding, motioning him back. Unafraid, he looked at the holo recorders. His voice rang out, "I am Friday Garcia Yellow Legs. I would have the peoples of the Directorate know the name of Spider. From my home, World, I have been called here." He smiled, friendly, knowing, extending himself toward the invisible masses, trying to touch each person's soul.

"Let me tell you about Spider. Let me tell you what we Romanans have learned. We're not your enemy. Instead, we bring you a new religion . . . a new life. We're not death. We're a way to a better future. Listen now while I tell you about Spider and the sacrifice He made that men will be free. . . ."

From the side, Iron Eyes watched, feeling Friday's mag-

netism, curiously swayed by the power of the little man's
words.

"How's it going?" Rita asked as she stepped in.

"If there aren't Spider cults all over Sirius in a week, I'll
make Old Man Wattie a war chief!"

CHAPTER XXI

Cold, dead, and dark, the corridor faded into blackness—a
tunnel of night and death. Damen Ree waited, bobbing
slightly on his tether in zero g, the grav plates long since
deactivated by power failure or cut by blaster bolts.

Movement. Ree lifted the heavy shoulder blaster.

"Passed my section," Hanson whispered, the voice echoing in Ree's helmet comm.

"Let 'em come," Ree hissed back. "Easy now, try and get
one or two alive. I want to know what they're after. They
keep trying for the bridge. Why? What's up there but comm
and dead screens?"

He could make them out now, human forms appearing
out of the dark square of receding corridor. They moved
warily, as well they might. The deep recesses of *Bullet* had
become a battle ground. Death lurked throughout the ship,
hidden in booby traps, rigged explosives, barricaded and
defended hallways, and waiting in the power packs of desperate Patrol personnel, fighting for their ship, their honor,
and their lives.

*Only we're losing, bit by bit. They're wearing us away.
Slowly but surely, they learn the passages. No matter that we
cut and weld and mine and kill, still they come, searching
through the corridors, learning our strengths. But why? What
do they seek in* Bullet *that so many would die to kill the
handful of us?*

"Now!" Ree ordered, triggering his blaster, laying a burst
across the advance. The sonic concussion slapped him around,
bouncing him on the tether despite the vacuum in the evacuated corridor.

Swirling crystals and frozen fluids twisted and danced in

the lights that flooded the corridor. "Careful, people," Ree reminded. "We don't know how stunned they are."

"Got one," Hanson called. "Looks like he's an officer of some kind. Got a funny insignia on his suit. Yep, here's another."

"All right. Take them. Shoot the others and dispose of them. Ought to be more discouragement. Maybe make the rest think a little before they try it again." Ree unhooked his tether and shoved off the wall, winding down to a hidden crawl space. He lifted the latch, slipped his blaster inside, and followed, turning in the narrow confines to restring a detonator and trip wire over the flap.

He floated ahead another thirty meters, dropped to crawl across gravitized deck, floated again beyond it, and finally made a hatch. He tapped the right sequence and waited until the heavy door opened. Inside, he waited again while a temporary air lock pressurized, and stepped out into a dimly lit corridor, a marine helping him off with his helmet.

"Hear you got 'em, sir." The private grinned.

"Yeah," Ree slapped the man on the back. "Hanson's people are already towing them to throw out the lock. I wonder if Ngen's crew is getting tired of snagging up dead bodies?"

The private's expression hardened. "If they're not, we'll send them some more. Teach 'em to mess with *Bullet*, we will!"

"That'a boy. Keep up the good work." Ree gave him an encouraging smile and started the long trip back to the bridge.

"Call from med," Neal told him as he passed the bridge hatch.

Ree settled himself. "Already? Yeah, I suppose so. Takes a while to get around anymore! Put them on, Neal."

"Colonel?" a voice asked.

"Here."

"Major Glick got that psych machine wired up just fine. We put the Sirian captain under the cap first thing. Had to work fast since his arm had been blown off. Anyhow, here's the information. Ngen wants the ship to rebuild. I think we all knew that. The other thing—the thing most important to his troops—is that they don't hurt the comm. Ngen has made it clear. They are to take the comm intact: period."

"So, they'll keep coming no matter how many dead Sirians

we throw out the hatch each day?" Ree tapped his command chair.

"Hang on, I'll ask this guy." A pause. "Yes, sir. Ngen wants the comm intact. Uh, Colonel, I'm losing this one. You want the lieutenant hooked up?"

"Sure."

The story was the same. Capture the comm no matter the cost.

"Yeah, okay, thanks a lot, Phil. I appreciate your work down there." Ree cut the connection, head propped on his elbow. "The comm?"

"Intelligence?" Neal wondered from his chair. "You think they're after Patrol secrets?"

"What Patrol secrets?" Ree wondered. "What couldn't they have gotten from *Brotherhood* . . . oh, hell, you don't suppose?"

"That he knows we have Brotherhood secrets?" Neal finished the thought.

Ree swallowed hard. "Sarsa's communication came after Ngen had taken Arish's ship. All right, let's assume Arish didn't have time to demolish the comm. That means that anything Rita sent would have come through *Brotherhood's* communications center."

"So he would have heard the transmission. She also sent a copy of the data." Neal ran grimy fingers through his yellow-blond hair, the angle of his jaw shining in the dim light. "So why worry about what's still in *Bullet's* comm?"

"Unless he didn't get it all. That was raw data. Maybe someone just overheard it, you know, monitoring, and didn't get it recorded? That . . . or he thinks Susan's material is just the tip of the iceberg. That there's more buried in *Bullet* than Hans and Susan dug out." Ree tapped his stained armor, reaching down to chip at a charred spot where a Sirian blaster had almost tagged him.

Neal grinned. "Well, after all we've been through, it's nice to know someone still cares! And I thought he just wanted us, to test our heroic resistance!"

"Maybe he's trying to collect you. Heard about that paternity suit on Capetle IV. Ought to be quite a reward out for you, Neal."

"He'll earn it then," Neal chuckled. "I didn't go willingly in the first place. She got me drunk and took advantage of me. Now, I don't mind fessing up on the paternity suit—but marry that woman? Ouch! He'll never get me back there alive!"

"Colonel?" a call came through. "This is Deck Nine; we've got invaders trying to come in the transduction tubes. We're preparing a hot time for them."

"Good luck," Ree called. "If you need backup, holler. I'll get someone down there."

"I think we can hold, Colonel. But . . . well, it'll be tight."

"Neal, send them some backup." Ree made a motion with his hand, looking up at a schematic on one of the few screens they could still get power to. "How do they keep finding so many holes?"

"They have somebody who sure knows a lot about Patrol ships," Neal growled. "Probably the same person that told Ngen's gunners how to break us down so thoroughly."

"And when I get my hands on him," Ree grunted, "I'll break every bone in his body! If we live that long."

"That's the most important if for the moment." Neal straightened. "We've got another group coming down from the AT locks. Whoops, this is big, Colonel. We've got alarms going off all over the place."

Ree sighed, pulling himself wearily to his feet. "Tell the troops I'm on my way." He shouldered the heavy blaster. "If anything happens, Neal, you're the last. Blow that comm to pieces. I want it to be dust!"

Neal looked up, tension in his blue eyes. "You sure that's wise, Colonel? We lose you and, well, you're the heart and soul these days."

Ree clapped him on the shoulder. "And why is that, Neal? Yes, you know. It's because I'm down there with them, fighting for *Bullet* just as hard as they are. See you around. They keep this up and we'll have two crews shoveling bodies out the lock tomorrow."

"If we live that long," Neal whispered.

The Sirian problem deteriorates before our very eyes. Public opinion continues to grow in support of the Independence Party. The military situation at Sirius continues to stalemate. The Pirate, Damen Ree, has lost his ship, although armed personnel continue to hold certain portions of the dead vessel. On the ground, the Romanans continue to advance, the Patrol following up, maintaining defensive positions despite continual orbital bombardment by Van Chow's warships, Skor Robinson reported.

Navtov digested the information, accessing the public opinion polls flooding in from all parts of human space. *We have the option of scrambling Kamakazi, Uhuru, Gregory, and Ganges. Perhaps it is worth risking the entire fleet on a crushing defeat of the Sirian Rebels. One severe blow would—*

No! Skor decided firmly. *We can't abandon our presence for that amount of time. To do so would admit we're fallible— even more so than the loss of three Patrol ships off Sirius would indicate. If people see us running for Sirius, they will know our present weakness for what it is. Keep in mind, Santa del Cielo is a hotbed of sedition.* Uhuru *must make an appearance in her skies—a reminder of Directorate security. I have already scheduled* Gregory *to appear over New Maine and Zion—a calming presence there. Cobalt Station has suffered riots and sabotage.* Kamakazi *is already stabilizing the situation and has been ordered to head immediately for Respit where the miners are threatening a strike in support of Van Chow. New Israel is demanding the reinstitution of their old religion. Frontier, too, is beginning to stir. Do we want renewed interest in the Brotherhood and their subversive policies of indiscriminate education?*

Navtov considered for several seconds. *No, I can see the rest of the fleet is needed to stabilize society. One Sirian disaster is enough. To remove our presence from the rest of space could become a critical mistake. Looking back, I can tell that we made an error allowing the people access to transduction receivers. They should have been controlled along with weapons, books, travel, and education.*

Skor experienced a tinge of sorrow. *Indeed. Yet transduction composed an integral part of the economic structure of the Directorate. Did our predecessors not think it enough to control access to sending devices? Who could have thought receivers would prove so troublesome? A sender can be monitored—but a receiver? To have had people waiting for transduction reception would have doubled Directorate personnel workloads. We would have drowned in our own population monitoring.*

Roque, who had been monitoring the exchange, added, *So instead we shall pay the price with social turmoil? By cutting 6.758 percent of the people's luxuries, we could have afforded the extra monitoring. I can see no reason for humans to have chocolate, perfume, liquor, and sleep stim. The bare requirements for survival are well documented right down to the calorie. To provide recreational food serves no*

*useful social value. On Salam alone, they drink fifteen per-
cent more sugar than necessary in their coffee, and of that,
each male drinks three cups per day more than the Directorate average. We should have restricted—*

*There are learned behavioral differences stemming from
their Arabic ancestry,* Skor reminded. *Take away their coffee, and resentment will rise among them. On planets like
Bazaar, the Shi'ah still hate us, keeping their religion alive in
the desert enclaves despite regulation. To stop them, we must
kill them all. They wean their progeny on stories of Hussain
the martyr—and damn us. Take away one of their behavioral
crutches—like coffee—and we'll have violence feeding on
itself, breaking planetary and station boundaries until everything is chaos.*

Navtov added, *I fear it is already too late. From the
statistical predictions, I see a swell of interest in the Sirian
situation. Van Chow's broadcasts, following so closely upon
Leeta Dobra's, have caught the imagination of the people.
Perhaps we should have instituted a program to breed that
out of the species? Nevertheless, the proverbial genie has
escaped the bottle. We cannot return to the status quo. Our
strategies must be amended for the new situation.*

Skor felt a twist in his gut. He'd feared to think it might
have progressed so far. The computations he'd run on the
effect of the Roque broadcast showed that it had fed dissent. How could they have misjudged so thoroughly the
human response to their arguments?

*Perhaps. For the interim, are we agreed to allow the fleet
free reign to stop sedition and end dissent?*

Roque registered his agreement before adding, *Toby
Kuryaken and Yaisha Mendez have noted that an available
option with regard to Sirius would be to simply destroy the
entire planet and Ngen's fleet through antimatter and nuclear
devices.*

Skor pondered the idea. *It would be an easy remedy. But
let us consider. Suppose we blast Sirius and Arpeggio revolts.
We blast Arpeggio next. Depending on how insane the people
become, we could end up with nothing to Direct. No, Sirius
represents a considerable manufacturing capability. The planet
is rich in metals and centrally located for trans-shipment
throughout the Directorate. I would hate to lose so valuable a
resource base. And the thought of Chester Armijo Garcia,
and what he would say stilled Skor's desire to agree to
sterilization. We need Sirius!*

*   *   *

Susan sipped the cold coffee. The magic cups that heated by turning the bottom had shocked, amazed, and delighted all the Romanans. This one—two weeks old now—had worn out. The coffee stayed cold.

Any sense the war might have once had—like the innocence of the Romanans—had long fled. Sectors of the capital that declared for the Directorate were suddenly bombarded from space. That panicked the people even more and they fled screaming, burned, blinded, or dying from radiation. The city thronged with refugees, the arteries jammed with a constant human chain bearing last possessions over their heads as they fled for the suburbs and the mining lands beyond to starve before trickling back into the city.

Rebel sectors—like the one she squinted out at now— were fair game for any kind of raiding, coup hunts, sabotage, or reprisal.

Never mind that it made no sense; it worked. District by district, the capital had fallen. Each group suing for peace swore fealty to the Directorate to avoid further raiding by the Romanans. Rumors of the Romanan slave camps grew by the day and fear built to the point where so many Sirians were convinced the barbarians were invincible—never mind that their Prophets saw the future—that all thought of resistance was pointless.

"They ought to be coming soon," Hans growled to himself, his new half-inch beard giving him a fierce appearance. He still scratched at it. "Those informants couldn't be wrong. We should clean house today!"

"I'd think you had enough action last night to soothe your battle ready soul," Friday jabbed in a ribald whisper.

"Me?" Hans shook his head. "She does all the work, I just sleep through it."

"You, too?" Friday wondered. "I thought I was the only one." Laughter erupted in the tunnel.

"Hey! You're the holo star. How many Spider effigies have been cropping up? Heard a whole squad of Civil Guard turned on their pals the other day. Got an order to charge a bunch of Romanans, turned, and shot the hell out of their officers. Then took coup!"

"Yeah, well, you'd a been more hologenic, you know, with that haggard look after Susan—"

"Cut it, both of you! You'll wish you could sleep next

time." Susan growled, embarrassed enough to blush. Her? Could she still blush?

Her relationship with Friday and Hans had already caused more than a few rumors. She slept with them both; but never on the same night. Each had his own particular hold on her affections.

Further, whenever Friday or Hans talked about it, they joked. Privately, she suspected they'd sat down somewhere, drunk a half bottle of whiskey and decided how to divvy the spoils—namely her. But it worked. That's all she cared about. She could love them both, serve them both, and they in turn loved her.

Friday continued to be strong, virile, muscular, indefatiguable in bed and at the same time, joking and carefree. He engendered support for her mad schemes. He gave her a link to her People and could talk about the way the three moons glowed on spring nights and what the Prophets would say about their war. She depended on him for field evaluations and tactical judgments. He also supplied discipline if the team needed it.

Hans met other needs, his strength more spiritual. He saw and defined good and bad, right and wrong. Careful to avoid hurting her when they made love, she could confide her fears to him. He would hold her afterward like some precious vessel to be nurtured and cherished. He provided her team with a technical expertise that had saved them more than once. He heeded the cry of her soul and mind while Friday answered her body and emotions.

Intuitively, they seemed to know what each did for her. Further, they respected that her needs differed, and that neither could provide for all of her. Flushed with appreciation for such qualities, she also felt it unjust that she couldn't roll them both into one.

"Patience," Friday whispered with a grin. He turned to the man behind him and passed back a sandwich. The long line of warriors who crouched in the semidarkness of the powerlead tunnel acted bored, claustrophobic, and irritated.

"Shush!" Susan snapped rigidly to the alert. Here they came. Home Guards. "Ten, twenty, thirty, by Spider, there's a million of them!"

They weren't the same Home Guards. With time, they'd grown tough, desperate—but they still fled given half a chance. The Romanans had learned to keep from cornering them if possible. With an out, they broke and ran. Trapped, they fought like mad wolves.

"Must be a major offensive," Hans almost cried out as more and more of the soldiers trotted past. He pulled out his comm and whispered low and excitedly into the pickup. "Talked to Moshe, ATs'll hit 'em within minutes. After they pass and blast, we clean up what's left."

"I'd say there must be a thousand of them," Friday grinned. He grabbed the shoulder of the man just below him. "Think, that means there are twenty apiece out there." The soft chuckle went down the line into the darkness.

The whistle grew. Before the Home Guards could react, the ATs were on them, strafing the columns of screaming Sirians. The ground shook as the blasters did their terrible work. For three minutes, death rained from the skies from Patrol ATs. Then came a low roar and the ATs whistled away as a Sirian battleship in orbit tried to pin them.

Another four or five minutes passed while the big beam sprayed the neighborhood. In the end, silence lay heavily on the street. "Let's go!" Susan led the way out of the tunnel. The smoking rubble of blown apart buildings and the stink of cooked human flesh hung everywhere.

She led them forward in a skirmish line. Occasional Sirians pulled themselves from the rubble. Most whimpered, blind, severely wounded or half-crazed with fear. Whipped already, silent knives dispatched them, and coups were taken off the living and the not-so-badly-burned dead.

"Take cover!" one of the men called. Susan dove into the rubble. She pulled up her blaster and, to her surprise, observed another marching column. They came warily this time, nervous at the sight of the destruction.

"Friday!" Susan motioned him to one side. "Hans!" She sent him off to the other flank with the rest of the warriors. If they took this sector of the city—Angla they called it— Rita would control the rest by the end of the week.

This had to be a last determined push to demonstrate control before the entire city fell. If it did, Ngen's revolt would crumble like the wreckage around her. She spit dryly into the dusty blocks of concrete and sighted down her blaster.

Van Chow had become frantic in his broadcasts. He was appealing on an emotional basis now that support had eroded away from beneath him. For two weeks he'd been fighting a losing battle with *Bullet*. The ship might be dead in space, but Ngen's men couldn't take it.

The Patrol had tried one more antimatter torpedo, but the Sirians knew the trick this time. They shot it up as *Victory* dropped it and huddled next to *Bullet* on the off chance there had been two.

Hans had Iverson working on the Brotherhood data from the ship's computers. All they needed now was a source of hyperconductor: the big glitch in the system.

The Civil Guards continued cautiously. Susan's team waited. Within fifty yards of the enemy, she settled the sights on one of the lead men. Another ten steps, she decided, counting them off as the column advanced. Would they never learn to use cover?

Susan triggered the firing stud and watched the man's body explode. Her squad opened fire, shooting with that cool accuracy that came from many fights. Like green harvesters before a bear, the Home Guards ran for the sides and right into the concentrated fire of Friday and Hans' guns. Confusion and despair in command, the Sirians broke.

Susan motioned her team forward, running in a crouch. Quickly, efficiently, they pursued. Each time the frantic Sirians began to stop and regroup, Susan would let them— at the same time setting her flankers out to enclose the head of the column.

The roar caught her off guard. The sky flared purple. Susan sprinted for the nearest powerlead access. Blasting the cover off, she dove feet first down the shaft, almost braining herself as her feet slipped off the thick cable at the bottom.

Frantically, she rolled away from the violet stream of light that seared through the open manhole. Terrifying screams sounded from beyond. A constant wave of explosion followed the center of the focused beam. The half-burned corpse of a Home Guard rolled down the accessway, uniform melted and smoking on his charred hide, crisped hair looking like shiny plastic.

She caught herself trembling with fear.

"Spider is all
With Spider I walk in courage
See this woman walk in courage
Spider is the one and the all
Praise be to Spider
And to Harvester his Prophet
I came to the Mountain

I slew the wicked one on the Mountain
Praise be to Spider
I will sing the praise of Spider

Susan sang her medicine song, heart racing in her body. Somewhere out there, Friday and Hans had already found shelter—or they were dead.

And if they were? Something in her throat caught, making it impossible to swallow. Her hands began to tremble.

"Susan?" in the tongue of the People, the call came down the powerlead access.

"Who comes?"

"Friday Garcia Yellow Legs and ten men!" he answered, voice echoing weirdly in the confines of the tunnel.

The blaster fire had ceased. Susan winced as she climbed up the hot, searing rungs and stuck her head out. Desolation greeted her. Out of habit, she popped a polymerase capsule for any radiation which might have gotten through her combat armor. She crawled to a nearby pile of rubble, stifled by the heat rolling out of the collapsed wall.

"By the beard of Haysoos!" Friday muttered as he crawled out of the manhole.

"They must have used several beams together," Susan decided, shaking her head. She pulled out her comm. "Spider team one-three, Hans? You there?"

Her heart skipped a beat. She swallowed hard. "Where was his position?"

"There." A man pointed. The surface he indicated shimmered, glassy, too hot to even walk across. As so often after the big blasters had lanced the clouds, rain began to fall.

Susan suffered herself to trot across the burned area, heedless of the pain in her feet. A huge furrow of exploded soil met her searching eyes. Hans was dead. Nothing lived through that . . . nothing

A strange howling shrieked through her brain, a painful keening. Reeling, she walled it off, wincing, clutching at her heart.

"They're running!" Friday pointed to the Home Guards.

Susan agreed absently, "They k-killed H-Hans and . . . and . . . *Make them pay!*"

They did. Susan had to pick charges for her blaster off the bodies of the dead. The Sirians, of course, had manufactured Directorate equipment. For three days of violent ambush, hit and run, they harried the broken Home Guard, dodging blaster bolts from the sky, killing and burning their way through Angla on a mad rampage.

The howling in her mind lessened as she walled it in. A dike separated her thoughts from the memories she refused.

Susan knotted the coups and strung them around her body armor, heedless of the blood running out of the still fresh pelts. Her heart lay dead in her breast. Emptiness filled her soul.

"You want to talk about it?" Friday asked the next night while the men slept on the perimeter.

"Talk about what?"

"Hans," he said softly. "I mean, losing someone like that has to—"

"I'm fine," Susan said, voice faraway. "We live to kill Sirians. If we kill enough, and beat enough into the very ground they urinate in, we win. When the last Sirian has any will to resist, I'll be the one to blow his stinking head off."

"You don't sound all right," he whispered. "I see a deadness behind your eyes."

"I'm fine," she told him levelly, dry-eyed, keeping the wall in place. A wonderful thing, that wall, it blocked off memories of Hans. Pain and terror lurked beyond it, brooding. So long as the wall stood strong, she'd be safe . . . and Hans would live.

Friday's soft brown eyes probed hers. "I think there is more to it, Susan Smith Andojar. You've been out front ever since the blaster attack. No one reaches the Sirians before you. No one takes coup first." He hesitated, attempting to see past the veil of her eyes. "You've begun to cut them, Susan. Used to be, you stopped that kind of behavior among your men."

She met his eyes. "I will cease cutting their manhood when I meet men! Sheep like these are better cut. Keeps them docile."

Friday nodded slowly. "I loved Hans, too. I owed him my life . . . and yours. Something in your head snapped that day, Susan. You're not yourself. You're taking this too far. Killing Sirians is fine. Counting coup is fine. Cutting men is not."

"I cut who I will," she snapped, turning away, leaving him staring at her tangled hair.

"Cutting is a demonstration of superiority for a sick soul," he insisted. "You need not degrade the dead. Take their coup, that is symbolic of victory."

"I take my victory in any way I want, Friday." She glared at him from hot empty eyes.

He noted the flatness, the dullness in that look. *I am seeing part of her soul. But which part? Will I ever see the rest of the Spirit that was Spider's come back to her eyes? Will fate leave only this monster in the woman I love?*

Like thunder from a silent sky, he remembered the words on the mountain so long ago, so far away across the starry skies. Wincing, Friday whispered, "I have paid the price to spread Spider's word among the stars." He blinked, empty inside, staring at his bloodstained hands. "Sirius will fall to Spider. And Susan?"

His heart twisted.

The little that remained of Angla fell that day. Citizens left the few standing homes and drew spiders on the sidewalks and walls to show their defeat and one by one, they lined up to swear allegiance.

Friday watched the frightened eyes as they passed lines of defeated Sirians. They rode across a flattened waste, a landscape of shattered glass, twisted steel, and scattered wall panels. Runnels of dirt like wide flat ditches showed the crisscrossing of the orbital attacks seeking the scattered Romanan forces or trying to pin darting ATs.

"So much devastation," Friday mumbled even after having lived it for so many days.

He could hear the whispered words muttered behind Sirian hands as they passed. "There goes the Spider woman. She who cuts the men and is first to kill." People lowered their eyes as Susan passed, fearful of being recognized, fearful she would turn her wrath on them.

"It is because Ngen killed her lover!" Friday heard the whispered explanation. "When her lover died, he became a Spider and jumped into the sky!" another added. "A Prophet foretold her madness," still another insisted. "That's what happens when Spider touches your soul!"

Then one saw him. "*Look! It's Friday Yellow Legs!* He's the one, the one Spider sent to tell us!"

"Friday?" another called aloud. "See? See the Spider I have drawn on my shirt?"

"We heard you!" a woman screeched. "We have declared ourselves for Spider! Is it true Ngen killed her lover?"

Friday looked, nodded soberly, seeing them recoil from his expression.

And Hans? Friday wondered. Yes, Spider would take good care of his soul. He shot a quick look at Susan's ramrod straight back as he followed her toward an aircar. She'd made Hans Yeager into the man who'd hung by a foot from a pitching AT to save the life of Friday Yellow Legs. She'd taken that self-conscious little corporal who couldn't talk to women without blushing, and made him into a legend.

But at what cost? Friday climbed in next to Susan. She never looked right or left as the aircar lifted. She only stared straight ahead, eyes on the road, expression dead.

CHAPTER XXII

Below, Patrol ATs controlled the Sirian skies and Ngen Van Chow was helpless to prevent them. His powerful blasters—devastating to the landscape—proved unable to track the darting, corkscrewing ATs as they rained every sort of death or destruction on the Home Guards or manufacturing sites.

Ngen stared frostily at the monitor.

"First Citizen, we must do something! Our people watch helplessly as their world crumbles around them! They starve in the ruins." Pika Vitr spread weary arms, his black clothing stained and spotted. His face had thinned; worry lines gave his features an unaccustomed graven look. A faint cast of dullness dimmed the old fire in his eyes.

"Not only that, but more than our world crumbles. So does the resolve of the people, Ngen." Pika lowered his voice, suddenly uneasy. "This Iron Eyes, the Romanan War Chief, they call him. He made a holo documentary, showing your blasters ripping apart large tracts of Ekrania. He used witnesses—Sirians who called you the devastator. The people, well, they fear *Hiram Lazar* more than they fear the barbarians!"

"I thought my broadcasts had made clear the exact nature of the retaliation," Ngen countered coldly.

Pika filled his lungs. "You did. It isn't working, Ngen. I can tell you no more bluntly than that. Each time you let loose with the blaster, the Romanans and Patrol are flying around in their Ats broadcasting live with this Iron Eyes giving a running commentary. They've turned your threat of retaliation against you. The people, Ngen, are turning against you, embracing this Spider religion, talking of this Friday Yellow Legs and his foul insect God."

"Spiders are not insects, Pika, they're arachnids."

"Whatever. I care not for phylogeny. What I care about is the number of Sirians who now walk boldly through the streets with spiders drawn on their shirts in imitation of the Romanans. To our astonishment, the subversion has even seeped into the ranks of the Civil Guard. Not just the Home Guard oafs . . . but the Civil Guard!" Pika shook his head. "All this over some abstract mush concerning souls? *Ngen, we're in trouble down here!*"

Ngen chewed the knuckle of his thumb. "We have taken all the options available from orbit, the rest lies in your hands, Pika. You control the troops. Even after the crushing defeats, you outnumber the Romanans and Patrol. Unless you take the reins of responsibility down there, all I can do is try and support your people from orbit. If I leave to chase the Patrol above . . . the Patrol below will exterminate you on the ground. And, I remind you, I can't chase the Patrol above until you bring the situation under control down there."

"I am *well* aware of the situation," Pika practically moaned. "At the same time, there's a vicious rumor that the Romanans have one of their Prophets hidden away somewhere. How can the Civil and Home Guards fight when they believe the outcome is already known . . . that the Romanans wouldn't be doing battle if they didn't know they'd win? How can you convince fighting men there's—"

"Foolish superstition!" Ngen snapped. "A mere fantasy created by that woman anthropologist's report. Would they have attacked me, knowing they'd lose half their fleet? A—"

"I know!" Pika cried desperately, "but the soldiers in the streets won't believe that! To tell them rationally—well, who's more superstitious than a soldier?"

Ngen sighed. "And my speeches? Don't they touch the souls of the people anymore?"

Pika rubbed a hand over his high forehead, smoothing patrician silver-white hair over his long skull. "They help some. Every time you broadcast, the people take heart, that

is, those who haven't been hit by orbital bombardment."
Pika looked away. "First Citizen, there are places . . . well,
I've told you."

Ngen considered, face tightening into a emotionless mask.
For the first time, an element of doubt had entered the
picture. "I have told the people that I have no choice.
Those who do not rally against the Romanans. . . . What
other option is there? Tell my people—if they would save
themselves—they must fight! It's their battle, too!" He
thumped the panel with a fist.

*What has happened? Where is the heart of the revolution?
Surely the fools can see the alternatives? How has this come
about, that primitive savages—men who can't even read for
the most part—can route my superior forces?*

"We've come too far, Pika. We are on the verge of
bleeding them dry! You must wring that last bit of commitment from the People. They must see the precipice upon
which we now stand. Talk to them, Pika, exhort them, urge
them on!"

Pika nodded. "Of course, I just . . ."

"Yes?"

"They're tired, horrified at the destruction. The thought
of dying for—"

"*Pustulant Gods!* It's their fight, their freedom at stake!
Their survival! How many times must I tell them, it's their
war!"

Vitr swallowed hard, raising pained eyes. "I just wonder
if they're willing to fight it, First Citizen."

Giorj Hambrei methodically continued his study of *Bullet*.
How did the Patrol hang on in there? For every new approach Giorj devised, Ree's people adapted a counter
strategy.

He placed thin white fingers on his eyelids and rubbed
them, feeling the aching exhaustion behind the tired orbs.
He needed more sleep. Nevertheless, *Bullet* fascinated him.
The men in her fascinated him still more. For the first time,
he'd come up against an innovative genius capable of testing
his mettle. Whoever ran engineering on *Bullet*, the man had
proved uncanny at rerouting powerleads to produce atmosphere and gravity. No sooner did Giorj discover the location
of a generator and prepare to take or destroy it, then the
Patrol engineer had it moved someplace else. As long as the
game continued, the Patrol couldn't be starved or frozen out.

And there remained the possibility that they'd linked up to the huge antimatter reactor. If so, they could control the stasis and isolate enough antimatter to turn the ship into a bomb as Ree had tried to do over the Romanans' home world.

"They're dumping the bodies," the shuttle commander commented dryly. "Right on schedule, too."

Giorj looked out the observation dome, seeing the mass of limp, tumbling bodies blown from the hatch. Within minutes, a second evacuation spilled the dead into decompression, a halo of crystals around the cartwheeling bodies.

"Send someone to go net them. As usual, drop them into atmosphere over the poles." Giorj settled his chin on his knee, looking over *Bullet's* white sides, eyes absently on the big transduction disks, powerless now, wondering at the messages they'd sent over three hundred years of service. No, *Bullet* didn't defy him, the men inside did. A ship could be conquered, manipulated, understood and dealt with. A ship offered nothing more than an engineering problem—but men?

Ngen's face formed on a holo monitor to one side. "Engineer? I've been apprised that the latest sally into *Bullet* has been . . . shall we say, less than successful? Could you please delineate the nature and extent of the problems involved?"

"I am not a general," Giorj said with a heavy sigh.

"Nevertheless, you are my authority on Patrol ships of the line. What's the problem? Why do we make advances so slowly?"

Giorj straightened. "First Citizen. I can reduce the ship to slag. I can irradiate it, blast it, induce gravitational fluxes to paralyze the resistance within. All of those things—however effective against humans—would destroy the information in the computers. At the same time, it's become apparent from the manner of their defense that Damen Ree has determined the objective of our assaults. While I might employ blasters from *Hiram Lazar* to destroy knots of opposition, those defensive positions have been established around critical areas of the ship. You see? Destroy the Patrol personnel through our superior technology—destroy the ship and the data."

Ngen's eyes narrowed. "I'm running out of patience, Giorj. Not to mention that every time they evacuate our casualties, morale drops."

Giorj stared at him flatly. "I await your orders, First
Citizen."

Ngen sucked his lower lip, brow lined. "You are making
progress; very well, continue. Perhaps they're to the point
of breaking. Step up the assaults; give them no rest. Maybe
we can wear them down."

Giorj nodded.

"Engineer," Ngen continued, "at the same time you will
personally see to my yacht. Make sure all systems are one
hundred percent and all stocks and stores are properly
provisioned."

"I will do so."

"Thank you." The holo comm flickered off.

Giorj turned to stare thoughtfully out at *Bullet*. Ngen—
for the first time—had begun to evince the old behavior
patterns he'd espoused before the Sirian revolution. Giorj
let his gaze play along the lines of *Bullet*. Perhaps the planet
below was proving as stubborn as *Bullet*? The Romanans
had been close to Angla when *Bullet* had been disabled.
Ngen had carefully given him the chore of routing the Patrol
from the battleship. If anything happened to his mother. . . .

"Colonel?" Neal brought Ree out of a sound sleep.

"Hmm?" He blinked, yawning.

"I've got Ngen Van Chow on the other end. He's patched
into one of the few powered lines from an outside dish."

"Put him on."

Ngen's petulant face formed on the sooty monitor.

"Ready to surrender, Ngen?" Ree asked, glaring at the
screen.

"I find your attempt at humor amusing, Colonel Ree. No,
I was going to deal for your ship. Your lives, free passage to
whatever planet or station you desire along with—"

"Ngen, maybe you don't get the point. We don't—"

"Colonel, it's a very reasonable offer I'm trying to make.
Martyrdom is distasteful considering the way the Directorate has—"

"Go to hell!"

"It's a matter of time. Helg and Apahar are the only
major centers of resistance left on Ekrania." Rita took a
breath as she looked around the room. "Colonel Ree is still
holding out in *Bullet*, although from the renewed use of
blasters on the ship, Ngen may be running out of patience.

He could destroy them at any time. Further, he has already threatened to do so if we don't capitulate."

Rita leaned over the table, mouth tight. "I told him no."

Friday glanced over at Susan, seeing no change of expression. She kept her eyes on Rita, half-focused. The deaths of so many of the crew she had known didn't faze her.

"Is there any way we can get up there and take that ship from him?" Friday asked suddenly. "His blasters can't track us on the planet where we're maneuvering in atmosphere and at the bottom of the gravity well. What would happen to a spaceborn assault on his ships?"

"I've considered it." Rita nodded slowly. "The one thing we can't do yet is break off our pressure on the planet. In the event the ATs departed suddenly, can you guarantee the Sirians wouldn't believe we'd been beaten?"

Friday grinned. "No, but wouldn't you hear them groan for a half a galaxy if they did—and we came back!"

"We'll do it eventually," Rita explained. "The only thing is, we have to have Helg and Apahar. Ngen is still running a reduced shuttle service out of Helg. That will be our first priority. We take Helg and Apahar might fold on its own. With all of Ekrania in our control, opposition should collapse rapidly."

Moshe stood and sighed. "Another problem we have is the casualty rate. The longer we fight down here, the fewer of us there are. Look around the room. We've lost fifty percent of our strength. Almost sixty percent of our Romanan forces have been killed or so severely wounded that many—if they survive—will never be combat capable again."

"On the other hand," Iron Eyes looked grimly about the room, "the warriors we have are better than ever. We've learned a lot about Directorate warfare. Of our Romanan casualties, perhaps fifty percent were suffered in the first two days. Thereafter, losses have decreased significantly. I'm not trying to belittle the problem. It's serious."

Friday chirped, "Yeah, I've thought Sirius was a problem since I set foot on that spaceport!"

Iron Eyes winced and took a deep breath.

"Which brings us to another difficulty." Rita rubbed the back of her neck. "Romanans don't perform well on garrison duty. The more area that falls to us, the more we extend our dwindling resources, the fewer men we have to assault Sirian controlled sectors."

"On the other hand," Iron Eyes nodded, "and meaning

no disrespect to the marines, our Romanan forces take more ground and have fewer subsequent problems with uprisings."

Friday tapped the table in front of him. "We go through like a harvester into a green field. Marines think in military terms—we think in terms of out and out conquest. When marine garrisons come in, the people greet them with open arms. Now, if I was a war chief, I'd think that—properly used—I'd have an excellent psychological weapon, a follow-up strategy to our early broadcast. Areas which revolt after conquest will be occupied by Romanans."

"Good point," Rita nodded with satisfaction. "That's what these meetings are for."

Iron Eyes rubbed the back of his neck. "Then, perhaps with the exception of our marine advisers, we should let it be known that Helg and Apahar will be taken by Romanan forces?"

Friday shot a glance at Susan. A grim smile curled her lips. He cleared his throat. "They know we're not as strong as we once were." All eyes turned toward him. "They also know that most of our casualties come from not being able to reach cover before the space blasters hit us. Consequently, they've started boobytrapping the powerlead accesses. They plug them, mine them, or leave open powerleads to electrocute us. Sometimes they gas them. I don't think I need to mention the effect of that purple light when you know you don't have a hole to use."

Iron Eyes nodded thoughtfully, fingering his chin, eyes narrowed. "We've considered everything. To our knowledge, there's no way to stop the blaster until we take *Hiram Lazar*." He added slowly, "And when we do, I want Ngen Van Chow!"

"At the same time, they're killing so many of their own! That's got to have an effect on their morale." Moshe shook his head.

"From what we can see in the streets," Friday shrugged, "it's fifty-fifty. Some units fight harder knowing they might be shot by their own ships, others cave in, completely defeated, knowing they're going to die. So much depends on the individual unit and who commands it."

"There's another thing to consider," Rita said slowly. "We have the potential to lose a large part of our strength on these last two cities."

Friday studied her, nervous at what she was thinking. Susan leaned forward, the hard glitter in her eyes sharpening.

Rita marshaled her thoughts. "Prior to this, the front has been ever expanding. Only within the last two weeks have we been decreasing the area of our assaults. At the same time, Ngen used his blasters with limited success against us as we dispersed. He had less chance of killing our people. Now we're becoming more concentrated and with powerlead accesses uncertain at best, how do we limit our casualties to ground fire?"

The room was silent while it sank in. If Helg were to fall, Ngen could eliminate most of the Romanans by burning the whole city to the ground and killing every living thing in it. Who'd pay the price? Friday found himself looking around at the others.

"Small teams." Susan spoke into the moody silence.

"How?" Rita asked, eyes softening as she looked at the girl.

"Get us in and we'll burn our way through the city. Disrupt their activities, move constantly so they can't find a position to hit from space. We move fast enough, they'll blast places we've already left.

Iron Eyes grinned, nodding admiringly at Susan. He stood and accessed a map of Helg on the wall. "Suppose we employ five ATs in a patterned sweep, flying low. They can drop small teams of no more than twenty warriors at these strategic points." He demonstrated on the board. "If we use our crack troops, we can create confusion and chaos in the rear. I think we ought to infiltrate the suburbs, too."

"Small units?" Rita wondered. "Maybe a thin skirmish line?"

"What keeps them from massing and overrunning you?" Moshe asked.

"Mobility," Susan said flatly. "We move constantly."

"Susan's right," Iron Eyes said soberly. "Part of our purpose is to strike, escape, strike, escape, and strike again. If they're constantly trying to pin our people down, they have to dedicate the troops to the effort. If they do, defenses are weakened on the outskirts. The teams move in from the outside with smaller numbers just as effectively as with massed forces. If they choose to keep their perimeters strong, we're free to rain terror—and terror makes a very good ally."

"Leave terror to me, I'll rain it all right . . . on their

cursed heads!" Susan slammed a fist into the table, looking her challenge around the room.

"It could be suicide," Rita pointed out.

Just what she'd want, Friday thought to himself; his heart cried out.

"Wouldn't it bring honor?" Susan asked, expressionless. "Wouldn't taking the city with massed assaults bring infinitely more death and loss? I'm suggesting you let Romanans work as they do best. We raid, Major. We raid fast and deadly. We'll leave reminders of our power all over the city. Show them a few of us can make them into sheep. Will they resist for very long?"

"I back Susan's idea." Iron Eyes stood firm. "She'll bring the Sirians to their knees. Maybe make Ngen's big blasters do our work for us."

"It is worth a try," Moshe agreed. "If, for some reason, Andojar's plan doesn't work, we can always hit them from strength."

"Who picks the suicide teams?" Rita asked. "You know we can't get them out without exposing the ATs to considerable fire."

"We volunteer," Susan hissed vehemently. "We're Romanans and we have honor. Spider will keep those who die and," she smiled, "those who live."

Why not? Risk a few on the gamble of greater returns? Sure. But why, Friday thought, did it have to be Susan? "We should make use of the fact that in every city the Romanans have targeted, Ngen has done more damage than we have. Maybe if we yell it from the rooftops, he won't shoot just to spite us." And he'd have to go. She'd get herself killed if he didn't go along to watch out for her.

"Indeed," Rita grinned.

"Put the word out that we will attack Helg in three days," Susan said suddenly. "Instead, we strike tomorrow."

"Can we put it together that quick?" Rita turned to Moshe.

"It's a simple operation." Moshe shrugged. "We send however many ATs we need through in sequence, bringing them in from random directions. Skip them through town, setting down at whatever interval Susan wants. The Romanans hop out and we're gone to the next drop."

"At the same time, warriors are dropped at the outskirts in long continuous skirmish lines. They don't even need to hold an area. They can move as they wish," Iron Eyes reminded.

"What keeps them from wiping you out by patrolling in strength?" Rita asked. "You can't be decisive."

Susan shook her head. "Of course not. We don't need to be. All we need to do is wear them out, Major. We don't defeat them. They defeat themselves. Our teams teach them they're helpless to control their own city. We cut power, water, and food supplies. They'll fall."

"And they'll believe the Prophet has decreed this, too." Iron Eyes pulled at his long braid. "Don't forget to use that any way you can. The thought that someone has seen their defeat can be as powerful as Ngen's blasters."

"Let's do it," Rita agreed grudgingly. "Susan, draw what you need. Get your volunteers. Leave whenever you're satisfied you're ready. We'll attend to the propaganda and slip advance information out via an informer."

As the meeting broke up, Friday managed to snag Rita's arm. "Got a minute from your busy schedule?"

" 'Bout Susan?" Rita's cool green eyes pinned his.

He nodded and let her lead him to her cabin.

Friday took the cup of coffee she offered and dropped into the little chair. "I don't know what to do about her."

Rita studied the cup in her hands. "I don't either. She's bent on destroying herself. I've seen it before. Last time it was me." Rita sighed and settled into the bunk. "The only difference was when I did it there wasn't a war going on. I buried myself in the Patrol and fought my way up through the ranks."

"The Sirians hate her," Friday reminded. "She's considered an embodiment of evil to them. There's a price of five thousand credits on her head."

Rita laughed. "So? They offer a million for me . . . alive!"

"You're not within their grasp," Friday reminded. "Susan is."

Silence stretched.

"You know what it is," Rita looked up. "Susan hasn't learned to live with her guilt. That's bad enough . . . but on top of it all, she hasn't grieved for him. She won't let herself." Rita shook her head, mouth twisting bitterly. "God, and I thought she might not be tough enough!"

"She's destroying herself!" Friday cried. "I can't reach her. Can you?"

"No." Rita shook her head slowly. "It's up to her, Friday. She's shut down part of her mind. There'll be a key somewhere to break it open. No one can force her to deal with it. It'll come in its own time—if she lives that long."

"I . . . I just can't stand it." He raised his hands helplessly. Then he sighed. "Well, I know what the vision was all about now. Some trick!"

"Vision?"

He nodded, eyes lifeless. "I offered myself to Spider. The spirit-helper—this light that twinkled—asked if I would give what was most precious for Spider. I answered yes. Now, I . . . I can only hope that didn't mean Susan . . . that she's going to die."

"We all die," Rita reminded hollowly.

"The one great truth."

"Look, Friday, if I could think of some other way to keep her out of trouble, I'd do it. You know that. I'd take—"

"I'm going with her," Friday said doggedly. "Maybe I can keep her from committing suicide. If I could just be there at the right—"

"You're not going this time, Friday," Rita said slowly. "I need you here."

"*Rita!*" He struggled to his feet. "You're crazy! I won't do it!"

"Yes, you will, Friday Yellow Legs." Her expression hardened. "I need you more than Susan does. Hell, the People need you! Your honor requires it. You see, you're leading the attack on the outskirts. I need someone I can trust to relay information to me, and I need someone to handle Spider propaganda. You don't realize how effective your broadcast has been. Sirians want to see you. They want to talk to you. You've been promoted to the back lines, Friday. The war needs you more than Susan."

He sank down again, stunned.

Rita gave him a moment before adding. "Iron Eyes and I have made the appointment official. You're number three in the line of command. Consider. What would the warriors think of a man who followed a woman off to battle instead of looking out for the rest of them? They respect you, Friday. You're a mixture of the old and the new. You're Spider's warrior . . . and at the same time, daring enough to love their greatest woman hero."

She hesitated. "No, you'll stay."

He looked at her, seeing the struggle she was having.

Rita shook her head. "I . . . I . . . can't do anything else. It isn't any easier for me than it is for you. I . . . love her, too. If there was any other way . . . I feel like I'm sending her to her death. If I ordered her back she'd disobey, go where the fighting is. It . . . it's Spider's will now."

He stood slowly, knowing she was right. Leaving the untouched coffee cup on the chair, he headed for the door.

"Friday?" she called after him. "I suggest you look up Moshe. Determine what you need and ask for volunteers. You can't take everyone—pick the best. Anything you need is yours."

Then he was gone.

Rita sat back in the bunk. Who . . . what had she become? Damn it all, she'd begun acting like a major. Where was that devil-may-care, wild, old-time Rita Sarsa?

"That Rita died with Philip," she muttered to herself.

Memories of the excitement stirred, blowing down the dusty corridors of her mind. She and Philip had fought the whole galaxy, taking on the Directorate and not caring. She remembered the feel of his body against hers. Remembered how he'd brought her soul to life. Even through the pain, she relived the wild climaxes of their passion—savored every precious moment they'd shared while teetering on the brink of destruction.

"And what do I live for now?" she wondered. "What's my goal? Where am I going?" She pressed tired eyelids with the callused palms of her hands.

"Spider, I'm so tired."

Akar Helstrom heard the whistle and cocked his head, trying to place it. He frowned. The Patrol used craft that whistled on approach. Could this be one? He stopped, lifting his belt comm. What if he called in an alarm and it wasn't a Patrol craft?

The whistle grew louder while Akar puzzled over what to do. Finally, it rose to a shriek like he'd never heard before. "Unit seven, reporting," he said into the pickup, yelling over the whistling.

"Go ahead," his comm responded.

"I've got a whistle here," he yelled. Then something black dove out of the sky and crunched on the pavement half a block away. Almost as suddenly as it landed, it was off again, the whistle rising in the night accompanied by a

blast of hot air. "We have any aircraft here?" Helstrom
demanded.

"Negative."

"Something landed down the street," Helstrom frowned.

"Wait," the voice returned, "They're all over the city.
Call out your unit. We're not sure, but we may have been
invaded."

The next three days became a nightmare. Akar led his
little patrol up and down the streets, answering alarms,
taking unexpected fire from phantoms. At the same time,
he saw the results of the Romanan activities. The bodies of
his men were located, throats slit, hair cut off. Most grue-
some of all, the genitals had been violently hacked from
their bodies.

The citizens flocked to him in fright, telling of a horrid,
black-haired woman with a spider drawn on her battle armor. When Akar led his troops to the scene they found only
the dead and mutilated.

At the same time, rumors circulated. Refugees clogged
the streets fleeing from the Romanans who crept ever closer,
fighting from house to house. Only one or two were seen
here, five or ten there, never enough in one place for an air
strike to be called down.

As the net closed, Akar began to look fearfully at the sky,
noting which of the powerleads happened to be close, marking which ones sported booby traps.

With the setting of the sun came terror. In the long hours
of darkness, creatures prowled the shadows. No matter how
they tried to find the Romanans by day, they lurked, ever
present, in the night. Explosions sundered powerleads, buildings were blasted and toppled into the dark streets. Water
supplies reeked of poison. Ambushes decimated patrols of
Home Guards.

"Patrol seven!" the comm cackled as Akar kicked his
men awake. "Disturbance at A-10. Romanan raid. You are
to converge immediately. Support groups are on the way."

Akar felt his heart sink. How many of these had he
answered? Each time they arrived late, or worse, found the
Romanans. Of the thirty men he'd been in charge of, nine
remained.

"Their Prophet wouldn't have sent them if they weren't
going to win," a man muttered behind his back.

Akar winced. *Foolishness! Sure, Akar, tell yourself that.
The barbarians have crushed the whole planet! And how,*

*huh? It's their God. It's this Spider and the Prophets he lets
see the future! What are we doing with Ngen when we could
be winners. Hell, the Romanans will take over the whole
Directorate!*

The corner of A and Tenth seemed quiet as he led his
men up the street, hugging the walls the way his new experience taught. The explosion took Akar by complete surprise.

Outside of the flash, the noise, and something smashing
him painfully to the pavement, he remembered nothing.
The first sensation he felt came from the rough gritty surface under his cheek. He tried to breathe, slowly pulling
cool air into his burning lungs.

The ringing in his ears didn't go away. It made up his
universe along with the pain and the hard concrete he lay
on. Suddenly, something grabbed his hair and twisted. He
experienced a sting and his vision jerked as his head popped.
Hot wetness—blood—ran into his ear.

A shadow moved in the blackness around him.

Careful! Play dead! Fear sent tremors through his limbs as
he gathered his wits. Moving fingers and toes, he proved
nothing had been broken. Slowly, he gathered himself, tucking his blaster to his chest.

*What do I do? Just up and shoot? Play dead? Blessed god,
just let me live through this!*

Fingers pulled at his pants. Terror petrified him, made
him tense. The sting from his head became unbearable. He
fought to clear his vision and in the dim light of the night,
he saw the figure bend down over his white legs.

The glimmer of shining steel caught the light as it lowered. He felt a hand on his male parts and sudden realization gripped him. He was living the most terrifying of
nightmares! He screamed suddenly as he kicked out with a
fear-induced burst of energy, shoving her away. Then he was
on his feet, swinging the blaster with all his terror crazed
might.

He heard the soft thunk as it connected and watched her
sprawl limply to the pavement. Trembling, he backed away
as a second figure rushed from the blackness behind him. A
hard arm blocked his throat, bending him back over a
muscular body—crushing his cry inside.

Akar caught a shimmer of light, grabbed at the knife, but
was unable to fend off the point that lanced coldly through
his gut. Panicked, the triggered the blaster, the discharge

blowing a section from a building across the street. The knife flashed into his flesh again and again as the muscular forearm tightened on his throat.

Blaster bolts laced the air overhead. The assailant turned, shouting something in a strange language, running into the dark with a confusion of others.

Akar slumped, blaster clattering to the street. Suddenly cold, he felt at the wetness of his stomach. Warm, it carried a certain stench of . . . of. . . .

He wiped at the blood that ran into his eyes. More blaster fire laced the night, blowing out parts of buildings.

"Who . . . who goes there? Who is it?" He heard himself shrilling in his desperate fear. His bladder let go and he sank to his knees, praying to Allah as his grandmother had taught him so long ago. Suddenly, he needed to believe in God.

Forms surrounded him in the night—black forms of the Home Guard and Akar Helstrom shivered in relief at his salvation. "I killed one," he whispered, heedless of the blood gushing between the fingers gripping his throbbing gut. More blood dripped down his head, leaving cool tunnels on his hot face. "I killed one."

Akar Helstrom trembled. Something tight constricted in his chest. The world grayed as hands were placed under his shoulders. He coughed on the frothy blood that bubbled into his mouth, panicked again, suffocating.

Through the misty exhaustion that settled on him, he heard. "She's alive! He knocked her out! Oh, my God! *Do you know who this is?*"

But Akar Helstrom sank wistfully into an eternal blackness.

CHAPTER XXIII

"Pallas! Pallas Mikros!" Ngen greeted with a sly grin as the image formed on the transductor. "Good to see you again. So tell me, how's business?"

Pallas spread his pudgy hands, causing the fine fabrics draped over his fat arms to shimmer in the light. "Business, as always, is most profitable . . . if dangerous. Perhaps, today it is even more profitable than the day before? I trust the toron met your specifications? You have called for more? I have some excellent crystals, large, with good quality."

Ngen lifted a shoulder in a shrug. "Maybe. How's the market?"

"Tight." Pallas smiled, the effort stretching his fat face. "Toron—on the market—is becoming most actively sought after, old friend." He sighed. "Ah, and I owe it all to you and your Sirians. Throughout the Directorate, unrest seethes. Rioting flares here and there. The Patrol shuttles madly from world to station to world, pretending that everything is fine. Blasters sell for unheard of prices. Wondrous thing. Between you and the Romanans, I am becoming a rich man where once I had to be furtive as a rat under a board. Now governmental heads seek me out."

Ngen chuckled. "Then perhaps you could tell me what I need to know?"

"I will tell anyone anything," Pallas replied smoothly, hands clasping over his bulging stomach. "For a price."

Ngen shook his head. "Not me, old friend. Not the man who made you rich. Not a man who will make you richer. Call it a partnership, hmm?"

Pallas' heavy jowls dropped. "I don't have partners, Ngen. You are well aware—"

"Even partners with warships capable of blasting Patrol ships of the line out of space? Even partners who could bring you riches and power beyond your dreams . . . or a death so terrible your fat would sizzle off your—"

Pallas straightened. "Then again, I might be convinced to form a partnership. Tell me more."

Ngen laughed. "I appreciate your practical approach, Pallas. Indeed I do."

"And now that you're the leader of the glorious revolution, you need a partner? What, Ngen? The manufacturing might of Sirius can't supply you with women or pleasures? What do you wish?"

Ngen settled back in his chair, pointing a finger. "Suppose a man wanted to find a planet populated with a group of fanatics capable of being led? Suppose he needed ignorant men, the dolts who can't think for themselves, who will believe what a leader tells them? If he needed fanatics—fundamentalists—where would he go?"

Pallas narrowed his eyes, the fat pads leaving them recessed and dark. For a long moment he thought, chubby fingers rubbing sensually back and forth. "Ah, could it be that the Directorate propaganda is correct? Could it be the glorious revolution isn't all it's cracked up to be by the Independence Party?"

"It could be the people here don't deserve the glorious revolution," Ngen admitted freely. "I've learned a lot from the Sirians. With the right combination of ignorance and zeal, I could make even more—"

"How bad is the situation there?" Pallas tilted his head. "Let's say I'll trade information . . . a partnership, as you say. Tell me, what is truth at Sirius and what is lie? Have you destroyed three Patrol ships of the line?"

"I have."

"And are the Romanans gutting the fierce Sirian rebellion?" Pallas raised an eyebrow on the pasty expanse of his forehead.

Ngen made a futile motion with his hand. "To be honest, I don't know. Sirians don't have a stomach for war. They never did. Intrigue, plotting, skill at manufacturing, yes, those are Sirian virtues. Considering what I've had to work with—"

"You're looking for another hole to run to," Pallas decided bluntly.

"Perhaps." Ngen narrowed his eyes to slits. "The situation here is currently stalemated. It could go either direction depending on key factors falling one way or another. Right now, we teeter in the balance . . . and I must depend on a gutless people for the decision."

"So? If Sirius falls apart in your lap, what do you want from me?"

Ngen smiled. "You say the profits have never been better? You say people are clamoring for weapons? Consider, my crafty friend, the old order is passing before our eyes—vanishing into the past. The Directorate's control has been loosened. As you note, a lot of money can be made. But then, perhaps you're setting your sights too low. With what I know, and what you know, we might make a wonderful combination."

"I've seen your speeches, Ngen. Marvelous. I might have believed them myself. Things must be terrible if the Romanans can overcome even such heartrending rhetoric." Pallas waved a hand. "And now, so much for speeches of passion? So much for dying in the arms of your brothers? Hmm?"

Ngen laughed. "I'm a politician, Pallas, surely you don't expect *me* to tell the truth! The purpose of a politician is to mislead the people, bend them to his will and gain. Any leader knows his keenest sword is the lie. If these Sirian sheep waver, I need only find others, employ my skills with a more zealous population. And the Romanans have taught me a valuable lesson about the power of religion to motivate. Such a vehicle for social control should never be overlooked."

Pallas nodded. "I'll consider your offer. At the same time, I'll keep in mind the requirements you've mentioned. How soon do you think you might need my recommendation?"

Ngen chuckled. "A week planetary time? Next year? Five years from now? Let's see how fortune smiles."

"May fortune smile warmly upon you, Ngen Van Chow. Good luck with your . . . barbarians."

"Good luck with your merchandise. In the meantime, you might help your situation. Any social disturbances can only result in increased sales."

"Indeed. I'll be waiting to hear from you." The comm went dead.

Ngen Van Chow chewed on his lip, looking to the other monitors. From his headset, he accessed comm, standing and dressing before leaving the moaning wreckage that had been Arish Amahanandras behind him. Walking through the corridors, he located Giorj on the bridge.

"First Citizen, you called me?" The pallid engineer seemed haggard, preoccupied.

"Yes, Giorj." Ngen frowned. "You've seen to my private yacht?"

"I have, First Citizen."

Ngen took a deep breath, searching Hambrei's washed out eyes. "Giorj, the situation on the planet looks like it might turn against us."

"I'm aware of that, First Citizen." He hesitated. "May I ask about Angla? I haven't been able to get through to the Party Chief there. My mother—"

Ngen raised a hand. "Yes, I know. Angla is threatened. I have given orders for the evacuation of your mother in the event the fighting gets close. You know how much I care for her, Giorj. You know I'd never let anything happen to her."

The gray man lowered his eyes. "I . . . I've always appreciated you for that. She . . . she gave me . . ."

"I know. She's a wonderful woman." Ngen dropped a hand on Hambrei's shoulder. "But in the meantime, Giorj, you know the situation. I'd like you to go about making some modifications to the reactor. Just a precaution—you understand—in the event we lose the ship. As always, I'm covering my tracks. If you'll see to that matter with discretion, I'll make the arrangements to evacuate your mother to the *Hiram Lazar*. Should it turn out that we need to abandon the entire situation, we'll bring her with us on my yacht. I promise."

Giorj sighed. "Thank you, First Citizen. You can't know how I've worried. The thought of her—"

"For you, anything. You know what I owe you." Ngen gave him a reassuring clap on the back. "Any progress on *Bullet*?"

"Another deck. I think we've begun to wear them away. We've pushed them back so they can't thrust the dead out the lock anymore."

"Very good." He frowned. "You know, there is a possibility we may have to blast her, to keep her from falling back into Patrol hands. The *Brotherhood* secrets within her are better no one's than theirs."

"I'm aware of that possibility," Giorj looked pained.

"Yes, well, perhaps they'll capitulate in time to save themselves.

"Uh, First Citizen?"

"Yes, Giorj."

"I do have good news. Vitr called while you were on transduction. He reports they have captured a Romanan woman . . . alive."

*   *   *

Maya ben Ahmad perched before the monitor, glaring helplessly at the long-distance scan. "Isn't there anything we can do?"

"Nothing remains within our power, ma'am. To dive down and harass Ngen might cause him to blast *Bullet* out of space. For the moment, I'd suggest holding on, seeing if Rita Sarsa and the Romanans can crush the Sirians on the ground. If the planet falls, we can act in concert with the ATs. Anything more might cause Ngen to cut his losses."

"And *Bullet* would be a loss." Maya slapped her knee. "And the worst part is, *Miliken* and *Toreon* just sit there. No, Toby won't lift a finger! Damn bitch! She and Yaisha are just tickled that Damen's bleeding to death in that wreck down there. Hell, he deserves more. He's a warrior!" She pointed at the image of *Bullet* on the monitor, now swarming with Sirian fighters. "He's still fighting in there! That's what the Patrol was all about! Honor, guts, courage!"

The First Officer shook his head, looking up from the comm monitor. "I've run every permutation, ma'am. *Victory* could take no more than five minutes of combined fire from *Hiram Lazar* and *Helk*. After that, we'd be junk just like *Bullet*. If *Toreon* and *Miliken* were to—"

"They've refused!" Maya spat angrily. "Called Ree a pirate because that's what the damn pumpkin-heads call him." She gestured helplessly. "Crap! By Spider, look down there! The Romanans are *winning* the damn war! And . . . and they're the people Skor wants to be rid of most!"

Maya stood and paced across the bridge, muttering. "I don't know, Ben. The way it's shaking out; it looks like the Romanans are going to subdue the planet. You've heard Sarsa's reports. If they can take Helg, the Sirians on Ekrania will fold. Apahar can't stand against them. It's the same on the other continents. Our people clean up after the Romanans go through.

"So tell me, Ben. The Romanans take the planet. We launch a coordinated strike with the ATs rising to orbit while we drop, providing covering fire. We take *Hiram Lazar* and *Helk* because we know—if Ngen doesn't—that ATs can outmaneuver his fire control. And then it's all over and we're supposed to cut the throats of the Romanans, the people who won the war?"

She looked into his hard eyes.

"How's that make you feel, Ben? Huh? Like some royal hero or what?"

He tilted his head. "A lot of the crew came to like the Romanans while we had them on board, Colonel. Sure, they were a pain in the ass and all, but they taught us a lot. You haven't noticed the spiders in the corridors? They keep cropping up—and the Romanans have been gone for weeks now."

Maya crossed her arms, scowling at the two Patrol ships hovering off to one side, repairing battle damage.

"We're going to have to make a choice sometime soon, Ben."

Her First Officer nodded. "Yes, ma'am."

"What will the crew do?"

"Back you."

She looked down; his stylus made a doodle of a spider.

"Whichever way I decide to go?" She raised an eyebrow.

A pounding agony lived behind her eyes. The position of her arms proved even more uncomfortable, however. They were pulled back and tightly bound behind her, stretching the pectorals and making it difficult to breathe.

"She's coming around." The voice, oddly accented, sounded impersonal.

Susan tried to think. She was on Sirius. She had been on a raid. They'd shot up a couple of buildings to get a Sirian response. The Home Guard had come. They'd dropped grenades on them. She had taken coup and cut two, and while her team retreated, she stopped for one last one.

She remembered nothing after that. Carefully, she used her mind to explore all of her body. Everything still felt attached, although she'd seen examples of phantom pain in blasted men.

She opened her eyes to slits. The room was bright, almost making her wince. A ring of faces looked down at her. Sirians, uniformed Home Guards! She opened her eyes wide and glared her hatred, despising the pain that kept her wits at bay.

"There." A white-haired man nodded with satisfaction.

"Where am I?" Susan asked.

"Helg, barbarian." The white-haired man ran long fingers through his hair. "We've tried very hard to capture a woman Romanan. The First Citizen desires to question you. We've had very few Romanan prisoners. Like yourself, they've been incapacitated somehow."

Susan swallowed hard, wishing she could get her fingers around his thin, aged neck. She imagined the bones snapping hollowly.

"Like you, they say nothing." The white-haired man paused, crossing his arms and raising the fingers of one hand to his chin. "We've tried psych treatments on several . . . but in all cases the results were less than spectacular.

"You see, we've read the information Doctor Dobra transmitted. We know that your brains are different. It distresses us gravely that we can't psych you. It would make things so much easier."

"Pika," another man called. The white-haired one turned. "I have the First Citizen on the comm." The man called Pika leaned over and spoke quietly. He stood, face twitching slightly.

Something had been decided. Her death? A flutter of relief mixed with sorrow crossed her mind. It would hurt Friday so badly. On the other hand, her soul would fly to Spider with all it had learned. There were worse fates than to be the servant of God.

Pika leaned over her and she caught the slight scent of his perfume. The odor revolted her. Here stood no *man*! He was a fop!

"The First Citizen requests that you be sent to him immediately." Pika's face showed disappointment. "I had hoped to let my men have you for a couple of days first." He seemed genuinely distressed.

"Will I have the chance to kill you first?" Susan asked, nerving herself. "You and me, Pika the weak. Knife feud! You understand that concept of honor?"

Someone grunted. "Perhaps we have misjudged. She is even more primitive than the men."

"Indeed," Pika muttered, fingers resting lightly on his chin again.

The bud of an idea planted itself in Susan's head. They didn't know much at all about the Romanans. The men they'd taken must have been psyched on the chance they'd get a take, milk them for intelligence. Psych either drove a Romanan mad—sometimes; didn't take at all—mostly; or worked—rarely. The others hadn't broken.

"Let me kill you," Susan added a bit of a grunt to her voice. "Prove you are man—not sheep!"

"Sheep?" Pika asked.

"Sheep!" She replied and spit at him. "Cowards! We butcher you like sheep!"

"The Patrol must give them their orders," a thin man suggested. "Certainly they can't conceive of strategy."

"Well, no matter," Pika said distastefully. "She's the First Citizen's problem now. I regret our men can't have her. They'd probably be the tamest entertainment she's had in years." They all broke into laughter. Susan's lips curled into an insolent snarl.

Bound and trussed, they tossed her onto an anti-grav and pushed her out like a side of meat. She made herself study everything as they wound their way through the corridors. Passing the hard-eyed guards, she spat at them, leaving them with a returned hatred as deep as their own.

They dumped her unceremoniously in an open aircar. The breeze played over her hot cheek, cool in the night. How long since she'd been knocked out, hours, days, who knew? The aircar dropped underground and slid into a spacious room. Gantries, fuel lines, and large awkward looking equipment stood under the harsh lights, casting shadows on the side of a shuttle craft.

The aircar climbed until it rested even with a hatch. Rough hands yanked Susan through and strapped her to the cold deck plates.

"Thirty minutes until sunrise." A disembodied voice overcame the whine beneath her ears.

"No sign of Patrol ATs. Let's get out of here. They'll be running recon real soon."

"The main shield doors are opening. Five minutes to lift-off."

The whine grew louder until she couldn't hear the faint voices of the crew. A giant hand smashed her down into the steel plating, driving the breath from her body, turning the world first hazy and gray then black.

She was falling when she came to. Panicked, she realized the ship had been hit after all. Heart racing, she allowed herself to think about Hans, recalling the tenderness that had been his. She winced, aware of the hurt through the wall in her mind. How it would have tortured her had she let it out.

She forced herself to wonder about Friday, leaving the pain of Hans hidden in the depths of her mind. She visualized the humor in his eyes, the quick smile and outrageous appreciation he bestowed upon her. Would he let his pain kill him the way she had let hers? She closed her eyes and prayed to Spider to die quickly and gracefully.

"Matching," a calm voice called from the cabin.

Susan frowned. The pilot didn't sound like he was dying.

Weightless! This tiny little shuttle didn't have grav plates!
Why not? All it took was a little hyperconductor. If they
had so damned much to build those huge blasters, why not
spread it around?

Susan squirmed and looked around the compartment.
The decks and bulkheads were bare. Faintly, she could see
the thin seams where they would have laced the hyperconductor
for the grav plates. One should be right behind her head.

For a second she thought she would twist her already
strained shoulders out of their sockets, but she caught a
fuzzy glimpse of the bulkhead. The weld appeared new, the
proverbial white paint fresh only on the seams.

Susan grinned to herself. So Ngen had stripped his whole
world of amenities to build his blasters. Now, if she could
only get a close look at the blasters and get a report through
to Colonel Ree or Rita.

Her body shifted as the shuttle changed attitude. Minutes
passed. She heard a clunk and felt a scrape through the
thick metal. She jerked to one side as the shuttle docked.

The crew came down and unstrapped her. She flopped
helplessly and they literally caught her and carried her into
gravity. So Ngen hadn't stripped his warships!

"That is a Romanan woman?" The man who peered
down at her looked sick—pale, almost gray. No expression
marked his face.

"She is in your charge, Engineer." The shuttle pilot
shrugged. "Any food in this bucket? Rations are getting real
scarce down there. Feels like I haven't eaten for a week."

"How bad?" the engineer asked. "Are there still supplies
going into Angla?"

"You mean you haven't heard?" The pilot bent to check
a monitor. "The Patrol got that last week. *Helk* burned
that whole suburb off the map! God, it looks like the moon
down there. I heard the First Citizen was mad to get every
Romanan he could, no matter the price!"

Susan kept her eyes on the engineer. He'd tensed up,
fingers knotting on the board that controlled the antigrav
she rode. Pain now contorted his dead eyes. Why?

"I was there," Susan whispered softly. "It was terrible.
The people had surrendered and driven out the Home Guard.
I only lived because I got to a powerlead."

"My mother . . . lived there," the engineer whispered before
he realized who he was talking to. "He said he'd protect her."
His voice caught, muscles around the mouth pulling tight.

"Hey, sorry to hear that," the pilot commiserated, looking nervous. He nodded and left quickly.

Susan let herself feel a spark of hope. "My . . . The man I loved was burned off, too," she whispered, surprised that the pain came so easily to her voice. "God, it was horrible."

The engineer looked down at her, seeing the hurt in her eyes. He started the anti-grav on its way. "You would tell me about it?"

Susan looked deeply into his odd, pale eyes. Could she gain leverage here? How much could she compromise her cover of ignorance? "It would hurt you," she whispered. "There's been enough hurt on both sides. Suffering is all this conflict has brought."

He nodded. "My mother was my only—" He snapped his mouth closed, and swallowed.

"You loved her," Susan finished slowly. "Nothing wrong with that. Bless Spider that you had a mother. My mother, well, she died when I was little. I would enjoy hearing of yours. I always wondered what it would be like to have parents."

His eyes narrowed. "You had no parents?"

She shook her head, trying to read his hidden reactions. "I was an orphan. I guess that's how I ended up here."

"That may not have been any stroke of luck," his soft voice warned.

"What is your name, engineer. Why would I expect my luck to change?" She kept her voice soft and vulnerable.

"I am called Giorj Hambrei." He looked at her. "You will never leave the First Citizen's room alive. He has had you brought here at great expense to see if he could break you. He enjoys dominating weakness in other men. In women, he enjoys degrading them. He cannot deal with adversaries as equals. To break you, gives him strength."

Susan remembered similar words from Friday's mouth. "The symbol of a sick soul," she whispered.

"I couldn't have put it into better words." Giorj paused, as if making a decision. His eyes darted nervously to one side and then the other, his mouth worked and he licked his colorless lips. "How strong are you, Romanan?"

"No one ever knows how strong they are," Susan answered. "I suppose strength comes from doing the most difficult. I've overcome many difficulties. How about you, Giorj?"

He stared straight ahead, impossible to read. A muscle

ticked at the corner of his mouth. "I don't know. Maybe I've never done anything difficult. Maybe I've always had too much to lose." He looked down. "I don't know what I can do to help you. But what I can. . . ."

"Why?" she asked, suddenly worried. "I'm a Romanan, enemy to your people."

Giorj seemed to wilt inside. "Maybe you are not the only enemy to my people."

"In that case," Susan grinned, "I'll help you, too. If I can. The planet is just about all Patrol property. Won't be long before they have space, too. The people are starving, broken; they can't fight us. When Ngen tries to burn us, he kills thousands of Sirians."

"He lied! He looked me, *me*, right in the eyes and lied! Said he'd order her taken out when he knew . . . *knew* she'd been blasted by his own weapons!"

"I'm sorry," Susan whispered. "So many have died. It's all been for . . . for what? Would there have been a war without Ngen?"

"I can't tell you more now. Be strong," Giorj whispered. "We're there." The engineer palmed a doorway and it slid open.

From her position on the anti-grav, Susan could see a large padded room with subdued lighting. Two beds jutted from the wall around the sides, a doorway passed into what she assumed was a commode. Two women, one on each bed, stared vacantly at her in the changing pastel light of the room.

Giorj reached down and the restraining straps fell loose. Susan sat up, wincing at the pain in her shoulders. Giorj, silent now, unfastened her combat armor and piled it on the anti-grav.

"The facilities to wash are there." He indicated the doorway Susan had inspected. "I must place these on your wrists." He held out two thin bracelets.

"I don't want 'em!" Susan growled, aware they must be under close observation.

Giorj's eyes may have flickered for an instant at the change in her manner. He held out a thin rod that glowed on the tip. "I use this. Please, I assure you, there's no choice."

"I don't want stinking sheep jewelry!" she growled, standing straight, arms crossed insolently.

Purposely, she left him no choice. When she came to, she

lay naked on one of the beds, she'd been washed—the first time in weeks—and Giorj was gone.

"Where am I?" she demanded of the two women who sat on the bed across from her.

One, the younger, laughed and babbled hysterically. The second looked at her from dull, pained eyes. Susan studied the face. Something familiar about the nose and eyes. . . . It hit her! Colonel Arish Amahanandras! Here! The haughty Colonel, naked and broken?

"Where am I?" Susan demanded with authority. "What is this place? Where are my weapons and armor?"

Arish moaned, turning her head away, panicking.

Susan sprang from the bed only to bounce back on her rump. A curious field surrounded her: something like a shield. A dull chill ran up her spine as she looked over at Arish, frightened by the odd light in the other woman's eyes.

She fingered the little bracelets on her wrists. Another pair graced her ankles. Looking around the room, she could identify nothing resembling a weapon. Everything appeared padded with no sharp edges. She had only her own body . . . and the knowledge that with her bare hands she had killed more than one armed man.

She sank back on the bed, aware of the exhaustion that lay heavy in her limbs. Letting her eyes roam around the room, she rolled into a ball and closed her eyes.

Could Giorj be counted a friend, or an enemy? How could she communicate with Colonel Ree or Major Sarsa? What were they going to do with her?

That last bothered her. Gang rape? Could be, she wouldn't blame them in fact. Maybe she was first prize in some sort of contest? The fact did remain that they'd keep her alive—at least for a while.

So? How are you going to deal with it, Susan? she asked herself.

Her thoughts twisted around that, the memory of Rita's warnings stirring in her mind. She remembered women she'd seen the Romanans take. Mostly they lived through it. Friday told her it was the same as her cutting men. A chill skittered under her heart and up her back. Spider was giving her a taste of her own medicine.

She couldn't help thinking of Arish and the other woman with whom she shared this prison. Arish Amahanandras was no one's weakling. Patrol command didn't breed such people, yet, Arish had broken. How? Why? Cold fear clutched her intestines.

Guts, she told herself. Guts would either keep her alive or kill her. Either way, she'd made a difference. Indeed, she'd come a long way from the ignorant girl who'd wanted the stars. Well, she'd gotten this far. Further, she'd won the respect of her men, led them in combat, and even made Iron Eyes approve her plans.

Now, if she could just hold on here until the Patrol attacked. If the ATs made it through, they'd find her. She had to live at least that long.

"Ah!"

The soft, delicate voice took her by surprise. She looked up into the gentle eyes of Ngen Van Chow. Like lightning, she jumped to her feet, ready. Just a little closer and she'd kick his heart right out of his body!

"Hostile greeting, wouldn't you think, dearest girl?" he cooed. "Come, let us be friends." A deep frown lined his face, as if he were truly distressed. "I have come to teach you pleasure."

On the edge of her vision, Susan could see Arish cringing. The idiot one was relaxing at the sound of the voice, vacant eyes glowing as she ran her fingers along her own flesh. A wash of terror ran through Susan.

Ngen took a step closer as Susan's body tensed. She started the kick; but it never landed. Instead, she crashed to the bed, arms and legs pinned fast to each other, pain already welling under the bracelets.

"Dear one!" Ngen cried as he began stripping the clothes from his body. "We must teach you that pleasure comes through submission . . . not violence."

Susan fought to free herself from the clinging bands on her arms and legs. Twisting, she tore her flesh in the effort. The bands didn't budge, despite her tiger's body.

"Here, my wonderful angel," his voice cooed. She turned and glared her hatred at him. When she tried to bite him, he artfully stuffed a gag into her mouth.

"Such a shame, my beauty, but we do have a lot of time to work on pleasure. Look at my dearest Leona over there." His fingers began caressing Susan's skin as she glanced at the woman.

Leona Magill! It caught her interest, as she watched the onetime First Citizen caressing herself and moaning.

"You, too, will be mine like that, my wondrous, magnificent beauty!" Ngen chortled.

She struggled, half-hysterical, pitching this way and that.

"Now, sweet gem," Ngen added gently, "let's see what's in your mind." He lowered a curiously large headset over her temples.

Instantly, a calmness filled her, the machine reading her mind, lifting images from deep inside, swirling them around Ngen's smiling face, transforming enemy into friend.

"Hans," she called, seeing him smiling down at her as he moved to caress her body.

NO! The warning flashed through her mind. *Hans is dead! DEAD! This is Ngen! You're being raped! Fight!*

Only to her horror, her body responded, feeling Hans' gentle touch while the eyes that met hers were black, hot, passionate.

Her lips kissed him eagerly, while her brain recoiled. In the recesses of her mind, a hideous scream began, building, blasting through her brain, leaving her hysterical and whimpering as her traitorous body rose on a height of passion.

CHAPTER XXIV

Rita Sarsa stared woodenly at the monitor. "You're sure?"

The warrior nodded, bitterly. "We've caught members of the Home Guard, made them talk. They took Susan up to Ngen's ship."

Rita's heart dropped in her chest. "I see. I guess we'll just have to do what we—"

"*We* already are. Blood will run. Helg will tremble this night. The Sirians will know what it is to take a woman of the People!"

Comm went dead.

Rita froze, miserable. Only her eyes moved. Susan Smith Andojar merged into a series of memories. The sunlight had been so bright that first day she'd seen the girl being beaten by her uncle. The thrashing had become a spectacle, almost a circus event, with cheering spectators and a whooping, jubilant crowd.

The defiant expression had touched her. The disheveled

black hair flying out in strands had given the girl a ridiculous appearance. But that spark had been there behind the hurt and the humiliation.

Again, the day she and Iron Eyes had ridden back from the duel with Big Man, they had found her, still defiant, headed she knew not where. Heedless of both the creatures that lived in the mountains and the even wilder men, she'd taken her own destiny in hand.

The next time had been as an eager, somewhat uncertain young girl with a fresh coup at her belt and the solemnity that comes of a first vision quest. She'd driven herself, bright-eyed and enthusiastic, into her studies, overcoming each challenge and surprising them all.

Rita remembered the day Susan and Hans had been caught coming out of the computer access. She smiled grimly. The little witch had stood there and brazenly lied her way out of the whole mess. Rita nodded to herself. Brilliantly done, too.

She thought of how Susan had looked after that first day's combat, the haggard look, the blood spatters, the shiny hair of all colors that hung from her belt while she struggled to understand.

Susan had been so much more than Rita had let herself see. All through the campaign, she'd been too busy to know that Susan had grown past her perceptions. After Angla fell and Hans was blasted, the dream had died in a violet reality. Then it had been too late.

She recalled the way Susan's wooden face and dead eyes stared out at the world that had bitten back. And Friday, eyes worshipful, heart beating for her, had suffered along like a martyr.

Rita bent her head forward, resting it on her arms, willing herself to what came next.

She straightened, and accessed comm.

Friday's face formed on the monitor. "Major," he greeted, eyes bleary, features dust streaked. "I was just about to reach for the comm myself. We're closing in on Helg. Home Guards and civilians are streaming past us, every building has a spider on it. We've won."

"They got Susan the night before last," Rita said, as if she hadn't heard him. "Her people tortured the captives until they learned she'd been taken to *Hiram Lazar*."

Friday's face tautened. "I see. I . . . I . . . I'll talk to you later." The comm went dead.

She stared at the monitor, as if the afterimage still reflected Friday's stricken eyes. "Susan, Susan," Rita moaned.

"And there, kid, is the end of your ambition," Rita whispered to herself. "I wonder, was I wrong? Should I have let Friday go with you? Was it all my fault?"

She pulled herself numbly to her feet. Teams led by Iron Eyes had been dropped in Apahar only the night before. Already they were using Susan's tactics to bring the icy fingers of fear to the city. It would only be a matter of time now. Susan's gift to her People.

Moshe ducked his head in the hatch. "Just got a message over the frequencies. Helg is surrendering."

Rita gave him a forced smile. "Great."

One last stronghold and Romanan worms were already chewing holes into the wood of resistance. Ngen hadn't blasted Helg either. As long as Romanans didn't crop up in strength, the big blasters in space remained quiet. Their master, though, made broadcast after broadcast to the Sirians to overthrow Directorate tyranny. For once, the Sirians weren't buying it. They simply stared at the passing Romanans and Patrol, physically and emotionally exhausted.

The other continents, too, fell under the Patrol's thumb as their Romanans seeped through defenses like acid into Sirian morale. There, the smaller cities had fallen to the ATs and marines with only minor resistance. Ekrania proved the real seat of Sirian power.

Comm signaled for her. Apathetically, she accepted the signal. Iron Eyes stared at her, flintlike eyes glittering in his angular warrior's face, braids on both sides of his throat. "Want to catch an AT and drop over? Apahar's leading citizens are suing for peace with the expectation that we'll feed them."

Rita felt a little bit of a lift. "I'll be right there," she agreed, not feeling the elation that should have risen on this occasion. Accessing comm, she got Friday again. He looked ashen, as if someone had kicked him in the gut. "Beam your location, we're coming to get you."

Moshe had the AT off the ground at a split second's notice. Rita watched the clouds flying toward them like a wall of cotton only to fall before the AT's reinforced nose. Around her, battle grimy marines squinted into the monitors, watching for the first signs of the nasty violet blasters. Out of habit, the AT dodged and ducked to fool the tracking computers on the orbiting Sirian ships.

Twenty minutes later, having stopped to recover Friday's party, AT22 dropped from the heavens to settle lightly in the center of Apahar. As the dust whirled away, Iron Eyes walked out of a nearby building, ten Sirians in revolutionary black, rank and file behind him. Wary Romanans watched them from the sides, whispering behind their hands.

Iron Eyes led them up the rear ramp as Rita unbuckled from the crash harness and made a quick check of her appearance. Even a blind dock rat could tell it wasn't her wedding day. Her face had thinned, green eyes pinched by a permanent squint around the corners. She looked tired. She looked forty-five instead of closer to thirty.

She followed the progress of the delegation through the AT until they seated themselves in the conference room. Paging for Friday, she waited, letting the delegates be served coffee, tea, or whatever was their pleasure.

"Major?" Friday appeared in the hatch. He didn't look any better.

"You wouldn't happen to have a set of skin clothing in here, would you?" she asked, eyes gleaming.

"Of course." Friday shrugged. "I didn't know how long we'd be here."

"Go get dressed." Rita laughed and turned on her heel. What the hell, it wouldn't hurt to let the damn delegates wait a while longer. This was her party.

She slid the cool tanned leather over her body and pulled her coup belt tight. Dropping the heavy Romanan fighting knife into place, she picked up the rifle she'd taken from Big Man so long ago and walked into the companionway. The marine there gawked but said nothing. Friday appeared—likewise clad—the Spider colors dyed into the sleeves of his garment.

"You're my honor guard." Rita told him with a wry smile. "Get in that conference room and announce me, first in Romanan, then in Standard. Be sure to use both of my titles."

"What's going on?" Friday demanded, his eyes ringed with fatigue and pain.

"Didn't you hear?"

"Hear what?" His voice betrayed irritation.

"The Sirian ground forces are surrendering," Rita said calmly, watching Friday's jaw drop only to be snugged up in a bitter smile.

He entered the conference room in his rolling stride and

banged his blaster butt on the floor four times—the sacred number of Spider. Sonorously, his voice boomed forth, first in Romanan and then in Standard, "Attention! Red Many Coups, slayer of the enemies of Spider, Major Rita Sarsa of the Patrol, Commander, Romanan and Patrol forces of the Planet Sirius." He ended with a snapped salute.

Rita took her cue and entered, snapping a reply. She could hear wheezing intakes of breath. Slowly she turned to let her eyes play over face after face. Iron Eyes's craggy features beamed. The Sirians gaped, almost apoplectic.

"Gentlemen, I've been informed you wish to talk over terms of surrender." Rita didn't let her eyes waver. All men, how odd.

One man, white-haired, patrician, stood, meeting her eyes. "We would bargain for the . . ."

Rita held up a hand and stopped him. "There will be no bargain, gentlemen. We demand your unconditional surrender. Your Home and Civil Guards will present arms and retire to their places of business. There's a lot to be done, gentlemen, to put this planet on a stable economic footing. I intend to see to it that just that happens."

Rita's eyes narrowed. "What is your name, sir. You will be spokesman. I don't like talking to committees."

He bowed, taking a deep breath. "I am Pika Vitr. I am the Boardmember for the Union."

"Do I have your surrender?" Rita asked softly.

Pika Vitr looked helplessly around the table, finding only nods or expressions locked in futility. He straightened and looked Rita in the eyes. "You do, Major. We throw ourselves on your mercy. Hunger plagues the land; our children are failing from malnutrition. We can no longer watch them wasting away."

And you've completely lost control of the planet. Ngen can't help you. The Romanans are in your last retreat and there's nowhere else to run, Rita concluded the unsaid.

"Very well." Rita bowed. She reached into her pouch and produced a contract. "Sign there, each of you, along with whatever titles authorize and bind your signature. I realize that I still need the First Citizen's . . . but he remains an outlaw."

Slowly the paper went around the table. When complete, Rita witnessed it and gave it over to Iron Eyes. He laboriously scribbled his name, tongue hanging out the side of his mouth, brow furrowed with effort.

The Sirian delegation winced, lips quivering, trying to look elsewhere.

Rita handed the document to Friday who'd stood at attention. "Witness this, warrior." She nodded slightly. "I'll write your name. Make your mark next to it."

Friday bent down and took the pen. Carefully and with great ceremony, he made the figure of a spider next to the name Rita pointed out. He straightened back to attention, pride in every line of his body.

"You will attend to the return of all prisoners of war and order the immediate disbanding of your military force," Rita ordered.

Pika nodded. "If you don't mind, could we talk about food?"

"We'll signal the GCIs to come in just as soon as we clear Ngen's battleships from the sky." Rita settled herself into a chair and studied her enemies. They didn't look like so much.

A silence stretched, Iron Eyes speculatively chewing on his lip.

"What happens to us?" one of the men asked. His eyes shifted to Friday and his blaster.

"That's up to the Directorate," Rita told him, shrugging. She'd wondered how long it would take before they'd ask about their precious hides.

"And the Romanans?" asked yet another.

"The Romanans will, in all probability, retire to their home world taking whatever they wish to carry with them. We'll appoint administrators to see to the interest they have won here. We weren't joking when we said areas occupied by Romanans would remain Romanan."

Sirian eyes widened with shock; one man shook his head as if he hadn't heard right.

Rita saw the apprehension building. "Gentlemen," she chided. "You don't throw a revolution without some risk. They won't take that much with them. You have an entire planet. The population of Apahar alone is greater than their whole world's."

"And our young women?" Pika asked, voice a hollow whisper. He shifted his eyes from Rita's face to Friday's—thoughts evident.

"What of Susan Smith Andojar?" Friday asked suddenly, voice like a lash. "You have her. Is she still alive?"

Iron Eyes started. "They have Susan?" His eyes hardened, the muscles in his body knotting. The corner of his mouth worked. "She had better be well treated or I'll have—"

"I don't know who you're talking about," Pika protected.

"The Corporal was captured in Helg some three days back." Rita watched with narrowing eyes. "We at least want her body."

"You mean the Spider woman?" Pika realized. He added quickly, "We don't have her. She's on *Hiram Lazar*. We sent her up on the last shuttle out." He thrust out his hands. "She was safe when she left us. We didn't harm a hair on her head!"

"Aptly put!" Iron Eyes growled, fingers on his coup belt.

A desperate silence hung around the table. Friday's eyes glittered. Rita felt some of the pressure release around her heart.

"So our young women are made slaves," a gray-haired man murmured as he dropped his head into his hands.

"Not at all," Iron Eyes replied, still defensive. "They'll be taken as spoils of war. On our planet, they'll be married to warriors and adopted into the clans. You no doubt heard the Major's proclamation."

Iron Eyes gave them a reassuring smile. "It's really not such a horrible fate. As you can see from the example of Friday, our men are handsome. I myself might take one for a bride. I can promise you that I would love her like any other wife. And our planet is not nearly so miserable as yours. We haven't had a terrible war. Our air is pure. Your grandsons will grow strong and learn to ride free across the grasslands.

"Your young women shall provide our people with a wealth of children. They will learn the ways of the Prophets, and of Spider, who is God. Your young women shall find the joy of keeping a warrior's house. They will . . ."

"War Chief," Rita interrupted, seeing horror grow on the old men's faces as Iron Eyes began to wax enthusiastic. "I don't think these men have a framework for understanding just how lucky the women will be."

Iron Eyes looked about, mystified, and shrugged. "Who would have their daughters marry Sirians and stay here?"

Rita ignored him. "The bottom line is that the action of the Independence Party has brought us here, gentlemen. You have been in revolt against the power of the Directorate. Your own battleships have decimated the planet's surface and killed far more of your civilian and military population than all the Romanans and Patrol put together.

"If you wish, argue your case with the Directorate. They may ransom your young women back for you. That is between you and the Directors—not the Patrol.

"Further, you may deal with individual Romanans as well. Any you can persuade to leave their spoils are free to do so. We promised them loot for the taking as their fee to help us. If you can better the price, you're welcome to it." Rita gave them a challenging stare.

"How do you plan to knock Ngen Van Chow out of the sky?" Pika Vitr asked. "Your own Patrol battleships can't touch him."

"That is for us to know and Ngen to find out, Boardmember Vitr. May I remind you, you're not in our circle of trusted friends. I can see no reason why we should tell you about our allies. We definitely can't do anything with only ATs." Rita indicated that the subject was closed.

Allies? Friday asked himself behind his masklike face.

"And in the meantime, what do you wish of us?" Pika asked.

"You are the most familiar with the government of Sirius, Boardmember. Please, continue your duties. All decisions will be cleared either through me or my captain, Moshe Rashid. If you want, clear decisions through Iron Eyes, but I should warn you in advance that the Romanan concept of government is very different from yours. He is the War Chief. What he tells you, you *will* do." Rita smiled grimly. After Iron Eyes' enthusiasm about his planet, they'd check with her: assiduously.

Pika looked like a weight had been lifted off his shoulders.

Rita stood. "That will be all, gentlemen. Please, go about your business. Inform your people that everything is fine. The Romanans will cease their depredations and marine patrols will take over police duties.

"I would warn you that while I personally will do nothing to punish you, I would heartily suggest that you demonstrate your good faith to the Directorate. Any evidence that you have violated that oath of surrender you just signed would make me and the Romanans very annoyed." She turned and, with Friday on her heels, left the room.

In her quarters, Friday immediately asked. "What allies?"

Rita grinned as she poured two glasses of seventy-year-old scotch. "Come, Friday, you didn't think I was going to tell them we're going up after that bastard, did you?"

Friday sipped and nodded at the quality of the scotch.

Iron Eyes joined them then and Rita poured for him. "To victory!"

"To victory!" They cheered.

"How soon do we rescue Susan?" Friday asked, almost bouncing on his toes.

"Probably tomorrow." Rita shrugged. "Right now, the Sirians are in shock. I've had the ATs down to replenish with fusibles for the last three days. We've topped up without making a lot of commotion about it. I want the troops rested and ready to go—what's left of them."

"That's why everyone's been sleeping on the ATs at night?" Iron Eyes guessed.

"Not bad for a heathen," Friday grinned, expression lightening as hope replaced grief and worry.

"She may not be that glad to see us," Rita reminded. "We don't know what Ngen's been doing to her."

Friday shook his head. "No, we don't. She's in the hands of Spider. He'll take her and do as he thinks best. When Spider is done—whatever his reasons—Susan will know her way."

"To Spider's way." Iron Eyes raised his cup, noticing Rita had an effigy drawn on the ceiling. A portent of things to come?

That night, Iron Eyes made one last round, checking the guards, sharing a joke here, listening to another's stories there. They covered just about every approach to the AT. Such a different world, this Sirius. He looked up, missing the moons of his home planet. The stars—what he could see of them—had a different configuration, the clouds hung sullen and somber. He sniffed the breeze, smelling the acrid odors. The skyline, unlike the hills and bluffs of World, created a collage of irregular shapes, a pattern of darkness until the powerleads could be repaired and light restored.

A place of angles, lines, and curves, the geometry of the city made no sense to Iron Eyes. Sirius simply wasn't a warrior's land. How did a man track across the concrete? Where did he go to find a high place to pray? On top of one of the buildings? Would Spider talk to a man there?

A senseless place, a senseless war. Warriors were going home with their stolen aircars crammed full of coups. They were taking blasters, women, electrical and pulse power equipment. Of course, they'd picked up silver, gold, credits, heaters, comms, computers, and a host of other material.

Spoils beyond a man's imagination, all would be carried home to World.

The spoils might indeed be great, but the price had been, too. So many stayed here, blown to bits, their bodies turned to atoms. Others had been buried in the hostile ground. Some had been left to lie where they'd fallen . . . or had been thrown into converters. No matter what, World would never be the same again.

Slowly, thoughtfully, he walked back to the AT. He nodded to the marine on guard and spoke his clearance to the hatch. Inside, the lights blinded him. He made his way to the little cabin that was his. The message light blinked in insistent red.

"Comm?" Iron Eyes asked.

"John? Could I see you?" Rita's image formed.

He smiled, happy that her hair hung down in red waves and that she looked relaxed for the first time in ages. Her eyes beckoned, deep green against the bright red of her hair and the scatter of freckles on her nose.

Reaching her cabin, he palmed her door and entered, surprised to find her out of uniform. Her clothing consisted of a single wrap cinched about the waist and exploiting her curves admirably.

"More of that delightful scotch?"

"Yes." He took the glass she offered, feeling awkward and tongue-tied.

Her fingers moved deftly as she undid his body armor. Iron Eyes hesitated, catching a whiff of his body. He hadn't had a chance to get to the shower for a couple of days, because he'd spent most of his time on the line.

As if she read his mind, Rita offered, "Step in there. Make yourself at home, John. This is a night of celebration."

"I don't have any clean clothing," he protested as she pushed him in and took his dirty laundry when he handed it out.

"Don't worry about it." Her voice teased him, lilting in the old way, as if the last months had slipped from her.

When Iron Eyes reached out, she handed him a loose fabric. "What do I do with this?"

"Step out here," she ordered.

He came, holding the fabric around him. Rita fought a smile as she saw how nervous he was.

"How about just letting go of yourself tonight." She raised an eyebrow as she took the corners of the garment and folded it around him.

"Nice stuff," Iron Eyes grunted as he let the thin fabric run through his fingers. He didn't protest as Rita pushed him down into the bunk and slid in next to him.

She looked at him from tilted green eyes. "So, how does it feel to conquer a planet?"

He laughed and took a drink of the scotch. "I was just out trying to find out. I don't know, doesn't seem real. The values are different here, all changed. There isn't the glorious joy of a raid well plotted. Instead, there's a vast relief that this part is . . . is all over."

She rubbed his corded back muscles, easing the tension. "That's the difference between war as a game and the real thing."

"I can't help but . . . I mean, I wonder if Spider is satisfied by the change it will have on His People?" Iron Eyes sighed heavily. "We're changed now. Older."

Rita kept her silence, letting her fingers soothe him. Finally, she asked, "What about Leeta? Have you managed to make sense out of her death? Can you live with her loss?"

His expression was detached. "I'll miss her forever. She gave me so much. I'll always regret . . . Damn it! We didn't get time to spend with each other! It isn't right. All we ever did was plot against the Directorate. We never had a chance to . . . to love."

"I've realized how to justify and accept Philip's death," Rita said. "I figured it all out when I heard about Susan." She looked at him. "I've lost my way, Iron Eyes. There's no love in my life except for the dead. I don't have anyone to hold—to just be human with. I'm always the tough Major. I guess I need more in my life."

"So who's the man strong enough to keep you satisfied?" Iron Eyes asked, eyes half-closed as she continued to massage him.

"You . . . if you're interested."

"You know I love you," he told her, turning to look into her eyes. "You wouldn't mind sharing me with a ghost?"

"I have my ghosts, too. That bother you?" She breathed deeply. "Philip was very special. I loved him more than I realized at the time."

Iron Eyes pulled her down close. "I think we'd better give it a try. You're the best friend I've ever had, Red Many Coups. No one would ever understand me but you. I've missed a warm body all my life. Maybe I'd like to get used to one."

"I was hoping you'd say that," she whispered as she hugged him close. "Now, let's see you make another conquest."

"I can't," he murmured into her hair. "I'm already conquered."

"You see, First Citizen, we have had no choice. Surrender is the only option. The people have simply lost heart. And I . . . Perhaps, I don't blame them." Vitr looked crushed, the spark gone from his eyes, those square shoulders stooped with defeat.

Ngen hissed an epithet and cut the comm connection, turning to Giorj. "So you see, Engineer, the planet has fallen."

Giorj nodded, eyes impassive. Ngen squinted. "Is there something wrong? You look upset, angry."

"And my mother?" Giorj inquired, a tightness in his voice, his voice clenched tightly at his sides.

How do I use this to my advantage? Enough that I've kept information from him concerning her well being. Still . . .

Ngen molded his face into an expression of true contrition. "My old friend," he began softly, "we had her. My people had evacuated her to Apahar. I ordered her placed on the last shuttle. They tried to lift from the planet. The pilot did everything he could. The Patrol ATs caught them . . . well, I offer you my deepest condolences. This is just more blood on Patrol hands."

Giorj looked away, the sound of his grinding teeth loud in the room. When he looked back, Ngen noted the throttled anger on his normally emotionless face.

Exquisite! Handled correctly, I can bind him to me even more securely! His love for his mother can be turned to hatred for the Patrol and Directorate—another emotionally motivated weapon in my hands.

"We'll get our revenge for her, Giorj," Ngen added, tone soothing. "For the moment, however, given the turn of events, I need you to do certain things for me. You've installed the destruction device in the reactor?"

Giorj nodded.

"Very good. Now, the next thing. I need to have the coordinates for *Bullet*'s reactor room, comm, and structural centers placed into the fire control system. If I can't have her—and the Brotherhood information in her banks—no

one will have her. Should the Patrol turn the final tables on
us, we'll blow her to junk, tumbling her into the atmosphere."

Giorj nodded, making mental notes in his comm. "And
the planet?"

"Yes, as to the planet. It isn't wise for Sirius to become
an example of our failure."

"No," Giorj agreed, a curious hostility in his voice. "Do
you have a suggestion?"

Ngen smiled. "I think you can see the direction of my
thoughts. We have the coordinates for all the major power
plants across the planet. Enter them into the fire control.
Like *Bullet*, if we can't have Sirius no one shall."

Giorj's brow flicked a momentary hesitation. "They are
our people, First Citizen. Our brothers in arms. They have
supported the Party through—"

"They let us down." Ngen's face tightened in pain—the
expression a parent would use with a recalcitrant child. "It
will hurt me a great deal . . . but we must look to the future
of humanity, Giorj. As I've said so often—in so many
ways—sacrifice is a prerequisite for growth."

*Are you buying that, Engineer? No? Do I see hesitation
mixed with the anger in your eyes? Let me see if I can sell
you like I once sold them, Giorj.*

A sour twist to his mouth, Ngen jumped to his feet,
pacing, smacking a fist into his palm. "Consider, Giorj,
what we started here! We broke the back of the Directorate! Met their power head on and stopped it cold—would
have won but for those barbarians! We have stalemated the
most powerful fleet in space! While outnumbered! And we
did that because we thought! Used initiative."

He turned, peering into Giorj's eyes. "And if we give up?
What then? The status quo reestablishes itself on Sirius, and
humanity is still locked in the same old stagnant trap! No,
Giorj, you and I, we have a greater destiny."

He waved an arm at the screens displaying the stars. "Out
there is a people worthy of our skills . . . a people ready to
pick up the torch dropped by the Sirians and lead humanity
to a new genesis! A birth of freedom and expansion and
knowledge!

"Too many martyrs have died! Think! Consider the dead!
How many noble men gave their lives, lost everything for
the heart of revolution? They stood on the barricades, facing hideous barbarians with nothing but their courage! *And
their own people sold them out in the end!*

"I can't just drop it now." Ngen raised his hands, desperately. "God! What a slap in the face that would be to the people who died in the belief that human existence could be better . . . grow again, live again!"

Giorj cocked his head, eyes inscrutable.

"Think!" Ngen thundered. "Think of what your own beloved mother gave so that you could get a break! She suffered just so her boy could have his magnificent gifts recognized! Is that right? Can you walk away from her grave and say it was all for nothing? No, *you* can't! Neither can I! You're part of it, Giorj, part of the dream. Your mother can't have died for nothing. For her, you have to go on. *You owe it to her!*"

Giorj nodded. "I think I understand, First Citizen. Would you like me to blast *Bullet* now? We can put the tractors on her, spiral her into atmosphere."

Ngen chewed his lip, brows tight as he thought. "No, not yet. I'd rather take one more shot at assaulting her. *If* we could take that ship, we could still rebuild her. We'll have some time before the Patrol can reinforce. Time enough to rebuild her, correct . . . yes, I thought so. I *want* that ship! With our technology and her power, no one in space could stop us!" He sighed, slumping back into the command chair. "We can make the dream live for millions."

Giorj inclined his head. "Very well, First Citizen, I shall order a final full scale assault in an attempt to overrun the ship. And if that fails—destroy her!"

Ngen nodded approval and took a deep breath. "Then we blast the planet. Hitting the power plants will destabilize the antimatter reactors, the explosion will literally crack Sirius in two. Then we rise, shoot up the remaining Patrol battleships in high planetary orbit, and see if we can't take one of them to rebuild."

Giorj bowed. "I will see to it, First Citizen."

"Oh, and Giorj," Ngen cautioned. "Please, say nothing of this to any of the crew. You've the skill to see to the blasters, don't you? The gun crews need think only that they missed when we destroy the planet—that there was a glitch in the targeting computers. You can program them for that, can't you?"

Giorj nodded, a slight smile on his lips. "First Citizen, I can program the system to leave the gunners believing they scored direct hits on the Patrol positions. From their monitors, they'll never know what they hit."

"Very good, you have my permission to make whatever adjustments to the fire control are necessary—so long as they're capable of pinpoint accuracy when we engage the Patrol for the final battle." He hesitated. "Are you still with me, Giorj?"

"Of course, First Citizen." Giorj bowed.

Ngen watched as the man turned on his heel, walking stiffly from the bridge.

Friday Garcia Yellow Legs stood atop the broad flat roof of one of the arcologies, looking out over the dark city. Here and there, columns of black smoke rose into the sky. With the night goggles, he could see large effigies of spiders that had sprung into being on the buildings below—the price his God had demanded for his love. The air still smelled bad to him, leaving a foul burning feeling in the back of his nose.

Friday lifted the night goggles, dialing the magnification up to make the stars jump at him. Knowing roughly where to look, he picked out *Bullet* first, her bulk being the brightest in the flickering light of the binary.

From *Bullet* his search expanded, finding the gleaming hull of *Hiram Lazar* where she rested slightly above *Bullet* and to the right. Little flickers of light that had to be spacecraft inched back and forth between the two ships.

He centered the goggles on *Hiram Lazar*. The light reflected from the converted GCI, leaving it mostly silhouetted against the stars. A tightness constricted around his heart, pain throbbing deep inside him.

"Hang in there, Susan," Friday gritted. "I'm coming to get you."

CHAPTER XXV

Susan came instantly awake as the doorway slipped open. She tensed, heart pounding, praying this would be her opportunity to escape . . . to kill.

The soft steps came slowly closer. The bracelets hadn't snapped together yet. Would she have a chance to strike?

"Susan?" The hesitant voice wasn't Ngen's.

"Giorj!" she cried, looking quickly around, eyes slitted.

"The monitors are off." Giorj seated himself at the foot of the sleeping platform, indicating that the restraining field had been deactivated. "I won't hurt you. I just came to talk. You seem . . . kind. I thought maybe you would tell me how it was when they burned off Angla. I can only offer you my . . . my verbal support."

"I'll take it," Susan sighed miserably. "That bastard's been here three times! By Spider's hairy legs, he makes me want to puke!"

"You realize he's after your mind," Giorj waved at the two other women.

Susan shivered suddenly. "It works. The way he uses the psych, oh God. It splits my mind and body. Makes my body think he's Friday Garcia Yellow Legs . . . or Hans." She swallowed, starting to shake, almost going into convulsions. "I don't know what to believe of myself anymore. When he talks, my body starts to respond—so quickly—while my brain screams.

"He almost drives me to trying to break my neck. His voice comes over the comm and Leona . . . she starts to stroke herself." Susan began trembling, hugging herself fiercely. "Colonel Amahanandras is just about as bad, she just whimpers and fouls herself."

"Be strong," Giorj smiled, eyes darting away. "I can't understand all this. It makes no sense to me, but then my physical drives are dead. There was an accident once. The radiation made me different." His head dropped. "I am not a man you see. I—"

335

"Neither's Ngen!" she spat. "You wouldn't understand!
No one sane and human would! Ngen's a . . . a despicable
beast! I'd gut him like a worm. He's . . ." She shuddered,
dropping her head into her hands, shaking out of control.
". . . *He's using my own mind against me!*"

A warm arm settled on her shoulders, drawing her tightly
to him. He spoke softly until she got control of her spasming
limbs, drying her eyes.

"I know. I, too, cringe . . . wondering what women would
say about me. If they knew, they would laugh at me!" His
pale eyes pleaded with her. "If you don't laugh at me . . .
I'll come. Try and talk to you like . . . like a friend?"

"I . . . I'd like that." She raised his chin with her fingertips. "That's why you felt so strongly for your mother,
wasn't it? She was the only woman in the world you thought
could love you?"

He nodded miserably. "And she did so much for me."

"Tell me about her."

"What is there to tell?" Giorj shrugged. "I wanted to be
an engineer. We weren't rich. Father left us years ago. She
worked at any job she could get, but that wasn't much. My
mother sold her body, worked in bathhouses, was a servant
for parties. She even sold one of her kidneys." His eyes
gleamed with pain.

"I took every course I could, I spent all my time studying
so . . . so mother would be proud. I was naturally adept at
physics and engineering. They appointed me to servicing
GCIs. I did well there and they promoted me . . ."

"Go on," she prompted when he hesitated.

"Then I went home one day and she was lying on the floor.
Hair falling out of her head. She'd given me so much, carried
me through all that study, paid with her very life's blood!

"I was frantic, I called the ambulances and they put her in
a med unit. She had a very rare disease. For the rest of her
life she would need a very special, very expensive medicine.

"My steriliz . . . the accident . . . happened while I was
installing an antimatter reactor in a private smuggler's vessel. Smuggling isn't much of an occupation anymore, but it
still paid Ngen to handle certain things. In this case it was
weapons for the Independence Party. I was too useful, he
couldn't let me die and he couldn't let anyone know about
his smuggling. I was important to him . . . and a liability at
the same time."

"And Ngen kept your mother in the drugs so she'd live," Susan finished.

Giorj spread his arms and met Susan's eyes. "She did so much for me. Could I do less? She sold her soul that I might learn . . . and make something out of myself. Look at me! I'm the greatest engineer Sirius has ever produced. I'm challenging the secrets of the Brotherhood." His eyes saddened. "And mother will never know. Ngen killed her, lied to me. Now, he's going to betray all those people who worshiped . . . Oh, my poor mother!"

She held him close, feeling him fighting. "Do you know of our God?"

"This Spider? God is of no concern to an engineer."

"Our Prophets teach that the soul is part of God, who we call Spider. When your mother died, she didn't suffer. There was no suffering that day except among those who lived. The space blasters were quick—efficient. Her soul—her spark of God—went back to Spider and is one with His knowledge. You see, not only your mother, but God also is proud of you."

He stared at her skeptically.

"I'm proud of you." Susan hugged him reassuringly. "What you have done for your mother is worth coup. You have honored her and there is honor in knowing you, Engineer Giorj."

"And the soul is of God? Why?" He seemed puzzled.

"To learn," Susan told him. "I'm not . . . You really need to talk to a Prophet about all this." She paused. "Perhaps you are a cusp."

"And what is that?"

"Our Prophets see the future . . ." Susan began.

Giorj shook his head. "Causality proves . . . Impossible!"

"Oh, yes. They do. I know your physics proves different. But neither the Patrol nor the Directorate believed either. They do now. Cusps are the choices of free will which affect the future. If you need a purpose in life, Giorj, seek out the Prophets. Perhaps there, you will find a suitable challenge for your intellect."

He stared at her, frowning, finally asking, "Why do you play a savage with some and a human with others? You're an intelligent—"

"For the same reason you hide your emotions from those around you: protection. My savagery and your lack of emotions belie our innate capabilities. We're not perceived as threats. Keeps our options open."

"These Prophets would talk to me, who is not a man?" Giorj pondered.

Susan nodded seriously. "They would understand you better than you think. The Prophets have no need of physical identities. They live with time . . . and space . . . and God. They're devoid of emotion, just like you pretend to be. I guess when you see the hand of God, human emotions become foolish trivialities that—"

Giorj actually laughed. "And I thought the Brotherhood immensely clever."

Susan studied him, thinking of what he'd said earlier. "Did Ngen have my comp unit sent up when I was?"

"He did," Giorj was lost in thought.

"Could I get ahold of it along with a comm access?"

Giorj cooled, watching her intently, eyes gone flat again. "Why?" his dull voice asked.

"Quit that," Susan said, not acting all of her hurt. "It may be a way to help us both. I've trusted you. You've trusted me. Let's build on that. I want to be your friend. I need you to . . . to talk to me if nothing else. With the comp, maybe, I can get you more Brotherhood data in exchange for what you've got. We can work on it together."

For a split second Giorj's eyes lit. "You know something about the material Sarsa sent to *Bullet*?"

"I swear a blood oath in the name of Spider!"

"Take me with you. To see a Prophet. Promise . . . and . . . and I'll get you your comp and help you," Giorj said, a sliver of relief working through his wooden exterior.

A faint chime sounded. Giorj jumped. "He's up. I'm sorry, but I must turn the field on. Perhaps later I can help you . . . bring you the comp." He hesitated. "In the meantime, be strong . . . friend."

Susan watched helplessly as he hurried out of the room.

It took Ngen another two hours to arrive. He slipped through the hatch, smiling as she glared at him.

"Need milk again, sheep herder?" she asked, curling a lip.

Ngen's face fell. "Dearest one, sarcasm will get you nowhere. It only builds friction between us. You're my greatest beauty. Think of harmony, my wild darling. Think of pleasure and passion. Think of the heights I will lead you to. Your mouth may speak harshly, but your body sings louder than words."

He began stripping his clothing off as Susan watched dispassionately. He moved with a certain elegance and grace. Effeminate! So how should she handle this?

Susan didn't have much time to formulate a defense. He touched a control stud and her bracelets were drawn irresistibly to four areas of the bed. Spread-eagle, she raised her head to glare at him. *"You sheep-sucking bastard!"* she screamed. "If I could get my hands on your stinking body I'd rip your guts out with my bare hands!"

Ngen's mood lightened subtly as he watched her rage. "My, such anger, sweet angel. Come, let me show you the way to peace and pleasure." His eyes were solicitous as he bent over the bed. He began stroking her legs lightly and, as before, Susan felt her body relaxing, anticipating.

"What? No psych this time?" she hissed. "Going to take your chances?"

He looked up at her. "No, no need. Feel your body? I've trained it, Susan. And this time, I don't want to share you with images. This time, you're mine."

She was exhausted when he finished. Lungs heaving, she gasped for air . . . and her body literally glowed from the climax she'd experienced. Damn him! Damn *me! I BETRAYED MYSELF! BETRAYED . . . BETRAYED. . . .*

That's it! A little voice in her head wailed. *You're supposed to hate yourself.*

"There, sweet flower," Ngen cooed, letting his fingers play over her hot moist skin. "Isn't that better than rage and anger? Do you feel uplifted, dear one? Do you feel the passion seeping softly from your body. Is your mind remembering the flashes of rapture? Have you ever before experienced such bliss and joy?"

Susan looked over, struggling within for control. "Once. I was had by a . . . a mad bull in the pasture. He was bigger than you, skinny Sirian. The rapture he gave me was like light bursting into a dark sky. He at least fulfilled me. You," she shrugged. "You're good . . . in fact . . . better than most. But that bull, Sirian fop, was superb. When a woman has been had by God, what's a mere man?"

He'd straightened, voice tightening. "Clever lie, barbarian. I don't believe that for a minute." He chuckled. "Oh, you are a delightful challenge, sweet Susan. I shall enjoy making you beg for my touch."

"Perhaps," Susan told him nonchalantly. "Maybe if you were bigger, longer. And then you lose your manhood so quickly! To be sure, you bring pleasure—Sirian sick man—but you should ask yourself—can you really fulfill a woman?"

Ngen swallowed bitterly. For a brief instant blinding rage flickered in his eyes.

"Come," Susan suggested, mildly. "Try again. Perhaps you will do better this time?" She looked at him, lids lowered in boredom.

He threw himself on her, taking her violently. Trembling from pain, she asked, "And again? You do learn, civilized sheep! No wonder your warriors fall before ours like blades of dry grass!"

"Dear one . . ." Ngen's eyes flashed, jaw clamped tight, "I do have to run this ship and the government of Sirius. I can't spend every hour with you. You may think you're—"

"Then go back to your Directorate sheep over there." She indicated with a nod of her head. "When you can truly devote time to my pleasure, come back." She twisted her lips into a grimace and looked up at the wall, ignoring him.

"You *are* a challenge," Ngen whispered. "I think I could come to love you, Susan. I think I have finally found a woman worthy of me." He got to his feet, headed for the shower.

Susan drew a deep breath and squeezed her eyes shut. It had cost her. Degraded and disgusted—but she'd held her own for the first time. By Spider, how long could she outsmart him? What happened if she actually defeated him? How long would she live?

Her bonds snapped off and she pulled herself to a sitting position. The light over the toilet blinked on, indicating she could take care of her bodily functions. She got slowly to her feet and winced. He'd hurt her. Dripping an occasional spot of blood, she forced herself to stroll leisurely to the toilet, vowing to beat him.

Giorj woke her from a sound sleep. She sat up too quickly and gasped.

"You're in pain?" Giorj asked, suddenly frightened.

"A little," she grunted. "He hurt me last time. But . . . but I think I may have found a way to handle him for a while."

"He's preoccupied." Giorj agreed. He did something to the wall and surprised Susan as a med unit slid out. "The planet surrendered. Pika Vitr and the Union board signed the contract. On top of that, he left here in a frightful rage. Med gave him a sedative to sleep on. He's a very dangerous man right now."

She groaned as she let Giorj slide her into the unit. Her eyes widened as the med unit prodded her tender areas. "Don't be alarmed," Giorj said easily. "There, you should heal soon. If he sees you vulnerable, he'll exploit it."

She sat up, the pain gone. Giorj slid the unit back into the wall before sitting on the side of the bed. From under his tunic he handed her a battered but familiar comp unit. Susan clutched it to her breast, then hugged Giorj. Hans had held this once.

"Come on, let's find a comm access. I'll show you what I've got." She didn't ache when she stood, but the bloodstains frightened her.

"I wish I could get you out of here," Giorj whispered as he saw the mottled areas on her body.

"In time, my friend," Susan muttered as she cast a glance at the two blank-eyed women across the room. Leona stared into space or ran her fingers over her flesh. Arish vigorously avoided Susan's eyes.

From his comm unit, Giorj got her into the system. Susan donned a headset and gave her code. Information danced across the screen.

"Where did you get this?" he asked, breathless. "This is priceless! If we could just get a schematic of how they designed their ships!"

"That's everything I found in *Bullet's* comm." Susan sighed. "I don't know anything about the engineering data. The man who did . . . died in the same burnoff as your mother."

"How did you break their security locks?" Giorj cried. "This is magnificent!"

"Here, wait." Susan found the blaster schematic. "Is this the blaster here on the *Hiram Lazar*?"

Giorj ran his eyes over the drawings. "No! Not only that, but this is a much later design. That Fujiki Amplifier is completely new."

"Could you build that blaster for me?"

"Yes, of course, if you can get me the materials." Giorj rubbed his hands together.

"How about these shield generators?" Susan asked, accessing another file.

Giorj's pale eyes skipped across the diagram, following the lines and leads in a manner that indicated he knew exactly what he saw. "Superb! They were brilliant! Get me the materials and I can build any of these."

"Has Ngen destroyed *Bullet* yet?"

"No, he still has a slight hope he can take the ship. But he's pushed. I've input the data to destroy the ship on his order." Giorj frowned.

"Would there be enough hyperconductor left in *Brotherhood* and *Bullet* to build these devices? If we had them in *Bullet*, the ship would be invincible, wouldn't it?"

"Absolutely! Look at *Hiram Lazar*! Why, with a converted GCI we destroyed *Brotherhood* and *Defiance* and your *Bullet* lies at our mercy."

She reached over and hugged Giorj desperately. "My friend, my wonderful outcast of society . . . how would you like to join the rest of us riffraff?"

Giorj studied her. "What are you suggesting?"

"You said Sirius fell to the Romanans? What do you owe Ngen? The man's a monster. He owned you! Come with us—a free man! We—the People—need an engineer. We have a lot to offer you, Giorj. Our Prophets will fascinate you. They see the future because Spider wills it that we learn. And you can rebuild *Bullet* . . . with all the technology you want."

"I . . . I . . ." He looked baffled.

"You do us honor by your dedication to your mother. We value honor. We don't use it against our people. It's your cusp, Giorj. I think I've been sent to find you. I believe Spider's will is that you join us."

Giorj leaned back, eyes playing over the menus. "You know there's more on Frontier. I couldn't access it because I didn't know the codes. The blaster I built for Sirius was almost declassified as obsolete."

"I broke these codes" Susan said, face lighting. "Perhaps we can go to Frontier and break others."

He looked at her curiously. "There are more than military secrets there. There are bits of information that would benefit all men."

"If we can get there, " Susan said softly, realizing just where she was and how hopeless it was to think of escape.

"I can't get you off this ship," Giorj said sadly. "At least, not for a few days. With the planet fallen, who knows what Ngen will do. The Patrol is no threat. They can't harm us."

Susan's eyes smoked. "Perhaps not the Patrol," she said with a wry smile. "Perhaps it's Spider Ngen should fear."

"Your God?"

"And his Romanans," Susan's eyes glittered. "Who took the planet from under Ngen's nose and his super blasters?

Who backed the Directorate down against incredible odds? We will not be defeated, Giorj . . . not even in death. We are the way of Spider. We are here to stay, to bring a new life to humanity."

"That makes no logical sense," Giorj protested.

"Doesn't it? *Brotherhood* and *Defiance* were staffed with Patrol personnel. Even the ones who turned their back on Colonel Ree were aboard *Brotherhood*. She's dead junk. *Bullet* lies right out there, damaged, ready to be rebuilt. Why wasn't she destroyed, too?"

"Chance," Giorj muttered. "And the guts of her commander."

"Who also believes Spider's message."

The chime sounded. "He's waking up." Giorj shut the system down quickly and sighed as a blank wall slid over the comm unit.

"Keep that comp unit, Giorj. Get my weapons if you can. If anything happens to give us a chance to escape, all we have to do is make it to *Bullet*." Susan was trotting for her bed.

Giorj paused at the door. "You know, you're hard to believe. Here you stand, naked, EM restraints on your arms and legs, bruised from rape, tethered to a bed. In the midst of this huge ship, defended by the most powerful blasters in the galaxy, you're plotting a new universe!"

"And I'll have it, too, Giorj." She winked. "That is, if we live through this, if the right people make the right choices, if Spider doesn't call me first."

Then he was gone.

Bravado passed, she swallowed hard, closing her eyes. Knotting a fist before her, she willed, "I'll have it! All I have to do is survive! *Just survive!*"

"Comm's cut to med, Colonel. That means they've pushed through Deck 6." Neal said, voice clipped. "I've still got Glick in Engineering. He's holding the reactor room, but air's getting bad. Still no way he can turn the reactor up and make a big bang out of it. He's got to have powerlead to dump into or the reactor will only make a big enough bang to take out his part of the ship. Oh, and some of the alternate atmosphere plants have been cut."

Damen Ree scowled sourly into his helmet. "Damn it!"

"I'll keep you apprised, Colonel."

"Thanks, Neal. We get out of this, you're getting commendation."

"Got intruders all over, Colonel. Just about everybody i making contact. Could be a big push. And besides, I though the Patrol had second thoughts about us?"

"They do! But I'll make sure the Romanans give you you own horse herd."

"I . . . uh. Sure thing, Colonel. If I thought we'd liv through this, I'd worry. Horses? Me?"

"I'll . . ." He didn't finish the thought, unleashing th energetic fury of his blaster into the dark figures who cam ghosting down an unlighted companionway. A vortex o decompressing bodies blew crystallizing blood and body fluid through the frigid zero g in the airless main accessway. A limp arm bounced off the ceiling panels overhead, a strean of blood sending spirals of crimson crystals behind the shat tered shoulder. Random blasts of blue-violet puffed silen explosions of matter out of the plating in front of Ree.

Damen pushed off, easing up to peer around the corner seeing the Sirians fleeing in panicked retreat. He lined u the heavy shoulder blaster, scoring hit after hit amid th fleeing throng, bodies finally blocking his shots as the floated lifeless or dying in the darkness.

Hell must have looked like that—or a psychotic man' nightmares.

"That'll teach you to set foot in *my* ship, you Siria scum!" True, the only person to hear him was Neal Iverson sitting, rock solid, eyes haggard, beard stubbly, helping t coordinate the crumbling defense of *Bullet*—but it sure made Ree feel good.

Ree backed away, a fusillade of violet lights blasting a fo out of the bulkhead behind him. He bent to clip anothe charge into the blaster as one of the dead rose from unde his feet, spilling him, an iron arm circling around the fron of his helmet. Ree could feel the fingers reaching for the helmet latch. Release that hook, and it meant decompres sion and death.

"Got you, Patrolman!" a voice reached his ears, the Sirian' helmet pressed against his in the struggle.

"Think so, Sirian trash?" Ree gritted, flinging himself thi way and that, aware of the blaster bolts which had blown the bulkhead into ribbons and now peppered the inside o gun deck mess three.

"Yeah, Patrolman. I got you so you can't get loose. Can't get that big blaster reloaded or pointed at me. You're dead."

Ree let go of the big blaster, hearing blood rush in his ears, fear charging him. He batted at the suited fingers seeking his helmet latch, his other hand fumbling at his own belt. He clamped on the man's fingers, keeping them on the latch, grunting with the effort, sweating in his suit. The stink of his fear came rankly to his nose.

"One last thing, Sirian . . ."

"Yeah?"

"A present from the Romanans." Ree's fingers drove the big fighting knife Iron Eyes had used to kill Antonia Reary past his hip, lancing it up, feeling it pass through the Sirian's suit, feeling the sharp edge grating off bone as he withdrew it. Ree jabbed again and again, despite the man's horrible screams and the floating haze of blood and gases boiling out of the suit.

Ree double-checked the latch at the side of his helmet. Floating out of control, he bumped, gasping, into one of the walls, body limp, face flushed.

"Colonel? *Damn it! Damen, you all right?*"

"Here, Neal." Ree swallowed a knot the size of a fist. It went down his throat like a lump of wood. "Hang on, I gotta get this guy out of his helmet. I got coup to take!"

"Uh, sir? Coup? I thought you didn't believe in . . ."

"Damn it, man," Ree gulped, trying to still his heart. "I earned it."

"Please hurry, Colonel. The situation's looking pretty grim. They've never hit us this hard before. I . . . Well, sir, I'm not sure we're going to make it this time."

Ree looked at the big knife in his hand, blood frozen in glinting crystal patterns on the heavy blade. "Then make your soul ready to send back to Spider, Neal. We don't give up until the last man is dead."

"Yes, sir. It's honor now."

Ree nodded in the dark hallway, taking his coup. He snaked up his blaster, patting the charred graphsteel around him. "Well, old gal. I promised no one would get you while I was alive. Here's to it, *Bullet*, it's you and me now . . . clear to the end."

The worst part of her captivity was the constant waiting. Never in all her life had Susan been so incredibly bored. She stared over at Leona's blank eyes.

That was why, of course. Ngen's prizes had nothing to do but think about their plight. Bored stiff, with minimal sensory imput, they could only dwell on their time with him . . . and how far they had fallen.

Amazed, Susan shook her head. In spite of it all, she had to admire the man's genius. Once the women had cracked, they fell the rest of the way on their own . . . and wallowed in it.

No, Ngen was sick, twisted in the head, a degenerate aberration. He needed to be disposed of like a cow with blackleg. His brilliant, twisted mind—coupled with his need to dominate—brought nothing but suffering to humanity. At the same time, he talked a good fight.

She leaned back, remembering the times the Sirians had been beaten, their cities blasted by Van Chow's blasters, their people dispirited as the young women were hauled off to be brides, their industry pulverized. Then Ngen gave a speech and they fought on while he stayed safe in his impregnable ship.

And he'd killed Hans and . . .

She stopped the thought, a cold sweat breaking out. She swallowed hard and gripped her knees to her chest.

Hans? Dead? A soft whimper choked in her throat as she looked up at the psych headset beyond the confining field that imprisoned her. She was holding Ngen's threats to her sanity and sense of worth back. Hans' pain tried to make itself felt again. That wouldn't do—not when dream and reality mixed in Ngen's rape.

"No," she croaked, "think of something else, Susan. He wants you to think of Friday and Hans, and how your body reacts when his god-cursed machine implants them in your mind—all the while knowing it's him. Him inside, rotting everything precious, playing with your mind."

She forced a deep breath into her lungs, shaking her head. "Playing . . . playing with your mind, Susan. Trying to break you, turn you against yourself."

She jumped to her feet, padding over to slam an angry fist into the rubbery field, having it bounce back with equal energy.

"Why, Ngen? Why do you do this to people?"

Because it was degrading! He had no soul. He treated all humans alike. Doing the same to anyone who'd believe his smooth sell. He called and crooned, and they did his bidding. Ngen had destroyed Sirius just as assuredly as he had destroyed Leona and broken Arish.

· "But not on World, you social maggot!" she howled at
the sound-proofed ceiling panels.

In the presence of others, the Prophets would have asked
him to what purpose he needed to torture his enemies so
thoroughly that he wasted their souls for Spider—and the
crowd would have torn him apart.

The root of the evil lay elsewhere. She bit her lip, knowing where her thoughts led. The Directorate provided the
breeding ground that enabled the rise of a man like Ngen.
The Directorate had metamorphosed into humanity's benevolent enemy. The Directorate bred human sheep the
likes of which Ngen could herd so easily.

It would be so easy to fix, Susan realized. *Bullet* could be
made invulnerable. But why? What business was it of hers
that men be sheep? They, too, had brains. Were they to
think, they could see the stagnation of their lives.

Her thoughts scattered as Ngen entered, face drawn. "Dear
barbarian," he greeted. "I'm afraid I have but little time to
dally with you."

The bracelets pulled her resisting body spread-eagle again.
Suddenly, the bed shifted, pulling up against the wall. Susan
felt her skin pulling and tearing against the metal that held
her.

Ngen watched her sadly as he pulled an electronic whip
from behind him. "Your Romanans have dealt me a severe
blow, Susan," he said smoothly. "They've taken my planet.
I must punish you because you're like them. Romanans
must learn they cannot betray me with impunity."

"Beat them, Sirian sheep herder." Susan growled, feeling
fear spreading in her gut.

"Oh, fear not," Ngen smiled. "I shall not continue to do
this. Pain will provide a simple lesson for you. You see, it is
called conditioned response. Our last time together was an
omen. You hurt my feelings when all I want for you is
pleasure—to know the joy of your own body. And now I've
lost Sirius, too.

"But that's all right. I can go somewhere else and start
over. After I am through with you, I shall leave this planet.
We will rise and destroy the last of the Patrol Ships. They've
been waiting for me, you know.

"As for Sirius, they betrayed me. They betrayed all I
tried to do for them. I'll burn them on the way out. Leave
them and their world a pile of slag. The Directorate will
inherit a molten ball. That, dearest Susan, will be a lesson

to the rest of the galaxy should they ever try and resist me
. . . as you and your Romanans have."

He lowered his eyes as he ran a finger lightly along the
whip. "You don't realize that I can give you two feelings,
dearest Susan." He touched the whip end lightly to her side
and she almost bit her tongue off, avoiding the scream.

"There, see?" Ngen granted her a wistful smile. "Just a
light touch. I'll give you some more light touches." The
whip played along her skin in dripping, blinding, searing pain.

"Remember, Susan, you should never resist me. I want to
bring you pleasure and you make me give you pain. I can do
so much for you, for all humanity. If you would only let
me," his gentle voice pleaded.

Through the red haze, Susan heard herself shrieking. Each
time the darting lash brought greater pain, she struggled to
draw a breath into her burning body. During a slight hesitation while Ngen stripped, she realized that as superb as his
knowledge of erotic points was, he knew the pain centers better.

The lash touched her again and again and even through her
half-glazed eyes, she noted that her writhing aroused him.

She struggled against her failing mind to remember that
she was Susan Smith Andojar, warrior of the People, that
God was Spider, that truth existed in the universe.

She didn't realize the bed had shifted again. She lay
supine. Ngen forced something between her lips, made her
chew it. Life flushed through her shivering muscles, her
breathing slowed, her mind cleared.

Ngen ran his fingers down her body. "Here, dear one, now
that we have learned pain, let us learn pleasure," he cooed
happily into her ear.

"Think you're better than that bull?" she croaked hoarsely.

He stiffened, a hollowness in his eyes. "Oh, dear Susan. I
had hoped you'd learn."

She felt him shift, felt the coolness of the headset on her brows.

"NO! Damn you, Ngen I . . . I . . ." Warmth flooded
through her as she looked into Friday's loving eyes, his
features blurring into Ngen Van Chow's when he moved.
Friday's warm fingers stroked her flesh.

She thrashed her head back and forth, trying to blur the
image, to see the real Ngen, knowing the truth on an intel-
lectual level, living the lie emotionally.

"You see, I can teach you so much!" He nibbled lightly at
her neck. "There," he noted her responding body, "my
wonderful Susan, delight will be yours. You will have learned

the lesson. No longer will you deny me the opportunity to bring you to bliss."

The voice, roiling her brain, belonged to no one but Ngen. The cloying tones raked her, tearing her thoughts to shreds, leaving ripped fragments of resistance behind.

"Sweet Susan, before this week is done, I will hear you call for me. I will hear you tell me how wrong you were. Tell me you want rapture instead of pain. Tell me how much you want me to fulfill you!"

Susan's numb mind rocked with the impact of his words. Her fragmented thoughts wouldn't form into an identity. She cried out as she realized he was winning. His assualt came while psych left her emotions numb, her rational mind defenseless. Her brain still reeled from the physical explosions of pain—never mind the underlying euphoria of the stimulant. His new strategy had her beaten . . . and she hated herself, knowing it.

Curiously detached, she lay exhausted after he had left. In the emptiness of the room, she remembered her body trembling under his touch. She remembered the blinding ecstasy of her climax. She couldn't help but whimper, her body tucked into a fetal position.

Shaking, she clamped her eyes shut, beating frantic fists against the sides of her head, trying to beat out the memory of Friday Garcia Yellow Legs, eyes shifting, ever shifting, turning from Friday . . . into Ngen Van Chow . . . and back again.

"Susan?" Ngen's voice called through comm. Horrified, one portion of her mind realized she responded physically.

"No!" she screamed. "No! NO! *NO!*" But her body continued to warm, waiting for his soft touch.

CHAPTER XXVI

Friday Garcia Yellow Legs kept his eyes glued to the monitor. Acceleration jammed him back into the crash webbing. Even with his excitement budding to bursting, the sensation of leaving orbit awed him.

The changing colors of the sky showed their altitude. Around him, he knew another hundred and eight ATs rose, reaching for the Sirian ships. One hundred and eight—all that remained of the Patrol ATs.

Hopefully at the same time, *Victory, Miliken* and *Toreon* were diving out of high orbit to bait the Sirians into a response, to divert their scanners from the planet and keep their attention on the sky above them. Friday and the rest would know soon enough.

His breath came quickly. Action on the ground didn't bother him like this. His bladder began complaining, his colon tying itself into knots. His heart thumped against his ribs. Why did a man's tongue and mouth always go dry?

To calm himself, he began muttering his war prayer. A simple case of nerves, right? To a man who, except for the war on World and the flight to Sirius, had hardly been farther off the ground than being bucked off a horse, the idea that he was even now miles above the planet proved disconcerting—to say the least. On his first flights, he hadn't really understood that only a thin skin of metal wrapped around him and beyond that. . . .

Friday stilled his fidgety fingers and took a deep breath. His fate belonged to Spider. All men died. When they did, their souls went back to God. That was everything: truth.

But the way of dying is important! his mind screamed in protest. Falling for ten or twenty miles to one's death wasn't in Friday's book of good ways to go. A bullet stopped during a raid for horses or women, on the other hand, well, that seemed a nice safe death.

He puzzled at his reactions. Why be so concerned? He'd ridden up to *Bullet* from World. He'd ridden down from *Bullet* to Sirius. Between those trips he'd crossed enough space that it would have taken light—which he knew was very fast—one hundred sixty-five years to cross! So why did this trip worry him?

Because the first trip up, no one had shot at him. Because the second trip down, he didn't understand *what* they were shooting at him. Because this third trip up, they would be shooting that damned violet blaster that had blown three Patrol ships to the line of junk!

And because Susan is waiting at the end of this trip!

Friday ground his teeth. She scared him as badly as that nasty violet blaster. Ngen's blaster had cost him too many friends—it had cost him Susan when it killed Hans.

"Wave one splitting off as per schedule," came over the comm. That was *Helk's* assault team.

Friday's guts shifted suddenly as the AT changed attitude, his stomach rising into his throat. *Right. How am I ever going to handle combat in zero g?* He and the others had only had a month of part-time practice. Zero g made him giddy; he wanted to throw up, and he never knew which end to grab for!

Suppose the grav plates went out when they rammed *Hiram Lazar*? He craned his neck to look back into the grim faces of his team. Eyes—shiny with worry—met his, glittering like those of cornered wolves. Some were working their jaws, grinding their teeth, as they thought about where they were and where they were going.

Anyone could die on solid earth. Dying in nothingness? Well, that was something else. They'd embarked on the first space battle where they got to do the shooting. Last time, those who'd been aboard *Bullet* had had a great big ship around them.

And thinking of that took his mind off Susan.

He sighed and leaned back, helmet pushing against the webbing. What would she do when she saw him? Run? Hide? Pretend she didn't recognize him?

For lack of anything better to do, Friday composed speeches. He tried everything from "Hi, Susan," to "Look, I know you've been though a lot, but. . . ."

He bit his lower lip and wished he could do anything but cling there like a fly in honey. A world of energy burned in his body and he had no place to expend it.

On the monitor he saw the thin streamers of light flashing out of the sky. Even through his helmet, he could hear men muttering to themselves.

"That firing you see is directed at the Patrol ships. They're diving on *Hiram Lazar* right on schedule," the comm told them. "To date, no AT has been fired on. Ladies and gentlemen, perhaps this is our lucky day!"

A mutter of relief ran through the assault deck. Friday said another quick prayer to Spider.

What would a Prophet tell him to do about Susan? What would the lesson be? Frustrated, he realized he really didn't have any idea. He'd seen a holo show on *Bullet* where the pretty lady—rescued from space pirates—flung herself into the young hero's arms, showering him with kisses.

Friday closed his eyes, imagining. Unlike the story, Susan couldn't be called a blushing virgin; he'd shared her with another man. Unlike the woman in the story, she could damn well care for herself, having piled up more coups than had Friday Garcia Yellow Legs.

Feeling a growing anxiety, he wondered if perhaps she hadn't grown too far away from him. He hadn't fulfilled all her needs when things were rosy. Would she even look at him now that she had been kept as a Sirian toy for so long? Would she allow him to try and help her?

Worse, could he ever understand what she thought, how she felt about it?

Wincing, Friday visualized Susan's muscular body being abused by fat, sweating Sirians. He could see the desperate fury in her eyes as she was raped by sheep.

Hans had taken part of her soul when he died. What would the Sirians do with the rest? Friday let that crawl through his consciousness. He'd ignored it for a long time. Now, he faced the reality that he would see Susan again. And if she'd become a bit of vacant-eyed wreckage?

He closed his eyes and gripped the crash webbing.

AT22 jolted violently to the side. The monitors showed a violet streak off to one side. *Hiram Lazar* had found their range.

With skill, the pilot threw the suddenly wild AT about the sky. "Sorry, soldiers," the voice on comm greeted. "It would appear that our friends upstairs have divided their time between us and the Patrol."

"Yeah," Friday gulped, accessing his comm. "You just keep us out of that blaster bolt. You do that, laddie, and I'll give you a sorrel pony with four white feet!"

Laughter sounded around him.

"Who said that?" the voice asked. "I've never even seen a horse except in the pictures of Atlantis."

"This is Friday Garcia Yellow Legs. You keep me alive to see that horse right up close. You keep me in one piece and I swear I'll never belt that pony in the ribs again when he farts in my face."

The laughter intensified. Good, he could keep their minds off the situation.

"Horses fart?" the pilot asked as he weaved around a searching blaster bolt.

"Uh-huh, usually they save it up until you walk around behind them. But that's only the good part. Nobody's trained one yet to use a freefall toilet!"

"Maybe I won't take that pony after all, Friday," the pilot sounded crestfallen.

"Well, I've heard the Sirians say we Romanans don't know what one's for either." Friday quipped. "So, if you wouldn't mind, just pull this thing over 'cause I need out now! This here space suit will be full of gooey stuff if you let that light get close again!"

Laughter seeped through from the bridge comm, too.

"Sorry, Friday," the pilot never missed a beat as he darted away from a shaft of violet. "I don't stop for nobody once I get this crate moving. You see, we ain't got no braking reaction. The way I stops this thing is by bashing into the side of that battleship up there."

"Now I *really* need out!" Friday yipped. "You ever done that before?"

"Nope!" the pilot confided. "I read the manual one time. They said it could be done. There's a little picture, too."

"You know," Friday admitted. "There's times I'm more than a little happy I can't read! Us illiterate types are a hell of a lot smarter than that!"

"Are you?" the pilot asked.

"Yep," Friday nodded in this helmet.

"Well, if you're so damn smart, why am I flying this thing up front while you're riding way back there?"

"'Cause you're in the end that rams that battleship filling the monitor, that's why. You're closer to the crunch!"

"You got a point there," the pilot agreed. "Thirty seconds, folks. We're going to slow down some first."

Reaction mass spewed out of the front of the AT. Friday thumbed off his comm and sang his medicine song, knowing the AT would make one hell of a bump when it hit.

Suddenly the monitor went blank. A half-second later, the crash came. The webbing took most of the force—Friday bouncing around like a stone on the end of an elastic band.

When things quit happening, Friday almost cried. They were falling. The AT must have pulled loose, dead, to tumble back toward the planet.

"We got 'em!" a marine voice called over the comm. "Let's go, people!"

Friday hit his quick release and floated out of the webbing, turning as he fought for control. Catching a bench, he dove for the hatch.

Men started whooping behind him as they fought free of the webbing. Friday fingered his comm. "My team, form up on me. Come on now, let's show the marines what we learned. Just like drill now!"

It worked. They all twisted and pulled themselves along, training coming through. Friday undogged the attack lock from under the hatch and—with his team—moved it carefully out of the AT.

Lights played around a shattered rec hall, the hull peeled back where the AT had sliced through, ablative material scarred and stripped in the process. Atmosphere could be heard whistling out into space through rents in the hull. The marines formed up behind bent plating, blasters covering the darkness. Around them, the ship shook as other ATs smashed into the *Hiram Lazar*.

Friday positioned the lock against a bulkhead and sealed it in place. He triggered the seal mechanism and motioned his men away. Metal grew hot around the edges and glowed from dull red to orange to white. The metal gave, pushed by the air pressure on the other side. The lock shot out into an expanded tunnel, the still hot piece forming the rear wall.

"Hey!" Bull Wing Reesh called. "That's pretty slick. These Patrol folks can be almighty sharp sometimes."

"Let's go," Friday ordered. The marines beat him to the hatch. For preliminaries, they cycled a grenade through. A marine, hand on the bulkhead, nodded at the concussion.

The marines went through first—not that Friday really minded.

He stepped into the lock. It held a total of ten—half his crew. He felt the pressure increase around him. The inside hatch opened quickly and Friday almost killed himself when he landed in gravity.

Two ripped bodies lay on the deck. Grenade victims? Friday motioned his stumbling party forward, gravity making all the difference in the world. His confidence returned as he charged along a long, lighted corridor, hurdling the dead where the marines had left them.

Friday had no idea where he was going. He palmed a hatch and it swung open to a gun deck. The crews didn't even look up as Friday stepped through and shouldered his blaster. He calmly began executing them before they could react. Running and firing, it became ecstasy to pay those gunning bastards back! Concussion flipped him up and over to slam down on the deck. He tried to jump up, only to flop, staring in horror at the red gushing below where his knee had been. Long splinters of tibia and fibula had become lances of blood.

He barely heard himself scream.

"So, this is it." Ngen settled back in the command chair, watching the Patrol ships slipping out of orbit, *Victory* slightly behind and below the other two.

"Attention, all personnel," Ngen ordered. "The time has come to destroy the Patrol. Combat stations, everyone. When their fleet is crushed, we will take back the planet."

Ngen watched the monitors fluctuate as the main reactor built energy to power the shields and blasters. *Hiram Lazar* pulsed around him. Such a heady feeling, this power—and all at his control.

He gripped a knotty fist, shaking it in exultation. Like he'd broken the Romanan girl, he'd break the rest now. Everything was falling back into place. How foolish of him to have doubted. In the end, his ship, *Hiram Lazar* proved the be the invincible fortress which would hand him victory from the very gullet of defeat!

"Range!" the weapons officer called. Brilliant lances of violet shot out in taut strings of death. Fire control took over, searching to pin the Patrol battleships.

Ngen jumped to his feet, pacing, watching the lines shift. The Patrol remained elusive, the bolts lacing around them, but never connecting. "Refine your targeting, Weapons Officer."

"I am, sir." The man looked up at the monitor, frowning. "We're having some problem with doppler computations. Comm spits out the numbers . . . gunnery responds . . . and we're off just a couple thousandths of a degree."

Ngen sniffed and smiled. "Let them close a little more, we've got some leeway with our superior shielding."

"*Helk* is firing," comm informed. The second ship's blasters, while closer to being on target, slipped past the Patrol, wavering, resettling to light the shields in brilliant displays.

"First Citizen!" the pilot called. "I'm getting doppler off something from the planet. Looks like missiles, sir."

Ngen spun, turning to the monitor. "Give me a detailed picture."

The resolution refined, Ngen could make them out. ATs, a whole swarm, rising on a hundred different trajectories. "What?" The implications settled in his mind. "Weapons officer, destroy the ATs. Attention, all personnel. Prepare to repel boarders."

Ngen turned, leaving the bridge. He stepped into a lift,

accessing the cargo deck. Through his headset, he listened to the chatter from the bridge, hearing:

"Damn! They're fast."

"Why can't we track them. Never mind, I've got a track. Fire! Got him—no, I missed! Luck with them, or what?"

Ngen stepped out of the lift and into the main hatch of his yacht. "Giorj?" he called through the system. "Giorj, I need you immediately in my private craft."

Silence. The engineer didn't respond.

Ngen accessed the intraship, activating every speaker in the vessel. "Engineer Giorj Hambrei, report to the First Citizen."

Ngen waited, settling himself into his command chair, the monitors springing to life around him. He scanned them quickly, seeing no change in status among the Patrol ships. *Helk's* blasters still flared on the shields, *Hiram Lazar's* fire—so clearly decisive—slipped harmlessly past, arcing into the blackness of space.

"Weapons Officer, refine your targeting," Ngen ordered, a sensation of impotent rage burning in his breast. This was it! the final combat—and his guns hadn't connected with a single target yet! Why? What could be . . .

"I'm trying, sir. Seems like every correction we make on the Patrol, the AT targeting drifts. We correct the AT defense, the shots go wild on the Patrol ships. Sir, we've got a major glitch in the comm. Where's Engineer Hambrei, perhaps he could iron it out. Situation's getting critical, sir."

"*Giorj!*" Ngen screamed into the system. "Giorj, get on that targeting! *Now!*"

"Sir," the pilot called. "The ATs, sir. They're closing. Given the range and velocity, there's little chance we can get them all, even if targeting straightens out."

Ngen leaned his head back, mind racing. "Giorj?" he whispered. "Is this your hand at work?"

To comm he ordered. "Very well, Weapons Officer, you will destroy *Bullet*. Blow her into wreckage. You *can* hit a dead ship, can't you?"

"Yes, sir. Uh, First Citizen? Our people . . . Well, they're still fighting over there, sir. Are you sure . . . I mean . . ."

Ngen stifled a violent outburst. "I'm well aware of that. Shoot. Immediately thereafter, you will target the Patrol strongholds on the planet and eliminate them. Do you understand? Or would you rather argue tactics while your skin is slit by Romanan knives?"

"Complying, sir."

Ngen chewed his lip, watching the Patrol ships closing, seeing their shields holding despite the hot fire from *Helk*.

"Why have you betrayed me, Giorj? After everything I did for you, why have you done this to me?"

Suffering a burning anger, Ngen Van Chow powered up the systems of his personal craft, feeling the two huge reactors building their power. Once free, nothing in space could catch him, least of all the Patrol line ships.

"Have to time this just right," he murmured, feeding data into the comm, watching the Patrol ships as they closed. They'd pass, of course, having too much delta V. This maneuver was simply to provide tactical support for the ATs.

The Patrol blasters ceased to flare on *Hiram Lazar's* shields, leaving him a clear view of the closing ATs. His own ship's fire darted here and there, always just missing the darting, corkscrewing ATs.

As Ngen felt the first shuddering impacts, he slapped the cargo bay door control. As a last measure, he initiated the destruct sequence Giorj had planted in the reactor. At least he himself had double-checked that.

"So," he said softly to himself. "No one gets anything." The reaction mass climbed into the red zone. He'd have to go fast. Around him, *Hiram Lazar* trembled and shook as AT after AT battered into her thin hull.

Toby Kuryaken tapped nervously on the arm of her command chair. The battle below loomed on the screens. The shields flared as *Helk* got her range.

"Steady, people." She swallowed in a dry throat.

Her Weapons Officer looked up from the targeting comm. "Ma'am? *Bullet's* under assault again. Are you sure you—"

"Your orders stand, mister. At the first sign of life from that hulk, you blast *Bullet* out of space. Understood?"

He nodded. "Yes, ma'am. I've got a subroutine laid in. If *Bullet* shows any evidence of powering up, we'll cut her to slag."

The door slipped open. She watched with dead eyes as Giorj padded quickly across the floor. "Susan?" he called. "Susan, come on! I need you!"

"G-Go away!" she cried out hysterically, huddling, folding in on herself.

Giorj leaned over her, noting how she trembled. "My

God! How did he do this to you?" She felt his hands on her wrists. The bracelets slid away from her skin.

She bit back the tears. "W-Why am I here?" she asked in panic as she flung her arms around his neck, sobbing, out of control. "W-What have I d-done wrong? Why d-did he d-do that to . . . to me?"

"To break you. Has he done it? Are you broken, Susan Smith Andojar? *Damn it!* It's your dream! They're coming! The Romanans are attacking! You started it. *Damn you, help me!*" He shook her violently by the shoulders. Seeing nothing, he slapped her hard.

"W-What is the . . . the n-name of G-God?" Susan stuttered, eyes clearing slightly as her cheeks reddened. "Th-the n-name of G-God? W-What is . . ."

"The name of God is Spider according to you." Giorj's eyes blazed. "We have our chance to strike back! We're not beaten! It's up to you! I need your courage now. Hear me? I need you! *I can't do this alone.*"

"S-Spider . . ." Susan muttered, blinking, forcing herself to sit up and rub her face. "Spider. You have w-weapons?" She pushed herself up, weaving on her feet, and grabbed the combat armor he handed her. Hers, washed, cleaned, the effigy of Spider shining black on the white background. She hugged it to her breast, shuddering, drawing strength from the drawing.

"Here," he handed her her blaster and fighting knife. He hesitated over the hairy belt of coups, nervously offering them.

With practiced hands, she slipped into the undersuit and began snapping the armor in place. She hefted the fighting knife and shivered. "T-Turn the field off around them." She pointed the knife to where Leona and Colonel Arish Amahanandras watched with no comprehension.

"We can rescue them later!"

"Now!" Susan hissed, and Giorj nodded.

He shrugged and played with a control at his belt. At his nod, she went forward and quickly broke both of their necks.

"Why?" he demanded, horrified.

She stepped back, face grim. "Figure it out for yourself. I . . . I did them a favor. W-Where's Ngen? I want him . . . now!"

The ship jolted. "The ATs," Giorj whispered. *Hiram Lazar* trembled again. "I think they'll all get through. The targeting computer developed a slight, um, technical problem. We've got to get to the reactor room, Susan."

"*I want Ngen!*" she demanded as they ran into the companionway. Instinct took over, taking her mind away from the gibbering horrors inside.

"Follow me," he shouted. "Come on. *There's no time to lose!*"

Susan sprinted after him, her mind struggling to pull itself together, searching for missing pieces that had shattered and slipped away, gibbering into her subconscious.

Again and again, the ship shuddered under her feet. Every AT on the planet must have been slamming into the Sirian battleship. Two crewmen rounded a corner. They paused at the sight of Giorj and pawed for blasters as Susan instinctively blew them apart.

Giorj gasped, shaken by the sight and flinching from the feel of bits of exploded flesh that spattered him. He pawed futilely at the blood spots. Nevertheless, he pushed on. Susan fought her way through two more small groups of crewman. A mad rage possessed her by the time they reached an open hallway.

"There," Giorj gasped, pointing, lungs starved from the run. "We need to get behind that door!"

Sirians turned, dropping to their knees, weapons steady, unsure whether to shoot with Giorj standing there.

"Too many armed guards," Susan gritted. She gave Giorj a quick grin. Stepping forward, she forced herself to shout. "You boys want to see the Romanan who'll hang your hair off her belt? I'm going to kill you now, *sheep!*"

"Romanan!" She heard one call. Another lifted his weapon. She blew his chest apart. The rest backed away, white-faced, and ran.

Susan jumped for the big hatch. "Locked!" she called, sending blaster fire after the fleeing Sirians. "Hurry up, they'll be back. Even sheep can talk themselves into a fight."

Giorj went to the hatch and palmed the lock. The great portal slid slowly open. "Inside! Quick!"

Susan leaped as the hatch began to close. Men were springing to their feet all around the room.

"Don't shoot!" Giorj cried, stepping in front of Susan, arm out to block her. "You hit the wrong panel in here and we're all dead!"

"This is the reactor room!" she cried. *Where's Ngen?*

The Sirians erupted in a babble of questions, starting forward.

"Use your knife, Susan! Stop them until I can explain!"

Giorj screamed, half out of his mind. Squinting, Susan pulled the big Romanan fighting knife and dropped into a crouch. The Sirians stopped cold, eyes flashing from Giorj to her.

"What is this?" one of the engineers asked. "We're under attack, Giorj, and you . . . you bring *her* here?"

"We've got to shut the reactor down now!" Giorj thundered, pale face breaking out in sweat. "Ngen's got a detonator in the main comm reaction control. As soon as he's a safe distance away, he'll trigger it!"

"*What?* Have you lost your—"

"*I'm not lying!*" Giorj spread his hands. "Do you think for a minute that we can hold off the Romanans? There are thousands boarding. Now! As we speak! Do you think the man who could burn off our planet would hesitate to explode this ship when we lose it?"

"That true?" another asked, head cocked.

"I w-was there," Susan stuttered. "I've been under your b-blasters. Ngen . . . Ngen's killed more of your people than we have by . . . by scores. Let Giorj disarm the device . . . or I start cutting." Advancing, knife held low, she roared, "Live or die. *Now!*"

"All right!" the head engineer agreed with a nod. "All right. Ptor, shut the power down. Giorj, which console?"

Giorj flew to a panel and began unfastening the cover. Susan watched, blaster ready, eyes skipping from man to man, alert for treachery. Black shadows shifted in her mind, scratching at the wall that hid Hans.

Hans? Friday? Their images formed in her mind . . . only their eyes began to shimmer, blackening into Ngen Van Chow's. She fought to keep from screaming her fear out at the room, jumping at each sound, fearful that Ngen was creeping up on her. She backed up against the wall, but it reminded her of being cornered on that damn bed. She started to shake, pulling her finger from the firing stud lest her violent reaction discharge the weapon.

"The launch has just been released," a man called.

"*Damn!*" Giorj exploded. "We've got to hurry!"

"You mean, *he's . . . he's escaping?*" Susan demanded, gritting her teeth, fighting to replace terror with rage.

"We'll catch him later!" Giorj pleaded, not looking up from the box he'd located. "You can't get him if you're dead, Susan!" Sweat stood out on Giorj's face in clear beads. The engineers had turned ashen when they saw the box.

Susan walked over, looking down at the black square that had tiny powerleads running to it. She forced herself to watch, to fear the box and fiery death more than the ghost of Ngen in her shredded brain.

"So there lies death," she mused. How long before Ngen triggered the box?

"Launch accelerating at forty gravities!" The engineer watching the scanner groaned.

"Come on, Giorj, you're the best of us. Hurry up!" Another rocked from foot to foot, pulling on his fingers.

An explosion hammered at the hatch. Susan ran to cover it, blaster up and ready. The sound of violent fighting beyond carried through the thick steel.

"How's the reactor?" Giorj called.

"Seventy percent and falling," someone hollered back.

"One percent is enough to kill us all," a burly man remarked and laughed nervously.

Another explosion shivered beyond the heavily armored graphsteel. The hatch began to move. Susan dropped down, blaster at the ready, heart pounding.

"This is the Patrol!" a hostile voice called. "You're to surrender immediately and turn over control."

"Too late!" Susan called back. "A Romanan beat you to it, Joey! Come on in and pray with us."

A helmeted head snapped a quick look and ducked back. The marines trotted in nervously, battle armor scarred.

"Got it!" Giorj cried. He lifted the box out and ran for the door.

"Get clear! Explosive!" he bellowed in warning and threw it past the hatch. A second, two, then a hollow bang sounded in the corridor.

Susan hugged Giorj, who wiped sweaty hands on his tunic. Behind her the head engineer sniffed loudly, tears of relief tracing down his cheeks. The marines looked dumbfounded.

"Now I get Ngen!" she swore.

Damen Ree winced, pulling himself behind a bent section of steel plate. From the front, it looked like a giant flower, petals of grayish white graphsteel unfolded. A blossom of death, twisted out from an exploded mine.

It made a perfect shelter for a sniper like him. Blue-violet lanced past his ear.

"Damn Sirian scum suckers," Ree gritted, wishing he had feeling in his leg. Close call with that sonic grenade. He slid the muzzle of his heavy blaster past a bent curl of steel, sighting into the the darkness. At least they had better night sights than the Sirians. So far, that was all that kept them alive in the stygian blackness of *Bullet's* corridors and silent rooms.

A human form—crouched, running forward—filled the sight picture. Coolly, Damen Ree blew the man in half, feeling the telltale buzz of a weapon going low on charge.

He clapped in yet another charge, sighting into the darkness, finding a head, exploding if off the man's shoulders, the corpse recoiling, flopping out on the deck plates.

Too bad they'd been pushed back so far. The Sirians fought worse in zero g.

Ree swallowed, taking his time. Two charges left. He caught another Sirian as the man dove for an impeller induction tube. The shot took both the man's legs off below the hips. The fellow screeched and wailed, flapping his arms on the deck as he bled his life away.

"Colonel?" Neal's voice came through. "I can hear fighting. Sounds like they're closing on the bridge from Deck Three. I've had Amira rig sonics all through the comm— even Hans' and Susan's hatch."

Ree chuckled, hearing the bristly sound of his beard rasping on the helmet chinpiece. "All right, Neal. Don't let the bastards shoot you in your chair while you're having a pleasant chat with someone like me."

"No way, Colonel. You guys have been having all the fun. I want one or two of these guys to take back to Spider myself."

Neal sounded particularly chipper considering the circumstances. Hell, they all did. Grim jokes and inanities crackled back and forth over comm. Amazing how a person savored every second, made the most out of what little life remained, when he'd accepted himself as dead already.

Ree snapped a shot at a running man, missed, and resettled himself, seeing where the fellow went to ground. He claimed his reward a minute later when the man leaned around the corner to look.

"Half a head's better than none," Ree grunted, pressing the firing stud. He blinked at the grit in his eyes. He squinted, feeling the fatigue in all his muscles, yawning. "Damn trouble with Romanans, since I met the first one, I haven't had a decent night's sleep."

Neal laughed through the comm. "You can bitch about it to Spider."

Farther back down the corridor, several figures turned, running the other way. Ree wrinkled his face into a scowl. No, he saw right. They were all withdrawing. "Neal, everybody, watch out, they're withdrawing from my section. Might be a flanking maneuver."

"Got it, I'm checking with Hanson now." A pause. "Huh. Hanson says they're running on his front, too. Ngorikuku says the same thing where he's holding out. They're pulling back everywhere."

Ree waited, worrying his tongue with his teeth. "Aw, maybe they set charges all down that hall, figgering to blow us all to high hell."

"Hanson says he thinks they quit," Neal reported.

"Sure," Ree growled. "And I'm a pumpkin-headed freak, too! Quit? They've got us in the end!" He frowned, trying to shake the cobwebs from his exhausted mind.

Sighing, he mumbled, "All right, let's retake what they took from us. Move up, people. But for Spider's sake, be careful. We're getting to be few enough as it is without losing any more to their booby traps."

To himself, he moaned, "What I'd give for a night's sleep." On his numb leg, he slowly hobbled forward, eyes sharp for ambushes, trip wires, proximity sensors and self-propelled anti-personnel mines.

CHAPTER XXVII

Maya watched as *Victory* passed overhead. ATs—hers among them, darted for the sides of *Hiram Lazar*, sticking into the sides of the ship like white splinters.

"*Hiram Lazar* is firing on *Bullet*, Colonel," Ben called from behind her.

She looked at a second monitor, watching the deadly violet threads spin past the dead bulk of *Bullet*, a Sirian lighter exploding brilliantly in the process. Maya shook her head. "I don't understand. How can they miss? His targeting comm can't be that bad! Not after he mauled us as severely as he did."

Victory's shields flared and dimmed as the ATs slammed into *Helk* where she rested on the horizon, the fire going askew, threads disappearing as one by one, blasters went dead.

Maya rubbed her chin. "Looks like the end of it, Ben. The ATs—and whatever ruined Ngen's aim—won the war for us."

He nodded, frowning as he processed information from comm. "The Romanans won the war, Major. They took the planet. They crewed those ATs. We wouldn't have had the assault personnel otherwise—not and maintained any sort of presence on the planet during the attack."

Maya cocked her head, narrowing her eyes. "I suppose so."

"Got an escapee from *Hiram Lazar*," Ben called. "Timed perfectly, he waited until we'd passed and is accelerating one hundred and eighty degrees from our vector."

Maya looked, seeing a monitor locking telemetry on the fugitive. "Make any bets that's Ngen abandoning the fight—saving his skin?"

"Look at him go!" Ben whistled. "Must be pulling forty gs. Where'd he get power like that in such a small ship? Must have cost a fortune in credits!"

Maya cursed. "Get me . . ." But Yaisha and Toby's faces formed on the monitors.

"Looks like one's getting away, we're breaking with all we've got, tough to turn with this much V." Toby shook her head. "Maya, can you take him while we settle the situation in orbit?"

Maya opened her mouth to accept the challenge, and hesitated, looking over to where Ben watched her, eyes veiled.

"Negative, Toby, he's all yours. Battle damage. We took some hits from *Helk*," she lied guilessly.

Toby shot a furtive look at Yaisha Mendez and replied curtly, "We'll get him."

Maya straightened, eyebrow lifting as she faced the Colonels, waiting for accusations. *Why the furtive look between them?*

"Maya?" Yaisha asked in mellow tones. "Are you and your crew loyal to the Directorate?"

Maya bobbed her head, sighing. "We are. All of us."

Yaisha seemed relieved. "Very well. Let's see what the situation is down there."

Maya cut the comm and looked at Ben. "Something's not right. I can smell a rat."

"Neal? You still there?" Ree called into the comm, tethering himself, looking warily about through one of the rents in *Bullet's* hull.

"Affirmative. What've you got, Colonel?"

Ree turned his head, eyes seeking every shadow, every nook and cranny where humans might hide. "Nothing! Looks like they abandoned this section. Now why would . . . Hang on, I'm moving up."

He unhooked, pushing off and floating through the shadows, avoiding the starlight. Grabbing hold, he pulled himself along the melted graphsteel, easing his head slowly over the lip of the hull breach.

"Got 'em!" he growled. "Must be a couple hundred. They're packing up, cycling through the lock on a lighter. But why give up? *Blessed pulsars!*"

"What? What's up, Colonel?"

Ree turned the magnification up on his helmet. "It's *Hiram Lazar*, Neal. She's prickly with AT butts. Rita and John came through. *They've taken Ngen!*" He let out a whoop that almost deafened him in the confines of the helmet.

"Colonel?"

"Glick? That you? You alive back there?"

"Affirmative."

"We lost contact with you a long time ago, what happened? Where are you?"

"Aft of AT Dock 34, Colonel. I'm not sure how it happened, but they didn't bother us much. Seemed more interested in the bridge. Not only that, but in the last moments of the fight, Ngen tried to blow us away. His guns missed our hull by no more than five meters, just barely kissed the ship with each shot until Sarsa stilled *Hiram Lazar's* guns." A pause. "Hell! I could shoot better than that blindfolded!"

"Colonel?" Neal's voice came through. "Uh, we're getting a signal from the Sirians, sir. They want to surrender. What do you want to do with them?"

Ree hooked himself to the gutted wreckage of the hull. "Tell them to ship over to *Hiram Lazar*, we can't keep track of them here." He blinked at the exhaustion burning in his eyes. "Hell, we don't even know who's alive."

"Yes, sir. I'll tell them." Then, "Sir? They want to know if they can depart unhindered."

"Yeah, it's an order. People, no shooting at Sirians so long as they leave in peace. Glick?"

"Yeah, Colonel?"

"How's *Bullet*? Can we fix her?" His heart felt like a lump of lead, heavy in his chest. He held his breath.

"I think that was Ngen's plan all along, Colonel. Despite how she looks there's really not much wrong that powerlead, lots of plating, and a good cleaning won't fix. Most of all, we need to damp the reactor into the system and we'll have power."

He exhaled a blast of relief. "Thanks, Glick. Your first priority is to get a line to Rita on that Sirian ship. Next, reestablish comm to the bridge. After that . . . well, it'll come to me."

Unhooking, he looked around, enjoying the sight of the last Sirian lighter jetting reaction as she turned slowly and headed for *Hiram Lazar*.

"Neal? I'm on my way down. See you in a bit. Got any coffee in there?"

"Dispensers are down, but I think I can milk a cup or two. It'll be cold, Colonel."

He pushed off, headed for the black guts of the ship. "Yeah, well, you can't have everything."

"Affirmative, Colonel Kuryaken, that yacht's carrying Ngen Van Chow. My information is that he has jump capabilities, but his ship is shielded poorly and carries only two blasters with limited targeting capacity." Rita shot another quick look at the gray-complexioned engineer. "Anything else?"

"I doubt they can catch her," Giorj said guiltily. "I put that second reactor in. He has a terrible advantage of power to mass and the grav plates can absorb an awful lot of g, to the point of about forty-five."

"Did you get that, *Miliken*?" Rita asked.

"Affirmative. We view this as a challenge. Will you make us a wager, Major?" Toby's face showed a flush of excitement, the look of a predator on the hunt.

Rita shot a quick look at Susan's livid face. "Negative, Colonel. You'll get him. *Hiram Lazar* out." The comm went dead.

Susan's voice sounded gritty, forced, strung to breaking. "We need to see you, Iron Eyes, and the Colonel, alone. Right now, Major."

Rita studied Susan for a moment and decided. "All right,

I got a call from Neal a moment ago. They're all alive over there.

"Moshe," Rita waved her senior officer over. "Things seem to be pretty well under control here. Send the Sirians planetside under guard and see to pulling the ATs out. *Helk* is under our control so give me a call at *Bullet* in the event you need anything."

In the lift, Rita looked closely at Susan. The girl had a glazed, haunted look that sent a cold shiver down her spine. Susan Smith Andojar seemed to teeter on the brink of some inner darkness. Her face remained as expressionless as the odd engineer's. And Hambrei? A friend and ally, Susan claimed. Supposedly the man who'd jimmied *Hiram Lazar's* guns, saving thousands of lives.

Rita clamped her jaws, a smoldering anger within. Friday Garcia Yellow Legs lay in the med center, his short right leg blown off at the knee and Susan appeared completely disinterested.

And I lied pretty poorly when I told him Susan was all right. Why did he look at me that way? All I said was Susan was just too busy to see him.

Friday, almost screaming with pain, had nodded too quickly and dropped his eyes. Rita's guts twisted into a Gordian knot at the double dose of suffering he'd taken into med with him. She studied Susan through slitted eyes, fighting the urge to strangle the silent girl—only she wasn't Susan anymore. Not any Susan Rita had ever seen.

So the odd Sirian engineer had saved their bloody lives? Did that make him so damn precious? And Friday lay in med, loving Susan Smith Andojar, worried sick about her.

The AT they'd commandeered had trouble finding a dock on *Bullet's* scarred hull. "By Spider!" Rita heard herself breathe as they looked at the damage. "Will she ever fly again?" It almost choked her.

"I think we can have her fit within a month," Giorj declared, eyes devouring the ship he already considered his. Oblivious, he didn't react to Rita's steely glance.

Iron Eyes shook his head. "There are many holes running clear through. You can see stars!"

The AT settled down at Dock 25 where, so long ago, Doc Dobra had led her Romanans onboard. "Status banks show the other side in vacuum," the pilot called.

They donned helmets and went through the hatch into

airless darkness. Iron Eyes flailed around in the zero g until Rita hooked a hand around his waist. Giorj similarly towed Susan who had floated off the deck and had sense enough to stay still.

An emergency hatch loomed out of the blackness, outlined in their suit lights. "One at a time," Rita told them. "Iron Eyes, I'll follow you through. Just step inside. When the light blinks green, open the inside door and step out and close the door again."

He nodded and entered. After a minute, the outside light flashed and Rita sent Susan in. It proved an eerie sensation to stand alone in the dark with the anemic looking Sirian.

Rita sent Giorj, then took her turn, surprised to step into light, gravity, and air when she herself came through. Susan, Iron Eyes, and Giorj had doffed their helmets and stood to one side.

A figure dressed in scorched battle armor decorated with a giant spider effigy greeted her and extended a hand. "Greetings, Major. Good to see you again." Ree's gritty voice came from a blackened, bearded face. "Sorry the accommodations aren't exactly the way you remember, but we've had us a time here."

"Yes, sir," Rita agreed, shocked by the smoke-grimed walls. "How's the ship's condition?"

Ree looked tired. "Since the day she was commissioned, she's never been this bad. I'm not sure we can save her, but Glick is. I don't even know how he keeps the reactor from going up between one second and the next."

"If you'd give me a tour," Giorj said from the side, "I could make an estimate."

"Who're you?" Ree asked, frown indicating irritation.

Susan pushed forward. "Before we get too involved here, could we go somewhere and hash this all out. I have a feeling we can all help each other."

Rita nodded, curious herself about Susan's desperate motivation. Ree shrugged and led the way, hobbling on a leg that obviously pained him. Even through the armor, Rita could see the swelling.

They wound through patched corridors that showed burned areas where pirated plating had been welded over holes. He avoided corridors which should have taken them straight to their destination. Here and there, bodies—mostly Sirian— lay piled, blood and gut stink heavy in the air. Ree stepped over them nonchalantly, while Rita's gut flip-flopped.

"Why not the main corridors?" Rita wondered.

"Booby trapped dead ends," he grunted in explanation. "The whole ship's a rat's maze of aired-up corridors. Some even have gravity if the power hasn't been cut. The fusion system has been pumping out oxygen as fast as we can convert. Even so, it'll be a while before we can generate enough to refill most of the ship."

"That could work to our benefit," Giorj at last showed some animation in his pale features. "Structural changes can be more easily incorporated along the three major burn throughs. We'll need to reroute the powerleads some, but it will make a better defensive structure in the end."

"What do you know about the powerleads?" Ree demanded, stopping short, wheeling on his good leg.

Giorj smiled nervously. "Well, Colonel, I was the one who . . . who burned them out."

Rita thought for a second that Ree's heart would fail. The Colonel raised up on his toes, face working, fists clenched at his sides. Giorj backed up a step as Susan moved between them, her gaze deadly.

"Easy, Damen. I think we'd better hear all of this," Rita said coolly, defusing the situation.

"Uh-huh," Ree grunted, struggling to regain his temper. "When Romanans are involved, why do I let myself be surprised anymore?"

"Yeah, well, let's get all the facts." Rita placed a reassuring hand on his battle-chipped shoulder plate.

He growled to himself, shaking his head as he started down the companionway in his awkward limp, flakes periodically peeling off his charred armor. They had to float through several sections of zero g, along the way passing blasted bodies which looked fresher.

"Sirians paid a hell of a price." Ree made a futile gesture with his hand. "Before things got hot, we threw the bodies out every day."

The war room appeared the way Rita remembered it, but gloomy, the walls dingy. Everyone sat while Ree dispensed coffee all around.

"You might want to ask your engineer to be present," Giorj suggested. "I'm not sure, but talking to Susan I gather time might be of the essence."

Ree gave him a measured look from under lowered brows and sent a message to Glick. "It will take him a bit to get here. He has to cross three stretches of vacuum."

Rita looked over at the wooden expression on Susan's face. "Corporal, tell us what this is all about. I'm sure that when we get to the areas which concern Major Glick, we can wait."

Susan hadn't touched her coffee. "We want to rebuild *Bullet* into a better ship. We see no reason why she can't be the finest ship in the galaxy, not counting what the Brotherhood has. They remain a constant unknown."

Ree rubbed a hand over his jumbled hair. "To be honest, Susan, we haven't had a chance to go over the data you and Hans accumulated. We've been too busy making stop-gap repairs and fighting off boarding parties."

Susan nodded. "I'm well aware of that, Colonel. On the other hand, Giorj here converted three GCIs to satisfactory combat capability within three months. He and I haven't had much time to work out the details, but *Bullet* provides better raw material to work with."

"I think I know the way of the future, Colonel," Giorj agreed. "No matter that you've retaken Sirius, there will be others. The mystique of the Patrol has been broken."

Ree nodded. "You do have a point there." He leaned forward. "I have a question for you, young man. What do you get out of all this? What's your percentage in—"

Susan answered for him. "He wants the chance to rebuild *Bullet*, Colonel. Ngen used his mother's life as an inducement to build the Sirian fleet. *Hiram Lazar* killed her when it burned off Angla. I promised blood oath that I would take Giorj to World where he could build to his heart's content. I want a battleship to take back to my home planet . . . and I want the best."

Ree reddened, bloodshot eyes narrowing as a vein pulsed at the side of his head. "*YOU* want? Now just a minute here, Corporal, I—"

Rita raised a hand, feeling the tension crackling. Susan had stiffened, combat ready, a hand on her blaster. *Damn! She'll snap in two at the wrong word. What happened on that ship to metamorphose her into this stranger?*

"Easy, Damen." She turned to Susan. "Isn't that a little presumptuous?"

"No," Susan answered flatly. "I'm never going to stay on World. *Bullet* is my home now. I fight for my People. If this is to be my ship, why should I settle for second best? You see, Giorj and I have the data to make *Bullet* invincible

against anything humans can build for the next generation
. . . and perhaps beyond."

At that moment, Glick entered, body musky with sweat,
his combat armor grimier—if anything—than Ree's. Rita
couldn't help but wonder how they kept the computers from
fouling with all the smoke and junk floating in the air.

"Major Glick," Susan greeted, "may I present Engineer
Giorj Hambrei from the *Hiram Lazar*."

Glick's eyes were guarded; he shot a quick look to get
Ree's reaction, then took the engineer's hand and sat down.

"I would like to compliment you," Giorj said with true
admiration. "You have managed to effect an amazing number of repairs . . . considering the conditions."

"Thanks," Glick responded warily.

"Very well," Susan stood and inserted her tired comp
unit into comm. Picking up a headset, she accessed the
Brotherhood information. "Giorj, would you please explain
all this to the officers?"

She sat down as Giorj stood and began delineating the
ship he saw in his mind. Susan sat there like a bump on a
log, eyes blank. Giorj's excitement infected Glick first,
then Ree, after the Colonel caught the gist of the diagrams.

Iron Eyes—completely lost by the entire proceedings—
waited, eyes never leaving Susan's expressionless face. Rita
could see the reserve, the worry and concern he hid so
carefully.

Neal Iverson arrived, the excitement quickly sweeping
him up.

Like Iron Eyes, Rita watched Susan, wondering what was
going on in that quick mind. Wondering if she could ever
again reach this sudden stranger.

Glick began playing with comm as he and Giorj chattered
on about the materials they'd need. "So we strip *Brotherhood*
and *Hiram Lazar*? We still need more to build her all the
way." Glick frowned.

"We'll find it," Susan said easily. "We can always order
the Directorate to give it to us."

Ree frowned. "Think they would?"

"Could they seriously turn us down?"

A long silence passed as they mulled it over.

"Glick, what's your proposed turnaround on all this?"
Ree finally asked, leaning back in his chair and sipping his
coffee.

"From what Giorj tells me, we should be able to do it in

just over a month. At the same time, we can design a lot of changes to be added later as more hyperconductor is located.

"Majors?" Ree asked, looking at Rita and Iverson.

"Let's go for it, Colonel," Iverson agreed, eyes glued to the picture that had risen on the monitor from Giorj's and Glick's doodles.

Rita squinted up at the picture, imagining what a ship with those capabilities could do. "I say we don't strip *Hiram Lazar*. She's got to protect the Romanan home world. We can mine Sirius for whatever hyperconductor is left. We have to keep an eye on the planet for at least that long. Further, we have to see to the Romanan interests and load all their booty. If it gives us the edge for the next go-round, let's do it."

But she kept her attention on Susan. Where there should have been victory a hollow blankness stared back. There was only an eerie, half-dead quality to her eyes.

You have seen the report? Ngen is fleeing the Sirian system. From trajectory, he could emerge from jump anywhere along a hundred light years of space, revector, and jump again. Miliken is currently in pursuit. Colonel Kuryaken regrets to inform that he is outracing her. We must accept the fact that Ngen will remain loose. Skor allowed his fellows to process the information.

And the Romanans? Roque demanded. *They are loose, sowing discord on the planet. Spider cults are appearing in the wake of Romanan broadcasts. The people flock to this philosophy—this way of Spider—clamoring for Iron Eyes and this Yellow Legs. They have found new motivation. They have learned the use of space vehicles. They will—*

Worse! Navtov entered. *I have been informed by John Smith Iron Eyes that his people will keep* Hiram Lazar *and* Helk *as spoils of war. We cannot allow them access to space. Such a possibility would be totally impermissible, especially in ships able to reduce a Patrol ship of the line as both* Hiram Lazar *and* Helk *have been proven capable.*

Skor sent a warning through the system. *We did promise them spoils of war in return for their—*

Spoils? True. But two combat capable starships? Of THAT potential? We know if would take at least four Patrol ships of the line to destroy them! How can you justify allowing pirates by nature, BARBARIANS, loose among Directorate citizens whose protection is our purpose? Navtov demanded hotly.

We did promise. No— Skor began.

Promise? Did we promise them our hearts and souls, too? Roque countered. *No, there is a limit to our generosity.*

Soul, Assistant Director? Skor asked. *Have you absorbed something from the Romanan Prophet after all?*

There is no need to make derogatory remarks, Director, Roque countered.

The fact remains, Navtov insisted, *that we cannot allow such violent beings loose in the Directorate with battleships. I make my position clear. I cannot allow it.*

Roque? Skor asked.

I second the Assistant Director's decision. I cannot allow it either. Roque entered a series of highly detailed statistical projections following on his statement's affidavit.

Very well, the Romanans will be denied the two converted GCIs. Next, we must deal with the captives taken by Romanans. Sirian citizens have been placed into slavery for the purposes of concubines. According to the Pathos accords—

We are familiar with the Pathos accords, Director. Roque interrupted. *At the same time, since the Romanans are not subject to Directorate law, I believe we should let them have the young women and technicians in question. The—*

I cannot agree! Navtov entered vehemently, files of legal proofs following on the heels of his assertion.

In this case, Robinson interjected, *I must side with Assistant Director Roque. I believe there is a salutory lesson for others who would revolt against us. The reminder that citizens in revolt have placed themselves beyond the law will keep others from taking such liberties in the future.*

Ree lives. They will repair Bullet, Navtov informed. *I suggest we remove that potential immediately. Never again will the pirate be so vulnerable. He has sustained losses from the combat. His ship is damaged. I propose a detachment of marines enter* Bullet *and place Ree under arrest.* Victory *can then return the surviving Romanans and their spoils to Atlantis. Having done so, the damage will be sufficiently contained and we can continue with the chores of directing humanity to more profitable pursuits.*

Skor considered. *Assistant Director Roque?*

I agree. Then Roque added, *We need to try Ree and his crew for insubordination. The time appears most propitious now. We had best use it. Order the Patrol to seize his vessel and imprison him and his crew.* Toreon *can return them to Arcturus for trial.*

Skor Robinson hesitated. Two votes against. A slight tinge of unease lay in the bottom of his thoughts, a curious reluctance. He actually sighed aloud. *Very well, Directors, the orders are sent.*

For long moments, Skor floated in the blue haze, mind in an uncommon turmoil. A feeling he'd never experienced had seized him, leaving him upset. On an impulse, he accessed Chester Armijo Garcia, hearing the dying strains of some baroque piece in the background. Skor found himself oddly tongue-tied, the words refusing to come to him as he attempted to begin a dialogue.

Chester looked up, smiling, face warm and friendly. "What you really want me to explain is why you feel so strange." Chester waved a hand serenely. "What baffles you, Skor Robinson, is guilt. A very human problem. The roots of the emotion—and it can be very damaging—come from your perceptions of injustice. You feel you have just committed such an injustice against Colonel Ree and the Romanans. You are dissatisfied with yourself . . . afraid you have not lived up to your preconceived standards."

Skor's heart began to pound. He blinked, an uncertainty to his words. "Have I done ill, Prophet?"

Chester spread his arms wide, shimmers of delicate fabric unfolding in waves. "That is up to the cusps, Director. Decisions rest in the hands of others as well as your own. What will be is up to free will—yours, Ree's, ben Ahmad's, Colonel Mendez's. Others will then act."

"What will happen?" Skor snapped.

"One of several alternatives. A situation this complex depends on many cusps. A person makes a decision. Another person's actions hinge on those. The future unfolds exponentially."

"And you will not tell me what to do?"

Chester smiled regretfully. "Would I have you come to depend on me? What would become of *your* free will? How would you feed your soul? Do you want to see your sense of responsibility erode like the wind? No, Skor, I wouldn't, even if I could. Your future is filled with enough trials without adding dependence."

"I . . ." He stopped, realizing the truth in the Prophet's warning. "That will be all, Prophet."

Maya ben Ahmad stared uneasily at the missive. "So that's that." She looked up as Yaisha's face filled the holo.

"You have received orders?" Mendez asked, face stiff. "I . . . yes, Yaisha, I have." She sounded old and tired. Balefully she glared up at *Toreon's* Colonel.

"Be easier if we just blew him out of space."

"The Directors want him alive. Along with his crew. I'll follow orders and keep him alive, Yaisha. A thing of mine, you understand, a quirk."

"Your ship is closest to *Bullet*. I'll send a detachment of my people over. We can assault Damen Ree together."

"Send them." Maya looked up at the stat board. "Ship them in at Dock 7. I'll have people there waiting."

"Affirmative." Yaisha hesitated.

"Yes, Colonel?"

"This bothers you, doesn't it?"

Maya nodded. "You know how I feel about it. Duty, Yaisha. I got a thing about that, too. Even if I think it stinks. But you know, Colonel, you gotta believe in something." She cut the comm, looking over to where Ben had stiffened in the command chair. She flipped him the flimsy with the orders.

He looked up, having scanned the text, the lines around his mouth going tight. "They cut their throats!"

Maya slouched on the comm console, bracing a foot, fingering her dark chin. "You've talked to some of our people? The ones who were down on the planet?"

Ben nodded, eyes guarded.

"Who took the worst of the beating all through this? Who really broke the Sirian will to resist?"

"The Romanans," Ben replied evenly. "There have been constant calls for interviews with their Prophet. Holos of the Dobra broadcast and that Yellow Legs lecture on Spider are selling like deuterium breeders down there."

"Why?"

Ben lifted a shoulder. "It's a common social psychology. If the other guy won, he's doing something right, has an edge. Something in the way he does things is somehow better. Then there's the feeling that if it's the way of the future, why not hop on the bandwagon now? It's adaptation at work, Colonel." He frowned before adding, "And the Sirians see something else. Honor. The way the Romanans go on about Spider and the need to learn—to feed your soul—appeals to them after Ngen's lies. Spider gives a purpose to everything that happened here."

She turned, looking at the monitor where *Bullet* lay waiting in orbit, repair crews already swarming around the ship. "And how will the Sirians react when the Directorate undercuts their new Romanan heroes?"

Ben took a deep breath and shook his head. "I don't know." A pause. "You going to call for volunteers to go take Colonel Ree's ship away from him?"

She turned, a dullness in her chest. "You think it's a good idea?"

He looked away, voice barely audible. "Yes."

She narrowed her eyes, seeing the small effigy of a Spider drawn on the shoulder of his uniform. "Why?"

He lifted a shoulder, eyes still averted.

Maya chuckled hollowly. "I see, Ben. Sure, call for volunteers. Get a feeling for the sentiment of the crew, eh? See how many want to take that ship from Damen after he and his people paid so dearly to keep her?"

He looked up, the muscles in his jaw jumping, eyes hard. "Maya, you and I, we've spaced for a long time. We've gotten along better than most top grade officers because I never tried to cut your throat, never tried to stab you in the back because I respected you. I just . . ."

"Shhh!" She raised a hand. "On the monitor I see Yaisha's assault team disembarking from *Toreon.* We got a veteran assault unit back from the planet? Who's got the best record?"

He bit back a protest. Sullenly, he supplied, "Captain Dyad. He'll follow orders to a tee, Colonel."

"Have him and his people meet me at Dock 7," she said, pulling herself upright. "In the meantime, sound battle stations and power up the reactor. I want the ability to blow a ship into plasma at my command."

She felt his eyes burning into her back as he stepped to the locker, pulling combat armor from the shelves.

CHAPTER XXVIII

"Colonel?" Neal's voice brought him out of a sound sleep.

Groaning, Damen Ree pulled himself to his feet, grabbing for combat armor out of habit. "Don't you ever sleep, Neal?"

"Uh . . . yes, sir. You've been out for hours. Uh, sir, we've got ATs coming in from *Victory,* I know you wanted to be alerted if Patrol made any move."

"Thanks, Neal. Any word from Maya?"

"Yes, sir. She's on the way over. Uh, and sir?"

"Hmm?"

"*Victory's* powering up, sir."

"Powering . . . Sound alert. Damn it! It's happened. They've had time to think it over! Scramble Rita on the *Hiram Lazar,* tell her to power up, put a lid on any visitors from *Victory* or *Toreon.* They're coming to get us!"

"Yes, sir!"

Ree snapped the carapace around his chest, rubbing the grimy spider effigy clean, suddenly proud of the coups on his belt. He stopped for an instant, hand on the cold steel of the hatch.

"Well, old gal," he told the ship, gentleness in his voice. "I guess they're at it again. If it's not Ngen, it's Skor Robinson. Well, let's see who wins this time."

Panting, out of breath, he reached a lock in time to watch the AT slide into one of the working docks. A second craft slid into the lock behind. That one bore *Toreon's* markings.

"Must think we're real pushovers," Ree grunted, happy for the first time that *Bullet* was a rat's maze of corridors and traps. "That or they think we're asleep and surprise is all on their side."

"Colonel?" Neal's voice came through, unflappable as always.

"Here."

"We're ready. Same plan we used on the Sirians. Damn! If they just weren't . . ."

"Yeah, Neal, I know," he added quietly. "It's World all over again. Two to one, huh?" Only it wasn't.

"That's right, sir. I got Major Sarsa, she's powering up. They've got all Ngen's blasters on line over there."

"Then maybe we aren't dead after all," Ree whispered, running his fingers over the Spider effigy. Only, if Maya opened with *Victory's* guns, they'd be blown away before *Hiram Lazar* could reply.

A lock cycled, Patrol marines stepping out, combat armed. Precise, they formed up in a defensive perimeter.

"Hold your fire," Ree ordered. "We don't want any costly mistakes."

"Good thing!" Maya's stiff voice cracked on his frequency. "Damen, that you? Didn't catch you napping, huh?"

"You came to take my ship?"

"Got the orders an hour ago."

"We'll let you take the first shot, Maya. After that, well, devil take the hindmost. We're not giving up the ship."

Silence.

"Damen?"

"Uh-huh."

"I think maybe you and I'd better have a long talk. Face to face."

"Won't change anything."

"Maybe. You and me. Alone. On your bridge."

He frowned. "All right, Maya, come on through." Heart in his throat, he stepped out, waiting as she came striding into the lock, advancing from behind her nervous looking marines. More than a few Spider effigies spotted their armor. They didn't look happy.

"Could be a real bloodbath," Ree greeted, slightly annoyed by the dazzling white of her armor.

She looked up at him, piercing eyes taking his measure, a grim smile reshaping her smooth dark features. "You look like you've been through the mill, Damen. Every time I come to visit, you're more ragged than the last time. And this wreck you're so attached to looks more like junk!"

"Must be the company we keep. You wanted to talk? Why on the bridge?"

"Need the communications," she growled, "Come on."

"Not that way. Another ten paces and you'll be blown to bits. Follow me." And he led off through the bent and ruptured corridors to the bridge. "Uh, close your nose as you step over the corpses. They're high on the list, but we just haven't had time."

She nodded, placing her feet disdainfully as she picked her way through a pile of twisted dead. "Jeesus, what are you doing? Running a morgue here?"

"They came to us."

Silence hung between them as they crossed a section of zero g, the walls pocked by blaster fire.

"You taken to wearing hair?" she wondered, hooking a thumb at his belt.

"Earned them," Ree grunted. "You had to be there. We were prepared to die in honor."

"Honor," she repeated under her breath, nodding slightly.

Maya took Neal's salute as he passed the hatch; her armor had become grimy along the way. Eyes slitted, she stared around at the soot-streaked consoles. Of the several that worked, some showed the outside of *Bullet's* ripped hide. Another displayed a stern-faced Rita Sarsa, a white bridge behind her.

"Dyad? Everything all right? Good. I'm on the bridge. Stay alert . . . and out of trouble." She turned to Neal, "Major Iverson, please open a line to *Victory*."

Ree nodded approval, arms crossed, waiting.

Maya looked up to see her First Officer's face form. "Ben? I'm here. Status report?"

"We're all ready, Colonel. Um, *Hiram Lazar* has powered up, she's swung slightly, the gun decks are pointed our way." He swallowed, waiting.

Maya chuckled. "And how are Yaisha's people doing?"

"Hopping mad, Colonel."

"What the hell's going on?" Ree asked.

Maya ben Ahmad scowled. "You know I got orders to seize your ship and crew. I also got orders to take *Hiram Lazar* and *Helk* from the Romanans. Or, I should say, we all did." She wiped a finger across a console and grimaced at the black.

Ree cocked his head. "You can always try, Maya."

She pursed her lips, working them, a deep frown lining her brow. "Major Iverson, open a line to Colonel Mendez on *Toreon*."

Ree once again nodded approval.

"Time to pay the fiddler," she said wistfully as the remaining comm filled with Mendez's face.

"I take it you've succeeded? Yaisha asked tersely. "I see

you've gotten Ree. I must say, I didn't think it would be that easy. I didn't exactly expect you to put yourself at risk either."

Maya dropped her head, rubbing the back of her neck. "It wasn't easy at all, Colonel. I *had* to come. You're not going to take *Bullet*. The other ships belong to the Romanans. *Victory* sides with Ree and the Romanans. The Directors are—"

"*You? Maya, you've gone over to . . . to them?*" Mendez started forward in her command chair, arms braced.

Maya glared hotly at the screen. "You want to make a party out of this, Yaisha? Ben's on my bridge, and *Toreon's* filling the targeting comm. And Yaisha, we're powered up to cover *Bullet* from you or Toby when she finally returns."

She hesitated, the desire plainly there. "My orders are to—"

"Die?" Maya wondered. "That's what it will be, Yaisha. You're outgunned and I don't think you're powered up. *Victory* will shoot on my order, Yaisha."

Rita Sarsa added, "And I think *Hiram Lazar's* guns will get you first, Colonel. I have only to say the word and we'll use these great Brotherhood batteries." She glanced to a monitor, "I see from the displays, Moshe has *Helk* powered up, too."

Mendez shook her head. "Why, Maya? Why you . . . for them?"

Colonel Maya ben Ahmad gave her a tired look. "Duty, Colonel. Respect? Yes, that, too. We can't just use these people and throw 'em away. I didn't come all this way to demonstrate hypocrisy to Sirians, or to go back on my word to the Romanans. No, Damen and his people taught me a lesson. Maybe it's time we recognized we all need each other. Like it or not, it's just beginning out there. Sirius was only the first. Other planets will follow. It's a time for loyalty and honor again, Yaisha." She looked over to Ree. "Maybe that's the way of Spider, huh?"

Mendez looked up, obviously having accessed her comm. "And my people?"

"On *Victory*. Ben tells me they're a little mad, but they're safe. Had to hijack your AT to make sure Damen and Sarsa didn't get caught by surprise.

"Colonel?" Ben called from his monitor. "I've got communication from Arcturus. They're requesting that we disregard the previous orders. Director Robinson himself notes it was a . . . an unfortunate error—a mistake in transmission."

Maya looked curiously at Ree. "What the hell? The old boy's learned to lie!"

Ree sagged into his stained command chair. "Shut it down, Rita. Maybe we've been saved by the damn bell again. But stay on your toes, people."

Friday Garcia Yellow Legs watched *Bullet* change as the days passed. He stumped around *Hiram Lazar* on his temporary prosthetic. The gadgetry fascinated him. The fake leg contained an electro-stim unit that regenerated tissue. Someone had told him about DNA and regeneration and gene nodes. Words. Still, as the days passed his leg got longer and longer.

In the meantime, he taught himself to read, devoured space warfare tactics, and studied the engineering changes Patrol techs were making in *Hiram Lazar*—the first Romanan space ship.

Friday developed a liking for Sirian theater which he thought to be immensely funny. He studied the history of old Earth and read the ethnographies Leeta Dobra had stored in *Bullet's* comm after they transferred it to *Hiram Lazar's* banks. But most of all, he hung around hoping that Susan would eventually show up.

Friday periodically forced himself to go down to the chamber where a squad had found the dead bodies of Leona Magill and Colonel Amahanandras. Friday watched them cart the contents of the room away, piece by piece, as he looked at the one blood-stained bed and tried to imagine.

Rita had arrived one day and had shown him the holos a tech had dug out of Ngen's private files. He saw Leona and Arish break under Ngen's hand.

"Is there one of Susan?" he asked, voice hoarse and choked.

"Several," Rita replied, face like stone. "She was tougher. She almost had him for a while."

"I'm not sure I want to—"

"You won't. I destroyed them. There's nothing there any human wants to see."

"And Susan?"

"Ngen used a psych machine as part of the process. The techs who took it apart say it read the brain engrams—the synaptic tracks of memory. Used them against her. Friday, it was probably you—or Hans—who she saw when Ngen . . ."

"But is she all right?" he pleaded, his imagination spinning horrors.

"I don't know her anymore, Friday. She's . . . she's . . ."

He had reached up and patted her hand where it rested on his shoulder. In silence he closed his eyes, heedless of the tears.

A month later they fitted him with a new fake leg, his stub having grown an inch and a half that month. Across the way, *Bullet* had begun to shine whitely again, most of the outside battle damage gone. Scaffolding surrounded the ship in a delicate looking framework.

Susan was in there . . . somewhere.

"Friday!" Rita cried, coming up to hug him.

He grinned up at her and saw Iron Eyes tagging along behind. "Hello, Major. How are things going?"

"Can't complain. We got a message from the Directorate today. *Miliken* and *Toreon* are back on Patrol. The Directorate has a civilian council due here tomorrow. The food supplies are coming in regularly on GCIs and we got a little of the hyperconductor we asked for."

"And Ngen?"

Rita dropped her eyes. "No sign, Friday. He completely outran *Miliken*. He made the jump first. After that, he could have dropped in anywhere, changed his vector and jumped again."

"The galaxy isn't that big!" Friday protested. "He's out there ruining other innocent lives. We can't just—"

"He'll show up," Iron Eyes agreed. "We've advertised through the worlds and stations that when he does, the Romanans will provide a man's weight in toron. We have sworn blood oath as a race."

"That makes me feel better." He looked up hesitantly. "Any change in Susan?"

Rita took a deep breath. "No, she just supervises and spends most of her time with Giorj. They talk a lot where no one can hear." Rita looked down at her hands.

Friday felt his gut drop. "That's good, I guess. She needs someone. Do you think he . . . he helps her?"

"Yes," she whispered. "I think he does. Keep in mind, she's not the Susan you once knew. She's someone different, inhuman. She lives in her head. Like . . . like part of her soul's dead. Ngen twisted her, Friday. He may have broken her forever."

"She never mentions Hans or me?" Friday whispered dully.

"She moved in with Giorj. She's sharing his quarters. I'm

sorry, Friday. It's better than having you hear it from someone else."

"I've met him, you know," Friday said dully. "I spoke to
him when they were modifying the big blasters. He seemed
nice, but sort of preoccupied with all the work going on."

His vision blurred.

Iron Eyes laid a hand on Friday's shoulder. "I think you
should come down to the planet. I think you need to see to
your share of the material being loaded for transport. So far
you have nothing of your own but coups."

"Give mine to the widows and orphans," Friday tried to
keep his voice level.

"I am giving you an order, warrior." Iron Eyes' voice
didn't brook argument. "I need help there and you're capable. You made a name for yourself with the Spider broadcast. The Sirians, they want you. They respect your word. I
need you to handle my . . . what is it?" He looked to Rita.

"Public relations, War Chief."

"Yeah, you're going to do that for me, Friday."

"I—"

"It's an order."

Friday nodded, eyes straying toward the shining white
ship across that unbridgeable space. Something new was
being built there. Something Friday Garcia Yellow Legs had
no part in. Why hadn't that Sirian gunner shot just a little
straighter? Why hadn't the med team been just a little slower.

Chester Armijo Garcia turned the volume down at the
final strains of Beethoven's Ninth Symphony and as the
ending notes echoed, Skor Robinson's image formed.

Chester smiled. "I cannot tell you, Director. He has been
in Gulag Sector among friends who provided him with arms
in the past. He will make his next decision in several days.
He is moving constantly, making choices by the day. His
cusp is not yet complete."

The dwarfed blue eyes glittered under the bulging forehead. "You always make me nervous when I talk to you,
Prophet," Robinson's cracking voice declared.

"I regret that, Director." Chester inclined his head. "I
will take this opportunity to let you know I will leave for the
world you call Atlantis tomorrow. Would you be so kind as
to schedule a transport for me?"

Robinson's face twitched in distress. "Why should I do
that? Perhaps you serve our purpose best here?"

"Perhaps. At the same time, I have other duties I owe to Spider. I was brought here for a purpose, Director. Your decisions demonstrate glimmerings of enlightenment. Your soul has sprouted. I go where I am called. On the other hand, you, too, may exercise your free will. You may keep me here should you decide to create a cusp of your own." Chester smiled easily.

"Which is better for the Directorate?"

Chester shook his head. "I do not know, Director Robinson. One way will bring a birth by pain and blood . . . but through that will come new life as a new order is born. The other way may bring balance depending on the cusps—or sterilization and slavery. The knowledge gained will be different—though I see dead souls in one future—but perhaps the result is just as valid. I know not Spider's motives."

"Your God angers me, Prophet!"

"He angers many."

"There are Spider cults springing up all over Sirius." Skor's mouth twisted. "They seek a Prophet, too. Are you sure you would not go there?"

"Perhaps I might . . . eventually," Chester was thoughtful. "I will not for the present. I can see a young man who lives with visions. He has been praying for many days—singing to the glory of Spider. It is not his cusp yet, but I think he will go."

"Why Spider cults when Romanans have beaten them, frightened them? Committed atrocities?"

"Because we beat them, Director." Chester smiled benignly. "What frightens a human triggers him to understand. At the same time, Romanan ways provide a simple truth. Honor and knowledge and virtue—though savage—they can perceive. Their world is reeling, Skor. They have been lied to; their reality has been blasted, devastated by war. Spider provides them something to cling to. A hope for the future.

"Once, Director, we talked of souls. Among them the Romanans have talked of souls, first to the amusement of the Sirians, but now because the Sirians see a truth. Like yours, their souls are starving, crying for nourishment. They want to learn now, to experience, to improve their lives."

"That is not reassuring, Prophet." Skor swallowed uneasily.

"Life is not reassuring, Director. Were it, we would learn nothing and our souls would be sterile."

"Colonel Ree desires more hyperconductor—a strategic, expensive metal. That is not reassuring either."

"Can you stop him from getting hyperconductor for his ship?"

"I do not know." Skor worked his thin, bloodless lips.

"Would sending it to him be better than if he took it?"

"I do not know," Skor said woodenly.

"You will still order him to relieve himself of command," Chester said thoughtfully.

"He is becoming a nuisance," Skor replied. "He deserves retirement. There are younger men who should command. We will give him many honors and much credit for his years of service. It is better this way. He can retire on greater laurels than any Patrol colonel in the last three hundred years."

Chester nodded knowingly.

"What if we want you again, Prophet?"

"Send for me. I will come if you desire knowledge." Chester smiled as a bit of the future fell into place. Skor had made his decision. Chester let time flow through him as a vision formed.

"I have had enough of your knowledge for now," Skor muttered to himself—a trait he'd never demonstrated before.

"Perhaps," Chester agreed easily.

"Do you never argue?"

"Should I?"

"Have you no thoughts of your own?" Skor's brow developed faint lines.

"Would it make any difference if I did?"

"Questions!" Skor almost spat.

Chester was silent.

"Should I send the hyperconductor to Colonel Ree?" Skor's voice pinched. "Would he use it against me?"

"The question you ask should be considered thus," Chester said benevolently. "Does Ree have a reason to use it against you? Have you any evidence that they would turn against you? And—if they did—would the results be good or evil in the end?"

Skor Robinson watched him with his sharp blue eyes. "Enjoy your trip, Prophet."

The image winked out.

Chester smiled to himself as another piece of the future dropped neatly into place. He chose Mozart's quartet in A minor, K-581 for his next piece.

Techs and noncoms worked twenty-four hours a day.

Sirian shipfitters swarmed in the yards on the planet and on the rebuilding stations in orbit. Giorj called down specifications and in double time, the sections of deck, plate, or powerlead came up by shuttle or AT.

Pleas to release certain hostages or to accept gifts in place of some young woman, besieged the Romanans. Sometimes it worked, sometimes it didn't. While occasionally a woman decided to leave peacefully, others tried to commit suicide, fought constantly, or gave themselves up in despair. None of which bothered the smiling husbands.

Death threats circulated. Atrocities didn't die quickly in some Sirian minds, but on the whole the people had simply been worn out. Stunned, their planet in ruins, they simply accepted.

The majority, however, were more than intrigued with the Romanans. Their hated foes had become something of a cultural prize. Romanan warriors were invited here and there to speak to civic clubs and religious groups. No one wanted an aroused Romanan anywhere near. Tame, they were fascinating, exciting.

Iron Eyes, in particular, had even more to do in peace than in war. Outside of calls to release young women, businessmen ambushed him wanting to produce Iron Eyes dolls, market official Romanan war knives, sell official Romanan coups, and book vacation excursions to Atlantis, or World, as the Sirians had learned to call the Romanan home planet.

Authors clung to the Romanan headquarters like flies as they tried to get biographical information from the warriors who entered and left. Similarly, the holo producers cropped up everywhere, trying to sign steely-eyed warriors for holo productions entitled, "Romanan Revenge" and "Spider's Raiders."

Imitation leather clothing—dyed in Spider and Santos colors—sprouted on screaming Sirian youths, who charged through the streets with toy blasters and bits of fabric, carpet, or wig for coups.

Warriors were in great demand to sing war songs for the media. Essays, treatises, and lectures were published continually by news personnel and media hosts on subjects like the concept of God as Spider, Romanan morality, social structure on World, the role of women in Romanan society. Spider effigies decorated walls, aircars, business establishments, and logos.

Iron Eyes winced at the thought that along with Rita's and Ree's, his face stared out from holo ads, magazine articles, and billboards. Actors played him in the cheap holos, and a reporter he'd told tales to one night after too much scotch was making a fortune depicting Iron Eyes single-handedly killing Atlantean bears with one bared fist. That brought laughter to a lot of Romanans.

"None of it makes sense!" Iron Eyes almost shouted as they passed a billboard touting Iron Eyes' favorite restaurant.

Damen Ree had been surprised at the amount of reconstruction which had been accomplished in the short time since the planet had been devastated. He looked up at the new signboard. "It's doesn't hurt. Have the agents been at you?"

Iron Eyes groaned and nodded. "Constantly. They keep telling me how many credits I'm losing. I guess by letting them put my name up, I can make credit. What's credit to a warrior? What about my honor and my coup? Do they care? Why me?"

"Just lucky, I guess." Ree chuckled gleefully. "Must be that handsome face."

Iron Eyes didn't look amused.

"Look, you're a hero," Ree protested. "You're an image to them, something they look up to. Of course they're going too far with it. That's what heroes are for, for Spider's sake!"

Iron Eyes growled.

"Would you rather it was Ngen they were adoring?"

"Don't even say it. We bled enough here." Iron Eyes shook his head. "As much as I hated Big Man, Ngen is . . . is . . . foul."

"Got that right. But you're doing Spider's work here, my friends." Ree shook his head with a wistful smile on his face. "We have over twenty thousand young men and women who want passage to World for the purpose of learning to be warriors."

"Women?" Iron Eyes snorted.

"Susan made quite a reputation."

"They don't know what they're asking for," Iron Eyes said angrily. "And Susan's . . ." His lips twitched.

"No," Ree agreed, "they don't. But it's a start. We've accepted a lot of them, John. We need skilled men and *women* to replace our losses."

"Not as warriors," Iron Eyes protested. "Sirians don't—"

"No, as techs and comm specialists and gunners and so forth." Ree rubbed his chin. "We've got enough young Romanans who will want to go with us from World."

Ree dropped the aircar at the governmental center.

"Maya's already here," Iron Eyes noted, looking askance at the crowd.

"Good!" Ree crowed. The crowd parted to let them land. Holo recorders and cameras focused on them as Colonel Damen Ree stepped lightly to the ground, his dress uniform gleaming under the bright light of the double star.

Iron Eyes jumped down, resplendent in his leather clothing, cleaner than it had been since he'd skinned it off the cow. His fighting knife gleamed, polished, his belt of coups appeared small considering the ones worn by his warriors. His hair—freshly washed and braided—shone in the sun.

They climbed the steps and entered. A marine in sparkling armor brought them to Maya's temporary office. She looked up from a comm.

"Maya, how's it going?"

"Despicable, Damen," she grunted. "I'm a spacer, not a bloody colonial viceroy!" She pulled the headset from her brow, rubbing her face. "Nevertheless, we've got most of the major problems lined out. I'm not cut out to be a military governor but according to the word from Arcturus, Kimianjui is sending a gaggle of bureaucrats to take over. Ought to be here in a month or two."

"It *was* your sector," Damen reminded, dropping into a seat. He smiled weakly at her scathing glare. "Well, never mind. We're here. I suppose you have the papers ready?"

She swiveled in her grav chair, turning to Iron Eyes. "Have you given any consideration to my proposal?"

Iron Eyes nodded. "I have. For the moment, I think it's a good idea."

She handed him a contract. "There it is. Everything we've been haggling over for the last month. The Romanans own ten percent of all Sirian gross economic production. The military government will see to your cut for the time being. Thereafter, you'll have to have your own people here to watch out for your interests." Maya smiled humorlessly. "I wish you luck. Welcome to the cutthroat business of books, credits, and debits."

Iron Eyes smiled. "Cutthroat?"

"I don't suppose you'd understand all the ways of cheating that—"

"No, but a Prophet would." Iron Eyes winked ribaldly, causing Maya to start.

Ree stepped in. "The materials for *Bullet* have been right on schedule. We're space capable as it is, most of the ship's been cleaned, air's fresh again. We'll be shipping out as soon as we run a couple more checks on *Bullet*."

She looked at him, a sad smile hidden behind her professional exterior. "I'll miss you, Damen. Aw, I'll miss that wreck you space in, too. Been a hell of a campaign, huh?"

Ree rubbed his hands together. "You know, you're all right. I've always had a lot of respect for you. You went out on a limb for *Bullet*. In the Romanan way, we consider it honor to *Victory*. If you ever need us—call."

She looked at him, twirling the headset absently. "You know, Damen, there's trouble ahead. The Directorate's coming apart like a hypercharged molecular string. I always liked your style, Damen." A subtle communication passed between them.

Iron Eyes cleared his throat, standing. "For my people, I thank you, Colonel. I understand there are some young men who would stay with *Victory*? Tell them they do the People honor. Your ship is always welcome in our skies. You may have all the toron you ever need." On the way out, he looked at Damen and added, "Whenever you're ready, Colonel. Don't rush."

Ree looked back over his shoulder as Iron Eyes stepped out. "Good man, that."

Maya smiled, exhaling loudly. "Like all the rest of them. They grow on you." She looked at him, eyes softening. "I meant what I said. That I'd miss you."

He chuckled, relaxing for the first time all day. "Enjoyed having you come by for dinner during the last month." He paused. "You know, for years I never had anyone to talk to. Then we went to World and a whole bunch of people flocked into my life, Leeta, Sarsa, Iron Eyes . . . you. Now I'm off to World again . . . and you're here."

Maya stood, walking to the window to stare out at Sirius. "Command never leaves a person time for relationships, Damen. Leaves us exiles among the multitudes."

"I noticed Ben has a spider on his uniform."

She laughed. "Yeah, you warned me. It's the way of Spider. A creeping philosophy." She rubbed the back of her neck, face pained. "And I just agreed to keep Romanans on my ship? I'm out of my goddamned mind!"

They were silent for a time.

"Damen? You know, you could stay. I could run a transfer through." She turned, a vulnerability in her eyes.

"Think the two of us could live on one ship?" he asked softly. "The last woman I considered said she couldn't share me with *Bullet*. No, don't look at me that way. If it could be anybody, it'd be you. But we're who we are. Hell, we might not even like each other. Dominant personalities, you know?"

He sighed. "And I can't leave *Bullet*." He smiled fondly, fingering his palm where a faint scar marked his flesh. "My blood's in her steel."

She came close, looking up. "Never know about the future, Damen. Maybe someday."

Iron Eyes was joking with the Romanan warriors when Ree emerged a half-hour later.

After they'd climbed into the aircar, the Romanan honor guard retreated to glare at the curious and Ree took the aircar up. "So everything's taken care of. No occupation for Romanans, just a straight cut off the top. Ten percent of Sirius? Not bad."

Iron Eyes spread his hands. "We're happy. On top of the loot, that's fine. And Maya's a good ally." The question remained unspoken.

Ree nodded. "I, well, I don't know. I guess I always liked her. Hated to shoot at her that day over World. She's got sense."

"And?"

Ree lifted a shoulder, eyes softening. "Oh, I don't know. She asked me to stay. It wouldn't work out in . . . I guess we just understand each other is all. You know, common things. Maybe, if . . . Aw, hell. I made that decision years ago. My lady? Well, she's up there in orbit."

"How soon are we ready to go?" Iron Eyes asked, letting his eyes range over the Sirian capital. In the distance, the aft end of a wrecked AT thrust up at an awkward angle. The signs of war were disappearing, but not that fast. Angla remained a flattened waste.

"*Bullet* can go any time. We can send *Hiram Lazar*, er, excuse me, the *Spider's Treasure* whenever you want." Ree looked over curiously.

"Send it. A lot of warriors are anxious to see their families and brag to their clans. What's the point of all the coup if you can't show it off?"

"How about you? You want to go back with *Spider*?"

Iron Eyes laughed. "And leave Rita? What do you think I am, a crazy Romanan? No, I've lost too many loves in my life to take this one for granted." He raised his hands in supplication. "Besides, *Bullet* is a Spider ship. She's my home now."

"That tickles me where I sit," Ree nodded with a satisfied smile. "She'd follow you, you know. She loves World as much as she loves you. That'd hurt. I've lost too many good officers recently."

"You've got us."

Ree set the aircar down next to a washed, polished AT22. "Want to ride up? Rita's keeping an eye on Iverson, Giorj, and Glick to make sure I know what chaos they've committed in my ship." He raised his hands. "I get lost in there! In my own beloved *Bullet!*"

Iron Eyes looked out at the waiting line of sightseers, salesmen, agents, hucksters, promoters, and autograph seekers. "I could use a vacation."

The Romanan guard cleared the way, strutting proudly before the Sirians whom they still despised—even if they did preen before them.

Ree leaned back in the acceleration chair and let the kinks out of his body. He'd always hated the stiff, inhuman lines of a dress uniform.

"We're almost out of here," Ree repeated. "Did you ever think this was the end of the line?"

Iron Eyes lifted a callused hand. "Maybe. That was up to Spider. But me, no, I didn't." His eyes gleamed, predatory. "I'm a warrior, Damen. It's bred into me. I can't stand to lose. I told you that how many times?"

"Foolish me. Romanans! What do you want for dinner tonight? We'll make an occasion of it."

"I could use a good steak!"

"I think we have a couple left. The stock was dwindling as it was. Then some bastard Sirian gunner hit the galley. I think we can still find one or two though."

The AT docked smoothly and Ree complimented the pilot. Iron Eyes entered a freshly white corridor and followed the Colonel to a refitted lift. Ree settled his headset, checking on the ship.

"Rita's meeting us in my cabin. Drinks are on me. She says Giorj's new blasters work like a champ. That Fujiki Amplifier narrows the focus even further and accelerates the bolt somehow. Some sophisticated manipulation of complementarity. Hell, those particles already leave at light speed. How can they go faster?" Ree frowned. "Imagine that, fooling around with causality!"

Iron Eyes shrugged. "Until I met you people, I thought my rifle verged on magical!"

Rita waited in Ree's quarters, fingering one of the Romanan rifles hanging on the wall. Damen watched Iron Eyes kiss his gorgeous redhead and felt a slight twinge of jealousy.

Why didn't I noticed how attractive she was until after she'd started falling for Romanans? Lonely, old man? Maya's down there. She made the offer. Maybe a good bottle of wine, some music in a plush Sirian penthouse and . . . Hell, I'm too old for that. It's Bullet *or nothing.*

"Everything came off without a hitch?" Rita asked, green eyes melting when they met Iron Eyes'.

"Yeah," Ree began, "the Romanans own ten—"

"Subspace transduction, Colonel. Priority," comm intoned.

Ree began pouring scotch. "Run it."

Skor Robinson's bulbous head formed in the holo. "Greetings, Colonel."

"This is indeed an honor, Director." Ree felt himself tensing. Iron Eyes stared unabashedly, mouth open. Rita moved next to him—as if that iron woman needed protection.

"I have reviewed your actions on Sirius. I wish to thank you personally for your fine work. I've sent the hyperconductor you requested. It will be awaiting your arrival at the planet Atlantis."

"My deepest thanks, Director." Ree inclined his head. "Your kindness is greatly appreciated."

"I also wish to congratulate you on your promotion to Admiral, Damen Ree." Skor's expressionless eyes seemed to narrow.

"Admiral?" Ree almost gasped. "But . . . but what of Admiral Kimianjui?"

"The illustrious Admiral has picked this moment to retire, Admiral Ree. He is amply impressed with your abilities.

"Your orders are to supervise the shakedown of *Bullet* to the planet Atlantis where you may oversee the installation of the hyperconductor to your satisfaction. You will then board the Fast Transport which is returning the Romanan Prophet, Garcia, to World for your return here and assumption of the duties of admiral."

"Thank you, Director." Ree saluted. "You do me great honor. With anticipation I await my arrival at Atlantis. We shall space from this system within three days. I trust that's within your expectations?"

"Excellent, Admiral. Again I extend the gratitude of all humankind for the service you have performed. Good day." The image flickered off.

"That was a Director?" Iron Eyes whispered. "So . . . monstrous?"

Ree drew a deep breath and sipped his scotch. "Admiral?"

"My God, Damen, what are you going to do?" Rita asked, recovering.

"Probably call a staff meeting and have one of Glick's boys whip up a set of Admiral's sunbursts." He undid his dress coat and sighed with relief as Iron Eyes watched, eyes glittering.

"*Damen!*" Rita cried, "What the hell kind of talk is that?"

"We knew it was coming." Ree shrugged. "They're trying to take *Bullet* away from me. The hyperconductor's a gratuity."

"So, once again, what are you going to do?" Rita demanded.

CHAPTER XXIX

"Pleasure, my dearest Susan," Ngen's voice ripped through her, making her body shiver. "I've won, my angel!" he chortled happily. She tried to run, but her legs were trapped, bound in some sticky substance.

"*Get back!*" she screamed at him, terror wrapping around her like a web, enfolding her, making her soul shriek.

"But, dearest one, I am pleasure!" he whispered sensuously as her body began responding.

"Why have you done this to . . . to me. I hate . . . Bastard! I hate . . . hate you . . . hate myself!" Her voice broke in a curdling scream as darkness and pleasure closed around her in a muck of degradation. "*I hate myself!*" she screamed again, twisting to get away, fighting to escape from the memories and the body that betrayed her.

"Susan!" Giorj's voice penetrated the terror. "Susan! You're safe! Please! *Wake up! It's a dream!"*

She blinked, shuddering, jerking uncontrollably. Her resistance crumbled and she broke into violent sobbing, wracked with spasms of fear and frustration.

"Here," Giorj soothed, stroking her long glistening hair. "Peace, Susan. You're safe on *Bullet*. He's nowhere around. You're with me, surrounded by this big ship. It's all over."

"He's always there," she snuffled. "I walled off Hans . . . and Friday. I can deny the pain, Giorj. I can deny the guilt. Why can't I deny what that bastard did to me?"

His fingers smoothed her furrowed brow. "Perhaps the psych officer could do something."

"N-No!" She cried, voice trembling, shaking her head violently. "No . . . no one must know what happened to me. I . . . I c-couldn't t-take it, Giorj. It would k-kill me if anybody knew. I have to be perfect! Yes, perfect. I have to be strong! No one can know he . . . he b-broke me!"

Voice soft yet firm, Giorj reminded, "Friday still asks about you. Whenever I meet him, he valiantly hides his hurt. In fact, after we talk for a while, his concern for you overrides his pride and he asks. Susan, he loves you."

"No!" she whispered sibilantly. "He can't! It's impossible. He needs someone else." Her eyes clamped shut and she pressed shaking hands over her ears.

Giorj nodded sympathetically. "Sleep, Susan. The dream won't come back. I promise. I need to go check on the heat transfer system. They should be about finished with it. Rest, my friend."

"D-Don't leave me!"

"Strength, warrior," he chided, betraying his concern. Then he was gone.

Susan stood, turning to the shower. *Bullet* still rationed water; she couldn't stand in the warmth long enough. Dressing, she stood before the mirror until she had herself composed like granite—emotions carefully locked away. Her mind made numb, she palmed the hatch and went to the gym.

In her daily ritual, she fought the combat robots, wheeling, twisting, striking, kicking, dodging, feinting, trying to kill the machine.

She fought at expert status now, body reacting without thought. She pushed herself, stretching, ducking and slashing out. Bounding high, she smashed the robot's head with a lightning kick and crushed it to the mat with a spine-snapping body slam.

"I don't think I could've done better," Rita Sarsa's voice startled her.

Adrenaline pumping, she shot to her feet. In a combat stance she crouched, heart pumping fearfully, ready to strike.

Rita pushed off where she slouched against the wall. "You're hardly a novice at hand-to-hand combat anymore. Perhaps you should try out for the ship's title one of these days?"

"That's yours," Susan replied tonelessly, warily. With all her concentration, she turned her face into a mask.

"Titles change hands." Rita shrugged. "Of course, you'd have to take it away from me first."

Susan kept her peace. Nodding as she started for the shower.

Sarsa moved to block her way. "You know, we're landing tomorrow."

Susan nodded, heart racing, fear of discovery building.

Rita's gaze held hers. "Gotta hand it to you, you've been brilliant at avoiding Friday. You've been brilliant at a lot of things . . . except dealing with yourself."

"Excuse me, Major," she kept her voice even, fear rising to a high pitch.

"Afraid of a crack, Susan?" Rita asked, curious. "How long do you think you can keep going before you break yourself?"

Susan bit back her response. Her jaw muscles tightened until they creaked.

"I saw the holos Ngen took," Rita's voice was almost a hiss. "I know what you went through. I know how close you are to falling into little tiny pieces that you'll never pick up."

"I'm just fine," Susan managed, forcing her facial muscles to a faint smile. *Sarsa knows!* She felt hot. *Who else knows? Friday? Iron Eyes? Her men?* Fear hissed behind the walls in her mind. Sweat stood out in streams on her face.

"Sure," Rita nodded. "And as soon as you convince me you won't destroy yourself, I'll believe it."

"I suppose the holos are part of the record?" Susan asked, voice low. "That's good. I'd like to see them sometime. Ngen was amusing, don't you think?"

Careful! Control. Think. Keep your control. Can't break now.

Rita's eyes had turned an icy green as her head shook slowly back and forth. "No, Susan, he wasn't amusing. I destroyed the records. I suppose the wrong button got pushed—accident, you see."

"Too bad," Susan kept her front up, securing it with mental rivets. "Thought maybe psych would want them for their deviant file."

"Susan," Rita's voice held a thinly veiled threat. "As of this moment, you're on restricted duty. You're not allowed into secure areas. You're restricted to mess and recreational centers of the ship."

In her mind, she screamed. "Don't you think you're overreacting?" she asked, raising an eyebrow slightly. Iron will straining, she clenched her fist, stopping the tremors.

Rita looked at her head coolly. "You know, I've seen a lot of tough things, Susan. I also know a complete emotional breakdown when I see it. I told you about my husband. I watched him try and put himself together. Stopgap —just like you. He never made it.

"You're not completely broken yet. You still have that core of identity. Something's driving you and you're holding yourself together with bits of hope pasted here and there with courage. One of these days, the paste will crack and you will, too. If you won't let me help, I don't want you where you can hurt anyone except yourself."

Sarsa's voice softened. "Look, if you need to just come and talk, you know where I'll be. No questions, No pressure. You just tell me what you want and I'll listen."

"Very well, Major," Susan shot her a frosty grin. "Restriction suits me fine, I can use the break." She saluted and made her way to the shower, Rita's somber eyes following her.

In the stall, she collapsed, hands trembling from the strain. Almost whimpering, she hoisted herself up and doused her hot body with cold water until she shivered. With the icy streamers coursing down her freezing flesh as a distraction, she pulled her teetering mind together.

So close! The walls had been sagging under the weight that cracked them, bowed them out: Grief for Hans. Guilt over the way she'd treated Friday. Her own self-disgust and degradation. The memories waited to crush her into human wreckage. How much more could she take?

As much as I need to, she lied to herself.

*   *   *

The bright sunlight of World's sky caressed the land in golden tones. The late summer vegetation had started to turn from a bright to a yellowed green indicative of fall. Rita sat hunched in the observation blister as AT22 sank through the few thin clouds that fluffed the sky.

Below, the gray wreck of the *Nicholai Romanan* became a dot surrounded by the dingy hide-covered huts of the Spider settlement. She shot a look at the Romanans who waited anxiously, eyes mirroring their thoughts. Some were relieved. One man dabbed at wet eyes as he viewed his home world. Others were contrasting the miles of sprawling megalopolis of Sirius to this primitive sight.

What would they think of the beaten-dirt paths, the piles of night earth, the refuse thrown into the streets for the harvesters to eat? What would they think about the tallow candles, the hide waterbags with their horn dippers? What would they think about the firepits used for heat?

Did we do the Romanans any favors by taking them to the stars? Where cattle now grazed in the dirt tracks that passed for streets, aircars would soon prowl. Along the foot of the Bear Mountains she caught a glimpse of an animal—the huge, two-tailed, dragonlike Romanan bear that seized its prey with suction discs and that often served as a rite-of-passage challenge for Romanans eager to prove their manhood and honor.

A woman of the People had run off to become one of Spider's most feared warriors. Other women would want to follow in Susan's footsteps. At the same time, Sirian women were being forced into the clans—forced into a world that hadn't bred them. So many would fail; but their ideas would permeate World's culture.

A tempest unleashed, Rita realized. Not just the tempest of Romanan barbarians stomping Sirius under an iron heel, but that of bringing back a different sort of Romanan warrior. Change—a whirlwind dervish—would sweep World as violently as it ripped through Sirius.

And only the Prophets might tame it.

The ground rose to meet them. The pilot eased AT22 to the ground and shut the systems down. Romanans swarmed around as other ATs settled in the square near the wreck of the *Nicholai Romanan.*

As the ramps dropped, a wild rush of warriors ran out, whooping, shooting into the sky with their long neglected

rifles, shaking fists full of coups overhead. The People re-
acted with screams and cheers of wild abandon. Somewhere, the deep pulse of a drum sent its reverberations
through the crowd as men sang their songs of victory and
triumph.

Rita made her way to the hatch and heard, "Red Many
Coups!" They already carried Iron Eyes through the throng
on shoulders, his face lit with disbelief and merriment. Rita
found herself lifted and borne by joyous youths.

Through the milling bodies, she caught sight of Susan
Smith Andojar walking down the ramp to a lesser welcome
until someone realized the patchwork garment she wore
consisted of human hair.

"Coup coat!" someone shouted, and Susan, too, was carried about by wildly screaming young men.

And it went on, all through the morning, all through the
night. Bullocks roasted and hissed over open pits. Whiskey
gurgled down throats by the gallon. The People oohed and
ahed over cowed Sirian women and wide-eyed young men
who'd talked Romanans into bringing them back and making
them Spider warriors.

Aircars, comm units, generators, the wealth of Sirius was
laid out before shocked Romanans who tried to comprehend the wonders of Sirius as told to them by gleaming-eyed
warriors. Old men and women shook their heads, eyes
narrowing at stories of buildings sky-high and cities stretching farther than the eye could see.

Nor could the grim side of the homecoming be ignored.
Rita winced at the sight of young women, moving off,
blankets over their heads. A steady stream of people rode
horses or took wagons to the mountains where they would
pray to Spider. Many would cut a joint off their fingers,
burying it under a cairn of rocks, and with it their grief for
the lost dead.

Instead of the traditional display of bodies, personal me-
mentos which identified the dead lined the platform. Half
the warriors who'd left World would never return. Instead
of their bodies, the scaffold bore each individual's personal
possessions. The number of pieces was frightful to see. At
Rita's request, Ree sent a series of things to represent the
Patrol men and women who'd died. Rita herself placed
Hans' dress uniform on the scaffold.

She was saddling her gelding when S. Montaldo, the
Directorate planetologist, found her.

"Pleasure ride?"

She hugged him briefly. "No, I'm just overwhelmed by all of this. I need to ride out and pray and think. I haven't had the time for introspection. I need to know what's happened, and why. Iron Eyes already rode out on that black mare of his. I think he wanted some time alone at Gessali Camp. Me, I'll just ride by the Navel for a while and talk to the ghosts. Then I'll find a high place. Make my peace with Spider."

"We've started the toron operations." His face crinkled. "I've only got a couple of young men who're interested in mining. The rest are imported. Things are changing, and I can't get Romanan help."

"You'll get more." Rita snugged up the cinch, waiting for her red gelding to blow so she could tighten it. "The Sirians can't wait to get back on their feet so they can come be tourists."

"I thought tourism was discouraged."

"You can't pray from a high place on World while you're using a holo in Ekrania." She shrugged. "The Sirians want their own Prophet—but more want to come here on a pilgrimage."

"That's scary. I wish Doctor Dobra was here. She might be able to keep this thing from getting out of hand." He shook his head.

"Yeah, I miss Doc." Rita smiled wistfully. "Guess Spider didn't want her around. He called her back. She must have learned what she needed." She paused, squinting at him, "So what do you think the rest of us need to learn?"

"Guess we'll find out one of these days. It's in Spider's hands. At least, that's what the Prophets tell us." Montaldo seemed locked away in his thoughts.

"Spider? You gone native, S?" Rita swung up into the saddle. "Let's get together when I get back. Bend some elbows. Ree's seeing to his hyperconductor. *Bullet's* declaring independence from the Patrol as soon as the pressure builds up. Thought you might want some advance warning."

"Jesus!" Montaldo cried. "What if they send the Patrol?"

"What if they do?"

He nodded, grinning. "Enjoy yourself out there, Major." In a lower voice, he said, "Say hello to Philip for me, too."

She nodded soberly and waved as she rode into the evening, her rifle and blaster hanging from the saddle.

Szchinzki Montaldo watched the horsewoman ease into a

canter and then leaned back against a roof support. "Well," he muttered, "I suppose that makes me the new Minister of Economics and Development. I wish they'd learn to do things one at a time." He smiled wryly and shook his head.

Admiral Damen Ree answered the door and found himself staring into Chester's smiling face. The Prophet bowed and walked in uninvited. Comm explained that Chester had walked onto an AT and asked to please be transported to *Bullet*. In stately composure he'd walked by the security teams and straight to Ree's quarters.

"Chester? W-What're you doing here?" Ree stammered.

"Observe." He motioned.

Admiral Damen Ree watched each of the Directors appear on holo one by one. Shaking his head, Ree saluted, staring uneasily at the three huge heads and their glittering, out-of-proportion eyes.

"Greetings, Admiral." Robinson nodded. "I trust the hyperconductor was to your satisfaction."

"It was, Director," Ree said carefully. He shot a quick glance at Chester who nodded his support.

"Why have you not yet boarded the transport to return to Arcturus? Is there further trouble?" Robinson's voice barely inflected the question.

Ree shook his head slowly. The time had come to pay the fiddler for the jig. "On your screens, gentlemen, you will see the declaration of this ship's officers and crew. From the document, I hope you can see the necessity for keeping Admiral Kimianjui in his present position."

"Are you turning Rebel?" Robinson asked, aghast, face twitching.

"Absolutely not, Director." Ree shook his head vigorously. "We support the Directorate and *Bullet* will continue to conduct its patrol duties among the planets and stations which depend upon our support and protection.

"Further, in the event of insurrections such as the Sirian incident, we—and the Romanans—will be on call, for a cut of the profits. We're still yours to direct but with certain limitations. When you call us, we must be assured that your requirements meet the needs of the people. We are sworn to protect and uphold law and order. But more than that, we consider ourselves peacekeepers."

"And where will you get replacements and spare parts for your ship?" Semri Navtov asked.

"From the worlds we service. We'll also provide scholarships to university as the Patrol has done in the past. Similarly, Romanans will slowly take over our marine duties."

"What if we do not honor this declaration of yours?" An Roque asked, thin voice almost reedy.

"Then you don't honor it," Ree shrugged. "I don't think force will work either. For one thing, we've enhanced the capabilities of the Sirian blasters significantly. Our shields are superior to anything the Patrol can produce. And, last but not least, we would bring the Romanans to Arcturus if we discovered hostile action against any of our planets. Accept our independence with grace, Directors. We'd work better together than against each other."

A long silence passed while the Directors communicated among themselves. "We will do so, Admiral," came the response. "What does the Prophet do there?"

"I have come to see if my teaching has had an effect," Chester said easily. "I am pleased."

"Thank you, Prophet." Skor didn't sound enthused.

Chester nodded.

"We will honor your independence, Admiral. Please call on us if you have need of anything the Directorate can provide." The disembodied voice indicated Directorate unanimity.

"And do call should you need us," Ree bowed gracefully.

The holo went dead.

Ree drew a deep breath and dropped into a chair. "I didn't think they'd get nervous so fast. They must have been real worried about us."

Chester nodded. "It's bothered them for some time. Director Skor Robinson has planned for this eventuality. I think he's now a better Director. His Assistants will follow. He's learned much of himself."

Ree looked soberly at his hands. "I didn't think they'd give in so quickly."

"You have the Fujiki blasters and Brotherhood technology. Could they take a chance on refusing?" Chester paused. "Would you, Colonel?"

Ree grinned at the slow, concise tone Chester used. "And how about yourself, Chester? What've you been doing with your time?"

"I have had a delightful stay at Arcturus." His brown eyes gleamed with excitement. "I found books and literature and art and music. Truly! My time was spent rapturously!"

"Emotion, Chester? Is that a good thing for a Prophet?"
Ree poured two glasses of that superb Sirian scotch they'd
liberated.

Chester cocked his head. "Of course emotion, Admiral.
You must understand, the soul of a Prophet is no different
than yours. I, too, have a desire to learn and to understand
that which goes beyond what Spider has given me in my
visions. Any soul is like a sponge; it must absorb that which
it is provided.

"I've found that literature displaces the soul and makes it
something else for a brief instant. Music on the other hand,
sweeps the soul about and soothes it. Art is an expression of
emotion. All become different textures of reality which I'm
sure Spider has studied for eons."

"I've missed you, Chester," Ree admitted, touched by
the man's sincerity.

"And you have learned much, Damen," Chester praised.
"But I've come to talk to you of another matter. There's a
young man who will come to see you. He's still unsure of
the visions which come to him and he's resisting the future.
He'll overcome this, of course, just as I did, but he desires
passage to Sirius. Is there some way you could provide it?"

Admiral Damen Ree nodded. "I believe so. How'll I
know him when he shows—"

"Come, Damen, do you really think you will have any
problem?"

Ree chuckled, raising his scotch to touch Chester's in
toast.

Susan stood defiantly over the prostrate body before her.
She gripped her bloody knife, turned, and looked to the
elders. Two marines ran up and grabbed the man. They
sprinted for an aircar and—despite the cries of those around—
bore the dying man to the nearest AT.

"Why do they do that?" an old man asked from the somber
circle of faces.

"To save his life." Dreamlike, Susan heard herself answer.

"But this is *knife feud*!" another of the elders exclaimed.

"Raven Andojar Garcia's death would waste excellent
potential. He'll be a better warrior now," her wooden voice
answered. "Is there another challenge, men of the Andojar
clan? I killed Ramon Luis Andojar after he shot at me first.
I had no choice. I did as I had to do."

She whirled Raven's freshly cut coup through the air to sling the blood from it. She'd given him no chance.

"There's no other challenge," one of the elders muttered, shaking his head. "You've acted with honor—woman."

Dismay and apprehension that a woman had won knife feud hung heavy in the very air. Not just this combat, which was Andojar's, but one against Smith clan and one against Garcia clan, too. Those three coups that now hung on her belt meant something. Under Iron Eyes' orders, the marines had been present to hustle each man off to a med unit in an attempt to save his life.

New ways were diluting the old. Susan felt the loss dimly, somewhere in the sharp angles of her mind. The med units would grow their hair back and fix their wounds. Of course, she could have killed them, any warrior back from Sirius knew where to make a knife wound that med units couldn't fix. That wasn't important to her anymore. Nothing was.

She wove the coup into her belt and nodded briefly at the old men. Beyond the light of the fire, the night sky blazed in a passion of stars. There, reflecting the light of the Romanan sun, *Bullet* followed its orbit. Her ship, her future that she had to get back to. She had to pound the hurt and fear back into the depths of her mind. She had to beat herself. If she didn't Rita'd never let her back aboard.

Worse, she had no one here to hold her at night. Deeply engrossed in *Bullet's* blasters and shields, Giorj didn't set foot out of the ship although he'd been talking to the Prophet, Chester.

She stifled a cry. And she couldn't get back up to him. The walls in her mind trembled and bulged. Viciously, she pushed them back, seeking to suffocate everything within. Dreams of Ngen filled her nights. Only this time, no Giorj woke her to hold her and listen. Alone, deathly alone—and the shadows continued to creep ever closer.

When she walked in the bright daylight now, she heard Ngen's voice spinning out of the air around her, cooing, stroking, caressing. She shuddered and clutched the knife at her belt.

Rita had grounded her. Grounded! But . . . but if she killed Rita in knife feud? Could she get back to *Bullet*? Then she'd have to kill Iron Eyes. Who then could keep her from her beloved ship? Ree? Could she challenge the Admiral to knife feud? Would he agree? If she killed them all, who could stand in her way?

She was good—perhaps the best on the ship—when it came to hand-to-hand or knife fighting. No one could take her. The walls in her mind creaked—sibilant mumblings loud behind them.

Could she kill them all before the walls broke? Damn, Rita! The Major had almost broken her that day in the gym. She'd been so close—so near disaster. Susan cried softly into the night as she walked. First her body had betrayed her to Ngen; now her mind might break in front of Rita.

She slept that night in the corral where she'd hidden from Ramon so very long ago. She had been fighting for her survival then, as now. The dreams buffeted her all night long, the walls groaned and cracked, ready to crumble as she fought them back, bottling the memories, the grief, and the fear.

He was sitting next to her when she fought her way from the dream—away from Ngen's gentle voice. Frightened, she shrank back, using her knife blade to hold him off. She trembled with fear that he could have gotten so close.

"Who . . . who are you?" she hissed, afraid. This was a man! An unsafe man who might touch her, degrade her. A man who would try and break her—like all the others!

"Who I am isn't important, Susan Smith Andojar. Who are you?" He sounded kind, calming.

"You've come to swear knife feud?" She started, preparing to spring on him. "You've come to stand in my way—to keep me from my ship?" Eyes glazing with fear, she fought for control, only to see her hand begin to tremble violently.

The precipice yawned, calling to her.

"I've come to take you to the ship." He was a young man, perhaps thirty, handsome in a way. His eyes glowed with a subtle, knowing warmth she'd never seen before.

Giorj? Could he be a friend of Giorj's. "Who . . . who sent you here?"

"You called me to help you get to your ship." The man smiled. "I know a way that's easier than killing so many friends who love you. The choice is yours. I cannot tell you how to choose. I can only tell you the options. In the end it's all the same. Would you learn of yourself?"

"I know enough about myself," she snapped, feeling the walls trembling in her brain. "I need . . . need my ship!"

"Who are you?" the man asked. "Do you want to know?"

"Do you want to die?" she cried, feeling closed in—hemmed by his good will. She thrust the knife point closer to his body. "I'll kill you if you don't leave me alone!" Her voice broke hoarsely.

The man pulled his collar open. "Here, go ahead if you think it will help you." He indicated the pale skin at his throat.

"You're crazy!"

"You're killing your soul, losing yourself, Susan."

"No!" she screamed at him. "I'm strong! See me! See my coups! I'm powerful, powerful! I could kill you now! Leave me alone, don't make me kill you!"

The walls shivered, closing in on her will to resist. Her mind strained to push them back, to prop the denials in place. The image of Hans tried to form but she pounded him down, knowing he'd turn into Ngen. Friday's voice echoed in the dim hollows of her memories—his voice mocking Ngen's coo. She refused to listen. Ngen filled her, voice seeping through a crack in her defenses.

"I can't make you kill me," the man said softly. "Will you come with me and see someone who will give you back your ship? She wishes to see you. She wishes to ask you about your ship."

Rita! Susan's eyes lit. This man had talked her out of the grounding! She wouldn't need to kill Rita after all. It would have hurt to kill Rita—but death was part of life. Rita would understand. Rita knew.

"Yes," Susan breathed relief. "Take me to her. She'll get me back . . . back to the ship."

"That is your free will?" the man asked easily.

"Get up! Damn you!" Susan was on her feet, jabbing at him with the knife.

He got up slowly and led the way, Susan trotting along, trying to force him to move faster.

"It's a delightful day," the man said, smiling up into the sunshine that bathed them in the glow of the Romanan morning.

"Sure, where's the woman?" Susan demanded curtly.

"Follow . . ." the man smiled.

Susan shrugged, mind smothering sudden doubts. It had to be Rita, no one else could get her on the ship. "This takes forever," Susan complained. The walls pressed, shifting again. If he'd just get her to Rita and get the grounding lifted, Susan could beat the walls back.

"Here we are." He indicated a low hut, the floor dug deeply into the ground. Short poles supported the stiff rawhide that made the roof. Susan started inside, but he waved her back. "Better if you see her in the glory of this magnificent morning."

"Hurry up!" Susan snapped, fingers jerking on her knife. "If this is a . . . a joke, I'll split you right here!"

The man smiled happily. "I'll be right back," he said, ducking into the doorway.

Susan drew herself to her full height, arms crossed in defiance to meet Rita Sarsa. She beat the walls back again, bracing them with her resolution to have Rita see her strong. If the Major didn't let her go back to the ship, she'd kill her on the spot.

The man was backing out of the hut. Susan could hear his voice, soothing and easy. "Here, I've brought you Susan Smith Andojar."

He turned, a little girl with curly brown hair and deep worshiping brown eyes in his arms.

"It's her!" The little girl cried, struggling to get out of the man's arms. He let her down and the little girl walked shyly up, a hesitant finger in her mouth.

"My mama says I can be just like you when I grow up!" the little girl said as Susan fell to her knees.

"Yes," Susan whispered huskily. "You sure can." The walls burst and broke, flooding grief and shame through her mind, washing the horror away.

Tears blinded her eyes and she didn't see Friday Garcia Yellow Legs and Giorj walk out of the hut, grinning happily to each other. She didn't see Chester's knowing smile as he walked off, the bright sunshine pleasing him even as strains of Mozart echoed in his head. She saw nothing but the pain and guilt as she reached her trembling arms out and gathered up the little girl wearing the yellow dress.

Ngen Van Chow settled himself on the bridge, watching the stars blinking on the monitor. He amused himself by perusing the *Catalogue of Planets and Stations.* Frontier caught his eye.

Frontier? The home of the Brotherhood and lost glories. But then, Earth, too, lay just a jump away. Earth, the old weary progenitor of humanity, its hegemony lost since the overthrow of the Soviets. What did it mean to them to be ruled by a distant Director who'd never even set foot on a planet?

Earth, home of some of the finest foods and art in the galaxy. Earth, its economy stifled by colonies that had originally provided exotics which had eventually become the staples of life.

Ngen accessed his comm and drew up everything he could find on the planet. He let his eyes skip down the data. Ah, here! Perhaps a religious revival?

But why not Zion or Range? The older planets of the Confederacy might be ready to reassert their influence. Gulag Sector was ripe even now. He'd seen that before he'd countered that treachery by Blackov. So, the Romanans would buy him for his weight in toron?

Thank God for Pallas Mikros—who could see beyond today's greed. One day, he would reward Pallas.

Ngen Van Chow relaxed and sipped the brandy he'd called up from the dispenser. A man of his charm could always rebuild a dogmatic cult that would serve his purpose. Perhaps some sort of ecumenical revival? Ngen smiled happily as he punched in a new course. Somewhere, he would find the situation just right for his seed of dissension to grow and flower.

He downed his brandy and made his way back to his quarters. He suffered a feeling of loss as he thought about the Romanan girl. She had provided such pleasure. Just like that dream he'd had. How delightful to watch her squirm and scream as he played the lash over her voluptuous body. He'd never know if the interrupted dream ended like the live version. Their future-seeing Prophets couldn't have done better than he.

Damn Romanans, he'd have to teach them all a lesson some day soon. One never knew, perhaps he'd be able to retrieve his lost Susan. She'd been broken. He'd won. When he'd left, she was showing all the signs of destruction.

Could they save her? He shrugged. They should have just killed her outright.

Ngen grinned happily. All was not lost. He touched the control studs first. Stretching, he eased out of his shirt and dropped his pants. He accessed the holo and sank down on the bed. He watched Susan Smith Andojar again as he played the electric whip around her breasts, flicking the nipples and then dancing it between her thighs.

But the best was yet to come. He leaned over and admired the golden-haired girl next to him. Tall, station-bred, her body shone with radiant youth. Her wide blue eyes locked on the holo in horror.

"There, my dear one," Ngen cooed easily. "You need not learn that lesson of pain. I'm here to teach you pleasure . . . and we have a lot of time!"